TO CATCH A
THIEF

IMPECCABLY DEMURE PRESS

Prologue

London, 1855

JAMES RAFFERTY DIDN'T LIKE HAVING a knife held at his throat, even at the best of times. He was tired, he was dirty, and he'd just killed a man, and he was finding it particularly trying.

"What the fuck do you want, Stiles?" he said in an irritated voice.

Billy Stiles blinked, obviously used to men cowering when he threatened them with a knife. "You killed Judge Belding."

"I did," Rafferty said agreeably.

"You and I were his second in command. Don't you think I ought to kill you for it?"

Rafferty sighed. "What would that gain you?"

"Control of his men. They always listened to you, not me. With you out of the way, it should be clear sailing."

"I have no interest in running Belding's gang. I'm getting out of the business."

Stiles's scoff sprayed spittle in his face. "Once a thief, always a thief."

"I really don't care. Move the knife, would you? It's tickling me."

There was a moment's pressure, but he didn't even consider he might be misplaying this. Billy Stiles had been his enemy for the last five years of his life, but he was a vulnerable man, if you knew how to play him.

The knife lowered. "Assuming you really are going to just disappear, where does that leave me?" Stiles demanded.

"It leaves you with a gang of experienced men to do your bidding. They may not like you much, but they fear you, and you prefer it that way."

Stiles didn't argue. He hadn't put the knife away yet, but at least he was no longer holding it to Rafferty's throat. "What about his money?"

"What money?"

"Belding's cache. You and I both know he kept his money well hidden in case the police ever caught on to his doings. Where is it?"

"I haven't the faintest idea. I don't care. I have enough of my own."

"Bollocks! Everyone cares about money."

"I don't need Belding's money and I don't know where it is. If you can find it, you can have it," Rafferty said.

"Oh, no, boy-o. You won't convince me of that. There's no such thing as too much money."

"I didn't say I had too much. I just said I didn't need his. I didn't like some of the things I've done to earn it. Have it with my blessings."

"You know where it is!" Stiles accused him. "You're going to take it from me the first chance you get. I should cut your throat and have done with it." He began to raise the knife, but Rafferty knocked it from his hand.

"I don't know where it is, and I don't care."

"Maybe my men will persuade you."

Rafferty just looked at him. Judge Belding was barely cold and already Stiles was talking about "his" men. He wasn't particularly worried about the band of thieves loosely under Belding's and now Stiles's rule. They liked him better than they liked Stiles. Still, any of them would cut a throat for even a tiny portion of Belding's legendary fortune.

Rafferty sighed. "I tell you what. I'll find the cache and we can split it among the men. That would be more than fair."

"After I take my cut," Stiles said slyly, and Rafferty knew just how big a cut that would be. "I knew you knew where it was."

"I don't. But I have an idea or two."

"You wouldn't be thinking of taking it yourself and cutting me out?"

"Wouldn't dream of it."

"Because I'd gut you before I cut your throat. I'd..." Stiles went on for a bit on the gruesome things he would do to his body, but Rafferty stopped listening. He was a good deal taller and a great deal stronger than Billy Stiles, and he fought dirty. Stiles wouldn't have a chance.

"Then we're agreed." Rafferty interrupted him. "I'll find the money, you take your share and divide the rest with the men."

"What about you? I don't trust a man who lets money slip through his fingers."

"I'll take my share as well," Rafferty agreed. "It may take me some time..."

"You'd best hope not. I'm not a patient man."

"Don't worry, Billy. You'll get what's coming to you. I'll make sure of it."

Chapter One

JAMES RAFFERTY STARED up at the townhouse from his vantage point in the midnight shadows, his ragged clothes pulled around him in the frigid night air. In truth, he wasn't that cold—his body temperature tended to run hot, and he'd spent colder nights on the street. He had a cap pulled low on his shaggy head, his beard was ferocious, and his entire demeanor was that of the lowest of the low—a street beggar, veteran of Her Majesty's endless wars of conquest. The rough-hewn crutch was beside him, in case anyone would doubt his profession, and no one would notice his ever-alert eyes beneath the rough hat he was wearing.

Corinth Place had seen better days, as had the entire area. Once the home of aristocrats, it now housed merely the gentry, wealthy families down on their luck, the disgraced, even the bourgeoisie had found homes in the decaying neighborhood. The area would either rise back to the heights it once held, or it would deteriorate into the nearby slums. He was betting on the slums.

Number Ten had held up better than most. It had once belonged to his erstwhile employer, the renowned Judge Belding, though it had simply been an uninhabited rental property, seemingly unused and unwanted. The Manning family had moved in several months ago, and they showed no signs of leaving. He liked it that way. If they left, the crown would lay claim to the home, and he could kiss his chances goodbye.

A sudden gust of wind slammed into him, and he suppressed his shiver. It was past eleven—the night was just getting started, but the house at the far end of the square was dark. Clearly the Mannings had retired early, and for a moment he was tempted to see just how quiet he could be. He'd robbed any number of houses while the owners slept upstairs, and he had no doubt he could do the same at Number Ten. But he wasn't interested in their paltry possessions—a family down on its luck would have sold off most of their most portable valuables. The treasure he was seeking would be much harder to find, and he couldn't risk getting caught before he knew exactly where it was.

He didn't have that far to go—Corinth Place sat just on the edge of the slums, and all he had to do was turn a corner and he'd be back in his home territory. He moved through the darkness, as silent as a cat, slipping back into the shadows where he belonged, leaving Corinth Place behind him.

He heard the noise from a distance, and he halted his progress in surprise. These streets were far from deserted, but he could swear there was a carriage approaching this burgeoning slum. The few hackneys that made their way down this far sounded old and weary. These horses, and there were two of them, were young and lively, just the sort of horseflesh to be stolen by an enterprising thief or two. Either they belonged to one of the houses back at Corinth Place or they were coming to his slums. He wondered how far they'd get.

He heard the second pair with disbelief. What in the hell was going on, with the bloody toffs broaching his territory? He ought to give them the lesson they deserved, liberate the horses, and sell them. He had no doubt he could do it, no matter how many servants accompanied such prime horseflesh, but he had more important things on his mind. He needed to disappear, and fast, before whoever they were came around the corner. Whether it was his blood enemy, Billy Stiles, or the local constable, he couldn't be seen near Corinth Place.

He sank down in the nearest doorway, ducking his head and pulling his hat down, just another tramp with no home and nowhere to go. The carriages came into view, following his surreptitious trail into the slums, and he felt no gratification in knowing he'd been right. The first carriage was small and elegant, with two perfectly matched chestnuts. There was a driver up on the box, but no one else—easy pickings.

The next carriage followed, this one bigger, and the horses, while better looking than the everyday street hack, were older, a little thinner. They weren't worth the trouble—in fact, none of them were when he was in his present disguise. A crippled soldier didn't steal horses, and he had bigger fish to fry.

He watched them approach from beneath his brows, no more than mildly curious. The carriages were an anomaly on these filthy streets, and he was prepared to be entertained when someone decided to relieve their owners of their property, until he realized, to his absolute horror, that they were slowing to a halt directly in front of his ragged body. Had they seen him? He tried to retreat further, but the doorway was too small for his big frame, and he could do nothing but watch as the first, elegant coach stopped directly in front of him. The door opened before the driver could move, and an exquisitely dressed young gentleman of the ton stepped out, holding out a hand to the person remaining in the dark confines of the carriage.

The delicate foot on the steps was a hint of what was to come, and he remained very still as the most exquisitely beautiful woman he'd ever seen stepped out into the cool night air. She wasn't dressed for the weather—her perfect white shoulders rose above the pale pink gown, reminding him of just how grubby he was. She had raven black hair, adorned with diamonds that would have been worth more than the horses and carriages put together, assuming they were real, and she was looking directly at him as she descended.

She sniffed, a dubious expression on her face, as she approached him. "Do you really think he'll do, Alcott?" she asked of her companion, a man Rafferty had already dismissed as a useless fribble. "Couldn't we find one a little more...well, presentable? He probably reeks."

In fact, he didn't. The clothes were filthy—he wasn't. He tilted his head up to look at the beauty, enjoying the spectacle if not the conversation.

"But, darling," the man drawled, "that's exactly what we're looking for, don't you know." He said the last three words as if they were one. "A filthy beggar, the dregs of society. You said you wanted to win."

"I do," Darling said grimly, eying him like he was a skinned rabbit.

The other carriage had halted, with much less majesty, and before it had even stopped moving, another young woman tumbled out, a tall one, with a tangle of curly hair down her back like a schoolgirl and a spate of words.

"You're not being fair, Norah!" she continued, obviously in mid-sentence. "I was the one who told you where to find someone, and you ran ahead to beat me."

"I always beat you, George," the beauty said in an arch voice. "You might as well get used to it. " She didn't even bother to look at the girl. Instead, she approached him, lifting her skirts to expose delicate, exquisite ankles beneath that dress of shimmering silk. "Here you, my man. How would you like to make five shillings?"

He tipped his head back to look at her. He was cursed with memorable eyes, but they wouldn't be noticeable in the darkness. "Who do I have to fuck?" he said in his rich, rough voice. "You or the man?"

Her ladyship had heard that word before—for a moment, she was open-mouthed in shock, looking a little less like a fairy princess. "How dare you!" Her voice was icy with outrage.

The young woman behind her stifled a laugh. "Serves you right, Norah."

"Are you going to let him talk to me like that?" the woman, Norah, demanded, her arch tones getting shriller.

The man beside her looked alarmed. "What do you expect me to do, fight him? He's probably carrying a knife."

"Happen I am," Rafferty said agreeably. "Now why don't the two of you go back to wherever you came from and stop disturbing me in my slumbers? I don't come haring into your bedroom at night—you should do me the same courtesy."

"Alcott!" the woman cried, her voice getting shriller. "Do something about him!"

Rafferty rose, slowly, careful to balance on his so-called good leg, and towered over her. "I'm thinking someone should do something about you," he said, moving toward her with a small dose of the menace he could easily summon. She moved back, away from him as he advanced on her, tripping over her own delicate feet and landing on her backside on the filthy street.

He barely heard the smothered laughter from the second female. He glanced at her, but couldn't see much, just a tumble of messy curls and a plain dress. No bared, perfect shoulders for this one.

"I'll have you horsewhipped," Norah hissed at him, her fine eyes narrowed in fury. "I'll have you hanged."

"Miss Manning, you can't..." her companion began uncertainly.

"I can do anything I want," she snarled.

Manning? Rafferty froze. He wasn't a man who believed in coincidences. He knew that Sir Elston Manning had two daughters—what in the world were *they* doing here?

The young woman was making her way in their direction, her amusement unabated. "Not this time, you won't," she said cheerfully. "If I were you, I'd go somewhere else to find the dregs of society."

The beauty allowed her companion to pull her to her feet, and she looked up at Rafferty with pure hatred. "I will," she said, replying to the girl without looking at her. "But I still intend to see this man punished."

"Come along, Miss Manning. I should never had agreed to bring you down here—it's all my fault."

"She wouldn't have given you any choice, Mr. Alcott," the young woman said, sliding to a stop a full ten feet away from Rafferty.

But no one was paying any attention to her. The beauty scrambled into her carriage with less grace than she'd descended, and the young man followed, slamming the door behind them. In a moment, they were off.

But he wasn't alone. He turned to focus on the girl they'd abandoned in the worst streets of London. No, she wasn't quite a girl, though clearly not long out of the schoolroom. He'd heard that the fashion that year was for dark hair—the unpleasant young woman was most likely an absolute diamond. This one had hair that was neither blond nor brown but a tawny shade in between, coming down from a messy knot, and her evening dress was plain and unadorned. There was a faint streak of black on the side of her face.

"What are you still doing here?" he growled, hoping to scare her away.

She was made of sterner stuff, though. "I...I thought I should apologize," she said, stammering only slightly.

"For what?"

"For leading my sister here. For agreeing to hunt for the dregs of society and coming down here to you. It wasn't very nice."

She looked absurdly chastened, and he was tempted to laugh. He kept his expression a powerful glower, hoping to scare her away before she got a good look at him. Not that he was recognizable with the full beard and shabby hat, but he couldn't afford to stand chatting to an ingenue in the midnight air.

"No, it wasn't," he agreed. "And exactly why did you want me?"

"Oh, it wasn't you. Anyone would do. We were having a treasure hunt, you see, at Millie Rutherford's, and we each had a long list of things we must retrieve in order to win the prize. Except there is no prize, just the glory of winning, but Norah always wins, and just this once I really wanted to beat her." She stopped, a little breathless.

"Your sister deserves to be beaten in every sense of the word," he said. Why the hell was he extending this conversation?

The girl sighed. "It's true. She's so pretty she's always gotten her own way, and now she's too big and too important to punish."

"Too important?" he echoed, confused.

"Well, she's a beauty, you see," the girl said explained.

"I noticed."

"And our family is very, very poor. My father made some bad investments, and my brother Neddy gambles, and now we can barely afford servants. It's up to Norah to marry well and bring in a nice marriage settlement, but so far her nasty tongue has scared them all away."

"What about the young man with her?"

"Alcott?" she said. "Oh, he's like her faithful dog, following her and doing whatever she wants. He's in love with her, like half the men she meets, and she uses him. You'd fall in love with her too if she weren't being so unpleasant."

"I doubt it," he said. He was waiting for a chance to slip back into the shadows, when he thought he heard the most absurd thing. "Was that a goat?" he asked, astonished.

She nodded. "I've got the last things I needed, including two goldfish and a baby goat. All that was left was the dregs of society, but I've decided that's not fair, and I should probably get rid of the baby goat and the goldfish. I just don't know where." She took a deep breath at the end of this long, artful sentence, and he found he wanted to smile. He couldn't—fearsome beggars didn't smile.

He had to get rid of her, but for some reason, he was strangely loath to. "Shouldn't you be heading back rather than conversing with the dregs of society? How many men do you have with you?"

"Just Edgars, our coachman, and he's so old he doesn't provide much protection," she said cheerfully. "But I have a gun."

She'd managed to startle him. "You do?"

"Up in the carriage. Unless the goat ate it."

Rafferty sighed. "It won't do you much good in the carriage if I decide to hurt you."

"Oh, you wouldn't," she said with supreme confidence. "If you didn't interfere with my beautiful sister, then you're hardly going to bother with me."

He watched her, thoughts tumbling over and over in his brain. What seemed to be a disaster could be turned upside down. He made up his mind in an instant. "What would it take to beat your sister?"

She looked surprised. "Well...you. Or someone like you. But I couldn't ask you to come. It's degrading."

"It is," he said. "And you didn't ask me. I'm offering. "

"Would you really?" she said, her eyes shining brightly. "That would be so kind of you. But if we're to beat Norah, we must hurry. She could have found another dreg...er...gentleman already."

"Hardly a gentleman, miss...?"

"Miss Georgiana Manning, but everyone calls me Georgie. Except for Norah, who calls me George." She made a face.

He picked up his abandoned crutch and limped heavily over to her. "Then let's go, Miss Georgiana Manning," he said, taking her arm in his and leading her to the carriage like the gentleman he most assuredly was not. The coach started with a jerk and they were off down the street.

He turned his face to find himself nose to nose with an annoyed-looking billy goat. He glanced at Georgie, who smiled back, clearly pleased with herself.

"This will be wonderful!" she said. "Norah went around

making Mr. Alcott buy everything she needed, whereas I had to wheedle and beg. This is going to be truly a triumph."

"A triumph," he echoed, considering whether he might have made a very grave mistake. He wasn't in the mood to be paraded in front of some rich nitwits, even for Miss Georgiana Manning. But this was a coincidence he couldn't afford to waste.

The goat chose that moment to *baaah* loudly in his face, expressing his displeasure, before Georgie pulled him back to her side of the carriage. "I'm so sorry," she said. "He's not the best-behaved goat I've ever met."

"And you've met so many?"

She smiled that infectious smile once more. "My share of them," she said. "We used to live in the country. I hated to leave."

"What happened?"

"Well, we needed to launch Norah in society so she can marry a rich man and save us all, and there are very few wealthy men in Dorset."

"What about you? Couldn't you marry a rich man just as easily?"

She laughed. "I'm not a beauty like Norah. Besides, I'm not officially out. Mother says we can't afford to have two of us out, so I mostly stay home. I only got to attend the Rutherfords' tonight because they needed another female to make up their numbers, and their company is not too particular. Apparently, the older generation doesn't like treasure hunts. I love them," she added. A shadow crossed her face. "At least, I usually do. We've never been told to get a human being before, and I must say I don't like that part of it. Are you certain you want to come with me?"

Now was his chance. He could simply request that the carriage stop and he could disappear into the London night. The young woman was looking at him anxiously, and he wanted to laugh. She looked like a saint heading to the stake.

"I rather think I'd like to see you beat your so-beautiful sister," he said, and was rewarded with her sunniest smile.

"Oh, bless you. And don't you worry. I won't let anyone be mean to you."

The thought of an innocent young woman like Georgie protecting his own six feet four inches should have made him laugh—instead, he was touched. He'd spent days watching the Manning house with nothing to show for it—as far as he could tell, there had always been someone at home. He might as well do a favor for this slightly odd young woman with the earnest blue eyes, and maybe it would help him get inside the townhouse.

He glanced at her. If she were older, he could always take her home to bed and roam the place while she slept off the soporific effects of sex. She was out of the schoolroom, even if she wasn't actually "out," and he had a dislike of hurting innocent creatures. Still, he had to be open to all possibilities.

He was thinking better of it when they rolled up to a brightly-lit mansion in the heart of Mayfair. Crowds surrounded the place—he spied three more goats, eight bowls of goldfish, and various other detritus in the arms of over-dressed, overbred aristocrats. He didn't see another man who could qualify for the dregs of society, and he sighed. He'd agreed to this, bewitched by those blue eyes. He was going to carry it through.

He pulled the goat with him, striding up the front steps in Georgie's wake as she transported the goldfish, and he noticed with amusement that he was being given a wide berth, as if he might be contagious. She marched him straight into chaos, a room filled with people shouting, goats bleating, odd objects of furniture being passed overhead, when there was a sudden, thundering silence.

"Miss Georgiana Manning," a stalwart gentleman announced in a tempered bellow. "Have you brought to us a Dreg of Society?"

She scowled. "I've brought you Mr...." She turned to him and whispered loudly. "I beg your pardon, what's your name?"

"Rafferty," he replied.

"I've brought you Mr. Rafferty," she announced. "A man temporarily down on his luck."

The man looked him over, as if guessing his weight for market. "I'll have to ask some questions."

"Of course," he said in his deep, gravelly voice, using his best cockney accent. "What you need to know, guv'nor?"

"Where do you reside?"

"On the streets. Lately I've been sleeping in a doorway near the docks."

"How much money do you have on you?"

"Not a penny."

"Do you own any property?"

"Nuffink," he replied easily. "I'm fancy free."

"And would you term yourself the dregs of society?"

"Can't think of anyone much lower."

The man looked at him for a long moment, then turned to the waiting crowd. "Then I declare the winner of The Rutherford Treasure Hunt is Miss Georgiana Manning," he announced in a stentorian bellow, followed by enthusiastic cheers and huzzahs.

Rafferty was tempted, so tempted, to tell them exactly what he thought of them, but then Norah Manning might get her wish to see him strung up to the nearest tree. The British upper classes took their privilege very seriously, as he knew full well. Everyone had crowded around Georgie, shaking her hand, hugging her as an avalanche of congratulations poured around her, and he judged it a fine time to disappear. He would have time to get back to the deserted town house and begin his search before they returned. He moved through the parting crowds, very aware of the suspicious servants watching him in case he decided to take off with the best silver, and he'd almost made it out the door when he ran smack into the beautiful Norah, with some poor, rundown soul in tow.

"Too late," he announced cheerfully. "Your sister's beaten you."

The expression on her perfect face was so ugly it took him

aback. "You!" she said in tones of loathing. "How dare you show your face here?"

"Isn't that exactly what you wanted me to do?" he countered. She really was a looker, even with that mean expression on her face. Given time and inclination, he'd take her bed, and damned if she wouldn't go willingly if he put enough effort into the task. He wasn't interested.

"If you'll excuse me," he said politely, staring to move around her, but she forestalled him.

"I ought to call the police."

"What for?"

"You pushed me into the street!"

"You tripped."

"Alcott!" she called, but her faithful swain was nowhere in sight, and he gave into temptation, looming over her once more.

"I didn't push you," he said. "But I could remedy the omission."

She let out a noisy squawk, for all like a discomfited chicken, but before he could take a step closer, Georgie was by his side.

"Hullo, Norah," she said happily. "I beat you!"

Norah quickly regained her self-control, looking at them both with supreme arrogance. "So you did. I didn't really care, anyway. So, what are you going to do with our giant now that you've plucked him from the gutter? Next thing we know, you'll be wanting to reform him."

"And why not?" Georgie shot back. "Mother has her good works, why can't I? We bring baskets to the poor, don't we? I think that Mr. Rafferty simply needs a chance in life, someone to believe in him, and he can become a respected member of society."

He controlled his instinctive shiver of horror at such an idea. "I'll be taking my leave now..." he said, edging away, but Georgie immediately grabbed him by the arm, holding him fiercely.

"No, you don't. Norah is absolutely right, you're my project! I'm going to reform you, make you happy..."

"I'm fine as I am," he said uneasily, trying to free himself from her grasp. He couldn't, not without hurting her.

"No, you're not," she said. "I'm going to see you're gainfully employed. We need a butler—our last one took off yesterday, and we can't afford a new one. But you'll work cheaply, won't you, given that it's your first job?"

He looked down at her, into her shining eyes, about to tell her where she could stick her butler, when the beauty of the situation struck him. He'd spent long, endless nights looking for a way to get into the Manning household. Now it was being offered to him on a silver platter.

Norah was back to squawking her outrage like a chicken, and Georgie was looking determined.

"You want me to be your butler?" he said slowly.

She nodded, told her apoplectic sister to shut up, and then nodded some more. "Will you? Please?"

It was the please that did him in. That and the fact that it was the chance of a lifetime. Still, he'd be mad to do it. This was too good to be true.

He opened his mouth to tell her no when he caught sight of Norah's mute fury. "Yes," he said. "I will."

Chapter Two

GEORGIE MANNING SMILED up at the unkempt Mr. Rafferty. "Excellent!" she announced to no one in particular. "I'll reform you! You'll learn a trade, you'll have a purpose in life, and you won't need to sleep inside doorways anymore. I don't exactly know where the butler sleeps, but I would expect he'd have his own room in the servants' quarters. Not that that there are any servants, really, except Bertha, who cooks for us, and there's a girl who cleans, but it never seems to be the same one, and Mama said the last one took some of the silver, which is a shame, because the Manning silver is very old and very famous, but most of it was too big for her to cart away with her, thank heavens." She was talking too much, and she knew it, but she couldn't help herself. She always prattled when she was nervous.

The man towering over her made a noncommittal noise. "If you have all that silver, why don't you sell it?"

She made a face. "Oh, it's entailed, like the country house. It's considered a national treasure. The best we could do is donate it to the crown, and that wouldn't do us any good. Father is a baronet—he doesn't need to be a viscount or an earl, and that's about the only reward we could expect."

The man nodded, saying nothing as she herded him back out

the door and down the broad steps. For such a crowded venue, they were able to pass with relative ease, and she realized that all the guests were giving them a wide berth.

"You seem to terrorize the guests," she said. "Everyone moves out of my way. It must be because you're so fearsome."

"I doubt it," said her companion. "They just don't want to mix with the dregs of society."

She frowned at that. "Well, we'll show them. They'll have to mix with you when you're our butler."

"Not exactly."

They'd reached the carriage, and she waved old Edgars back to his perch as she reached up high for the doorhandle. Instead, an arm reached across hers, as Mr. Rafferty easily opened the door and let down the steps before taking her arm and assisting her up into the carriage. She had the impression of strength, and then he followed her in, the coach sagging beneath his weight. Her father really would need a new coach sometime soon, she thought with that nagging bit of worry in her stomach. Her father was going to need a great many things that were out of reach, but at least she'd provided him with a butler.

"Well, people have to be polite to the butler," she continued her argument. "What would the world come to, if people refused to converse with other people's butler?"

"Society, as we know it, would collapse," he said wryly.

She cast him a quick glance. He had a sense of humor—most servants were dreadfully serious. But then, this man was no ordinary servant. "Well, that might be a good thing." She sat back on her seat, surveying him. It was dark, of course, and he was nothing more than a very large, dangerous-looking shape. "Mother is always telling me I rush into things without thinking them through, and I expect she's right, but I really do think you're an excellent idea, unless you're a criminal and a murderer, in which case it's not so clever of me, but I trust my judgment and I can sense you're a good man."

"Completely harmless," he answered in his deep, slow voice,

and she could see the white of his teeth as he smiled beneath the shaggy beard. "Do you always talk so much?"

"Only when I'm nervous."

"Do I make you nervous?"

She didn't want to answer that. "You're going to have to shave, I expect," she said suddenly. "And bathe. And I suppose I'll need to find clothes for you—you really don't dress like a butler. It's a shame you're so awfully tall. We've never had anyone in service as big as you are, so we have no livery that would fit."

"Butlers don't wear uniforms, they wear black," the man observed.

"So, they do," she said thoughtfully. "You see, you already know more about the job than I do! You're going to be splendid. We just need to find you some clothes."

"I can take care of that."

"You can? But if you can find clothes worthy of a butler, then why do you dress in rags?"

"Because no one's going to give money to a well-dressed beggar, now are they?" he said reasonably.

She nodded. "You're very wise." She glanced out the window. "Here we are," she announced as the carriage slowed.

She almost thought there was a trace of hesitation in her companion, but he opened the door and let down the steps, moving out first so he could assist her down. For a man who lived on the streets, he was very adept at gentlemanly gestures, and she looked up at him in sudden suspicion.

"You're not some nobleman in disguise, are you?" she asked. "Some foreign prince or bastard son of the king or something like that?"

He appeared amused. "Not that I know of. Why do you ask?"

"Because you seem to know what you're doing. I won't have anything to teach you in your new position."

"You're not really that familiar with all the things a butler does, are you?" he said.

"Well, I suppose not, but..."

"Then you'll just have to hope I catch on quickly. Perhaps your cook will help me."

"Bertha? She always fights with the butlers."

Again, that flash of smile in his dark face. "I'm very easy to get along with."

"You know, you are," she said, thinking about it. For all she knew, she might have brought a criminal into the house, but she couldn't summon up any misgivings. There was something about him that just felt...right. She couldn't bear to think of him disappearing into the slums again. "I think my parents are going to love you."

"It's always possible. Your sister despises me."

"Oh, fiddlesticks!" she said. "Norah despises everything. She's been sulking ever since we came to London, and I don't see why, since she's the toast of society with every man falling at her feet. But she's not interested. Not that it matters. The family is going to be very pleased with me for bringing home a new butler." She started up the front steps, but he didn't move, and she stopped to look back at him, sudden worry assailing her. "Aren't you coming with me?"

"Butlers don't enter the front door, Miss Georgiana, they use the servants' entrance."

She breathed a sigh of relief. "Oh, of course they do. All right, we'll use the servants' entrance," she said cheerfully, taking his arm and leading him along the sidewalk to the iron gate.

"You're supposed to use the front entrance."

"You're going to be perfect at this," she said encouragingly, patting his arm. "You already know all these little details. And there's no use for me to use the front entrance since we have no butler to open the door for me. I'd just have to rouse the household and then I'd have to explain you and it would all be incredibly tiresome. We'll spring you on them in the morning—you'll be a lovely surprise."

"I'm not much for springing," he said wryly.

"Oh, they'll love you. And most likely they'll love you a lot

better after you're bathed and shaved and wearing decent clothes."
She took a deep, happy breath. "This is almost like Cinderella!"

"Cinderella?" he echoed, sounding puzzled.

"A fairy tale," she clarified. "About a girl who lives in rags and
cinders, which is where she got her name, and her fairy
godmother arrives and dresses her in a beautiful gown and sends
her to a ball where she meets the prince and falls madly in love
with him. I'm your fairy godmother."

"I don't have to marry a prince, do I?" he drawled.

There it was again, the flash of humor. It wasn't very butler-
like but she laughed anyway. "No, but you will have to shave yourself, unless Bertha volunteers, but I wouldn't let her if I were you,
because she's got a bad temper and she'd probably cut your
throat."

"I can manage." They'd reached the side basement door, and
he looked down at her. "This is where we part."

"No, it isn't. I can't get in the front door, remember?"

"How do you usually get in at night?"

"We leave it unlocked."

"So we won't have to wake anyone. Use the front door, Miss
Georgianna, and I'll use this one."

"But I need to explain you to Bertha," she protested, but he'd
put his hands on her shoulders and turned her around.

"I can explain. You go up the front steps and I'll stay here and
watch until you're safely inside."

A sudden uneasiness filled her. "You aren't just going to turn
and run away, are you?" she said suddenly. The thought was
wrenching.

"No."

"I'll see you tomorrow, then? You promise?"

"Yes. Now go on."

She was reluctant to leave him, but he wasn't giving her much
choice. She kept her gaze on him as she went around to the front
of the house and started up the steps, but he didn't move,
watching her as she reached the door. It opened, of course, and

she turned back to him, to wave, to wish him good night. But he was already gone.

&

RAFFERTY EDGED BACK around the side of the house and went up the two steps to the sidewalk, closing the iron gate behind him. If he was going through with this, and it looked like he was, he was going to need to shave off his beard and find a decent dark suit. He'd had a bath two days ago, but it looked as if another one was necessary, and he had an unusual fondness for bathing, something he hadn't been able to indulge in much during the last few months. If he was going to win over the mettlesome Bertha, he'd best be on his good behavior. Not that he had any doubts— there'd never been a woman he couldn't charm if he put his mind to it, and the Mannings' bad-tempered cook would fall as all the others had.

He hadn't set out to charm Georgie Manning. For one thing, she was too young. For another, he couldn't see any benefit in it, and he was always alert to what would benefit him. He also hadn't charmed Norah Manning, but he knew if he had the faintest desire to do so, he could change her mind about him. He'd sooner push her into a rubbish heap. He'd met other women like her, bedded them, and they were a tedious lot.

It was a good thing he didn't need much sleep. By the time he'd bathed and shaved and secured the proper clothes, it was close to six in the morning, and the Manning household would be awake and at work. He let himself in the servants' entrance to the old house, landing him in the kitchen, and he looked around him with interest. Bread was rising on the cookstove, and he could smell Earl Grey tea with its thick bergamot scent overriding kippers and bacon.

"Who the hell are you?" the woman by the table demanded, fixing him with a steely stare. She was in her fifties, plump and immaculate, and she was glaring at him as if he was a rat who dared invade her territory. The fearsome Bertha, no doubt.

"I'm Rafferty, the new butler."

"You are not," she shot back. "This household hasn't paid a servant in over a month. If you take my advice, you'll turn around and walk straight back out of here."

"I'm afraid I can't do that. Miss Georgiana hired me, and I promised I'd be here."

"Miss Georgie," Bertha said with a dismissive sniff. "She's as crazy as the rest of them, and what's she got to do with hiring a butler? That's her father's business, and he knows far too well that no one but a fool would agree to work for him."

"Then I'm a fool," he said easily. "You're Bertha."

Her gimlet eyes narrowed. "What did they tell you about me?"

"That you'd put the fear of God into me," he replied.

That surprised a bark of laughter from her. "Well, they told you true, at least." She looked him up and down. "You don't look like a butler."

He glanced down at his immaculate black suit. "Why not?"

"Too big for one. Too handsome. What kind of experience have you?"

"None."

"Well, that sounds about right," Bertha said with a sigh. "Sir Elston's awake by now—you may as well start by bringing his tea up to him. He lost his valet two weeks ago—are you any good at shaving?"

He touched his bare chin. "I've done it a few times."

"Good. You take care of Sir Elston and I'll take care of the ladies. Wouldn't want you to go traipsing around in their bedrooms anyway, though Miss Norah would likely bite your head off. Go on with you now."

"Who the hell are you?" Sir Elston Manning demanded as Rafferty let himself into the suite of bedrooms at the top of the stairs, and he stifled a grin.

"I'm Rafferty, sir," he said, setting the tea tray down on the small table by the bed. "Your new butler."

Sir Elston glared at him from under bushy eyebrows. He was a short man of impressive bulk, and he appeared less than thrilled with the new member of his household. "Who hired you?"

"Your daughter, sir."

"Norah?" he said, aghast.

"No, Miss Georgiana."

"What the hell was she thinking, hiring a butler we can't afford?"

"She knew I was in need of gainful occupation and she thought I might do."

"There'll be no gains from this household," Sir Elston said frankly. "We're on the rocks."

"A roof over my head and three meals a day is recompense enough for the time being. Once your fortunes rebound, you can pay me my back wages."

Manning's laugh was a harsh, grating sound. "You have more faith in my future than I do. What are your qualifications?"

"I believe I can carry out my duties to your satisfaction," Rafferty said smoothly. "Would you like me to shave you?"

There was no lessening of suspicion in Sir Elston's beady eyes, but he sighed. "Just don't cut my throat. If you're going to steal the silver, then do it. It's no good to me."

"So Miss Georgiana informed me. I have no interest in your silver, sir." That wouldn't have been true on any other occasion. He was a criminal, after all, a thief. A thoroughly bad man. But he had far bigger fish to fry.

"Hmmph. I trust you have no interest in my daughter," he said in his gravelly voice, "either of them."

"None apart from my employment, sir."

Sir Elston still didn't look convinced. "Touch a hair on their precious heads and you'll have me to answer to. I'll horsewhip you."

His new employer was almost a foot shorter than he was, and

well-padded. He'd have a hard time reaching him, but Rafferty simply nodded gravely. "Yes, sir."

"All right, then, Rafferty. You may shave me."

He managed a creditable job, given that he'd never shaved another man in his life, and saw Sir Elston neatly dressed and on his way downstairs before he heard the screech from one of the bedrooms. Since butlers were ostensibly in charge of an entire household, he went straight to the room, tapped on the door and pushed it open.

Norah Manning stood in the middle of the room, in the midst of throwing a brush, when she saw him. "Who are you?" she demanded in tones of deep loathing.

"I'm your new butler, remember?"

"Get out, get out, get out!" she screamed, throwing the brush at him.

He closed the door before it could hit him.

The door across the hall opened, and Miss Georgiana Manning stood there, her tawny hair in a braid halfway to her waist. "Who are you?" she said sleepily.

Introductions in this household were certainly consistent. "Rafferty, your new butler," he said politely.

Her bright blue eyes narrowed. "No, you're not! I hired a new butler last night, and he..."

"Shaved and bathed and bought a new suit," he said. "Good morning, Miss Georgiana."

A bright smile lit her face, and she came rushing out of her room, paying absolutely no attention to her deshabille. "It *is* you!" she said, taking his hands. "You look wonderful."

He gently detached himself. All he needed was the old man or the wicked sister to see him and his service would be at an end.

"Thank you, Miss Georgiana. Is there anything I might do for you? If not, I should go back downstairs..."

"Oh, no," she said. "I hired you, I should be the one who oversees what you do. Come into my room and talk to me."

"I can't do that, Miss Georgiana," he said solemnly. The

nightgown she was wearing was worn thin from use, whereas Norah's had been rich silk from the glance he'd had.

"Oh, call me Georgie," she said. "All my friends do."

"I'm not your friend, Miss Georgiana, I'm your servant. And it would be improper of me to come into your bedroom."

"Why not? Our old butler did when he brought me my tea. So did Harkner, Papa's valet. It's perfectly all right."

No, it wasn't, but he wasn't sure how he could explain that to her, when she herself came up with the answer. "You are remarkably handsome, Rafferty!" she said with a heartfelt sigh. "I never realized beneath the rags and dirt and beard that you were so pretty!"

He just looked at her. "Do you always say exactly what you're thinking?"

"I'm afraid so. My mother tells me it's a very bad habit, but since I don't go into society much, I don't see that it matters."

"You were out last night," he pointed out.

"That's because the Rutherfords aren't good ton," she confided. "And I don't really like society much. I wish we were back in the country."

"Why?" He shouldn't be having this conversation with her— he should be back down in the kitchen and away from temptation. Though why he should find her so tempting was a mystery. She was pretty enough, but no great beauty, and she definitely talked too much.

"I'm not supposed to talk about it," she said, and he hid his amusement. She talked about everything else.

Rafferty kept his face stoic. "Bertha said she'd bring your tea up to you. Would you like me to see what's keeping her?"

"Oh, she brought my tea ages ago. I was going to get dressed when I heard Norah having one of her temper tantrums. Was that over you?"

"I'm afraid so."

"Good," she said with a grin. "And you must have gone into her room. Why can't you come into mine?"

Because she doesn't look at me with shining eyes and call me pretty, he thought grimly. "Rules are rules, Miss Georgiana. You want me to be good at my job, don't you?"

"Yes, of course," she said earnestly.

"And you don't want to give your father any cause to fire me, do you?"

"Oh, he wouldn't. No one else would work for free."

He hid his own grin. "He's already warned me not to touch a hair on your head or he'll horsewhip me."

"But I didn't expect you to do my hair," she said, far too literal. "I just want to talk to you. You must have lived such an interesting life—I want to hear all about it."

He could just imagine her reaction to some of the harrowing tales of his thirty-one years. "Miss Georgiana, there's a great divide between those downstairs and those upstairs. Servants never converse with their employers."

Instead of looking chastened, she smiled at him. "See, you'll be perfect at this. How do you know so much about...about butling? Were you ever one before?"

He wondered how she'd react if he told her the truth. That the first fifteen years of his life he had lived in a great house, albeit on the edges of the family, and he'd had more than enough time to observe the duties of a butler. "No, miss. But I've read a lot." He threw that in for his own amusement, then regretted it when she latched on.

"You can read! Oh, that's wonderful. Except I'm disappointed —I had plans to teach you to read and write...oh, you can write, too, can't you?"

"Yes, Miss."

"Oh, don't call me miss. It's too formal."

"If there's one thing a butler is, it's formal."

She grimaced. "That's all right. I'll find something else to teach you. You're going to be the very best butler in all of London and everyone will want you but you'll tell them no and stay here because you're loyal and we're the ones who took you in."

"Very noble of you," he said, just a trace of ice in his voice.

"I said the wrong thing, didn't I? I always do." She screwed up her face in consternation. And then the distress vanished. "I know what we can do! I'll tell you all the little secrets of this household to ensure that you do an excellent job, and you can tell me when I've said the wrong thing. Not in front of my parents, mind you. They've given up on me and I don't want them knowing I'm trying to improve. But you can help me while I help you, and that way we can be friends, can't we?"

He looked down at her. *No, we can't be friends*, he thought with some frustration. *You need to stay in your world and I'll stay in mine*. But she was smiling up at him so sweetly that he couldn't bring himself to crush her spirit. Assuming it could be crushed—he was having his doubts about the irrepressible Miss Georgiana. Georgie. It was an absurdly good name for her.

"We can be friends," he said solemnly. "But for now, I've got my duties to perform, and you wouldn't want to keep me from them, now would you?"

"Of course not." Her brow wrinkled. "Will you come back later?"

"When I can," he lied. He knew what he was—Miss Georgiana Manning's new toy. She'd lose interest soon enough.

"Splendid!" she said, believing him, and he could have wished she weren't quite so gullible. Quite so talkative.

Quite so tempting.

Chapter Three

THE MANNING HOUSEHOLD was in chaos, Rafferty reflected a few hours later as he was polishing Sir Elston's shoes. The leather was worn thin, but he knew how to treat worn-out shoes, and he applied the polish in careful layers as he thought about his current situation.

The house was appalling—dust in the corners, shredded curtains in the sunroom, an almost empty cupboard as Bertha struggled to maintain what she could. He saw no sign of the lady of the house—apparently she spent most of the day in bed before she rose to go out on an endless succession of parties, and, while he knew Miss Norah Manning had risen, she had yet to make an appearance. He'd managed to avoid Georgie so far, but sooner or later...

"There you are!" she cried from the doorway. "What are you doing with my father's shoes?" She wandered into the kitchen, looking around her with interest.

"My job," he said reprovingly.

She turned and smiled at him. "I said the wrong thing again." She took the chair opposite and practically threw herself into it. She was dressed more appropriately now, though if his suspicions were right, the dress was too young for her, more appropriate for someone still in the schoolroom, which Georgie definitely was not. There was a stain across the front of the dress, and the hem had come loose, and her long, untended hair hung down her back. She looked more like a hoyden than a proper young lady, and he wished he didn't find her so...

He couldn't afford to think that way.

She didn't wait for his reply. "What else have you been doing? Have they got you polishing the silver yet?" She made a face. "It's huge—it'll take you days and days."

"No one's got me doing anything, Miss Georgiana. As the butler, I decide what needs to be done, and a gentleman needs more than one pair of shoes."

"I only have one pair of shoes," she confessed. "My dancing slippers, which is ridiculous because I'm not allowed to dance." She stuck her legs out from beneath her torn hem to display stockinged feet.

They were adorable. He frowned at her. "What do you wear when you go outside?"

"Oh, I have a pair of walking boots that are too small, but I can walk in them. I get blisters, so I tend to stay home, which is awful, but I think Mother prefers it that way. I miss the country-side, where I could go anywhere I wanted."

"How long have you been in the city?"

"A long time." She sighed, then smiled at him. "But life is going to get a great deal more interesting with you in the household. Do you want me to help you with Papa's shoes?"

"No, Miss Georgiana."

"Couldn't you call me Georgie?"

"No."

"What about Miss Georgie? That's what Bertha calls me. When she's not calling me a hellion and an imp of Satan and one of life's sore tribulations."

"What do you do to Bertha?" He was unable to hide his curiosity.

"She's teaching me how to cook, and I'm not very good at it.

But really, someone's got to help out around here, and we can't let the beauteous Norah soil her lily-white hands with menial labor."

No young lady of his memory would ever be allowed in the kitchen. "Does your mother know?"

"Oh, Mother doesn't care about anything but her parties and her cards. We wouldn't be nearly so destitute if she didn't gamble, or if she didn't always lose, but she says it's her only character flaw, which frankly isn't true, but I don't argue with her because she has a temper just like Norah, though she talks almost as much as I do."

"Impossible," he said faintly, setting down the shoe.

Georgie wasn't one to take offense. "Father adores Mother, but she really is useless."

"And Miss Norah is useless as well?"

"Oh, no! She's going to marry well and save us all." She sounded just the slightest bit doubtful of that happy outcome.

"And if she doesn't?"

"Then I'll have to think of something else."

"You could marry some rich toff," he suggested.

She shook her head. "Hardly. Norah is the beauty. No one can hold a candle to her. I expect that if I'm lucky enough to get married, it will be some ancient widower."

He could have explained to her in simple terms how wrong she was. Her tall, lush frame was just the sort of thing any man would like, and even her endless prattle was disarming. Despite not having a dowry, she could have her pick if the men in society had half a brain. Which he suspected they didn't.

She needed someone to show her just how pretty she was. If they were anywhere else, he'd take her in his arms and demonstrate, but she was too young and he needed this place too much. He told himself he wasn't even tempted, and he knew he lied.

"But that's neither here nor there," she continued briskly before he had a chance to come up with a response. "I've come to find you because I want to help. I'm quite good at it, you know. I can make beds, and dust, and—"

"Now you go leaving Rafferty alone, Miss Georgie!" Bertha announced as she trudged into the kitchen lugging a bucket of water and a mop. "He's got his work to do—he doesn't have time for the likes of you. And don't expect me to give you cooking lessons today—we've just about nothing to eat, and I don't know what we're going to do. The butcher and the greengrocer won't advance us any more credit, and while I can make a meal out of eggs and bread, it's not the sort of thing I like to set before the gentry."

"I wasn't bothering him, Bertha!" she protested. "He's my protégé, and I'm looking after him."

"Your what?"

"My protégé."

"He's no such thing, and you should be ashamed to think it!" Bertha snapped.

"Why?" Georgie asked, perplexed.

"Never you mind! You just go along back upstairs and see to some of the mending—that's a nice, ladylike occupation."

"I'm terrible with a needle and thread," Georgie confessed.

"I know you are. Practice makes perfect."

Rafferty rose then, setting the polished shoes on the floor. "I'll see what I can do about the larder."

Georgie looked up at him. "You're going out? Can I come with you?"

"No!" Bertha and Rafferty said in unison, but Georgie was far from cowed.

"Well, I'm coming, and if you leave without me, I'll just sneak out and follow you, so you might as well let me come. Besides, if the butcher sees my woebegone face he might take pity on us and extend us a little more credit." She came up with a creditably forlorn expression, and Rafferty laughed before he could stop himself.

"I doubt it," Bertha said. "It's a waste of time for both of you —Jenkins has a heart of stone and we're more than two months in arrears."

"I'm a butler," Rafferty said. "I'm supposed to work miracles."

"You'll need one for Jenkins."

"And I'm coming with you!" Georgie announced, brooking no argument. "Just let me get my boots." She was off before he could come up with another protest, and his eyes met Bertha's.

"Is she always like this?"

"Miss Georgie? Oh, she's the best of them—good as gold, she is, and worth twice her feckless family. The master's not so bad, but he's over his head and can't find his way out of the mess he's in. Sooner or later we'll all be out on the streets, and that's likely to be sooner."

That wouldn't suit him at all, Rafferty thought. He'd had a chance to make a preliminary inventory of the place—this ramshackle old house was huge, with a warren of cellars beneath the ground floor, attics overhead, and the rambling family quarters. Belding could have stored his money anywhere, and it was going to take time to find it. If the Mannings were thrown out on the street, he'd no longer have access to the place. Of course, he might be lucky and find the stuff on first try, but life didn't tend to work that way. And he had Billy Stiles breathing down his neck, just as determined to find Belding's cache as he was.

It should be simple enough—his erstwhile employer, the notorious Judge Belding, had left a fortune behind, presumably in this very house.

He also didn't fancy seeing Georgie destitute, though the rest of them could suffer for all he cared. Though he liked Sir Elston, and Bertha was a good sort.

"She needs to get married," he said, half to himself.

"Miss Norah's been scaring them all away, for all she's a diamond."

"I meant Miss Georgie."

Bertha didn't blink at the nickname. "She's not interested. The daft girl wants nothing more than to go back to the country and live a quiet life. What she wants is a farmer, say, or a horse trainer, and you can imagine what Sir Elston would say to that."

"She'll get married," he said firmly.

Bertha's brow furrowed. "It will be up to Sir Elston to arrange something, and he's got enough on his plate right now, trying to bring Norah up to snuff."

"I think you're underestimating Miss Georgie's charms," he said.

"I think that you're paying too much attention to Miss Georgie and not enough on your duties," Bertha said dourly. "She's not for the likes of you."

"Don't be ridiculous," he said, horrified at the idea.

"Just keep that in mind. And don't call her Georgie. She's Miss Georgiana to you."

Bertha was right—he was asking too many questions about someone who was none of his business. He needed to concentrate on Henry Belding's lost fortune.

"I'm going before she can get back," he said, heading for the door. "Stall her if she tries to follow."

"She's a stubborn young woman. Might as well try to stop a hurricane," Bertha said dubiously.

It was a beautiful day in Mayfair, the crisp autumn weather a treat for the mind and soul. If he still had a soul, which he sincerely doubted. No one even glanced at him as he strode, hatless, down the sidewalk.

He was walking too fast, ghosts and demons at his heels, when he suddenly remembered who he was pretending to be, and he slowed his pace to a butler's walk, a cross between self-important and servile, and was congratulating himself when he heard a clatter of footsteps behind him.

Chapter Four

HIS LEGS WERE SIMPLY TOO LONG, Georgie thought as she scurried after him. She was already limping slightly in her too-small boots, but she was determined.

"I told you I'd follow you," she said triumphantly, catching up with him. "Bertha said I was to bring this basket along as well, just in case you managed to talk someone into an act of charity."

"No one's getting charity," he said. "I'll simply explain to the shopkeepers that it would be in their best interest to advance more credit. They'll be reasonable."

"I doubt it," she said, looking up at him. She still couldn't get over the transformation—he was quite the prettiest man she'd ever seen. No, not pretty like Darcy Winderham, the town beau with the brain of a peacock, but pretty like some ancient Greek statue. He had high cheekbones and a strong chin, but it was his eyes, she thought dreamily. They were a beautiful clear blue with hints of silver—quite the most extraordinary eyes she'd ever seen on anyone, including her sister's limpid, violet gaze. Of course, when his eyes rested on her, they tended to be impatient, but she could deal with that.

She would have to work on him. After all, she wanted to talk to him, to find out all about his mysterious life and what it was like on the streets.

Rafferty let out a sigh. "You're limping," he observed.

"My boots are too small—I told you."

"So you did. We'll have to arrange for new shoes for you."

"That's not a butler's job," she protested, skipping slightly to keep up with his long strides, and he slowed down. "Besides, there's no money for frivolities."

"Everything is a butler's job, Miss Georgie."

He called her by her name! She smiled up at him. "I told you that you were a natural at this. But how are we going to get me shoes? You can't just go out and buy them, and the cobbler told father he'd see him in hell before he made another pair of shoes for our family."

"Who told you that?"

"Norah, of course. She likes to tell me things that will worry me. Not that I'm that worried about shoes—I can manage with what I have. It's the bigger things that trouble me."

"Such as what?" They'd fallen into step together, almost by accident.

"There's no money," she said. "You've seen how we're struggling. If I were beautiful like Norah, I could marry a rich man and save the family." She didn't sound happy about the idea. "But I'm not."

"You'll find a good husband," he said eventually.

"I don't really want to," she said. "But under the circumstances, I can make do with shoes that are too small. It's a small enough sacrifice."

"You can't."

She was learning his grumpy voice and liking it. He used it when he thought things weren't fair, which meant he cared about her.

"You do, don't you?" she said suddenly.

"Do what?"

"Care about me." She gave another skip to catch up and her

foot caught on something, tripping her up. He caught her, his hands strong and secure as he set her to rights, and she wanted to sigh with happiness. He probably wouldn't like it if she did.

"A butler cares about every member of his household."

"But you care about me more than Norah, don't you?"

"Your sister is a snake," he said flatly, and she smiled up at him.

"Yes, she is," she said cheerfully. "You know, I think you're the only person who likes me better than Norah."

"Then the world is full of fools." He stopped, and she realized they were outside of the butcher's shop. "Stay here and don't move," he said sternly. "Don't speak to anyone. You promise?"

"I promise," she said, holding out the large basket.

He shook his head. "I won't need it."

Georgie grimaced. "You're right—he won't change his mind."

"He'll change his mind, but the order will be large enough that he'll have to send it to the house."

"You don't know Mr. Jenkins," she said, shaking her head.

"You don't know me." The door closed behind him, and she stayed where she was, mainly because her feet hurt too much to wander. The sun was warm overhead, and she surreptitiously lifted one foot hidden under her skirt and wiggled it as she watched through the window.

Mr. Jenkins was there with his blood-stained apron and his pugnacious expression, glowering at Rafferty, and she sighed. Rafferty must be used to getting what he wanted, which didn't surprise her in the slightest. She'd certainly do anything for him. But Mr. Jenkins was shaking his head, and then he...stopped. Even through the fly-specked windows, it seemed as if Jenkins's usually ruddy face paled, and his glare faded, and Georgie would have given anything to hear what they were saying.

A moment later Rafferty was out on the street. "There'll be a delivery this afternoon," he said, taking the basket from her. "Do you know where the greengrocer is?"

"How did you get Mr. Jenkins to agree?" she asked in wonder, setting her foot down and hiding her grimace.

"I simply explained the situation and he was more than happy to oblige," he said blandly.

Georgie didn't believe him for a moment. "You are a miracle worker," she said.

"I do my best, Miss Georgie." For the first time that day, he smiled back at her, and the strangest thing happened. There was a ripple in her stomach that had nothing to do with hunger, a strange pinch between her breasts, and she almost wanted to cry. The sensation was most peculiar. Instead, she looked up at him brightly. "Let's see how you do with the greengrocers," she said.

Two hours later, they were nearing home, Georgie's basket was empty, her feet hobbled by the too-small boots, but her heart was filled with happiness. Rafferty had worked his magic at each of their stops, and though she tried to get close enough to hear his exchange with the merchants, they remained stubbornly out of reach, but everyone's reaction was the same. They went from truculent to servile in a matter of moments, and Rafferty was on his way again, with Georgie clattering after him.

She would have liked to have taken his arm, but she knew how frowned-upon that would be, particularly by Rafferty himself, and she resisted the temptation. She didn't particularly care if it would damage her own reputation, but it wouldn't look good for him. After all, he seemed determined to make a success of his new position, and she certainly didn't want to do anything to jeopardize it. But he had such strong arms.

They were almost home when she tripped again, caught once more against his strong body. There was something shockingly delicious about it, about the warmth and strength of him, and she let out a happy little sigh as she straightened herself. "Sorry," she said, not in the slightest bit sorry.

He looked down at her. "Lift up your skirts," he said in his low voice.

"In public?" she said. She should have blushed at his abrupt command, but she wasn't one for blushing.

He didn't even look around to see if someone was watching. "In public."

She did so, exposing her not so tiny feet in the far too tiny walking boots. "They're not so bad," she said, but Rafferty had let out a low curse, and a moment later he'd scooped her up in his arms.

She let out a little whoop of surprise as he carried her, and while she wanted to do nothing more than enjoy the sensation, she knew she had to look out for him.

"If someone sees us, you'll be in trouble," she said, unable to keep the anxiety out of her voice.

"There's no one around."

She turned in his arms to look, and sure enough, the street near their house was almost empty, save for a few delivery wagons. A moment later, he was down the few short steps to the alley leading to the kitchen, and she let her head rest against his shoulder for a brief moment. It was too tempting to resist.

"What is it now?" Bertha demanded when he pushed through the door. "Miss Georgie, what tricks have you been pulling?"

He set her down carefully, and she immediately sank into one of the kitchen chairs, determined not to show that she missed the feel of his arms around her. "No tricks, Bertha. My shoes are too tight."

"And well I know that. You should have taken Miss Norah's. Better yet, you should have stayed at home and let Rafferty do what he could. Maybe without you tagging along he wouldn't have failed."

"He didn't fail, Bertha," she said earnestly, rubbing her foot in the boot. "There'll be deliveries this afternoon."

"I'll believe it when I see it. In the meantime, you'd best go up to your room before your mother hears you've been out gallivanting."

"I like gallivanting," she said defiantly.

"You should know better!"

"You need to get those boots off," Rafferty interrupted. "Do you need me to carry you to your room..."

"She does not!" Bertha said. "She's been wearing those boots for months now—they aren't going to kill her. Go along with you now, and I'll bring tea up later. I have a few words to say to Rafferty."

Georgie looked between the two of them. Bertha was looking grim, Raffety his usual cool unreadable self. She wracked her brain for a reason to stay longer, but she was coming up blank, and she really did need to get these blasted boots off. She savored the curse word. Blasted. There was something deliciously shocking about it.

Slowly she rose, determined not to evince one sign of pain, and she smiled at Rafferty. "You could send Rafferty up with my tea."

"I could not. He'll have enough things to do. Go along with you."

She gave him one last glance before heading for the servants' staircase, over Bertha's objections, and she didn't start limping again until she was out of sight.

RAFFERTY TURNED BACK TO BERTHA, more than aware he was about to have his head handed to him. Too bad the deliveries hadn't arrived yet—it would sweeten her mood.

"You don't belong here," she said.

Rafferty smiled faintly. "No, I don't suppose I do, but it'll suit me well enough for the next few weeks."

Bertha scowled. "That foolish little girl is falling in love with you, in case you hadn't noticed."

"I noticed. She'll get over it. They all do." He moved over to the window to make sure no one had followed them—an old habit but one hard to break.

"Miss Georgie isn't like most silly young girls. She's got a heart of gold, she has, and I'm not going to stand by and watch you break it."

He turned back to her, unmoved. "That's the last thing I want to do. Don't worry—she'll forget all about me the moment I'm gone."

"Not planning to stay long? I'm not surprised. I've never seen anyone less like a butler in my life. The sooner you're on your way, the better."

"All in good time," Rafferty said. "But I think you underestimate Miss Georgiana." He used her full name on purpose, but Bertha didn't look appeased. "Give her the proper clothes and she'll have young men at her feet."

"I wish that were true. But it won't do anyone any good if all she wants is you."

"I told you, she'll get over it."

"Humph," Bertha said, a wealth of meaning in that one word. "In the meantime, where did you get those two girls who showed up an hour ago, saying they were maids? The Mannings can't even pay me, much less two able-bodied young women."

"You let me worry about that," he said. "I trust you put them to work?"

"Of course I did. Even if they're only here for a day, they can make a difference in this wreck of a house."

"They're here for as long as you want them."

"But the money..."

They were interrupted by a rap on the kitchen door, and a moment later, Mr. Jenkins himself was there, directing his men to carry in the loads of meat and eggs that Rafferty had ordered. Bertha took it all in, along with Jenkins's ingratiating manner, and said not a word till they were alone once more, and then she turned on Rafferty.

"Just who the hell are you?"

❧

GEORGIE HADN'T PLANNED on running smack into her sister as she emerged from the servant's staircase, and she tried to duck back in before it was too late, but Norah's beautiful purple eyes had already narrowed in on her.

"Been consorting with the servants again, George?" she demanded archly.

Georgie controlled her temper. "I was helping my protégé."

"Your what?" Norah's voice rose. "Good God, George, does Father know about this?"

"Of course he does. And he approved. Rafferty shaved him this morning."

"Rafferty?"

"Pay attention, Norah," she said impatiently. "Rafferty's our new butler, and he's my protégé, just like Mother has."

"It better not be just like Mother has," Norah said obscurely, "or your protégé will be back out on the street in no time. Come to think of it, a strange man did enter my bedroom this morning, but I'd forgotten. So, we have a butler again? Thank God for that!"

"Thank me for that," Georgie said. "I found him."

"What do you mean, you found him?"

"Don't you remember? He was the Dregs of Society. I decided to reform him and make him our butler. He doesn't even want any money for doing it. Or, at least, he may want it, but he knows he's not going to get it and he's willing to be our butler anyway."

"You're out of your mind!" Norah snapped. "That man assaulted me! God knows what he'll do to the household if he's given free rein."

"He's going to run the household, and there's nothing you can do about it," she said defiantly.

"Not if I have anything to say about it," Norah snapped. She raised her voice to an unpleasant shriek. "Mother! Father!"

"Oh, bugger off," Georgie said unwisely, stomping to her bedroom door and slamming it shut in her sister's face. It wasn't, perhaps, the most felicitous of phrases—she'd picked it up on the streets, but it had a satisfyingly vulgar sound, and she'd been looking for a chance to use it. Her sister deserved it.

They'd never been close, but at least when they lived in the countryside Norah hadn't been so determinedly mean. Georgie tried to be generous—Norah was unhappy and her sour outlook on life touched everyone but her army of would-be suitors. Georgie did her best to shrug it off—at least it was nothing personal. Everyone suffered from Norah's lash of a tongue.

She threw herself into the first chair she found. Stomping had not been a smart idea in these boots, and her feet were burning with so much pain that she had trouble unlacing them, her hands shaking with the effort. Once completely unlaced she tried to pull off the shoe, but it clung tightly to her foot, and she leaned back with a cry of frustration. Her feet had fit into the boots with only a little bit of effort—they must have swollen while she wore them. She could do nothing but listen as her sister and mother squawked in the hallway and her father's deep bellow joined in. She had the truly awful feeling that they were going to try to take Rafferty away from her, and she couldn't let them do that. Neither could she fight for him, at least not until she could pry the boots off her feet, and she didn't dare admit she'd worn them again. Her mother had tried to throw them out, her father would feel bad, and everything would be in an even greater uproar than it already was.

Her door slammed open, and she closed her eyes for a moment as her family crowded into her bedroom, the three of them talking at once. She let it go on for a bit, then finally raised her voice.

"Stop it!"

Needless to say it didn't quiet her voluble family for even a moment. "Norah says you've brought a beggar into the house and set him up as our butler!" her mother declaimed. Liliane Manning had a decided affection for drama.

"Best shave I've had in weeks," Sir Elston said. "And he'll work without wages."

"Don't be ridiculous—the man is a hoodlum," Norah said. "He assaulted me!"

"Assaulted you?" Sir Elston raised his voice. "When?"

"He didn't assault her," Georgie said patiently. "He merely scared her and she tripped."

"We can't have the butler scaring us!" Liliane said. "What would our visitors think?"

"He wasn't our butler when he scared her. She was being awful, and he merely—"

"That's right, make excuses for him," Norah cut her off. "Can't you see she's half in love with him already? You know how Georgie gets these crushes—two years ago it was the French master."

"That was just a crush, and I was a child. And besides, I am not in love with him," she defended herself.

Her mother frowned. "In love with the butler? How absurd —nobody falls in love with a butler. I could understand it with a footman—a matched pair can be quite striking," she went on. "But there's something pathetic about falling in love with one's butler. As if one couldn't reach any higher."

"I'm not in love with anyone," Georgie blurted out. "He's my protégé."

There was a deafening silence in the room, as the three other members of her family looked anywhere but at each other. "You can't have a protégé," Sir Elston said finally. "It's not done."

"Why not? Mother has protégés."

"Enough of that," Liliane interfered, unruffled. "Where is this new butler of ours? I want to meet him."

Sir Elston sighed. "He's a good-looking chap. You'll like him."

"Then why keep him around?" Norah demanded.

"I've learned to pick my battles," he said. "There are some things I can do nothing about, and that includes your mother's little pets. If I can get a good shave out of the bargain, I'll count it worthwhile."

But Liliane Manning was ignoring him, a contemplative expression on her ageless face. "What's the man's name?"

"Rafferty," Georgie supplied, feeling a combination of hope and despair. "And he's my protégé, not yours."

"Oh, I don't like Rafferty. It sounds so...raffish. Couldn't we come up with something a bit more English?"

"We can't allow him to stay!" Norah protested, incensed.

"Oh, I tend to agree with your father. We badly need a butler, and it sounds as if he's perfectly presentable. I think we should take him on."

Georgie knew that expression on her mother's face, and her heart sank. It was slightly predatory, if truth be told, and it would end with father shouting and her mother weeping and Rafferty out the door...

"We'll be murdered in our beds!" Norah said.

"You wish!" Georgie shot back, albeit illogically. "He's mine and I'm not sharing."

Liliane shrugged. "It is nice to see you take an interest in something, dearest Georgie, and heaven knows I've never been terribly gifted at household management. I have too much of an artistic temperament to bother myself with these matters. If you've found a presentable butler, then so be it. And Norah, you should be glad there's someone to answer the door when your Lord Felton calls."

"I've decided against Lord Felton," Norah announced. "He smells of the shop."

"That's why he has so much money, my dear," Sir Elston said. "And you've become a little too exacting in your demands. I've had three offers for your hand and you've rejected them all. The next time some poor fool asks me, I'm going to say yes."

"You wouldn't dare!" Norah seethed.

"Watch me."

She flounced out of the room, much to Georgie's relief, quickly followed by Liliane who was making cooing noises at her adored elder daughter. "Precious, your father didn't mean it..."

"I meant it," Sir Elston growled, turning to look at her. "Is your sister right? Is this man a danger to our household?"

"Of course not," Georgie said soothingly. "He's quite wonderful."

His face turned even more dour. "I trust Norah was simply causing trouble when she said you were in love with him. If I thought there was any chance of Rafferty being forward enough to…"

"Rafferty would never do anything!" she assured him, trying to hide her own regret.

"Because your mother's…affections for her protégés is something that is not acceptable in an innocent young girl."

"Oh, it's nothing like that," Georgie said earnestly, still not sure why her mother's affections for her protégés would be a problem.

"Then we'll keep him on, for the present at least. I imagine there'll be more than enough to keep him busy. You just keep your distance, young lady."

She didn't bother to protest. Her father was too wrapped up in his business worries to pay attention to what went on in his household, and besides, she had no wicked designs on Rafferty. Not that it would have done her any good. And he had no wicked designs on her. Alas.

When she was finally alone, she limped over to her bed, making one last attempt to strip the shoes off her feet, and then gave up, lying back. The window was open—she liked to keep one open even on the coldest days, and this autumn afternoon was no more than mildly brisk. She would lie there and wait until the swelling went down in her feet, lie there and dream of those strange, hypnotic eyes and his warm body, she would dream of…

Chapter Five

GEORGIE AWOKE with a start at the sound of a soft knock on her door. No one in the household knocked—everyone from Bertha on up tended to barge in without warning. "Come in," she said sleepily.

It was Rafferty, carrying a steaming pan of water. "How are your feet doing, Miss Georgiana?"

She resisted making a face at the formal address and quickly sat up. "They're fine," she said, trying to tuck the boots up under her skirts.

He closed the door behind him and advanced into the room, and Georgie felt a flush of happiness, one she tried to hide. "You need to soak them," he said.

He set the basin on the floor by the chair, and she looked at it dubiously. Maybe the hot water would loosen the boots' stranglehold on her poor abused feet.

"I will," she said, not moving.

He waited. She waited. Finally, he spoke. "Do you usually sleep with your shoes on?"

She made a sound of disgust, flipping back the hem of her skirt to reveal the boots. "I couldn't get them off."

Before she realized what he'd intended, he scooped her off the bed and settled her in the chair, kneeling down at her feet. "You should have called for me."

"I could have gotten them off my...self." She swallowed a groan of pain as he began to pull the boot. He was holding her foot in one hand, tugging gently, and after a moment, the boot came free. She had blood on her stockings.

He said nothing, merely applied himself to the other foot, and a moment later both were free. "Take off your stockings," he said, as calmly as if he were asking her for a biscuit.

"I can't!" she said, scandalized.

"Why not?"

She thought about it for a moment, then realized to her chagrin that he wouldn't care if she stripped naked. There was a challenge in his voice, and Georgie was not a one who backed down from a challenge.

"All right." She contemplated telling him to turn his back, then thought better of it. If he was daring her, she was going to call his bluff.

It was relatively easy to reach up under her skirts to her ribboned garter, easy to untie it and pull it out. It was originally pink silk, but use and many washings had faded it to almost white, and she suddenly remembered that the other garter didn't match. Fancy undergarments were one of the first things to go when they could no longer afford to go to the modiste.

And she was not going to let it bother her. With a calm efficiency, she untied the other one, pulling out a blue garter and setting it beside the pink one. "They don't match," she said disconsolately.

"Luckily, no gentleman will know that," he said, unmoved.

"You know it."

"But I'm no gentleman. I'm the butler. Do you want to unroll your stockings or shall I?"

That really did shock her. "I will." She hesitated. "Turn your back."

To her chagrin he did so, and she rolled the silk down her legs, pulling them free from the bloody patches with a hiss of pain. He turned back, and her skirts were to her knees, her feet completely bare, and she knew a proper young woman would blush and protest. She had never aspired to be a proper young woman.

"Put your feet in the water," he ordered, and she did so, letting out a soft sigh of pleasure as the warmth enveloped them. The water smelled of lavender and chamomile and she leaned back against the chair with a blissful smile.

"Who does the physicking in this household?" he said as he scooped up the boots and tucked them under his arm, preparing to depart.

She didn't want him to go. "No one. Well, me, I guess, when we've had servants and the like. Mother doesn't like illness and injury—they make her queasy."

"Your mother sounds useless," he said, a trace of harshness in his voice.

"Oh, she's quite beautiful. And very charming. Norah takes after her, but my mother is much nicer. She just doesn't like unpleasant or demanding things taking her attention."

"I see." He dropped the fiendish boots by the door and came back to her. "I'll take care of it."

"Take care of what?"

Once more, he knelt down in front of her, and she had the temporary fantasy of a prince begging for her hand in marriage. He'd make a very handsome prince, she thought dizzily as she looked down at him.

"Give me your foot," he said.

That was so far beyond the bounds of propriety that she hesitated, but he simply reached into the water and lifted her foot into his strong hands, drying it with one of the towels he'd brought. It felt lovely, being cradled by him, and it was all she could do to keep her expression bland when she wanted to purr. And then he brought out a tin of salve and rubbed it on her very bare foot, soothing it into the abraded skin, his fingers kneading the arch, the ball of her foot, the heel.

She couldn't stop herself; she moaned in pleasure, and he glanced up at her from beneath his lashes, absurdly long lashes for a man, and there was the trace of a grin at his beautiful mouth. "This is completely unacceptable," he said, "but I don't think anyone else is going to take care of you. I suggest you don't tell your mother." He set her foot down on the carpet and reached for the other one.

"Or my father or my sister," she said, squirming in delight as his hands massaged her foot. She wasn't used to people touching her, particularly so intimately, and she could see why it was considered indecent. Anything that felt that good must be shameful indeed.

He finished and rose, and she wanted to cry out in frustration. Her whole body felt taut, aroused in some way, and she wanted...she wasn't sure what she wanted, but it definitely had to do with his hands on her body.

But he'd picked up the basin of water and was moving away before she could stop him. And indeed, what could she say? He'd performed an act of such intimacy on her that she didn't feel she'd ever be the same again.

"Will you do that again?" she said forlornly as he headed for the door.

He stopped and grinned, very much not like a butler. "Not likely, Miss Georgie. I'd be horsewhipped if anyone found out."

"I won't tell anyone, I promise," she said earnestly. "But what if I—"

"I'm getting rid of your boots," he forestalled her.

"You can't throw them out!" she cried, envisioning a lifetime of imprisonment without street shoes.

"I won't. There are plenty of people down on the docks with smaller feet than you have. Someone will need them."

She looked down at her own feet, now pink and healthy looking. "Mine are awfully big," she admitted with a sigh. "Norah tells me I have the feet of a peasant."

"You aren't going to tell me you believe what your sister says?" he said.

He was across the room, too far away from her, the basin held in front of him, and she swallowed her sigh of pure longing. He was just so beautiful. Her mother would think so too.

With that depressing thought, she shook her head. "No. She just always knows what's going to upset me." She looked at him again. "Thank you, Rafferty."

His smile was a thing of beauty, without that trace of cynicism that usually accompanied it. "My pleasure, Miss Georgie."

And she almost thought he meant it.

WHO'D HAVE THOUGHT he'd find someone's feet that erotic, especially a proper young woman like Georgie? He should think of her as Miss Georgiana, but right then, with a hard cock and a hunger he should be ashamed of, he could only think of her as Georgie. And she wasn't that proper, he reminded himself. She needed to get married before her adventurous ways got her into trouble. For some reason, the thought troubled him.

He was being a fool. Marriage was the best thing for her—away from her poisonous sister and her strumpet of mother. Bertha had been surprisingly loquacious after a while, and it was clear the problems in the Manning household were legendary. They were on the brink of ruin, Sir Elston on the brink of divorce. Rafferty just needed them to hold together until he found Belding's cache and then he could return to...return to what? He was no longer sure it was the life he wanted to lead.

He could always join Billy Stiles in his criminal enterprises, assuming he didn't end up killing him, which was seeming more and more likely. They were both in search of the money Judge Belding had hidden away, and despite Billy's smiling assurances, there was no way the two of them were going to share it. Billy had no qualms disposing of inconveniences, and

Rafferty had it in mind to be very inconvenient indeed. With Stiles gone, the rest of his men would fall in line, and he could have a rich, happy life. After all, there was no such thing as having too much money, despite his own healthy assets. The only problem was...he didn't want to. He'd been in the game too long—he wanted something else, and he hadn't the faintest idea what.

Jane and Betsy were in the servants' hall when he reached it, scrubbing away at the long table that should have fed at least a dozen servants, and they greeted him shyly. They were whores and pickpockets, and he'd had some doubts about bringing them into the Manning household before he realized there wasn't much left to steal. Anything of value had already been sold, and besides, the two girls were in awe of him. They'd think twice about displeasing him by pocketing their employers' silver. Though, in truth, he was their employer, not the Mannings.

He moved on to the kitchen, where Bertha was plucking one of the quails Jenkins had brought, and he realized the household needed at least one more servant for the kitchen, to help Bertha and to wash the dishes. Young Polly might do for that, he thought. He'd make arrangements in the morning.

Bertha was unaware of the treat in store for her, and she jerked her head in the direction of the girls. "Those two girls are terrible."

He raised an eyebrow. "They're not helping?"

"They can clean," she said grudgingly. "Wouldn't trust 'em for a minute."

"They won't take anything, I can guarantee it," he said, already accustomed to Bertha's dour attitude.

"No one can guarantee servants won't steal."

"I can. You want me to finish with that quail?"

She looked at him then, a suspicious expression on her face. "I've never heard of a butler helping out in the kitchen."

"Well, this isn't an ordinary household, and I'm not an ordinary butler."

"You're certainly not." She shoved the carcass at him and he rolled up his sleeves. "How's Miss Georgie?"

"She's fine. Her feet hurt, but the salve I used should fix her up."

There was a dangerous silence. "You put salve on her feet? Her bare feet?" Bertha intoned with awful menace.

"I did. And don't tell me that now I have to marry her—I didn't touch her above her ankles."

Bertha hooted with laughter. "The day I see a Manning marry a butler will be the day I give up on the world. She'd be sent to live on the streets before such a catastrophe."

He didn't react. "Well, then it's a good thing I was simply treating her injuries since no one else in the household seems to care about her."

"You *care* about her?" Bertha demanded in horror.

"I don't like to see any innocent thing hurting." He was starting to find this conversation highly annoying.

"And that's exactly what she is. An innocent, and you're to keep your wicked hands off her."

He sighed. "I have no interest in putting my hands on her. She's a child."

"She's twenty, practically on the shelf."

"And I'm thirty-one and not interested in virgins."

He half expected Bertha to explode, but she was a smart old bird. She simply nodded. "Make sure you don't change your mind."

There was a noise outside the green baize door, and Bertha was suddenly alert. "Christ!" she said in disgust. "It's herself."

Before Rafferty could ask, the door flew open and a vision appeared. For a moment he thought it was a particularly colorful version of Miss Norah Manning, but a moment later, he realized his mistake. The woman standing there in sapphire silk, dripping with jewelry, was at least twenty years older, for all that she was as great a beauty as her daughter.

"Cook!" she announced in a deep, extravagant voice. "I've

come to check on the household!" Her magnificent gray eyes focused on him. "And this must be the new butler I keep hearing about."

He rose from his seat at the table and his dead bird and bowed low. "Rafferty, Lady Manning."

The woman let out a trilling laugh. "You are a handsome one, aren't you? And so tall! I do like a tall man."

Rafferty wondered whether he dared stoop. She came closer, smelling of expensive perfume, and he could see that her jewels were paste. Excellent copies, but fakes nonetheless. He wondered if she knew.

"How very clever of little Georgie to find you," she continued, running her eyes up and down his body. "We've been simply bereft since our last butler left us. We're a very particular household, you understand, and we don't hire just anybody."

"I noticed, my lady."

She fluttered. "And such a deliciously deep voice. I may have you read to me when you bring my warm chocolate in the evening. Just the thing for falling asleep. You can read, can't you?"

He didn't miss the warning look Bertha shot him, but he simply bowed. "I can. Whatever your ladyship wishes," he said, raising the timbre of his voice slightly.

But Liliane Manning was past noticing, and he realized she was practically drooling at his feet. This was an unneeded complication, but one he was more than adept at handling. His face and height had attracted all sorts of unwanted attention over the years, and he knew what to do to discourage it.

The door flew open, and Norah Manning marched in, a militant set to her shoulders, exposed in a new and very expensive evening gown. Despite the Mannings' enforced economies, they clearly hadn't spread as far to mother and older daughter.

"Didn't I tell you, mother?" she demanded in a strident voice.

But her mother was still gazing at him fondly. "He's quite something, Norah. You forgot to mention how handsome he was. He'll do very well for welcoming our guests."

"Which guests?" Bertha muttered behind him, but Lady Manning paid no attention.

He braced himself, waiting for Norah's scorn, but those magnificent purple eyes simply followed her mother's, and she had a thoughtful expression on her face. "George picked him up in the slums," she warned.

"I do wish you wouldn't call her 'George.' It's such a manly name. And we should be more than grateful to her. Imagine finding such a diamond in a lump of coal."

Rafferty wasn't thrilled at being called a lump of coal, but he was even less fond of Norah's expression. She came forward, walking around him like she was inspecting a prime piece of horseflesh. Apparently. she decided she liked what she saw after all. "He's not bad," she said suddenly. "We just have to make sure George doesn't appropriate him."

"He wouldn't look twice at her," Liliane announced.

Bertha choked at that, then covered it with a fit of coughing. "Now you two go along with you," she said, bustling forward with the temerity of an old, valued servant. "I've got dinner to cook and Rafferty's got his own tasks. You've met him and you've approved of him, now haven't you, so all's well." She began shooing them toward the door.

But Norah Manning lingered, her cool eyes like a proprietary touch on his body. "Perhaps you'll do after all," she murmured, closer than he would like.

"I will strive to deliver satisfaction, Miss Manning," he said without inflection, keeping his gaze lowered when he'd rather meet it directly. She really was an astonishingly beautiful woman, from her unusual violet eyes to her perfect figure to her cupid's bow of a mouth. That mouth that was usually curled in disdain.

He liked beautiful women—what man didn't? And he could have this one, ruin her value on the marriage mart for his own pleasure. It would serve her right.

He'd sooner bed an adder. He lifted his gaze, and found she

was watching him, an arrested expression in her eyes, as if seeing something for the first time. He wanted to groan.

"I suppose we'll let George keep you," she said finally. "She has so little to amuse her, poor dear, and, of course, no prospects. Let her have her little pet."

"Not so little, Miss Norah," Bertha piped up, and Rafferty had forgotten she was there. "And Miss Georgie will do just fine if you ask me. You need to concentrate on your own business and find a rich man to marry."

Norah turned away from him with a wave of her hand. "They bore me," she said. "I might want to sow a few wild oats before I settle down. After all, my mother certainly does, and she's received everywhere."

"Your mother waited until after she married and had children," Bertha pointed out.

"But I'm even more beautiful than she was," Norah said with complete assurance. "If I happen to blot my copybook, then the right sort of man won't mind."

"It's exactly the right sort of man who would mind," Bertha said, eyeing her. "Get along with you, now. We've got work to do here, and no doubt you're going out again. That's a new dress or I miss my guess."

Norah preened, and even her self-congratulatory air couldn't dim her beauty. "You don't know the trouble I had talking Papa into getting me a new one. I reminded him it was an investment in the future, but he still fussed, and Madame Racette insisted, absolutely insisted on being paid up front. I've a mind to take my custom elsewhere. Oh, I am so dreadfully tired of worrying about something as tawdry as money."

"Tawdry," he muttered, and she cast a quick, suspicious glance at him, but he'd already lowered his gaze once more.

"See that you keep an eye on this one, Bertha," Norah said. "We don't really know where he came from." The green baize door closed silently behind her, and Bertha turned to look at him.

"You've got this household in a rumble, that's for sure," she said. "There's Miss Georgie half in love with you, the mistress casting eyes at you, and even the beauty giving you a second look. You'd best be careful. Touch any of them, and you'll be out on your bum so fast you won't know what hit you."

"I'll endeavor to know my place," he murmured dulcetly.

"Ha!" said Bertha. "I don't know if having food on the table is worth all the trouble you'll be bringing to this house."

"There'll be no trouble at all, Bertha. If you think I can't handle two difficult women, then you underestimate me. And Georgie's no problem."

"Miss Georgiana to you," Bertha snapped.

"She needs to be married and out of this household," he observed.

"That's not going to happen. Not until Miss Norah makes up her bloomin' mind," Bertha said. "And she's just not interested, I tell you. You're the only man she's looked at twice, and if her father knew, you'd be out on your arse so fast your head would spin."

Georgie might not want to get married, but he was going to see to it anyway. She didn't belong here, a punching bag for her beauteous sister. She needed a home and a man of her own, someone young who'd adore her, not some prosy old widower with a dozen children.

Getting her married wouldn't be that difficult—she was pretty, lively, sweet, and intelligent. He'd accomplished harder things in his life, and he wasn't about to admit defeat so early in the game. Finding Belding's money wasn't going to take all his time—he could perform this little act of mercy as well.

No, he'd see Miss Georgiana Manning happily married to an adoring young man with democratic views.

And Rafferty wouldn't mind a bit. Or at least, not much.

GEORGIE DREAMED ABOUT RAFFERTY. Of course, she did—in the twilight minutes between sleep and waking, she could feel the strength in his body as he carried her, remember the feel of his hands as they rubbed her feet. Who would have thought that would feel so delicious? She'd tried to rub her own, but the effect left a lot to be desired. She wanted his large, strong hands on her. On places other than her feet.

She wasn't going to think about that. She knew perfectly well what went on between men and women—living in the country had dispelled any mysteries, and Bertha had explained the rest. It seemed a strange thing to actually want, but then, women didn't want it, or so she gathered. They endured it, for the sake of their husbands, and so far, she had yet to see anyone who would make it tolerable.

But Rafferty was a different matter. She couldn't imagine him committing such indignities, but the thought didn't fill her with horror. She had the firm conviction that Rafferty would somehow make it all right. Rafferty could make everything all right.

She stared into the darkened bedroom, her eyes wide open, watching as the curtains fluttered in the night air. It was late—she'd gone to bed early, hoping to get back to her enormously satisfying dreams, and now it was well after midnight and she couldn't sleep. Something had woken her, a scratching sound near the hearth, and she wondered if some kind of nasty vermin had gotten into the chimneys. It wouldn't be that unexpected in this shabby old place.

The problem with living in the city was that everything felt grubby. Shabbiness in the countryside only felt cozy to her; shabbiness in the city felt like dirt. In the countryside, the dogs would get rid of the vermin. Their house didn't even employ a cat, and she missed both of them, particularly her cat, Bottom. She'd tried to bring him along when they moved to the city, but her father forbade her, and she'd given in with good grace since everyone seemed so upset about the move. She wouldn't mind living in the city half so much if she had Bottom with her.

She heard another clanking sound, and she sat bolt upright in bed, squinting through the darkness. That was no mouse, or even a rat. Sliding out of bed, she landed on the floor in her bare feet and caught up the shawl she used in lieu of a night robe. She knew what she ought to do—call Rafferty. There was a bell she could ring, but he was probably sound sleep, and even the biggest rat couldn't hurt her. Just to be on the safe side, she picked up the fire poker and headed for the door.

The room directly beneath her was her father's library, a dusty, musty old place with books on finance and animal husbandry and not a play or a novel in sight. When they'd bought the house, they'd bought the contents as well, and whoever had lived here had the most boring library imaginable. She moved through the empty hallway toward the back stairs, clutching the poker, telling herself she ought to go back to bed. Whatever it was wouldn't hurt her, as long as she kept out of its way, but she admitted to the grave character faults of curiosity and stubbornness. There was no way she could sleep until she found out what was causing the noise.

The door closed silently behind her as she stepped out into the second floor hallway, but this time the darkness was not absolute, and she realized with a little thrill of danger that there was a light on in her father's library, and someone was moving around in there. Gripping the poker, she moved forward, counting on the element of surprise, and then she suddenly shoved the library door open, announcing, "Stand and deliver."

It was an incredibly stupid thing to say, but she hadn't been able to think of anything else, and Rafferty simply looked at her. "Are you a highwayman, Miss Georgie? Come to rob me of my earthly goods? I'm afraid I don't have any."

She lowered the poker as she felt embarrassment flood her face. "I couldn't think of anything else to say," she admitted. "What are you doing in here in the middle of the night?"

He stood there by her father's disorderly desk, and she swallowed. He was in shirtsleeves, open at the neck and rolled up at the elbows, his long hair rumpled about his beautiful face, and he looked absolutely...

No, she wasn't going to think of him that way. Before she could say anything else, he answered her question.

"Tidying up. I didn't trust the girls in here, and it seemed like a good thing to do while your father slept. I'm sorry if I woke you, but you really shouldn't come after strange noises with a fire poker. What if I'd been a thief?"

"You'd never be a thief," she said, breathing in her sigh of relief.

There was something ironic about his answering grin. "What if I had been? I don't think 'stand and deliver' would get you very far. Neither would that poker."

"I was curious," she said. "What are you doing up at this hour? Aren't butlers allowed to sleep?"

"I couldn't. I'm not accustomed to a warm bed. I'll get used to it, I suspect, but tonight seemed like a good time to catch up on things."

She looked around her. "You could always borrow one of the books. They were here when we got here—in fact, most of the furnishings were. We were told when we took possession of the house that anything here would belong to us, and I thought maybe there'd be a lost treasure or something, but I searched and couldn't find anything more interesting than this incredibly tedious library."

"You searched the house?" There was a strange note in his voice, one she couldn't read.

"I did. Everywhere but the cellars." She gestured around the tedious shelves. "Are you interested in animal husbandry?"

"It's not outside the realm of possibilities," he allowed. "Now why don't you give me that poker and go back to bed?"

She moved toward him in the darkened room, an odd feeling in her stomach, and handed him her weapon. Her hands were sweating, and she felt absurdly vulnerable, though in a surprisingly good way. "Is there something wrong with the hearth?" she said. "That's what woke me up."

He smiled blandly. "A loose brick or two. I'll have the mason come in and check all of them, just to be on the safe side. Don't worry—I won't be ferreting around it again. Go back to bed, Miss Georgiana."

The shadowy room with the one lit lamp felt disturbingly intimate, and she knew she should simply agree and disappear. "I'm Georgie," she said.

There was an odd, almost gentle expression on his face. "Go to bed, Georgie,"

She went, back up the dark flight of stairs, an odd flutter between her breasts. By the time she got back to her room, she was shivering in the cool night air, and she was half tempted to set the fire herself, something she'd learned to do out of necessity. Instead, she leapt into bed, burrowing beneath the covers and closing her eyes. Because she knew what she would see when she did. Rafferty, standing there in breeches and shirtsleeves, looking like some Greek god. Smiling at her. If she were Bottom, she'd be purring. Instead, she slept, and she didn't dream at all, curse the luck.

Chapter Six

RAFFERTY LEANED back against the desk with a sigh of relief, pushing the drawer closed again. She'd searched the place, had she? If he could find out exactly where she'd looked, it could make his life easier, but there was no way he could come right out and ask her.

She hadn't seen what he was doing—there was no earthly reason for a butler to be searching his master's private papers, but she'd been too startled to see him to realize. He'd come up with the perfect excuse for the loosened bricks in the fireplace, and he knew that she was inclined to be gullible, at least where he was concerned. He looked around the room, one last glance to make sure he hadn't missed any possible hiding place, and then sighed. He hadn't expected it to be easy.

And Miss Georgiana Manning in her soft white nightgown with the lacy shawl had been far too potent a distraction. He wasn't sure if he wanted to spank her or to...no, he wasn't going there. She'd been unforgivably stupid to come searching for some intruder with a flimsy fire poker in her hand. Mind you, he'd known a woman who could cause considerable damage with one, but that didn't mean someone like Georgie would have the where-withal to use it.

He was going to have a talk with her, in the daylight, when they were both formally dressed, about the dangers of wandering the house at night when she thought someone might be afoot. First, because he couldn't have her walking in on him while he was searching, and second, what if it had been someone like Stiles? Billy Stiles wouldn't hesitate to use his knife, and he wouldn't want anyone left behind to tell the authorities about him.

And he couldn't have her running around in her nightgown. He was only human, after all, and he was having a hard time thinking of Georgie as a child. Most women he knew were mothers by the age of twenty, and even if she'd led a sheltered existence, she was still an enticing young woman, damn it. And he couldn't afford to be enticed.

He needed to keep his mind off his cock. He had a job to do and limited time before Stiles came after him - he couldn't afford to let Georgiana Manning get in his way. Even if he wanted her to.

GEORGIE LIKED to think of herself as a practical soul. Her lifetime of being Not the Beauty had convinced her that fairy tales and handsome princes weren't for the likes of her. She knew her future better than anyone. They would marry her off to the first man who showed the slightest bit of interest, but so far, few people even knew she existed.

In fact, Georgie had considered it most likely that she'd never marry at all, and she'd remain a comfort to her parents. Not that either of them found her that comfortable—she had an unfortunate habit of saying what she thought, which tended to make everyone angry.

And after they died, she'd become an unpaid nanny to Norah's brood of children, though the vision of Norah as a mother was equally elusive. Norah would probably want them drowned at birth.

In fact, her day-to-day life was mostly uneventful, and her

future had looked undeniably drab. Until Rafferty had walked into her life.

Well, in fact, she'd walked into his. If it weren't for her, he'd probably still be down at the docks, begging. Interesting that his supposed war injuries had disappeared once he'd joined their household, but then Norah had told her that those who begged were able-bodied enough to make an honest living. She still had her doubts, but clearly Rafferty was able-bodied.

Not that she should be thinking about Rafferty's body, but the last twenty-four hours had been such a whirlwind that she thought about everything possible to explain the state she was in. She was confused, giddy, depressed, energized, and exhausted, and she couldn't figure out why. All she knew was that it centered around Rafferty, and the way he'd looked last night, rumpled and gorgeous.

There was no denying he was handsome—without that beard, he had a strong face that bordered on beauty, as her mother had unfortunately noticed. His blue-green eyes were such a strange color that they practically seemed to glow, his dark hair was thick and still too long for his post, and his mouth was...

She could imagine kissing that mouth. It would be very different than kissing Harry Trenton, son of the only country neighbors her mother had found acceptable. That had been a sore disappointment—all slobbering lips and heavy breathing. She had the sneaking suspicion that Rafferty would know just how to kiss.

And she liked how tall he was. His long legs and his strong back and arms. Of course, that was probably just happenstance— every girl must have some perfect man in mind, and Rafferty just happened to fit her particular taste in men. There'd be other tall men with gorgeous eyes and beautiful mouths. Men with position and money.

And they'd be for Norah. Which was utterly fine with her— Norah could have anyone she wanted. As long as she kept away from Rafferty.

Not that Georgie was in love with him. That was absurd,

everybody knew that. He was the butler. But she felt responsible for him—after all, he was her protégé. It was no wonder she had a special...affection for him. Nothing wrong with that—she loved grumpy old Bertha too. In fact, she was much closer to Bertha than was considered proper in society—one didn't make friends of one's servants.

But Bertha was her friend. And so was Rafferty. And the fact that she was still buzzing from the feel of his strong hands on her feet was understandable—she'd been in pain and he'd soothed it. She certainly wasn't about to fall in love with her doctor, was she? No, it was simple gratitude.

She scooted up in bed, wiggling her toes. Despite her late night foray, she was up early, hoping against hope that Rafferty would bring her breakfast, but instead, a maid brought it, a young girl Georgie had never seen before, and when Georgie had asked her where Rafferty was, she'd shrugged.

"Dunno, miss," she said. "But Bertha says I was to bring this to you and you were to eat everything or she'd have something to say about it."

Considering that the breakfast was sumptuous compared to the lean meals they'd recently been having, Georgie had no problem devouring everything. But when a different maid came to retrieve the tray, she was even more confused.

"Who are you?"

"Jane, miss." The girl said. Her uniform didn't fit her gangly, undernourished form, but she seemed cheerful enough. "Me and me friend Betsey are learning on the job, Rafferty says."

"Rafferty hired you?"

"Yes, miss. It's a big house, but Betsey and me can make do. Easier than earning it on the streets, that's what I say, though Betsey's not so sure."

"You earned your living on the streets?" Georgie asked, fascinated. "What did you do?"

The girl glowered. "Never you mind, miss. Rafferty warned

me to watch out for you and your questions. There are some things you're better off not knowing about."

But Georgie was possessed of a lively curiosity. "Did you sell your body? Not that I'd blame you. I'd sell my body for food any day."

Jane recognized a sympathetic ear and her reservations fled. She shook her head. "Sometimes it's just to get off your feet for a few minutes. The ones I hates is when you're down on your knees on cobblestones. Good thing they don't last long."

"Why would you be down on your knees?" Georgie said, mystified.

"Uh...no reason, miss," Jane said hurriedly. "This is hard work, but the grub is good. And we'd do anything for Rafferty, me and Betsey both."

She felt a sudden, niggling sting of jealousy. "Are you in love with him?"

Jane grinned. "Who ain't? Not for the likes of us, though, unless we fancy a one-nighter. Rafferty's hard to pin down."

"Where is he now?"

"Don't know, miss. I can get you anything you want," Jane said helpfully.

Can you get me Rafferty? she thought with a pang. "When you see him, would you ask him to come to my room?"

"Sure thing, Miss Georgiana." Jane took a couple of steps closer, peering at Georgie. "*You're* not in love with him, are you, Miss? Coz that would be a big mistake. If he's not for the likes of us, then he's certainly no good for a real lady."

Georgie let out a convincing laugh. "No, of course not. I merely want to find out how his first day went."

Jane gave her a suspicious glance. "I'll tell him, miss. If I see him."

He didn't come. She'd waited, determined to still be abed when he came to her room. He could sit on her bed while she lay beneath the covers and tell her all about his day, and he would make her laugh, and he might even touch her, a casual touch. She could tell him her feet still hurt and maybe he'd rub them again, but no, that was a terrible idea, because it felt too good and surely something that felt that good must be sinful.

Not that she was overly concerned with sin. Despite the vicar's hell and damnation sermons, Georgie had a different view of God as someone forgiving of even the most stubborn sinner, someone who found her amusing, not wicked. It was much more comfortable that way. Her God hadn't gifted her with beauty like Norah, but he'd given her a strong back and an optimistic heart. She knew that however her life turned out, she could be happy.

And she knew she certainly didn't love Rafferty. She might, just possibly, have the tiniest bit of a crush on him, but that was all. Nothing to worry about.

She heard the light tap on her door and a little thrill ran through her. She sat up, a bright smile on her face, when Jane opened the door carrying a brown paper-wrapped parcel.

"What's this?"

"Dunno, miss. It just arrived," Jane replied, moving to the fire to sweep up the ashes.

Georgie reached for it. It was heavy, and she looked for a message, any kind of hint as to where it had come from. The paper was plain brown and the string unremarkable, but for some reason she wasn't going to open it while Jane was bustling around.

It seemed to take her forever, though in fact it couldn't have been any longer than five minutes to lay a new fire, scoop up the dirty dishes, and depart in a whirl of skirts. Only then did Georgie address the package on her lap, tearing off the wrappings.

It was the most beautiful pair of walking shoes that she'd ever seen in her life. Made of soft brown leather with blue leather trim, they were beautifully shaped, and she knew if she didn't fit them, she'd still wear them and suffer the consequences. But they would fit her perfectly, because Rafferty had provided them, though she had no idea how he managed in such a short time.

She slipped one on, and it was soft and buttery, like a glove, hugging her foot gently. With silk stockings, it would fit perfectly, and she sighed in utter delight, hugging the shoes to her breast.

Maybe she was in love with him after all.

Chapter Seven

RAFFERTY, however, was proving surprisingly elusive. Once she was dressed in one of her shabby day dresses, she went straight to the kitchen in search of her prey.

"He's gone out," Bertha said.

"Where?"

"Never you mind, Miss Georgie. He's the butler, and he's got all sorts of things to do. Everything's gone to rack and ruin in the last few months, and he's got more than enough things to do without you bothering him as well."

"I wasn't going to bother him," Georgie protested. "I just wanted to thank him for my shoes."

"What shoes?" Bertha demanded.

Georgie lifted her skirts to her ankles, exposing the beautiful leather, and Bertha shook her head in disapproval. "Where'd he get those?"

"I expect from Cooby and Sons. They've made shoes for me in the past."

"And where's all this money coming from, I'd like to know!" Bertha snapped. "We've got two new maids, enough food to feed an army, and God knows what he'll bring back whenever he decides to reappear."

"It can't be his money," Georgie said. "He was a penniless beggar when I found him."

"Well, maybe he's your fairy godmother or something, because this house is starting to look like it used to, and a new shipment of gowns was delivered just an hour ago."

Georgie felt a pang of envy. "Norah already has too many gowns," she protested.

"Don't be ridiculous, Georgie." Her mother swanned into the room, a predatory expression on her ageless face. "A girl can never have too many gowns her first season. We wouldn't want to look so desperate that she had to wear the same dress twice."

"I wear the same dress all the time," Georgie protested.

"Yes, dear, but the situation is very different. Norah was born with extraordinary physical endowments, and we need to take advantage of those while we can. In the meantime, your clothes will have to wait." Her eyes narrowed as she spied the elegant walking shoes, clearly visible beneath the too-short hem of Georgie's dress. "And where did those come from?" she demanded.

"Rafferty arranged for them," she said.

Liliane frowned at the footwear. "I wonder if Norah could fit in those? They're awfully cunning, and she could do with a new pair of walking shoes."

"They'd be too big," Georgie said quickly. She was not giving up her shoes for the sister who already had everything. "She'd trip in them, and you know she can't afford to look clumsy."

Liliane stared at the shoes a moment longer, then shook her head. "No, you're right. I wonder if they'd fit me—I have slightly bigger feet than you..."

"No!" Georgie snapped. "They're mine, and I intend to hold on to them."

"Really, Georgie, it's not like you to be so selfish. I've a good mind to tell your father."

"Her father would tell her to keep the shoes," Bertha piped

up, earning Liliane's look of displeasure. "Let the poor lass have something of her own."

"I'm hardly going to argue with a servant about what I consider necessary as far as my daughter is concerned," she said haughtily. "And exactly where is Rafferty at the moment?" She cast her sharp gaze around the kitchen, as if she expected him to pop up from one of the large pots on the stove.

"Off seeing to things," Bertha said, giving the same answer she'd given Georgie. "Best leave him alone—there's no quarrelling with success."

Liliane opened her mouth to say something, then closed it again. "I've had them put the new dresses in the mauve bedroom. It should have the least dust of all the rooms..."

"The maids have already seen to it, my lady," Bertha said sullenly. "And when's Miss Norah going to be going through them? There might be something she's willing to pass on to her little sister."

"They're not the same size, silly!" Liliane said. "Besides, why would Georgie need ball gowns? She's not out yet." She sighed, temporarily lost in her own thoughts, then became alert again. "I suppose we can thank Rafferty for the dresses. The modiste had refused to extend us any more credit, and then suddenly a large order appears, which I'm certain are the ones I ordered. There are even two or three that might do for me." She looked quite pleased with herself. "I think I'll wake Norah so we can go through them and decide what she should wear tonight. Viscount Rothschild will be attending tonight's rout, and while we might decry some of his heritage, his fortune is breathtaking, worthy of our darling Norah." She glanced at Georgie. "The Islingtons are not the height of society—you've been invited to attend, though I doubt you have anything to wear. Your one evening gown smells of goat."

Georgie looked at her in surprise. This was the second time she'd been invited to go out with her family, and for a moment she wondered if they were trying to marry her off without the expense of a season.

It didn't matter—her mother was right. She had nothing to wear. And she needed to remember not to wear her new shoes in front of her sister, or size or not, she'd lose them.

The shriek could be heard from several stories overhead, a scream of pure rage filtering down to the kitchen. "It's Miss Norah," Bertha said dryly.

"So it is," Liliane said with a sigh. "I would have thought she'd be happy with her new clothes, but then, her temperament is so sensitive. She feels things so dreadfully."

Another shriek, and it was enough to get Georgie moving. "Something's wrong!" she said worriedly, pushing through the baize door, Liliane and Bertha following close behind as she raced up the two flights of servants' stairs to the mauve bedroom.

Norah was standing in the doorway, her beautiful black hair pointing in all sorts of strange directions, an expression of such fury twisting her face that Georgie almost thought she might explode. She was wearing a dress completely unsuited to her—it was a soft rose, much simpler than the usually fussy gowns Norah preferred, and the dress was slipping down her narrow shoulders. "These are all wrong!" she said, and behind her Georgie could see the shambles of what had once been a modiste's pride and joy. Gowns lay tossed about, the colors muted but glowing, and Norah was already tearing at the dress she wore, yanking it off her tiny body, throwing it on the floor and stamping on it.

"But how could Madame Racette be so mistaken?" Liliane cried. "Those aren't even your colors, much less your size. I might fit them, but they would be entirely unsuitable. Those are the dresses for a young girl just making her debut..."

Lilianne Manning was shallow and selfish, but no one ever accused her of being stupid. She turned to look at Georgie, her face like a storm cloud.

Norah didn't miss that look, and after kicking the dress one more time she advanced on Georgie, her face contorted with rage.

"What are these doing here?" she demanded, her voice still loud and strained. "These plain, dumpy things are clearly for you. What did you have to do for Rafferty in order to get a whole new wardrobe? I warned you, Mother, that he was up to no good. How dare he buy clothes for Georgie?"

But Lilianne's anger had vanished, and she was looking at Georgie with a thoughtful expression. "You know, you might look quite presentable in one of those gowns, Georgie," she said slowly.

"I didn't have anything to do with them..." she protested, keeping a wary eye on Norah in case she decided to pounce. Norah was very adept at slapping and hairpulling.

"Of course you didn't, dearest. It's merely a case of our very zealous butler seeing to things we'd let slide. Stop your caterwauling, Norah!" she snapped. "We were ready to accept the clothes if they were meant for you. We shall count ourselves very fortunate if Madame Racette was moved to an act of charity."

"It's not fair!" Norah whined.

"Nonsense, my dear. And I'm sure this is not a complete loss —that shade of lavender would look quite striking with your eyes. We could see to getting it altered for you, if your sister doesn't mind."

Georgie did mind, but she was in too much of a daze to say so. Rafferty had done this? How could he possibly have arranged it in so little time? And why?

"I'm not giving up my dresses for Georgie!" Norah said. "They're entirely inappropriate—she can't even go anywhere important!"

"In fact, she's giving up one of her dresses for you, darling," Liliane corrected her. "I'm certain you'll look charmingly in it. And Lady Islington has been kind enough to invite her tonight. She can wear one of them." Lady Manning looked Georgie up and down with a calculating expression.

Words had failed Norah—she made a sputtering noise as she stared at her mother. Finally she spoke. "We need to send the dresses back," she announced flatly. "You know as well as I do that

Papa can't afford wardrobes for both of us. If you think a pudding face like George can attract as wealthy a husband as I can, then you've taken leave of your senses. We need to send the dresses back and request the ones you ordered."

"I don't think your father's paying for these dresses," Liliane said slowly.

"Then who is? The butler?" Norah demanded with a hoot of laughter.

"I neither know nor care," Liliane said. "If we've run into a sudden streak of luck, I'm not about to argue with it. Take your dresses, Georgiana. We need to see if any of them need to be altered. I expect Madame Racette would be happy to make certain her artistry is well-displayed."

Georgie wasn't going to give her a second chance. A moment later, she was heading to her room, her arms full of silk dresses and petticoats, the lavender one hidden between them as she went.

Bertha, who'd been an interested witness to all that melo-drama, followed her into her bedroom, closing the door behind them. "Now let's look at what we've got, Miss Georgie," she said briskly. "If there's something that needs a little adjusting, I can probably manage it."

"They'll fit," Georgie said, spreading them out on the bed to admire them.

There were five in all—three day dresses in soft shades of rose, blue, and, most surprisingly of all, pale yellow. Her mother had always insisted that most women could never wear yellow, but Georgie took one look at it and fell in love.

There were two elaborate ball dresses, one in a rich, creamy shade and the lavender one that Norah had coveted. She should probably let her have it—the neckline was lower than anything Georgie had ever worn, and probably indecent for a young girl.

Except she wasn't a young girl. At age twenty, she was closer to a spinster. And she was going to wear the lavender dress, even-tually, and shine in it.

She picked up the yellow dress and held it out. "I'm wearing this," she announced pugnaciously.

"What's stopping you?" Bertha said.

Stripping down to her worn petticoats, she reached for the dress, pulling it over her head. As the yards of fabric floated down around her, she emerged, pulling the neckline down. And down. And down.

"It's too low!" she said in shock.

"Not for a young lady, it's not," Bertha announced, moving behind her to begin fastening it. "Your sister wears day dresses that are much lower than that. You've got a fine bosom—it suits you."

Instinctively, Georgie clasped her arms around her torso, trying to hide the wide expanse of flesh, but Bertha simply batted her hands away. "I can't..." Georgie said.

"Don't be missish. Your mother may be a crack brain, but if I say it's all right, then you know you can trust me. Don't you?" Bertha eyed her with a dangerous glint in her eye.

"Yes, Bertha," she said meekly.

"Good girl." Bertha spread the skirt over her petticoats. "Now I want you to walk in this dress like you own it. Back straight, young lady."

Georgie had hunched over in an effort to minimize her chest. In truth, she wasn't that large, but her breasts were bigger than Norah's, and her sister had always mocked her. She straightened up, then caught sight of herself in the mirror and froze.

The pale yellow was perfect on her. Her cheeks were flushed, her blue eyes sparkled, and for the first time in her life, she no longer looked a poor relation. She looked like a young woman, and if she was still a far cry from Norah's legendary beauty, she was quite acceptable. Almost...pretty.

She turned, examining herself from every angle, while Bertha scooped up the dresses and put them in the clothes press. "Now don't be getting conceited," Bertha warned her. "We've already got Miss Norah swanning around. Pretty is as pretty does."

Georgie looked at her in surprise, then back at her reflection, and she gave herself a dazzling smile. "Where's Rafferty?"

"Oh, no, you don't!" Bertha said.

"You know he's responsible for these. I have to thank him."

"You get such thoughts out of your head, missy. He's the butler and you well know it."

"Yes, he is," she said dreamily. She turned to look at Bertha, whose mouth was set in a stern line. "He's quite wonderful, isn't he?" She sighed.

Bertha shook her head. "We need to find you a husband," she said, her voice a dire warning. "That will get you over this foolishness."

She didn't want to get over this foolishness, she thought stubbornly, running a surreptitious hand down the soft muslin of her skirt. She didn't want the only kind of husband she'd be likely to get. She wanted...

She wasn't going to think about what she wanted. She didn't dare. So she simply nodded demurely, trying to look biddable when she'd never been biddable in her life.

"Harrumph," said Bertha.

Chapter Eight

It had been an absurd thing to do, Rafferty thought as he strode through the streets in Mayfair. It had been one thing to arrange for food and maids for the hapless Manning family. It had even been acceptably quixotic to have a pair of walking shoes made for the forgotten daughter.

But a new wardrobe for a young woman was asking for trouble in every sense of the word. It had been simple enough to arrange—once he found out who the Mannings used as a modiste, it had been child's play. Madame Racette had been all graciousness once he paid her bill, and there were a number of dresses already on consignment that could be altered to fit the so-sweet Miss Georgiana Manning, for a price. One that he was more than willing to pay. He didn't want to see Georgie in her outgrown schoolgirl outfits anymore, the hems too short, the necks too high. She might look like a child, but she was twenty years old, old enough to...

Well, old enough. He still wasn't interested. He was too old for her, too experienced, too wicked for such an innocent. She was like a devoted little puppy dog, looking at him out of her big blue eyes in mute adoration that both unnerved him and...he wasn't sure he wanted to name what else it made him feel. She was off-limits, not because she was his putative employer's daughter, but because she was one of the few honestly decent people he'd ever met.

No, he was going to follow Sir Elston Manning's orders and keep his hands strictly off the women of the household. It had been a close call last night, alone with her in the study, that threadbare nightgown and the single light outlining her curves. He'd been too noisy in his search, and he could have kicked himself. At least it had been Georgie coming to investigate and not her irate father. Still, the thought that she might have run into Billy Stiles put the fear of God into him. He'd laugh at a fire poker.

But Billy wasn't going to bother him for the time being—he was happy with Rafferty doing the dirty work. As soon as he found the cache, Billy would be there, claiming the half that he didn't deserve.

Rafferty wasn't having much luck, and he needed more time to search, but the Mannings were demanding and their lives were in chaos. He shouldn't care, but he was having fun looking after her, and he had more money than he knew what to do with. Might as well spread it around for the undeserving upper class.

The kitchen was deserted when he reached the house on Corinth Place, though Betsey was industriously chopping vegetables at the table. She scowled up at Rafferty. "How long do we have to stay here?"

"Don't feel much like honest labor, do you?" he countered, closing the door behind him.

"Janey doesn't mind. As for me, it's a lot less trouble earning my living on my back. That way the men do all the work."

He raised an eyebrow. "If you lie there like a slug, I doubt you'd get many customers."

"I'm young, and I have all my teeth," Betsey said. "That's worth something. I'd rather be on my knees taking care of someone than on my knees scrubbing floors."

"Then it's too bad you're going to keep scrubbing floors for the foreseeable future."

"Rafferty!" she whined. "Can't you find someone else? Jane don't mind, but I do."

"Sorry, pet, but you two are the most presentable. Can you see someone like Dirty Rose in this household?"

That got a rusty chuckle from Betsey. "All right, but you owe me."

"You'll be well-compensated and you know it," he said. "And keep your hands off the silver."

"Speaking of which, the old lady says you was to polish it. Can't really see you doing that, though."

Rafferty took a moment to savor the thought of Lady Manning's reaction to being termed an old lady, and then he shrugged. "I've done worse things in my life. I'll survive this."

Indeed, there was something curiously soothing about polishing the massive silver—epergnes and trays, candelabra, and other assorted centerpieces. They held no secret cache, but then, he'd known it wouldn't be that easy. He'd taken over the massive kitchen table, and as he polished, he let his thoughts drift to places he knew he shouldn't. He was so lost in thought that he didn't hear her approach, so that when he looked up and saw Georgie, he was momentarily struck dumb.

Those clothes had been a very bad mistake, he thought, looking at her. Possibly fatal. He'd learned early on in his rough and tumble life that he couldn't afford weaknesses, and one was standing right in front of him, nervously tugging at her neckline.

She was...he couldn't call her beautiful. She was pretty, with a fresh-faced innocence and warmth that were a far cry from Norah's icy perfection. She was exactly what he didn't want and couldn't have, and he couldn't tear his eyes from her.

"What do you think?" she said nervously, her hand fiddling with the lace at her neck. "Does the color suit me?"

She was wearing the yellow dress that looked perfect on her—warming her cheeks, brightening her eyes. Madame Racette had tried to talk him out of it—the dress had been promised to a brunette, but he'd been adamant. He'd been right.

"It does," he said shortly, afraid of saying more.

If his faint praise disheartened her, she didn't show it—she simply moved into the room and took the chair opposite him. "Can I help? I like polishing silver."

"You'll ruin your new dress."

"I can wear an apron like you. Or I could put on one of my old dresses…"

"Those should be burned," he said darkly.

"Oh, you never know when they'll come in handy," she said. "Let me help."

"No."

For a moment, she looked hurt, and she started to rise, but he was fool enough to stop her. "But you can talk to me while I work," he suggested.

That sunny smile wreathed her face again. "All right," she said, settling back in the seat. "You can tell me why you ordered all those dresses for me. And how you managed to talk Madame Racette into extending more credit. I don't know how my father will pay for it."

He should have known she'd ask what he didn't want to answer. "She's not extending any more credit. The dresses were made for others who didn't need them." Not strictly a lie on his part. The dresses had been made for other young ladies of society, and they didn't need them half as much as Georgie did.

She cast him a skeptical glance, but she didn't dispute it. "But they really should have gone to Norah. She's the one who's supposed to get us out of this mess."

"Norah has plenty. Besides, she's not the only one who needs a husband. You're old enough to be in society as well, and my money's on you to bag a better match than your sister."

"You're biased," she said cheerfully, obviously pleased by the thought.

"Am not."

"Of course, you are. You don't like Norah and you like me. Naturally you think I'd beat her."

"What makes you think I like you?" he countered, rubbing paste on the serving tray.

She grinned. "Of course you do. You're my protégé. I've rescued you from a life of misery and crime. You're grateful."

Gratitude was a far cry from what he was determined not to feel for her. "Who says I don't like misery and crime?"

"No one wants to be a criminal," she said firmly. "They simply have no other choice."

He set down the tray. "Now there's where you're wrong, Miss Georgie. Crime can be a great deal of fun."

She looked at him doubtfully. "Are you a criminal?"

"One of the best."

She said nothing for a moment, blinking, then smiled beatifically. "Then you'll be an even better butler."

She really was the most frustratingly cheerful person, he thought. She wasn't safe out on her own—she needed a husband to look after her and make sure her innocence wasn't destroyed.

There was a sudden crashing sound from the ground floor, followed by a bellow, and Rafferty quickly rose. More noise followed, and it sounded as if an elephant had charged its way into the house. He quickly stripped off his apron and gloves and reached for the somber black coat that denoted his temporary profession.

"It's Neddy," Georgie announced in a disconsolate voice. "He must be back."

"Who the he— Who is Neddy?"

She had risen too. "My brother. He's been visiting friends."

"Does he always make so much noise?"

"Usually," she replied. "That's because he's always had too much to drink."

Another crash, and the sound of breaking glass. "I'd best see to him, then." And he started for the stairs.

Edward Manning was lying on the floor, his long limbs

sprawled out around him as he lay half in the hallway, half in one of the downstairs parlors, and he was, indeed, very drunk. He'd lost his hat somewhere, his cravat was missing as well, and his jacket was torn. He didn't move from where he lay, but his eyes, a match to Norah's lavender eyes, were wide open and staring at him in mild curiosity.

"Who're you?" he demanded in a genteel slur.

"Rafferty. The new butler." He reached down and pulled the man into a sitting position where he could better assess him. He was a handsome young man, but there were signs of dissipation around his eyes and his skin, and he blinked up at Rafferty in disbelief.

"We can't afford a butler," he said, sounding mournful. "Shouldn't have come back here. Nothing but trouble. Poor little Norah. Ruined her chances."

Norah was far from pitiful, but Rafferty refrained from pointing that out. He shoved his arms under Neddy's and hauled him to his feet, where Neddy stood there, swaying slightly, looking like he was ready to take another tumble.

"Which is your room, sir?" he questioned, doing his best to sound patient. He found drunks particularly annoying.

"Third one on the right," he mumbled, taking an abortive step toward the broad front stairs. Instead, he tripped, down on the floor again before Rafferty could catch him.

Rafferty reached down to hoist him up again when he heard light footsteps on the stairs, and a moment later Georgie was on her knees beside her prostrate brother. "Oh, Neddy," she said in a gently scolding voice. "When are you going to stop this?"

"Can't," he muttered. "Sorry, Georgie. Hate to do this to you."

"You're not doing anything to me, you're doing it to yourself," she said, catching his arm in an effort to pull him to his feet.

Rafferty immediately reached behind him and hauled him upright once more, keeping a strong hand on him as Neddy wavered. "His bedroom is third on the right?" he asked, needing to verify it.

"Second bedroom on the right," Georgie corrected. "I'll show you. He has a tendency to cast up his accounts when he gets this bad, and it's better that I look after him than you."

"I disagree. If your brother is ill, I'll take care of him. You don't want to ruin your pretty new dress."

That got a smile out of her. "Well, with luck, he'll keep everything down. Let's go."

Their procession moved slowly up the stairs, Georgie holding his hand, Rafferty keeping him upright. By the time they reached the door, Neddy was mumbling under his breath, a string of unintelligible apologies. He fell face first onto his bed, and a moment later, a loud snore erupted from him.

"Oh, dear Neddy," Georgie said miserably, as Rafferty lifted his body onto the high bed and rolled him onto his back. Neddy didn't respond, lost to the world in his claret-induced haze. She started to unfasten his shoes, but Rafferty gave in to temptation and put his hands on her, moving her away.

"I'll take care of him," he said, moving her toward the door.

"But I want to help," she cried. "He's always been so good to me."

"Then he'd appreciate it if you didn't have to see him like this. I'll see that he's properly settled and then you can check on him."

Indecision crossed her face, and then she nodded, reluctantly, before leaving them alone.

At least he didn't throw up, Rafferty thought as he efficiently stripped the young man of his ruined clothing. There were starched and folded nightshirts in a drawer, and he dressed him and put him beneath the covers before closing the curtains, plunging the room into merciful darkness. He was just about to leave when Neddy spoke up.

"Who the hell are you?" His voice was still slurred.

Rafferty thought of a dozen answers, but went with the

simplest. "I'm the butler, sir." And he closed the door behind him.

He found Georgie waiting for him in the hall, her eyes anxious. "How is he?"

"He's fine. Or he will be, once he's sober."

She started past him, and once more he touched her, stopping her. "He's asleep," he said. "Just give him time."

"Poor Neddy," she said, looking truly distressed, and he cursed the boy who'd upset her. "He blames himself for the mess we're in, and really, he's just a part of it. Mother gambles as much as he does, with even worse results, but we would have been fine if my father's investments hadn't gone terribly wrong. Something to do with a bubble that collapsed, which I don't quite understand. Suffice it to say we're quite destitute."

"I gathered as much," Rafferty said.

A shadow had crossed her face. "And we'll be out on the streets and homeless in a very short time unless Norah finds someone fabulously wealthy to marry."

"And she refuses?"

"No, she says she will. She just wants to have fun for a while before she agrees to someone. But no one is good enough, and she's starting to get a reputation, and I really don't know what's going to happen to us."

This wasn't a problem he could easily fix, Rafferty thought. Norah Manning was a spoiled bitch—sooner or later, her suitors would realize it and the Mannings would be out of luck.

All the more reason for Georgie to get herself a good, safe husband. He needed to find her someone, since her father seemed too caught up in the mess his life had become. Somehow the idea didn't fill him with any pleasure.

"So you see, Neddy blames himself, even though he's only part of the problem, and so he drinks." Georgie finished. "If only I could do something..."

"You aren't sacrificing yourself for your family," he said flatly. "What we need to do is find you a nice young man to marry."

She jerked her head up in sudden surprise. "I don't want to marry a nice young man," she said firmly.

"Then who are you going to marry?" he said, amused. "A bad, old man?"

"Yes," she said simply. Looking at him.

Oh, no, you don't! he thought. He ignored her shining gaze. "I'll come back and check on your brother in a couple of hours," he said, immediately changing the subject. "In the meantime, it's best just to let him sleep it off."

She was still looking at him with that odd, almost hopeful expression on her face. "But I—"

"You'll be going to out with your family," he said, his voice brooking no refusal. "I think you should look around when you get there and choose someone."

She looked startled by his sudden change of subject. "Choose someone for what?"

"To marry. There should be any number of suitable young men there—pick the one you want."

She was no longer looking so sunny. "And you'll arrange it like you've arranged everything else? No, thank you. And I don't want to go to the Islingtons."

"Too bad. You can't stay in this situation—I want you to have somewhere else to go if your family loses the house and you're homeless."

"I'll go with them," she said. "With you. You wouldn't abandon us, would you?"

He was planning on doing exactly that, but she was looking at him with a fierce gleam in her beautiful eyes.

"I wouldn't abandon you," he said. "Not until everyone is safely settled. Including you, with your new husband."

The expression on her face was suddenly blank. A moment later, she was gone with a flounce of yellow skirts, and he was watching her disappear, a rueful smile on his face. He'd said exactly the right thing, whether she liked it or not. Having her moon after him was going to make it damned difficult give the place the kind of search it needed. He needed to find Belding's cache, and soon.

That didn't mean he couldn't take care of other business at the same time. She was a sweet, lovely girl and he was going to find a husband for her, someone she could dote on, rather than her ramshackle family.

And he'd congratulate himself on a job well-done. Of course he would.

Chapter Nine

BY THE TIME Georgie reached her bedroom door, her cheeks were flaming and her eyes were full of unshed tears. Stupid, stupid man! Didn't he see what stood right in front of him?

Of course he did. He saw her very clearly, better than she saw herself. What with Norah's histrionics and Neddy's drinking, her parents barely noticed she was around, but Rafferty was the only one who looked in her eyes and actually saw her. The question was, what did that mean, besides new dresses and a sudden social life?

She threw herself down at her dressing table, searching her reflection. She didn't have Norah's elegant nose—hers was more the upturned sort. She didn't have Norah's mysterious lavender eyes—her own were blue and guileless. Her hair was an unremarkable brownish-blond, and brunettes were in style this year, and it seemed every year. She wasn't petite and slim—she'd been looking like an overgrown schoolgirl for so long that the young woman looking back at her was a stranger.

She tugged at the neckline again. It wasn't that low, but she wasn't used to so much being on display. Most women had much lower necklines, but most women didn't have her curves.

And Rafferty couldn't care less about her curves. He wanted to foist her off on some marriageable man—why? So he wouldn't have to worry about her? But then, why was he? She was the patron, he the protégé. She should be worried about him.

Not that she needed to be. He was the best butler they'd ever had—her mother flirted with him, her father liked him, even grumpy Bertha seemed to have a soft spot for him. Only Norah disliked him, and as far as Georgie was concerned, that was a point in his favor.

In fact, his only flaw was his sudden interest in seeing her married, when such a thought hadn't entered her mind. She didn't want to marry a...what did Rafferty call him...a suitable young man. She didn't want to marry anyone, she wanted to have her own household with Rafferty taking care of her. He could be her butler, or her friend, it didn't matter. She just didn't want to be saddled with anyone else. She stuck out her tongue at her reflection, only to jump when she heard a pounding on her door.

Norah flung it open, eyeing her with a malicious gleam.. "Had a fight with your little darling?" she cooed.

Georgie made a face. "What little darling?"

"Your new house pet, Rafferty. He won't stay long, you know. We can't pay him, and we're too much trouble. He must hate you fawning all over him."

"I don't fawn over him!" Georgie shot back, glaring back at her. "He's my—"

"Yes, he's your protégé. You've already told me that, several times. Much as it pains me to tell you, but a protégé is not quite what you think. Not nowadays."

"I don't know what you're talking about! Oh, do go away, Norah!" she said in frustration. One of Norah's favorite pastimes was to goad Georgie, to remind her of just how unattractive she was, but Georgie was no longer so vulnerable. She'd learned that if she didn't respond with tears, then Norah grew bored quite quickly.

Norah moved closer into the room, a spiteful expression on her beautiful face. "Every time you call him your protégé, you're telling him you expect his services," she hissed.

Georgie sighed. Norah was in one of her moods, and her only choice was to ride it out. "I do expect his services," she said flatly. "He's the butler, after all."

"That's not the kind of service I'm talking about."

Georgie swung around on the padded bench to glower at Norah. "Then what are you talking about?"

But Norah simply gave her a cat-like smile. "You are such a child. I wonder that Father allows you out at all. A young woman should be discreet, innocent, charming..."

"You're playing off half the men of the ton. Why don't you marry and save us all the worry?" she snapped back.

"At least I'm not trying to seduce the butler," Norah said sweetly.

Georgie was shocked into silence. "Seduce?" she echoed.

"You heard me. Men don't like that sort of thing—they find blind adoration tiresome."

"They do?"

"Of course they do. They want to be the pursuer, not the pursued. They want to feel as if they've won the woman, not that they themselves were the prize."

"That has nothing to do with Rafferty and me," Georgie said firmly.

"Doesn't it?" Norah arched one perfect eyebrow, a trick Georgie had tried and failed to master. "You're embarrassing yourself and us with your fixation on Rafferty, the way you look at him and follow him around."

Georgie had had enough of her game. "You're being ridiculous. Rafferty wouldn't look at me twice."

"True enough," Norah jumped in.

Georgie turned to look at her reflection in the mirror. It was the sad truth that Rafferty wouldn't be interested in such a plain Jane. He might think he could marry her off, among all his other extraordinary accomplishments, but she knew just how unlikely that was.

"I'm going downstairs," she said smoothly, rising from her table.

She was hoping she could glide past Norah, but her sister reached out to pinch her arm, hard, another bad habit.

"You'll always be in my shadow," Norah hissed. "They may look at you, but they'll want me."

"And they," Georgie said calmly, "can have you."

FOR HER ENFORCED re-entry into society, Georgie would have chosen someone other than the Islingtons. The earl and countess were her parents' age with a tendency to throw lavish soirées to showcase any number of hopeful young ladies eager to display their meager talents. Since the Islingtons were tone-deaf, they seemed to particularly delight in off-key sopranos and the stumbling poetry preferred by romantic damsels, and Georgie was terrified that she'd be coerced into showing off her nonexistent accomplishments. Norah, of course, had a clear, bright soprano, and she could recite with drama worthy of a Covent Garden extravaganza, making Georgie's failings even more noticeable. If called upon, she would simply refuse. That, or she could recite "The boy stood on the burning deck" with all the fervor of one of her mother's blasted acolytes and bring the room to tears. That, or give them "the boy stood on the burning deck, eating peanuts by the peck," and be thrown out on her ear.

In fact, she'd be safe from showing off her wares. Too many other young women were determined to snatch their prize from the marriage mart—Georgie wished them luck. She would find a potted plant and hide behind it until it was time to go home. Back to Rafferty.

It was only her second outing into society—the ill-conceived treasure hunt had been the first—and she knew no one but her sister, who of course wanted nothing to do with her. Georgie, abandoned by her family, immediately went in search of cake.

Georgie loved to eat, and while the Islingtons' soirée tended to be painfully dull, they also happened to employ one of the best pastry chefs in London, which was just about the only reason Georgie had agreed to go in the first place.

She was wearing the lavender gown, and even she had to admit she looked...nice. But Rafferty's eyes had simply passed over her when he ushered them to their carriage, and while he helped her mother and sister up into the equipage he left her to scramble after them all by herself. It was no wonder she needed cake and solitude.

She found her potted plant in an alcove a safe distance from the painful performances and she placed her heavy-laden plate on the chair next to her. The cakes would keep her busy long enough, and then she could feign a headache. They would all have to accompany her back home in the family carriage, and Norah wouldn't like it. As the beauty of the season, she commanded adoration and obedience from the other young ladies, and she delighted in the glow of approval from all and sundry. She most definitely did not like having her awkward younger sister tagging along after her.

"You need something to drink." The voice came from behind her, startling her so violently that she almost lost her cake. The next moment a young gentleman came around in front of her, two glasses of champagne in his hands. "All that cake must make your mouth dry." He smiled at her, a crooked smile, and Georgie's original temptation, which was to throw her cake at him, faded, and she found herself smiling back.

"I'm hiding," she confided, reaching out for one of the glasses.

"I know you are. Would you mind telling me why?"

"I don't want to be called upon to perform. In fact, I didn't want to be here in the first place, but my parents insisted. They seem to think I'll make a good match." She made a face at the notion.

He laughed. "Don't you want to get married?"

"No. At least, I don't think so. I want to be an old maid with goats and chickens and Rafferty to keep me busy."

"I know what goats and chickens are, but I've yet to hear of a Rafferty. Is it some strange exotic camel-like animal?"

Despite herself she laughed. "Rafferty's our butler."

"A very wise part of your plan," the young man said. "I always prefer to have my butler as part of my plans for the future. May I sit?"

Georgie scooped the plate off the seat, dusting crumbs off her satin skirts. "Of course. I've been rude—excuse me. I haven't been out in society for very long."

"I'm astonished," he said with a straight face. "Since there's no one here to introduce us, would you mind if I was so gauche as to do it myself? My name is Andrew Salton."

She inclined her head with perfect grace. "I'm Miss Georgiana Manning," she replied.

"Manning? Does that mean you're related to that bewitching character over there?"

Norah was singing, surrounded by a dozen rapt young men, and they could hear her perfect, crystal notes from where they sat.

"She's my sister," Georgie said with a marked lack of enthusiasm. "Don't bother to fall in love with her. She's destined for an earl at least. Er...you aren't an earl, are you?"

He laughed. "Just a plain mister, I'm afraid. I recognize she's way above my touch."

He was busy watching Norah, an odd expression on his face, so Georgie gave herself permission to assess her companion. He was young—not much older than Neddy, which would make him about twenty-five. He had dark brown hair, warm brown eyes, and a very presentable face, with a good jaw, high cheekbones, and a ready smile.

He must have felt her eyes on him, for he turned back to her with his ready smile. "Forgive me, I've been rude."

"Not at all. Norah affects everyone that way."

But Andrew Salton was looking at her, not Norah, and there was clear admiration in his eyes. What would it feel like, if Rafferty were to look at her like that?

That wasn't about to happen. Norah finished her song on a perfect, sustained note, then fell back to enjoy the adulation that was *de rigeur* for everything she did. Georgie went back to her cake, prepared for Andrew Salton to abandon her in favor of Norah.

He did no such thing. In fact, he didn't even glance at her sister while he kept up an amusing line of conversation about his father's tiny church in Kent and the frequent attendance of the neighborhood livestock in the midst of his sermons.

"It's extremely difficult to contemplate the wages of sin with a goose staring at you balefully," he continued, and she laughed.

"Geese are dreadful sinners," she said, waiting for him to turn away. He didn't. That, in itself, was unusual—Norah drew the eye of everyone in the room, but Andrew kept his head averted, those soft brown eyes focused on her.

Rafferty had hard eyes, always wary, always alert. He'd never looked at her the way this man was looking. What was there about her to admire? And then she remembered her reflection in the mirror, so certain she was going to dazzle Rafferty.

Surely this was much more pleasant. Andrew Salton was an extraordinarily easy man to talk to, and she didn't even notice when she ran out of cake. He did, however.

"Let me bring you more cake, Miss Georgiana," he said. "You seemed particularly fond of the strawberry one."

She had been particularly fond of it. But she'd been brought up with manners, so she quickly demurred. "There's no need..."

"There's every need. And I need to find someone to make a proper introduction—I really shouldn't be back here with you without your parents' approval."

Her parents would approve of him. In fact, they'd probably approve of any halfway presentable suitor for her, not that this man was courting her, per se. Anyone but Rafferty.

She watched Andrew as he went in search of cake. He was a well-built young man, not as tall as Rafferty, more sturdily built. Rafferty was tall and lean, but Georgie suspected he would best most anyone in a fight, because he was deceptively strong. He'd carried her through the streets of London without any sign of strain, and his hands were strong, deft when he touched her, when he rubbed her feet, when he—

"There you are, darling!" Her mother loomed up, looking formidable in a silver frock only a few years too young for her. "What are you doing, hiding out here?"

Georgie didn't bother to state the obvious. "Eating cake," she said with a trace of defiance.

"Of course you are," she said soothingly, in a surprisingly good mood. "And you've managed to conquer at least one heart on your very first night out. Lady Tisbury made me known to a most exceptional young man named Andrew Salton. He's the son of a vicar, but he's also cousin to a viscount. I believe there's some money there. He's quite acceptable."

"Fascinating," Georgie said flatly.

"He wants to meet you—I hope you'll be on your very best behavior. If we could marry you off as well, then our fortunes would very much improve."

"I'm sorry I've been such a burden," she said in a low voice, but her mother was paying no attention.

"Of course, he's talking to Norah right now, so that might put an end to it. He's not wealthy enough for Norah, but you know how she affects people. That's the problem with having such a dazzling daughter—there's no attention left for the pl— The younger sister."

She was going to say "plain" and thought better of it. Georgie knew she ought to be grateful her mother was alert enough to censor herself, but her gratitude had vanished at the thought of Andrew fawning at her sister's feet along with all the others. He would be dazzled, he wouldn't be able to pull away from her, he would give her the strawberry cake...

"Here he is now," her mother announced cheerfully, as Andrew emerged from the crowds of people. She waved her hand in a flirtatious gesture. "Yoo-hoo, Mr. Salton?" she said in a high-pitched voice that made Georgie want to shrink in embarrassment. "I must have you meet my younger daughter, since you were so smitten with my dear Norah."

The cake was in one piece and so was Andrew, and there was a definite twinkle in his eye as her mother made the prescribed introductions.

"Miss Georgiana, might I interest you in a piece of cake?" he said smoothly.

"Oh, no," her mother tittered. "Georgiana doesn't eat cake. She's slimming."

Georgie wondered what might happen if she dumped the last of the champagne in her mother's lap? She'd have to leave them alone, and Georgie could have that very substantial piece of cake in peace.

But she loved her mother, even when she said utterly stupid things, so she simply plastered on a grim smile and shook her head. In the battle between pride and cake, cake usually won, but right then she was outgunned, with her disapproving mother and a chastened Andrew Salton.

Her mother had all the charm in the family, her father had once insisted, and that night she exerted it to her full potential. Within moments, she was on the dance floor with Andrew, the cake left forgotten on one of the chairs. Georgie snatched it up before a servant could remove it but took her time eating it. Her mother would monopolize Andrew Salton for as long as she could, and Georgie wouldn't see him again. It was a shame—if she had to have suitors, he was by far the best of the lot, but she could at least say she tried. Her father didn't have to know she hid behind a pillar most of the evening.

Her mother returned eventually, without Andrew. "He wanted to dance with you, but I told him you weren't officially out yet," her mother announced, looking pleased with herself. "I must say, he's quite delightful. Good for you for finding him." She eyed her daughter carefully. "He might do for you. I didn't know the son of a vicar could be quite so handsome."

No one would do for her, except the one man who couldn't, wouldn't, didn't. She managed an easy smile. "He was merely being kind to a wallflower."

"Most likely," said her mother with a singular lack of tact. "Shall we depart?"

"What about Norah?"

"Alcott will bring her home. She's having too good a time to leave now. And don't look at me like that—she'll be properly chaperoned."

"I'm sure she will," Georgie said meekly, rising from her chair with feigned reluctance. "I am tired."

"Such a whirlwind of gaiety," her mother said, eying the empty cake plate beside her. "You won't always be able to hide away like you did tonight. Sooner or later, you're going to have to get out there like Norah."

"Not like Norah," Georgie said. "I don't expect to have her success."

"Of course not. She's the beauty—you're not. But you could manage a respectable arrangement with some unexceptional young man. I should find out exactly what kind of money the Saltons have."

"I doubt the son of a vicar is particularly well-endowed."

Her mother cast her a sudden, sharp look, then tittered. "For your sake, I hope so."

"I don't need a wealthy husband," Georgie protested, wondering what her mother found so amusing.

"We do," Liliane said firmly. "You've done well tonight, and that dress looks lovely on you, though I still think it should have gone to Norah. Let us find our carriage and go home before anyone realizes the wretched state of our conveyance. We're lucky we even made it here in the first place." She took Georgie's arm and her heavy scent enveloped them both. "Your father will be very pleased."

So will Rafferty, she thought miserably. Andrew was exactly what he wanted for her. A good man, he'd said, and she wanted a bad man.

Too bad he didn't want her.

Chapter Ten

THE TAVERN WAS small and dark, with low ceilings and guttering oil lamps to aid the roaring fire in lighting the place. Just the right location for a man to meet with his old partner on the High Toby. It had been years since Rafferty had made a living as a highwayman—it was a little too risky for his peace of mind, and he had no fancy to be shot by an overzealous coachman.

They'd had a simple but effective routine—Martin was a small, skinny street rat with an affection for dressing up in women's clothes. He would appear at the side of the road, a seeming damsel in distress, and once a coach had stopped, Rafferty would move in, relieving the passengers of their jewels and their blunt and carrying off the supposedly fragile young lady. This had worked like a charm until Rafferty ended up with a bullet in his shoulder, too close to his nonexistent heart for his liking, and they'd decided to part ways.

Martin had stayed a true friend, and he'd exchanged his thieving ways for a career dealing in information. It was easy enough to come by—Martin worked at Mrs. Percival's Social Emporium, a brothel dealing in particular tastes. Martin, in his skirts and petticoats and maquillage, was a great favorite, and men never tended to be discreet in bed.

It was a cold night in late autumn, but not cold enough to give Rafferty the excuse to cover up with mufflers and cloaks and the like. He was going to have to hope the tavern was small and dark enough to keep people from noticing that Rafferty had reappeared in the neighborhood—he wasn't ready to deal with Stiles just yet, though he had no idea why he hesitated. Once again, he cursed his height and his bright blue eyes—it was damned hard to blend in, no matter how much he slumped and squinted.

Martin was waiting for him in the darkest corner of the place, like the good man he was, and Rafferty went straight to him, tucking his big body into a small chair before breathing a sigh of relief. He was getting too old for all this subterfuge—once he finally dealt with Stiles and his eternal greed, he was going to live an exemplary life, never having to look over his shoulder again.

"You don't look like yourself," Martin said, reassuring him, reading him like he always did. "And even if you did, no one here would squawk."

"Stiles pays well. He doesn't know where I am at the moment, and I prefer to keep it that way."

"Yes, but they don't like him. They like you," Martin pointed out.

"I don't know if people can afford to be so particular," Rafferty said.

Martin shrugged. "Maybe not, but if they have the choice, they'll choose you. What do you need, old friend? You know I'll do anything for you."

Rafferty took a good look at him in the darkness, the traces of kohl around his eyes, the yellowing bruise on his cheek. "Have they been treating you all right?" he asked suddenly, his own business forgotten.

Martin shrugged. "Some have, some haven't. I keep hoping I'll find someone who wants to take me on permanently, set me up in a nice little townhouse and shower me with jewels, but most men tend to hide their peccadillos when it comes to affaires with another man. So I earn my keep the best I can and hope for the best. Mrs. Percival's a fair one, and keeps the worst of them out of her establishment, but still, some slip through. I never did understand why someone would want to hurt someone they shag." He shook his head.

"You know as well as I do that that's the way some men take their pleasure," Rafferty said.

"Too bad I don't care for bedding women," Martin said. "But enough about my woes. I wish I had better news for you, but Stiles has everyone out looking for you. What's he got on you?"

"Belding's fortune. I'm supposed to find it and share it with him, or so he says. I've been looking for months how, and found nothing."

"He's not the sort to do his own dirty work," Martin said. "Where do you think it is?"

"Beats me. I'm not that interested, but I told him I'd give his men and him half. Assuming I can find the damned pot."

"Well, you knew Belding better than anyone else—you were his right-hand man. Who better to find out where he hid anything?"

"Who better?" he echoed in a resigned voice. "I haven't seen hide nor hair of Stiles in the last few months, not since we had our gentleman's agreement."

Marty hooted with laughter. "Neither of you are gentlemen—what good does that do?"

"It keeps him off my back for the time being. I'm not likely to find anything with Billy breathing down my neck, and I don't expect that to change. Do you think he knows where I am?"

"Where are you?"

"You wouldn't believe me if I told you," he said.

Martin chuckled. "Well, for God's sake, don't tell me. Leave it to my imagination."

"I'm a butler in the Judge's old house on Corinth Place."

Martin looked at him for a long moment. "No, you're not!" he said flatly.

"I am. For Sir Elston Manning, who has about as much

money as a church mouse. I'm trying to get him out of the mess he made for himself."

"Why?"

It was a logical question, one that Rafferty wasn't disposed to answer. It was pure whim on his part and had nothing to do with a certain young lady who...well, he wasn't going to think about her. "I don't want see them kicked out of the house. The Crown will claim it as they claimed all of Belding's other assets, and I won't be able to get close."

"You think the money's in the house?"

"It must be. I can ferret around and find it without disturbing anybody. If Stiles gets wind of it, there'll be a bloodbath."

Martin shook his head in disbelief. "It sounds logical. Somehow, I don't think that's the entire truth. You've always had a soft spot for someone down on their luck, but I wouldn't have thought that would extend to the gentry. Wouldn't it be better if the place were deserted?"

"I don't want to risk it. It's working out well enough as it is. I have plenty of time to search the place while they're out and about," he said.

Martin shook his head in disbelief. "There's something you're not telling me. James Rafferty, King of the High Toby, prince of the thieving classes, brought down to this! A butler!"

"I really am." Rafferty leaned back, surveying him. "In fact, I may have something for you in the same line."

Martin raised a delicately plucked eyebrow. "I don't think so."

"If you'd like to consider a new position. Your old one's growing too dangerous."

Martin sighed, leaning forward. "Tell me more."

GEORGIE DREAMED, as usual, about a pair of vivid blue eyes that haunted her, keeping her tossing and turning for half the night, and it was late morning when the sound of someone moving around in her room awakened her from her deep sleep.

The clink of china signaled her morning cup of tea, and a moment later, the curtains were flung open, letting in the fitful light of a gloomy autumn day. *Rafferty*, she thought, and struggled to sit up, only to be confronted by a stranger.

"Good morning, Miss Georgie," the woman said in a warm contralto.

Controlling her disappointment, she managed a sleepy smile. "Who are you?"

The woman was already bringing her tray over, so Georgie sat up in bed, unused to being fussed over. "I'm the new lady's maid, Martina," she said. "I'm here to look after you and your family. Rafferty says you've been too long without a proper maid."

"Rafferty brought you here?" Georgie said, immediately approving of this new addition to the household.

"He did, indeed, miss." Martina arranged the pillows behind her, then set the tray on her lap. There was a pot of tea and her favorite marmalade toast, and Georgie sighed in happiness.

"Rafferty is a saint," she said firmly.

Martina choked. "Not what I'd call him," she said wryly, and Georgie took a long look at her.

She was pretty in a strong-featured way. She favored heavy maquillage, and her dark hair was in a low bun at the back of her neck. She wore a flowered dress with an apron, rather than a maid's uniform, and Georgie remembered that lady's maids were the aristocracy of the servants' quarters—her mother's Havisham had been a terror even abovestairs.

Martina looked far from terrifying, and there was a decided twinkle in her eye. "I've never had a maid before," Georgie said. "And I promise I'll be the least of your worries. My sister is having her first season, and my mother is very fond of society. You can concentrate on them."

"I've met them," Martina said.

Georgie looked at her warily, recognizing something in the tone of Martina's voice. "Was everything all right?"

"Of course, Miss Georgie. They were both very happy to have someone help them with their toilette. I had hoped to provide you similar assistance. Have I offended you?" Martina's brow wrinkled.

"Oh, no! I'd love your help. It's just that one maid for three women is a lot of work."

"I'm bred for hard work. And the three of you managed with no one at all, though how you could is beyond me. I'm here to make everything better." She headed to the clothes press, looking through the new gowns with a practiced eye.

"I thought I'd wear the blue one today," Georgie ventured.

Martina shook her head. "That one's old and shabby," she announced, pulling it out of the pile and tossing it on the floor.

"Yes, but I'm not going anywhere today. I wanted to save my new dresses for more important occasions."

"New dresses, eh? Where did all these come from?"

"Rafferty," she said, and Martina raised one delicately arched eyebrow. "That is, Madame Racette, of course, but Rafferty arranged for her to extend us more credit and apparently she had some of my gowns already made up and..." Words trailed off as she began to realize how unlikely just such a thing was.

But Martina simply nodded. "Rafferty's very good at persuading people. And he told me I was to give you the majority of my time."

"He must think I need it," Georgie said in a disconsolate voice.

She almost missed Martina's understanding smile. "No such thing, miss. I expect he just thinks you've been left out in the past. You deserve as much attention as anyone."

Georgie said up straighter in the bed, pushing the breakfast tray away. "Have you known Rafferty a long time?"

"A long time," Martina said, and Georgie waited for the familiar tickle of jealousy. Martina was very pretty—of course

Rafferty would be attracted to her. Maybe they were even lovers in the past. Maybe they still were.

"Now what are you looking so gloomy about, miss?" Martina chided her. "This rain's going to let up and you can have a lovely walk in the park this afternoon in the...rose dress," she said, pulling it out from the others.

"Oh, no, that's my favorite," she protested.

"Exactly the reason why you should wear it. Pretty things are made to be enjoyed." She swooped in and removed the tray.

"And I can't walk in the park—I don't have a chaperone."

"Me or Rafferty will do the trick," Martina said. "In fact, it'll probably have to be Rafferty since I'll be helping your sister get ready for the Ormonds' ball tonight."

"Oh." She tried to hide her surge of happiness.

"Still want to wear the blue dress?"

Georgie glanced at the soft rose fabric. "No, I expect you're right. The blue is too shabby."

"Of course. if you'd rather go with me, we could go earlier in the day. I'd be too busy in the afternoon, but if you want to go out as soon as the rain stops..."

"Oh, I'd much rather walk in the afternoon," Georgie said hurriedly. "Though of course I'd love to have you as company."

Martina coughed something under her breath, and it sounded suspiciously like "liar." "You don't have to worry about my company, Miss Georgiana. I'm here as your servant, not your friend."

"Can't you be both?"

Martina's smile was crooked. "Society frowns on that sort of thing. Makes the servants too familiar."

"I don't give a hoot about what Society does or does not want. Rafferty's my friend, and there's no reason why you can't be one too."

"Oh, he is, is he?" There was a decided twinkle in Martina's eyes. "Then I can hardly object."

Georgie scooted back in bed, fixing Martina with a determined expression. "So, tell me about Rafferty."

Martina rolled her eyes. "I don't think that's proper, miss."

"How old is he?"

"I believe he's thirty-one."

Georgie made a face. "That makes him eleven years older than me," she said. "That's not a big difference, isn't it?"

"Big enough," Martina said in her low contralto.

"Is he...he's not married, is he?"

Martina kept her expression blank, but Georgie realized she could read right through her innocent questions. "No, miss, as far as I know, he's never married. He's footloose and fancy free. And he's not going to be looking at a young lady like you."

"Of course not," Georgie said hastily. "I was just curious."

"If you have any more questions, you'd best ask him yourself," Martina said firmly. "In the meantime, let's get you dressed. Your mother has been asking for you."

Now that the possibility of Rafferty being married had entered her mind, however, she couldn't let go of it. And it wasn't as if he would stay still long enough to answer her questions—every time she saw him he disappeared on some mysterious errand.

But she would have him to herself that afternoon. She would insist on a long walk, and even if he refused to answer her very reasonable questions, he would still be there with her, with no one to distract him.

By the time she reached her mother's salon, visiting hours were already in progress. She paused at the door for a moment, watching all the gentlemen surrounding her sister, and she tried to slip away, only to back into Rafferty. He caught her arm to keep her from stumbling, and she wanted to lean back against him, but he was pulling her away when her mother caught sight of her.

"Georgiana!" she trilled. "Come in and meet our callers!" For some reason, Rafferty's hand tightened, as if he was reluctant to let her go, but then a moment later he released her, and she decided she must have imagined it.

She plastered a demure smile on her face, one that turned genuine when Andrew Salton rose from his seat beside Norah and came forward. "Miss Georgiana," he said warmly. "I was hoping I might see you."

"Mr. Salton," she replied happily, still enjoying the memory of Rafferty's strong hand on her arm. For some reason, Norah's admirers were paying Georgie sudden attention, and she saw the hint of a frown at the corner of her sister's beautiful mouth. A moment later, disaster was averted when the gentlemen turned back to Norah, and Georgie was left with Andrew Salton.

"Did you like the flowers I sent?" he asked, once they were seated.

"They were lovely," she lied, having assumed all the floral tributes were for her sister. She glanced toward the door, some random instinct telling her that Rafferty was close by.

He wasn't watching her, a disappointment, but he wasn't watching Norah either. His attention seemed fixed on the man beside her, a disapproving expression on his face.

"I'm hoping you'll honor me with a dance this evening," Andrew Salton was saying, unaware of her distraction.

"A dance...oh, yes," she quickly recovered, and smiled warmly at him. "That would be lovely." She hadn't danced since the cotillions held near their country estate, and she'd missed it. Dancing with Andrew would be very pleasant. And she wondered if Rafferty knew how to dance.

Rafferty knew how to do everything. She glanced back at the doorway, but he'd disappeared, and she felt a pang. Why couldn't Rafferty be Andrew Salton, a perfectly unexceptional guest? It would make life so much easier. She planted a smile on her face and turned to Mr. Salton, trying to banish Rafferty from her mind.

Andrew and the horde of other gentlemen were rising, the strict timing of a morning call coming into play, and were gone before Georgie could get up the desire to even flirt with him. She watched him go with a sigh.

Norah looked at her from across the room, her eyes narrowing. "Why did you decide to join us this morning?" she demanded sharply. "Calling hours are for the senior members of the household."

Georgie ran a hand down the soft muslin of her new dress. "I thought that I should, now that I'm no longer dressed like an aging schoolgirl."

Norah let out a long-suffering sigh. "I think it would be better if you didn't join us for calling hours, at least not until I marry. You look absurd in that dress, and then you monopolize a gentleman's attention with that aging schoolgirl act. I'm certain Mr. Salton found you quite ridiculous."

"I think the dress is lovely. And I wasn't monopolizing anyone's attention. I was just talking with him."

"Don't be absurd!" Norah said. "He's only here to see me, and then he has to deal with your puppy-dog attentions. I thought you were madly in love with our butler. Keep away from my suitors."

"Mr. Salton isn't your suitor!" she shot back, ignoring the jibe about Rafferty. Not that she wanted Mr. Salton paying court to her, but she was so tired of Norah getting everything, all the attention, all the gentlemen, all the love.

"Oh, isn't he?" Norah said archly. "Why did you decide to join us this morning?"

"I told her to join us," her mother said with a trace of asperity. "You aren't the only one in need of a husband in this family."

Norah jerked her head upright in sudden disapproval. "You aren't giving her one of my admirers! I won't have it!"

"Don't be ridiculous, darling," Liliane soothed her. "None of your admirers would be willing to settle for her. I thought Mr. Salton would prove an admirable choice."

"Mr. Salton is completely unsuitable for a chit like Georgie."

"Don't be a dog in the manger, darling," her mother said. "You don't give him the time of day—you're almost rude to the man. Surely he's the last man you'd begrudge your sister."

"He's..." Norah's voice trailed off as she made an effort to pull herself together. She turned to Georgie. "Why don't you go in search of Rafferty and leave us alone? Mother and I need to talk."

Startled, she looked behind her, and realized to her relief that Rafferty was no longer looming beside the doorway. He hadn't heard that apparently she now had a suitor.

But Andrew Salton was a kind man. She was not the idiot everyone seemed to think she was—she knew her feelings for Rafferty could lead nowhere. But until she left this house, he was hers, whether Norah liked it or not.

He was in the kitchen, talking with Bertha, and she took a moment to admire his beautiful back. She hadn't made any noise on her slippered feet, but he stopped and turned, a frown on his face, and she wondered if he knew what Liliane had planned.

"I have a suitor," she announced glumly.

There was no surprise on his face. "So I gather. It's all settled then?"

"Of course not. I've just met the man last night."

"He's not the right man for a young girl like you," Rafferty said in a tight voice.

"I'm not a young girl."

"You are to me," he said in a clipped voice.

Georgie looked up at him, stricken. Was that really how he saw her? Her brand new grown-up dresses seemed to have done her no good.

"Then tell Norah you disapprove," she said. "She'll be happy to agree."

"Your sister is not my problem. You are."

"Why am I your problem?" she asked.

"Because I don't care about your sister."

Georgie had a swift intake of breath. "You care about me?" she said in a soft, hopeful voice.

"I don't care about anyone," he said, looking discomfited. "As a member of this household, you're my responsibility."

"So is Norah."

"Norah can take care of herself."

That stung. "I can take care of myself," she shot back. "I have been for the last twenty years."

He said nothing, but she could practically hear his silent scoff. "Then may I be the first to felicitate you on your upcoming nuptials?" he said smoothly.

Georgie ground her teeth in frustration. "I'm not going to marry Andrew Salton, no matter how nice he is. In fact, I don't intend to marry at all. I intend to live out my years in a house in the countryside, full of books and cats."

"And how are you going to manage that?" Bertha piped up, having watched their conversation with blatant disapproval. "You think you can look after yourself without a husband to see to things?"

"I'll have a maid and a butler," she said hotly.

She saw Rafferty jerk in discomfort. "I suggest you not count on me, Miss Georgie. This is only a short-term engagement, not a way of life. You'll need to find someone else to look after you."

"I can look after myself," she said again.

"Yes," said Bertha, "but who's going to—"

"I don't need anyone," she announced.

"Good to know," he said gravely.

"Particularly not you," she added, but if she hoped to crush him, or at least damage his *amour propre* a bit, she was doomed to failure.

"As you wish, Miss Georgie," he said gravely, and there was nothing Georgie could do but beat a hasty retreat.

She flounced off, there was no other word for it, turning on her heel and moving toward the stairs. When she turned back to see how he was appreciating her high dudgeon, he was gone.

Chapter Eleven

RAFFERTY MADE HIS ESCAPE, cursing himself as he went. It was all perfectly well to keep Georgie away from Norah's biting tongue—the young woman was a menace.

What made less sense was his efforts to keep her away from Andrew Salton. He wanted her to marry someone, didn't he? Salton should be exactly who he'd want for her. Salton could take good care of her without crushing her spirit, and Rafferty wouldn't have to worry about her or even think about her anymore.

Salton had brought her flowers, though that scarcely improved him in Rafferty's eyes. Baby pink roses, innocent and sweet, and all Rafferty's protective instincts were aroused. Georgie deserved peonies, pink and flush and luscious, though Rafferty had no idea whether they were grown in hothouses or not. But Andrew Salton saw what he wanted to see when he looked at Georgie—a simple, shy young lady cut from the same cloth as everyone else. She was no ordinary young lady of the ton, she was so much more, she was—

He cursed as he made his way to the kitchen. Bertha glowered at him from her seat at the table, a cup of tea in front of her.

"What's wrong with them?" she asked suspiciously as he tossed Salton's flowers into the trash.

"They have bugs," he lied. He wanted Georgie to find a good man, he truly did. Just not this one.

But none of the other hopeful young men who'd crowded around Norah today would do, either. Georgie deserved better than that, and he had every intention of finding the perfect man for her. No matter how long it took.

Bertha looked him for a long, silent moment. "I just hope you know what you're doing," she said finally, and he knew she wasn't talking about the flowers.

"I always do," he said, and wondered if that were true.

"She's a piece of work!" Martina announced as she flounced into the kitchen.

"Which one?" Bertha asked. "Miss Norah or Miss Georgie? They're all crazy if you ask me."

Martina cast a sly glance in his direction. "All of them?"

"Miss Georgie's the worst. Not a practical bone in her body."

But Rafferty wasn't about to react to this provocation from the women staring at him so meaningfully. "I've yet to see any sign of it," he said blandly.

"I was talking about that Miss Norah. Miss Georgie is an angel."

Rafferty gave out a derisive laugh.

"You're not fooling me, young man," Bertha said.

"I'm thirty-one—hardly young," he protested, ignoring the main question.

"Oh, don't be stupid, Rafferty," Martina said as she took a seat opposite Bertha and poured herself a cup of tea. "You know perfectly well that the girl's in love with you. Head over heels, in fact."

"Which one?" he said, deliberately obtuse.

"You know who I'm talking about," Martina chided him. "I tried to warn her."

"Try harder," he grumbled. "And she'll forget about me as

soon as an acceptable young man shows up. The right one," he amended, thinking of Salton.

"You underestimate your allure," Martina said. "She sees you as some romantic figure."

"No one finds their butler romantic."

"But you're not an ordinary butler and we all know it. She's at the age when she likes that edge of danger you try to hide."

"Butlers don't have an edge of danger, as you so melodramatically put it."

"You do."

Rafferty made a face. "She'll grow out of it."

"Hmmph," Bertha said again, and Rafferty glared at her. There was nothing worse than a woman who thought she knew more than he did. Particularly when she did.

"Miss Georgie says she'll be ready for walk at two," Martina said slyly.

"What?"

"Lady Manning promised you'd accompany her on a walk this afternoon."

"Why not you? You're her maid."

"Miss Norah and her ladyship have already claimed my time."

"I thought I told you to favor Georgie?"

"*Miss* Georgie," Bertha corrected him with a fierce gleam in her eyes.

"And why exactly was that?" Martina said. "She's the only one who's not interested in monopolizing my time."

"No one pays any attention to her."

"You do."

Rafferty ground his teeth. "I have to visit Sir Elston's tailor. I don't have time to shepherd a child around London. Her brother can take her."

"Her brother will be three sheets to the wind by then," Bertha said. "You wouldn't want to let the lass down, now, would you?"

"The tailor," he said firmly, and made his escape.

He was making a royal mess of things, he thought later when

he returned to the house on Corinth Place. He'd taken as much time as he possibly could, not returning home until the early autumn dusk was closing around the city. Georgie would have prevailed on someone else to accompany her on a proper, leisurely stroll—it was no job for a butler.

Not that he could envision Georgie with a leisurely stroll. She had a tendency to rush at things pell-mell, just like a schoolgirl.

But she wasn't a schoolgirl, and he was learning to accept that. Reluctantly.

Dinner was *en famille* that evening, to be followed by that damned ball at the Duke of Ormond's house. Rafferty almost dreaded to see what she would wear.

His worst fears were realized when she came downstairs. She was radiant in a pale blue that brought out the color of her usually mischievous eyes. They weren't mischievous now—she was looking at him with deep reproach.

Neddy had managed to dress himself, with Rafferty's help, and he was just barely sober enough to make it to the table, giving his mother an affectionate kiss on her proffered cheek before sinking into his chair.

The Beauty was in fine fettle that night, a malicious glint in her eyes as she glanced at her unhappy sister, but she waited until the third remove before she dove in like the harpy she was.

"Georgie is looking rather forlorn, Mama," she announced.

Lady Manning looked up, blinking. "Oh, dear. Are you feeling quite the thing, Georgie? Should I call the doctor?"

"We can't afford the doctor," Sir Elston grumbled.

"Don't be ridiculous," Liliane said with an airy laugh. "Rafferty can get him for us. Rafferty can get anything for us. I quite don't know how we got on without him—he's been an absolute miracle worker."

"Humph," said Norah. "Have you ever wondered how he's managed to perform these miracles? After all, we know absolutely nothing about him. We found him begging in the streets."

"Oh, surely not begging," Liliane protested. "He's much too

elegant for that. In truth, he's the most presentable butler we've ever had—I'm quite taken with him."

"You and George," Norah said.

"What do you mean by that?" Sir Elston demanded, roused from his usual habit of ignoring his unruly family.

"Why, only that Georgie is head over heels in love with him, and she follows him around like a puppy dog. It's a wonder he gets anything done with Georgie hanging onto him."

"I am not!" Georgie snapped with a little more force than necessary. "And even if I were, what business is it of yours?"

Rafferty considered beating a hasty retreat. He'd taken up his position by the sideboard in lieu of footmen, but the Mannings obviously considered him to be part of the furniture as they debated his existence.

"You see, Mother. Next thing we know, he'll run off with her and we'll all be ruined."

"Stuff it, Norah." Neddy roused himself from his abstraction. "Georgie's not going to do anything that embarrasses us."

"Well, I don't know," Liliane said worriedly. "She is awfully headstrong."

"And stupid," Norah added. "The first handsome man to pay attention to her and she's all gaga."

"I'm right here," Georgie said in a testy voice, and Rafferty was strongly tempted to add, *so am I.*

"He's paying attention to her?" Sir Elston said dangerously, glaring at him from beneath his heavy brows. "What do you mean by that?"

"Oh, just that he arranged for her wardrobe to be delivered, while my dresses still languish at Madame Racette's. I hardly think it proper for a man to dress my supposedly innocent sister who's barely allowed out in society."

Sir Elston was at the point of exploding when Liliane broke in. "Well, I do see your point, Norah dear. After all, it's your season. But she does look charmingly in her new dresses, though I don't quite remember ordering them, but I must have, or else how would Madame Racette know to deliver them? I swear, I'm all a muddle."

"I'm not," Sir Elston growled.

"Pretty dresses are a waste of time in George's case," Norah said spitefully. "You can put rouge on a pig, and it's still just a pig with rouge."

"Stuff it, Sis," Neddy said blearily.

"You're a beast!" Georgie stormed, finally having had enough. "You're just jealous because Rafferty likes me and he thinks you're a snake. He told me so."

"He did what?" Sir Elston thundered.

Norah laughed, but her eyes glittered. "You see what I mean? And don't fool yourself, George. Rafferty likes me very much. He merely feels sorry for you."

"He does not!" Georgie cried. "Do you, Rafferty?"

They all turned to look at him, and he cursed inwardly. This was bad enough when he was a piece of furniture—now he was forced to respond.

"I'm quite sure Rafferty loves us all," Liliane said brightly. "Don't you, Rafferty?"

"I hold the entire family in high esteem," he said in a grave monotone.

"Even me?" Norah purred.

"Of course, Miss Manning."

"I must say that new lady's maid you found us is a wonder," Liliane broke in, thankfully changing the subject. "I vow I haven't had my hair done properly in weeks."

"A new maid?" Sir Elston exploded. "We can't afford one!"

"We can't afford anything Rafferty has brought to us, and yet somehow he manages," Norah said with acid sweetness. "I just shudder to think what will happen when the bills finally come due."

"Nonsense, child. Don't bother your head about money! I never do," said Liliane.

"I'm well aware of that," her husband said stiffly.

"Must we talk about money all the time?" Neddy emerged from his semi-stupor to complain. "There's nothing we can do about it, so we may as well not think about it. It's depressing."

"May I point out that your gambling has contributed to our current impecunious circumstances?" Norah said icily.

"Mother has high gaming debts as well." His voice was sulky.

"I must admit you're right, Neddy darling." Liliane brightened. "Your father was complaining about my gambling bills for at least a year before he lost everything on that bubble thing. But that's neither here nor there because Norah's going to marry someone fabulously wealthy and then there won't be any problem. Will there, dear?"

She directed her last question to her husband, who simply made a choking sound and rolled his eyes.

Rafferty allowed himself a covert glance at Norah, and she wasn't looking any too pleased with this future, but for once, she said nothing. She was still focusing on her sister.

"I think it's dangerous to bring perfect strangers in and give them the running of the household," Norah said. "Who knows, we all may be murdered in our beds!"

"Oh, I don't think Rafferty's a murderer," Liliane said brightly. "If he was, I suspect we would be dead already. And just think of all the lovely things he's brought us. I can't remember how we ever survived without him."

"We had a houseful of servants," Norah said. "And indeed, I'm wondering how one man manages to accomplish so much."

"Rafferty is wonderful!" Georgie snapped, clearly having forgotten her displeasure with him.

"I told you, Mother," Norah purred. "Next thing you know, they'll be off to Gretna Green and we'd never live down the shame of it."

Georgie's face flushed, and she glared at her sister. "You're an absolute beast, Norah. Stop being so hateful."

"I'm not being hateful, just honest," Norah said with spurious concern. "This family can't afford any kind of scandal if

I'm to marry some titled nabob." She didn't sound particularly pleased by the idea.

"Well, why don't you just do it instead of talking about it," Georgie shot back. "Haven't you been in society long enough? Much more time and people will start to wonder what's wrong with you, that you haven't secured a match."

"Mother!" Nora cried in protest.

"Apologize to your sister, Georgie."

"I'd rather die," she said, rising dramatically and stalking from the room.

It took everything he had not to follow Georgie with his eyes when she left the dining room, but he was an expert at keeping his face impassive. It was never good to betray any emotion when it came to his line of work, his real line of work, that was, and his implacability served him well as the Mannings' substitute butler.

"Oh, go after her, Rafferty," Liliane cried. "I can't bear to see her so upset."

"He's not going anywhere," Sir Elston thundered.

"Of course, he is! Georgie adores him—I vow she hasn't been this taken with anyone since her spaniel died. He'll cheer her up."

Rafferty was sorely tempted to bark, but he kept his expression stoic, not moving as Sir Elston and Liliane devolved into a restrained shouting match. Neddy slid lower in his seat—another glass or two of the fine claret Rafferty had been able to procure and he'd be on the floor—and Norah simply preened, her work done for the evening.

He wasn't paying attention to the battle royale until Sir Elston finally addressed him. "Well, what are you waiting for? Go after her. But if you put one finger on her, I'll horsewhip you myself."

So Lady Manning had won. It wasn't the order he'd been hoping for, but he could hardly refuse.

"Yes, sir."

"And do cheer her up!" Lady Manning added. "Never let it be said that I am anything but the most doting mother. We prevailed upon our hosts to include her in the invitation for tonight, and it would appear quite dreadful if she failed to come." Lilliane made a slight gesture, and he came forward and filled her wine glass as well as that of her son, silently cursing. It was already clear he'd have to transport Neddy upstairs and get him into his night gear —he hardly fancied doing the same with his mother.

"Go along with you now, Rafferty." Lady Manning made a shooing gesture. "Cheer the poor girl up."

He had no choice, and he was hardly going to argue. With a slight bow, he left the room, in search of his wayward patron.

It took him a while to find her. To his great relief she hadn't immured herself in her bedroom, but neither was she in the lady's salon nor any of the other formal rooms. When he finally found her, she was in the place he should have looked first—in the kitchen, comfortably ensconced at the big table with a heaping plate of food in front of her.

Martina and Bertha were with her, and neither of them evinced the slightest bit of surprise when he walked into the room.

"What took you so long?" Georgie asked.

"Your father was threatening to horsewhip me." He took the seat opposite her and sank into it. The kitchen, unlike the rest of the house, was a democracy, and he had no intention of being on his formal best when he was there.

"And you were so frightened?" Georgie said. "My father wouldn't hurt a fly."

"He might if someone he cared about were compromised."

"Yes, but you don't like Norah," she pointed out.

"Don't be deliberately obtuse. She's not the only young woman in this household."

"But she's his favorite. She's everyone's favorite," she said with a sigh.

The two women were quick with their demurrals. "She's a bitch," Martina summed it up nicely.

"A bitch?" Georgie was quite taken with the word. "I like that. May I use it?"

"No," said Bertha, Martina, and Rafferty in unison.

Georgie shrugged. "Witch will do," she said philosophically. "You weren't really afraid of my father, were you?"

"He told me to go find you and cheer you up."

"Oh." There was no hiding her disappointment. "That's good."

"Apparently, I'm taking the place of your deceased spaniel," he said dryly.

To his absolute horror, her blue eyes filled with unshed tears. "You couldn't," she said flatly.

"You're making a mockery of the girl's dead dog? Shame on yourself, Rafferty," Martina said sternly.

"Told you he was no good," Bertha muttered.

"All right, all right!" he protested. "I wasn't mocking the dead dog, I was mocking being compared to it."

"You're a wretch," Martina said with clear affection. "Pay him no mind, dearie."

Georgie pushed her plate away, her appetite apparently gone. "You don't really like my sister, do you?"

"It's not my place to like or dislike her," he replied carefully.

"She's a snake," Georgie said flatly.

"Aye, that she is," Martina said.

"You're not helping." Rafferty gave her a disapproving glare, but Martina simply shrugged it off.

"No need to pretend she's anything else," Bertha said. "She's always been a spoiled brat. Comes from being too pretty—everyone dotes on her."

"Fortunately, that's not my problem," Georgie said, and Rafferty knew she wasn't searching for compliments. "I'm the clever one."

"You could have fooled me on that one," Bertha said dampeningly.

"Well, Neddy drinks too much to be clever, and Norah's more interested in what she looks like than what she knows."

"Your sister's no fool," Bertha warned her.

Georgie sighed. "No, I suppose not. I just wish she'd get married and go away." She gave herself a delicate little shake, as if to rid herself of her sister's onerous presence. "In the meantime, how do I get out of going to the Ormonds' tonight? Rafferty, could you tell them I'm ill?"

"He could but he won't," Bertha said. "You need to go out into society and find a gentleman of your own. Like that Mr. Salton."

Georgie simply shrugged, and if he hadn't been so preternaturally aware of her he wouldn't have noticed the strained expression in her eyes. "He's a very nice man," she said, but there was no softening in her voice—clearly, Salton didn't remind her of her spaniel.

No, the spaniel made her cry, and he was a thoughtless brute to joke about it.

"You could marry him and be away from this crazy family," Martina piped up, and it was all Rafferty could do not to glare at her.

And it was a good thing, because Georgie was looking at him when she said, "I don't want to marry anyone."

"Nonsense. Every girl wants to be married," Bertha said.

"Not if I can't marry who I want," she said stubbornly, still looking at him, and he wanted to groan. A crush was bad enough —she was too tempting for his piece of mind. Now she wanted to marry him?

He needed to get the hell out of here before things got worse.

"You all need to go away and let me do my work," Bertha announced in her irascible voice.

"I'm going," Martina said cheerfully. "Miss Norah has a list of tasks an arm long, and her ladyship is almost as bad. And that reminds me, Miss Georgie. What can I do for you?"

"Luckily, I don't need you for anything," Georgie said. "Norah is the one who's going to save us."

Rafferty snorted indelicately.

Chapter Twelve

RAFFERTY SHOULD HAVE BEEN RELIEVED when the obstreperous Manning family departed for the Ormonds' that evening. He was having a hard enough time dealing with Bertha and Martina's pointed remarks; he didn't need Georgie's big blue eyes starting at him longingly any more than he felt like enduring Norah's acid tongue. To his surprise, Neddy was just barely sober enough to accompany them, and Sir Elston went as well, complaining loudly, leaving the house to the three of them. Betsey and Jane had gone home for the evening, happy to get away from their domestic duties. He wasn't worried about whether they'd return or not. He was enough to put the fear of God into anyone who knew him, and the girls knew him very well.

Except that he didn't put the fear of God into Georgie. She just looked at him with those shining eyes that should have made him itch. Well, they did, but the wrong kind of itch. He liked voluptuous, experienced women who took what they wanted, not innocent schoolgirls. He had no intention of laying a finger on her if he could help it. It wasn't his fault that he'd had to carry her, and she'd been a cozy little bundle, or rub her narrow, pretty feet. He'd never found feet to be particularly erotic, but hers were, even abraded as they had been. He liked the idea of her wearing the boots he had bought her—it was as if he had a secret touch....

Jesus, no! "I'm going out," he said abruptly.

Martina looked at him, too wise for his peace of mind. "You're not going to be stopping in at the Ormonds' tonight? I doubt you'd be welcome."

He jerked, startled, then let his bland expression cover his face. "You never can tell," he said obscurely.

"It's only the crazy Mannings who'd bring a stranger into their house as a butler," Bertha pointed out. "You'd hardly be welcome elsewhere."

"Obviously not," he said. "Are they particularly close friends to the Ormonds?"

"Not really. They're a bit above the Mannings' touch. But the young heir is head over heels for the Beauty, and the parents dote on the boy, so the Mannings might get a step up in society."

"I see," he said, which explained nothing. There were some things he had no intention of sharing, and the Ormonds' adored son was one of them. Though he could wish something better than Norah for the boy.

The current Duke of Ormond was no fool—he would see through Norah's shallow behavior easily enough, saving his young son from heartbreak, and the dowager duchess had a will of iron. It wasn't a bit of his business what happened to the boy, Rafferty reminded himself. He was on his own.

The night was cool and rainy, something that bothered him not one whit, and he started down the sidewalk, in the opposite direction of the Ormonds' magnificent townhouse on Berkeley Square. He hadn't heard any word about Stiles, even from the two maids who were usually up on everything. Billy Stiles was keeping low, but Rafferty didn't make the mistake of thinking he'd lost interest. As long as Judge Belding's fortune was unaccounted for, then Rafferty was living on borrowed time.

He paid no attention to the time as he walked. If he'd had any sense he would have stayed at the house and searched through the attics again. Stiles was not a man with a great deal of patience, and he was going to show up sooner or later and demand to know where the money was. If Rafferty couldn't find it, he was going to have a fair amount of trouble. Stiles had a small army working for him, and Rafferty was unsure just how many men he could best at one time. No need to be cocky.

The rain was coming down more heavily now, and he tugged up the collar of his coat, cursing. His skin was wet and clammy, and he was ready for a warm fire and a tot of Neddy's brandy. Come to think of it, someone would need to put Neddy to bed, and he wasn't leaving that task in Georgie's arms. He looked up to get his bearings, and cursed.

He'd somehow ended up in Berkeley Square, two buildings down from the Ormonds' mansion, a place he knew as well as he knew himself. If he had any sense, he'd walk in the opposite direction, taking the long way back to Corinth Place. It was only a little out of his way, and it would do wonders for his peace of mind.

He walked toward the mansion, drawn against his will. The carriages lined the streets on both sides of the square—there must be a big crush going on in the massive ballroom on the third floor. The back gate by the rose garden was still there, overgrown but functioning, and he slipped inside before he could think better of it.

The tree was still there as well. The thing must be ancient—it had been old the last time he'd climbed it—but it looked sturdy enough, and the rain had lessened a bit. A moment later, he was climbing, as nimbly as a chimney sweep, up the massive height to the view of the crowded ballroom.

It wasn't as busy as the carriages had led him to expect, but then, some people were already leaving, even though it was hardly past midnight. It didn't take him long to find the Beauty—she was surrounded by young men and enjoying herself tremendously. Lady Manning was nearby, basking in Norah's reflected glory, and the two Manning men were nowhere to be seen.

He wasn't interested in them. It took another five minutes

before he finally found Georgie on the dance floor, moving smoothly enough in Andrew Salton's arms.

The growl he made startled him. Georgie's eyes were shining as he whirled her in a decent waltz, though the man was not graceful enough to be a fit partner for her. He was looking down at her, dutifully besotted, and Rafferty growled once again. He didn't deserve Georgie. No one did.

He was being an idiot. He wanted Georgie in love, with anyone but himself. He wanted her safely married and away from her family's ramshackle behavior, particularly Norah's wicked tongue. He glanced around the room, looking for a suitable alternative, still grumbling.

There were at least three other young men who might do, though he didn't recognize two of them. Still, they seemed young, strong and presentable, and they weren't fawning over the Beauty. And there was young Charles Ormond, with his tall, lean body and his vivid blue eyes staring raptly at Norah's face.

He was the perfect choice for Georgie, on so many levels, though Rafferty doubted she would enjoy being a future duchess. The Ormonds were a conventional lot, despite a few rare slips, and they would expect their son to marry the pattern card of respectability. That would crush the life out of Georgie.

No, perhaps Salton was the wisest choice, despite Rafferty's misgivings. He looked back toward the dancing couple and froze.

Andrew Salton was clearly a man in love—you could see it from every angle of his face, the way his brown eyes shone with adoration. But he wasn't looking at Georgie. He was staring, over her shoulder, at Norah Manning.

"Bastard," Rafferty muttered beneath his breath. His instincts had been right all along. For all the attention he was paying Georgie, he was using her to get to Norah, and Rafferty wanted to punch him. Georgie didn't deserve to have her heart broken, she deserved the best of the best, and he—

They turned with the movement of the dance, and he got a better look at Georgie, and cursed underneath his breath. She wasn't looking like a young girl in love—no, she saved that expression for his unworthy hide. No, she looked like someone at her first dance, having a wonderful time. Salton wasn't about to break her heart, at least, not yet, and it would be up to Rafferty to make certain that didn't happen.

Cold rain slithered down his back, and he cursed silently before starting his careful descent. He'd seen what he wanted to see—now he needed to get back to the house on Corinth Place before the Mannings returned.

The tree trunk was slippery, and some of the branches were gone from the last time he'd climbed the thing. He was about twelve feet up when his foot gave away, and he went crashing down the rest of the way to the hard ground.

He lay there for a moment, winded, when he heard the sound of the kitchen door open, and rose quickly, shaking off the momentary dizziness.

"Is someone out there?" came an old man's voice.

He froze, his worst mistake. And then he moved quickly, up past the rose gate, into the street that was lit by the newest gaslight. Illuminating his face to his pursuer, just for a moment, but the damage was done.

"My God!" said the man who'd followed him. "It's Master Jamie!"

A moment later, Rafferty was gone, disappearing into the shadows where no one had the unfortunate ability to recognize him. Robinson, the ancient gardener, was mumbling to himself now, calling himself an old fool, and Rafferty stayed where he was behind a huge outcropping of bushes, barely breathing.

A moment later, the old man went back into the Ormonds' garden, closing the gate carefully behind him.

And James Rafferty, born James Alexander William Ormond, disappeared into the rainy night, cursing himself as he went.

"OH, THERE YOU ARE, RAFFERTY!" Liliane Manning declared with a high-pitched giggle. I'm so glad you're here—Neddy has had a bit too much of the grape and he's asleep in the carriage."

"Let him stay there," his father grumbled.

"Don't be ridiculous, Manning," his lady wife protested. "We can't leave him out there all night—he'll catch his death."

"Let him."

"Now, you know you don't really feel that way. Rafferty will bring him in and put him to bed, and by tomorrow morning he'll be fine."

"Harumph," said Manning.

"And didn't we have a lovely time!" Liliane trilled, unmoved by her husband's bad temper. "The Ormonds were so kind and gracious. I vow, I never thought I'd see the day when we would become dear friends with a duke."

"We aren't dear friends, we were merely invited to a ball," Georgie pointed out unfortunately. "And it was just because of Norah."

But Liliane was not to be chastened. "I see a fond friendship springing up between us. Who knows, we may be so bold as to call them family one day." She turned. "What was that, Rafferty?"

"Nothing, ma'am," he said. "I'll go fetch the young master."

"Poor Neddy," Georgie said, hovering near him. "Let me help. I'm good with him when he gets like this."

"No need," Rafferty said briskly. "I have plenty of experience."

"So you do. I wonder where you got that experience from," Norah said in her silken voice. "Perhaps you worked for one of the families in the area."

"No, Miss Manning," he said, trying to move away from Georgie. Georgie followed. "I've never worked in service before."

"But then, how do you know so well what a butler ought to do?" Liliane asked in amazement.

"Rafferty can do anything," Georgie declared.

"Mother, are you going to let her continue to make a fool of herself and our whole family?" Norah's whine was far less pretty than her face. "If people knew we'd hired a criminal from the streets to be a butler, we would become the laughingstock of society! He needs to go!"

"Certainly not," Liliane said. "I fail to see anything improper in Georgie's affection for her protégé."

"You wouldn't," Norah said under her breath.

"And I don't think it's anything to worry about. Georgie has done surprisingly well for herself in only three public outings. She already has a most devoted suitor, and I count myself much shocked if he did not request an interview with your father in the near future."

"Georgie is not getting married before I am!" Norah's voice was shrill.

"Well, then, choose someone," Sir Elston broke in. "Enough of this shilly-shallying. You could be a duchess in the end! What's that, Rafferty?"

Georgie was still staring up at him with rapt eyes and an expression that had been notably missing from her dance with Andrew Salton, and Rafferty wanted to sigh in frustration.

"Nothing, Sir Elston. I'll fetch Mr. Edward."

"And just who is this devoted swain I have yet to hear about?" Norah was demanding as he reached the door.

"Andrew Salton," Liliane provided triumphantly. "He sent her flowers."

Jesus, did everyone in the household know that? He should have thrown them out, not just disposed of the card.

He was unprepared for Norah's shriek of fury. "Don't be ridiculous! Mr. Salton is much more interested in me than my frumpy little sister. They all are."

"Oh, dearest, you can spare one or two," Liliane said airily. "And both you girls belong in bed—you don't want these late nights interfering with your beauty sleep. Georgie, move away from Rafferty, there's a good girl. You really can't spend your time mooning over the man."

"You see!" Norah blared triumphantly.

"I'm not mooning," Georgie said at the same time, reluctantly moving away from him.

"To bed, all of you!" Sir Elston thundered. "And Rafferty, bring me my whiskey after you dispose of my son and heir."

"Yes, sir." He escaped before he could be dragged into another uncomfortable conversation.

Neddy was blessedly cooperative that night, and he waited until he was in the water closet before he cast up his accounts. By the time he was sleeping it off and Sir Elston had been well-lubricated, Rafferty was finished for the night, off to his rooms off the kitchen.

Butlers lived relatively well in the hierarchy of household servants, and his quarters were spacious. The bed was narrow but comfortable, there was a chair and a table and a faded Persian rug on the dusty floor. He considered getting the girls in there to clean, but there were more important places where their help was needed.

Stripping off his still-damp jacket and tie, he sank back into the comfortable chair, wishing he'd helped himself to one of Sir Elston's bottles. He'd cocked things up that night, sentimental fool that he was, and he needed to be prepared to make a hasty exit if old Clem Robinson decided to do some talking. Still, the man had to be ancient—no one was likely to believe him if he started talking about ghosts in the rose garden. He didn't need to worry.

Leaning back in the chair, he closed his eyes and considered the mess he'd made of things. Life would be a great deal simpler if he'd never given in to Georgie's beseeching and become a butler, of all things! He shouldn't have rescued them, he shouldn't hang around while Georgie was so obviously suffering from an adolescent crush. The last thing he wanted to do was hurt her, but the longer he stayed there, the more likely that was to happen.

The smartest thing he could have done was simply disappear, leaving Billy Stiles alone in his quest for the judge's money. But then, that would leave the Mannings with no recourse, and Stiles was a bit too handy with his knife. If he'd never met her, he simply wouldn't care.

But he had met her, curse it. And whether he liked it or not, she was far too tempting, no matter how hard he tried to resist. There was something about Georgie's sweetness that touched a part of him he thought long dead.

That part of him needed to remain dead. He'd been a fool to show up at the Ormonds, an even bigger fool to give in to temptation and spy from that old tree. The thought of how much hell would break out if someone other than old Clem saw him was enough to make his blood run cold. The Dowager Duchess was no fool—if she caught wind of it, she wouldn't let go until she found him, and he'd turned from that life long ago. There was no going back.

There was nothing keeping him in London. Italy was warm and sunny in the south—he could buy a place by the sea and forget about this unlikely sojourn, leave Belding's long-lost funds to Billy Stiles.

And die of boredom. Still, an escape was relatively easy, and it was exactly what he should do. Once he made sure Georgie had found someone suitable to love, not this stupid crush she had. If he went now, she might wind up married to a man who loved her sister, and Georgie had spent enough of her life being second best.

No, if he put his mind to it, he'd find a decent man for her and then take off, and she'd be too much in love to even notice his leaving. All he had to do was focus.

And keep the hell away from the Ormonds.

Chapter Thirteen

THE DAY WAS bright and cheerful when Martina pushed open the curtains, the first day Georgie had seen the sun in ages. "Time to wake up, sleepyhead," Martina announced, setting the breakfast tray across her lap. "You don't want to be wasting this beautiful weather."

Georgie pushed her hair back from her face and reached for her cup of tea. "Where is everyone?"

"Miss Norah's still abed, as is your mother. Your father's gone to his club, your brother is in the breakfast room with a pounding headache, and Bertha's in the kitchen. Was that what you were wanting to know?"

Georgie refused to rise to the bait. "Of course," she said. "Where are the maids? Do we still have them?"

"They're cleaning. That amounts to everyone, then, does it?" An impish smile tugged at Martina's strong mouth. "Oh, there's Rafferty, of course. But then, you wouldn't care where he was, would you?"

"You are a miserable human being," Georgie said flatly.

"I've warned you he's not for the likes of you," Martina said, not without kindness. "Besides, haven't you got a gentleman who's been showing you marked attention? Much better to keep your mind on him."

Andrew Salton's handsome face swum in her mind for a moment, and she considered her future. He seemed to like her, and he was very kind. But he wasn't as tall as Rafferty, and he didn't have Rafferty's piercing blue eyes. And falling in love wasn't a practical thing—she could hardly just decide to do it. If she could, she would have chosen someone more sensible than their unconventional butler.

"I don't know what you're talking about," she said, reaching for her toast.

"Certain, you don't," Martina said. "There'll be no visiting hours today, given that everyone else is still abed. You need something to take your mind off things."

"What things?" she asked innocently.

Martina just gave her a meaningful look, then sighed. "What were you planning to wear, Miss Georgie? The striped green one would suit the day."

"I can dress myself, Martina. I'm used to it."

"You shouldn't have to be," Martina said. "I've got my orders and I mean to see to them."

The sooner she was dressed, the sooner she could find Rafferty. It would be easy enough to come up with some excuse, or she could simply wander into the kitchen to talk with Bertha. Rafferty would turn up sooner or later.

He didn't.

"Don't look so morose, Miss Georgie," Bertha said briskly from her spot by the stove. "It's a beautiful day and you need to be out in it."

"I need Rafferty to accompany me," she said stubbornly. "Where is he?"

"Too busy for walks in the sunshine," Rafferty said from the doorway, and Georgie felt her color rise. "You'll have to take Martina."

"She's busy with my mother and Norah," she argued. "I doubt they'll let her go."

"I'll see to it," he said in his oddly classless voice. When they'd first found him, he'd sounded like he came from the streets, but now he sounded, if not aristocratic, then not like a shopkeeper either. He was like a chameleon—he could fit anywhere.

"I'm willing to wait for you to accompany me," she said, trying not to sound too desperate. He was avoiding her, and she knew it, but short of outright pleading, she didn't know what to do.

His extraordinary eyes glanced over her just briefly, not really seeing her in her beautiful green-striped dress with the pink ribbons. She might as well not exist.

"I have work to do for your father, Miss Georgiana," he said. "And your maid is a more suitable companion for an outing."

But I don't want to be suitable, she wanted to cry. *I want you!* But he'd already left the kitchen, whatever he'd come for forgotten in his need to escape her presence. For some stupid reason she wanted to cry.

Bertha was watching her with a sympathetic eye. "How about a nice cup of tea?"

"No, thank you."

"Your gentleman sent you flowers again."

"Oh? That's nice," she said, moving listlessly around the kitchen.

"Well, Miss Georgie, you can stay here and sulk, or you can go out with Martina and enjoy the day," Bertha said briskly. "Never let a man know his decisions matter—they take advantage of it, they do."

Georgie's eyes widened. "Why, Bertha, I didn't know you knew anything about men."

Bertha harrumphed. "A great deal more than you do."

"I know nothing about them."

"That's the God's truth. I was married back when I was a lass.

A handsome man he were, though not a patch on Rafferty. Still, I thought he hung the moon, I did. But it wasn't long before he began his cheating ways, taking my money and knocking me about. So I decided pretty is as pretty does and I could do much better without 'im. I've never regretted my decision."

"Rafferty would never take my money and knock me around," Georgie protested.

"Rafferty's never going to lay any kind of hand on you—you'd best learn to accept it. He's the butler, you're the young lady of the house, and a fine, prosperous man is courting you."

"How do you know he's prosperous?"

"Lady Manning told me. She seems to think it's practically all sewn up."

"He hasn't offered," Georgie said, aware of a tightening in her stomach.

"He will. And you'll be able to leave this crazy household and live an ordinary life."

"I don't want an ordinary life!" she cried. *I want Rafferty!* She didn't say it out loud, but she might as well have. Bertha was looking at her with a sorrowful expression.

"I'll tell Martina to hurry up. You know the weather—it could turn cloudy and cold before you realize it. Put on those nice new shoes you got, and I'll send her up to you."

At the thought of her beautiful shoes, she nearly burst into tears, but she stiffened her back instead, moving up the back stairs to her room. She was being a child, she told herself, weeping for the moon. It was time she grew up, and married, and had children herself. There was even a steady gentleman who appeared interested. Though she could hardly imagine lying beneath him and letting him do the things men did.

She didn't want a steady gentleman, she wanted Rafferty! Shockingly enough, she wanted his body in bed with her. The truth should make her blush. But there was no denying the fact— he didn't want her. It was time for her to accept it.

It was hard to stay morose when the sun beat down, she

thought several hours later as she and Martina made their way down the crowded streets. They spent a great deal of time in the shops, looking at everything, buying nothing, though Martina insisted that Rafferty would see to things. The only thing that caused Georgie a pang was a beautiful night dress they found at Madame Racette's shop, a sample, the modiste said, for a discriminating gentleman.

"A man wouldn't wear this!" Georgie said, scandalized.

Madame Racette laughed. She was a skinny woman with a long nose but cheery eyes, wearing the best of her trade. "A gentleman would buy it for his lady love."

"For his wife?" Georgie said, looking at it with interest. It was truly a lovely thing, if a bit...indecent.

"No, Miss Georgie, for his mistress," Martina explained patiently. "These things aren't worn by proper women. I wonder you brought it out!" She addressed the modiste. "Don't you know a lady when you see one?"

The modiste was all apologies, starting to pull the night dress away, but Georgie put her hand out to touch it. It was so soft, almost featherlight. How would it feel to wear something like that? What would Rafferty think if he saw her in it? Would he want to...?

"And I don't wonder at you blushing, Miss Georgie," Martina carried on, misreading her reaction as she hustled her out of the shop. "I can't imagine why that woman would bring out anything so outrageous. Hasn't she dressed you for years?"

"Yes," Georgie said, remembering all the childish frocks and enveloping night rails that had been her lot.

"It's that bloody Rafferty," Martina said, then bit her full lip. "I beg your pardon, miss. Clearly the woman got the wrong idea when Rafferty arranged for your new clothes."

"What kind of idea?"

Martina never blushed, a fact that Georgie found interesting. Instead, she sighed. "You are an innocent, aren't you? Well, stay that way. It'll be for your husband to enlighten you."

"Is that what you would want?" Georgie countered. "To be kept in ignorance until it was too late to do anything about it?"

Martina looked at her with real trepidation. "What do you mean by that?"

"The night dress is made for a man's mistress. And Madame Racette must think that, because Rafferty somehow arranged for my clothes, that I must be his mistress. Which is absurd—I'm hardly the seductive type. And why me and not Norah?"

"He didn't buy the clothes for Norah," Martina said grimly.

"He didn't buy the clothes for me," Georgie said. "My father did."

"With what money?" she countered, leaving Georgie in shock as she ushered her into one of the new tea shops that had recently arisen.

There was no way she could respond, as she followed Martina's swaying figure to a small table, but a warmth had flooded her insides, filling her with happiness instead of the mournfulness that had plagued her all day. It didn't matter if he was trying to avoid her. He'd bought her those pretty dresses, those beautiful shoes. He must care about her.

They had cake at the tea house, sweet bars of lemon and treacle, and she devoured three out of sheer relief, sipping at the hot tea. "What are you suddenly looking so happy about?" Martina demanded, eyeing her suspiciously.

Georgie couldn't keep the huge smile from her face. "I'm just happy." If she told Martina her happy conclusion, then Martina would try to talk her out of it, and the fact that Rafferty really did care about her was a precious secret, one to hold close to her heart. It didn't matter how much he denied it, she had solid proof. He hadn't done anything like that for Norah or Neddy.

She was distracted from these happy thoughts when a voice broke through their cozy meal. "Miss Martina! I never would've thought to see you here!"

Martina looked up sharply, and Georgie could see her color pale beneath her heavy maquillage, as her eyes lifted to the man beside the table. "Mr. Stiles," she said in a breathy voice that almost hid her strain.

He was an ordinary enough man to engender such an intense response from her companion, Georgie thought, surveying him openly. He was middle-aged, and well-dressed, though his clothes just bordered on the flashy, and he was handsome enough, with a full head of salt and pepper hair, fleshy lips, and an oversized smile. It was his eyes that told her there was something wrong. They were small, flat, and black, contradicting that toothy smile as he surveyed the two of them.

"And here I was thinking I'd have to take me tea alone," he said, pulling out the extra chair at the small table. "When who should I run across but my friend Martina. How is our old mate, Martin?" he inquired, and Martina jerked slightly.

"I haven't seen him in weeks," she said in a strained voice.

"Nobody has, or I miss my guess," Mr. Stiles said cheerfully, signaling for fresh tea and a new cup. And then he turned that black, empty gaze on her. "And who 'ere is this beautiful young lady?"

If Georgie had any doubts before, they vanished at that word. She wasn't beautiful and she knew it. Her face was pretty enough, if she were being fair, but a far cry from Norah's elegant features.

"My mistress," Martina said stiffly, coming out of her frozen daze. "And I'm afraid it would be improper for you to join us...."

"Naah!" He grinned at Georgie with too many teeth, and she decided right then that she didn't like him. "All you 'ave to do is introduce me to this young lady and things will be right as rain."

For a moment, Georgie thought she'd refuse. But eventually, reluctantly, she spoke. "This is Miss Georgiana Manning." She paused.

"Continue," he said in a silken voice that was clearly an order.

Georgie expected Martina to balk, but even she didn't miss the warning in those flat black eyes.

"This is..." she hesitated.

"'Er old friend Billy Stiles," the man broke in, that ugly grin still on his face. "Why, I haven't seen my friend Martina in quite a long time, though I heard you were working for some toffs. That's a new lay for the likes of you." He let his eyes drift over Georgie, and she suddenly felt unclean. "The Mannings, did you say?"

Martina just stared at him stonily, and Georgie looked between the two of them, deeply uncomfortable but wildly curious. Who was this man who seemed to terrorize her stalwart maid?

"And where is our good friend Rafferty?" he said casually, turning back to Martina. "I 'eard rumors that he'd gone into service, though I find that hard to believe. He never was the type to take orders from anyone."

"Rafferty?" Georgie spoke before Martina could reply. "What does he have to do with anything?"

"Ah, a pretty girl like you needs to be careful around the likes of him. He'd have you on your back with your skirts up in no time."

"Mr. Stiles!" Martina cried in a shocked, angry voice. "That's no way to talk to a young lady."

"Begging your pardon, Miss Manning. I'm a simple man from the country, and I'm not up on the ways of polite society."

That was a lie, Georgie knew it immediately. He was city-bred if anyone was, with the accent of one born within the sound of Bow Bells. But she couldn't get the picture out of her mind— Rafferty tossing her on a bed and lifting her heavy skirts. It was terrifying, and it was bewitching.

"Excuse me for a moment." To Georgie's shock, Martina pushed away from the table, leaving her alone with this jovial, sinister man, and she wanted to shriek in protest. But she was gone in an instant, and Stiles paid no attention to her departure.

"I'm a bit rough around the edges," he said. "I hope you can forgive anything improper I might 'ave said."

Georgie managed a weak smile. There was something very wrong about this man, with the fancy clothes that somehow looked cheap, the formal speech with the cockney accent, the brilliant smile with the dead eyes. She wanted to get away from him.

"Now this is nice and comfortable, ain't it? Tell me about my old friend Rafferty—it's been a dog's age since I seen him."

"Rafferty?" she repeated with a deliberately vague expression. She'd seen her mother avoid confrontation and direct questions with a silly little laugh, and she managed a good approximation of it. "Who's Rafferty?"

Stiles's smile didn't waver. "Now, miss, you don't need to be shy with old Billy Stiles. I know what's what. Sure and Rafferty's keeping clear of the police—who can blame him? We've got a bit of business to settle. Not the way Rafferty would like it settled, but then he should know better than to underestimate the likes of Billy Stiles."

"What do you mean?" she said, her eyes wide and gullible. She was out of her depth, but she knew one thing. This man was Rafferty's enemy, and as such, he was getting no information from her.

Stiles's broad grin tightened for a moment, but before he could ask another question, Martina was back, dropping gracefully into her chair.

"Miss Manning has been telling me all about Rafferty," Stiles said smoothly. "He never struck me as a man for domestic duty."

Martina looked at her with horrified reproach, and Georgie blurted out a denial. "I didn't tell him a thing!"

"Ah, but there's something to tell, ain't there?" Stiles said, that toothy smile still in place. "I don't mean 'im any harm—he's an old mate of mine too, and I thought I'd look in on 'im. Settle things right and proper."

"We need to go," Martina said, starting to rise, but Stiles's hand latched onto her wrist, pulling her back, and her mouth was white with pain.

"You're going to stay right here, little Martina, until I'm satisfied." For a moment, the smile dropped, and Georgie realized what a truly ugly man he was. The smile returned as he looked at her, and she felt a cold dread in the pit of her stomach.

She straightened her back. "Let go of Martina," she said calmly. "And I'll tell you all about him."

"Miss Georgie, don't!"

But Stiles had dropped her wrist, turning to Georgie with his past affability. "A man gets to a certain age," he said, "when he wants to track down his old mates. Me and Rafferty go way back —he'd tell you that himself. Now why don't you tell me where he is so I can go and renew my acquaintance?"

"Right behind you, Stiles."

Georgie breathed a sigh of relief. She hadn't seen him approach, she'd been so mesmerized by Stiles, like a rabbit with a snake.

The moment passed in an instant. Stiles rose, all bluff friendliness, clasping Rafferty's hand, but it looked anything but friendly. Martina had risen, and Georgie tried to follow suit, but a moment later, Rafferty's strong hand came down on her shoulder, keeping her in place.

"Well, ain't this cozy!" Stiles said in his hearty voice. "Why don't we all sit down and share a cup of tea, and you can tell me how you've been doing on our little venture?"

Rafferty didn't move. "Well enough. These things take time."

"I'm afraid I'm not a patient man, Sunny Jim. We 'ave a bit of a misunderstanding about certain things, and I wouldn't want you to have an unfair advantage. You're a bloodthirsty bastard, all right, and I happen to value my neck."

"Do you?" Rafferty's voice was silky smooth. And deadly. There was no missing the strain of violence in his voice, and for the first time in a long time, Georgie remembered where she had found him, who he said he was. A thief, a criminal, a bad man. She could believe it. And it didn't change her feelings one whit.

Stiles met the subdued violence in Rafferty's voice without a blink. "I wouldn't want to think you were holding out on me. You've had more than enough time, seems to me. And Billy Stiles is not the man to cheat. You wouldn't want anything to happen to your old friend Martin."

Rafferty's flint-like expression didn't change. "Keep your hands off."

But Stiles merely smiled as he turned his beady eyes on Georgie. "Then again, there are always other choices. Guess you like the ladies well-bred too. You're taking too much time. And I wonder if this little ladybird has anything to do with it."

Chapter Fourteen

RAFFERTY DIDN'T BOTHER to glance at Georgie, but with his hand still resting on her shoulder, holding her in place, he felt her initial jerk. So her knight in shining armor was in league with this horrible man? What did that make Rafferty? It was time she knew. She needed a dose of reality about him. He removed his hand, but she made no effort to rise.

"I'm not a man to threaten, Billy," he said in a low, seemingly affable voice. "Not unless you're ready for the consequences."

Stiles grinned his toothy grin. His large white teeth were a matter of great pride to him, and he took almost obsessive care of them. Rafferty wanted to slam them down his throat. "Oh, no, you wouldn't want to upset the little lady."

"The little lady is in the family of my employer. She doesn't mean anything to me. But if I gut you, I might get blood on her dress." He didn't have to be touching Georgie to sense her start at his brutal words.

"I'd like to see you try," Billy's rough voice was like the purr of a savage tiger. "You and me've a long history, one that needs to come to a close. I've waited long enough."

"Get out of here, Billy," Martina said. "You don't want to

make a scene, now do you? Particularly when you know if it comes to a one-on-one fight, Rafferty would win."

"You mind your own business, you bloody little catamite. I'm a dangerous man when crossed."

"Are you?" Rafferty said mildly enough.

"You're forgetting my bad temper," Stiles said in a deceptively amiable voice. "I might just have to do something about our good friend Martin here. He wouldn't like what I have in mind."

"And you're forgetting me, Billy," Rafferty drawled. "He's under my protection."

Even someone as brutal as Billy Stiles reacted when he spoke like that, but he wasn't cowed for long.

"We don't need to fight about it," he said in what he obviously hoped was a pleasing voice. "We've got bigger fish to fry. What's taking you so bloody long?"

"I don't work for you. We've got an agreement and you can bloody well keep it. You'll know when it's done." He kept his voice calm and level, at odds with the murderous rage that filled him. It wasn't so much that he couldn't kill Stiles in a public place and get away with it. He could disappear before anyone would notice.

But he didn't want to do it in front of Georgie. And the bloody bastard knew it.

"And what about this pretty little girl, then?" He nodded toward Georgie. Rafferty followed his gaze and cursed inwardly. She was looking dazed; of course she was.

"She's nobody."

"Seems to me you wouldn't 'ave come running to the rescue for just nobody, and Martin can take of hisself. Seems to me she's someone who matters to you."

"I told you, she's simply the daughter of the people I'm working for. She means nothing to me."

"Well, true and all she's not your type, boyo. I could almost believe that. Georgiana Manning, Martin said." He turned and leaned over the table. "Well, Miss Georgiana Manning, you might be seeing me again soon, unless your friend here gets a move on things. He may not appreciate a pretty little morsel like yourself, but I'm a man to notice things."

Georgie simply stared up at him, and Rafferty wondered if she were going to cry. Most gently bred young women would after being threatened by a murderous bully.

But Georgie was made of sterner stuff. She rose then, and he made no attempt to stop her this time. "I don't know what you're talking about, Mr. Stiles, but I assure you that Rafferty is our butler, nothing more, and he has no special affection for any of us —we're simply his employers."

Once more they got the full effect of Stiles's teeth. "I'll be looking forward to seeing you sometime soon, then, Rafferty," he said smoothly, ignoring Georgie.

"When the business is done," he said obscurely. If Georgie knew he was in her household to find a lost treasure, she'd tell her father. No, she wouldn't, she'd probably want to help him find it.

Once more, Billy smiled. "And don't be thinking you could do a bunk and disappear. I can always find Miss Manning."

And with that, he turned and left, leaving a cloud of cheap scent behind him.

Rafferty could feel the tension vibrating through Georgie's body, and he took her arm. "Come along," he said grimly.

She pulled away from him, her face blank and unreadable, and started from the tearoom. They'd gathered a fair amount of attention, and eyes followed her as they left. By the time they reached the sidewalk the bright sunlight was gone, but the hackney he'd hired was still waiting.

She allowed him to help her in, but she felt cold and stiff under his touch. Martina followed, a worried expression on her face, and Rafferty wondered how long it would take him to cut Billy Stiles's throat.

Closing the door after them, he stepped back, watching as they drove away, Georgie's pale face averted. Well, at least that particular problem was solved, trifling as it was. She would no longer moon over the inappropriate butler.

He should be delighted.

SHE MEANS NOTHING TO ME. Those words were swimming around in Georgie's brain as she stared blindly out the window of the hackney. She'd never thought she was particularly stupid, but so many odd things had been said that she was at a loss to understand anything. Anything but *she means nothing to me.*

"Don't believe everything that man says," came Martina's low contralto, and Georgie turned to look at her.

"Which man?"

"Either of them, for that matter," Martina said, a worried expression in her warm brown eyes. "Best not get between two fighting dogs—you're bound to get savaged yourself. They'll work it out."

"Will they?" she asked listlessly.

"In the end." Martina sounded resigned, and Georgie turned back to the window, more of that conversation drifting through her mind.

He'd killed someone. That should have shocked and horrified her, but for some reason it didn't. She'd never had any illusions that Rafferty was a gentleman, or particularly safe and gentle. He had been gentle with her, though she wasn't quite sure why. Why had he done all these things for her if she meant nothing to him? Why had he come back with her to be their butler if he was...what was he? A man who killed? A man who lied? And what was that awful man talking about? What was a catamite, and who was Martin?

"Did Rafferty kill a man?" she asked suddenly.

"What would you think if he did, Miss Georgie?" Martina countered, admitting nothing.

"That he would have had a good reason for it."

Martina's smile was so wide it almost cracked her maquillage. "You're a good girl, Miss Georgie. No wonder he likes you so much."

"He doesn't. He said I meant nothing to him." Her voice came out more strained than she would have liked, almost tearful. She wasn't going to cry, not now, not until she was entirely alone. If Norah were to hear of her distress she'd crow.

Martina looked torn. "You'd be better off believing that."

"It's the truth. You heard him."

"I heard him tell a man who was threatening you that you don't matter. You might want to take that with a grain of salt. And that's all I'm saying, so don't ask any more questions."

A faint hope, one that had almost been crushed beyond recognition, began to stir. "What do you mean?"

"You heard me. You can figure it out yourself, Miss Georgie." She glanced outside in relief. "We're home now. Why don't you go upstairs and I'll bring you a nice cup of tea?"

"I've just had enough tea to turn my insides brown," she protested, feeling oddly comforted. "But you could see if you can sneak me one of Bertha's cream cakes."

Martina's smile was warm and sympathetic. "Now that I can do."

RAFFERTY WENT through his duties with his usual unflappable calm, showing no sign that his brain was in a turmoil. He and Stiles had an arrangement—Rafferty would find the treasure and Stiles would get his cut. It was the only way he could have gotten Billy out of his hair while he searched. Rafferty could do a thing with delicacy—Stiles was more brute strength and a total lack of morals. Not that he trusted Stiles for a moment—as soon as he told Stiles where the money was, he'd then become superfluous, and Stiles had killed a man for a great deal less. This job had been a godsend in his efforts to locate the hidden cache, but he'd forgotten how it might affect the Mannings. How it might affect Georgie. Of course, Stiles had picked up on that right away—how could he not, with Rafferty flying to the rescue? He'd been a fool to underestimate him.

No, he hadn't been careful enough as he'd gone about resurrecting the Mannings' luck. He still wasn't quite sure why he'd done it—down on their luck aristocrats were hardly his charity case.

But he knew the answer perfectly well. Georgie had gotten beneath his skin, though he wasn't quite sure how or why. Well-bred virgins were probably the least interesting of womankind, and yet the only way he could keep himself from thinking about her was by concerted effort.

At least that was over now. She knew him for what he was—an ordinary criminal. No, that wasn't quite true—he was an extraordinary criminal, one who had proven impossible to catch.

Stiles was the problem. He was the one who would put a knife in his back the moment it was turned. He was the one who'd hurt Georgie if he thought Rafferty was cheating him. And Stiles was a suspicious man.

If it were as simple as disappearing, then Rafferty would consider it, as long as it kept Georgie safe. But the plain truth was, it would do no good. Stiles would just go after it himself, slaughtering anyone who got in his way.

Ice ran down his spine. He couldn't protect her, not all the time.

Things were a right cock-up, and that didn't even include the complication of the Ormonds and their sharp-sighted gardener. The best thing he could possibly do was take off, simply disappear for a few months until Stiles grew careless. It was what a sane man would do.

But that would mean he'd leave the Mannings unprotected, something he wasn't willing to do.

At least Georgie would be over her inconvenient crush—that would simplify matters, particularly if he now had to spend more time with her to keep her safe. Martin—no, Martina, wasn't enough. He was going to have to do better.

&

GEORGIE DIDN'T MAKE one of her unannounced visits to the kitchen, and she wasn't about to. He didn't have to worry about running into her on the servants' staircase, sneaking behind a baize door. She'd leave him strictly alone from now on, thank God, and he could concentrate on his duties—

"Did you really kill a man?"

He jumped and swore. If he were going to let people sneak up on him, then he wasn't long for this world. He turned slowly to look at her.

She was standing in the doorway of the storeroom where he'd gone to unlock the silver, and there was no bright, sunny smile on her face. In truth, it looked as if she might have been crying, and he wanted to curse. He didn't want anyone making her cry, particularly not him.

"Yes," he said, steeling himself. "More than one, if the truth be told."

She flinched slightly, and he congratulated himself. "Were they bad men?"

He hesitated for a moment. "Very bad," he admitted finally.

"That's all right then," she said, sounding much more like herself. "I wouldn't like it if you killed good men. Were they trying to kill you?"

"Most of the time." He waited for her to ask how many. He knew the number, and he didn't like it, and neither would she.

But she didn't. "Who was that man in the tea shop? Is he a very bad one?"

"Yes."

"Are you going to kill him?"

"Yes."

She let out a sigh of relief. "Good. Because I don't want him to hurt me, and he looked as if he very much wanted to."

That wasn't all he wanted to do to her, Rafferty thought. "He won't lay a hand on you. You're under my protection."

Her smile was slightly wobbly, not the usual bright, self-assured one. "I know," she said. And then, before he could guess what she planned to do, she reached up on her tiptoes and kissed him, so quickly he didn't have time to respond. And then she was gone, and he wondered if he'd dreamed it.

No, it had been no dream. Her lips had been so soft, pressed against his mouth for that brief moment, but it had been enough to send a fiery streak of desire straight to his groin, and he'd wanted to put her up against the wall and show her what a real kiss was like. Thank God she'd gone before he could give in to temptation. Miss Georgie Manning was the most dangerous creature he'd met in years, and with Stiles onto her, she just might prove fatal.

THE MANNINGS WERE at home that evening, gathered around the dinner table once more. The beauty was in fine looks, as always, except for the petulant expression on her perfect face. Neddy was sliding down in his seat, and he'd be under the table before the fifth course, but Georgie looked almost serenely happy, and he wanted to growl. He could still feel the imprint of her mouth against his own, and it was driving him crazy. He should have shoved her away from him, he should have grabbed her and deepened the kiss, he should have...

He should have never run afoul of the bloody Mannings. It didn't matter how damned much Belding's cache was—he should have left it strictly alone. He had more than enough money on his own—it was sheer greed that made him search for it. Greed, and the desire to thwart Billy Stiles. He stood as still as a statue beside the sideboard, his face a blank, his eyes alert, his mind a mass of confusion.

"I must say, Sir Elston," began Lady Manning from the foot of the table, "that Bertha has been outdoing herself in the kitchen recently. I do wonder what has inspired her."

Manning grunted, basically ignoring her as was his wont, but Georgie spoke up. "That's because she has good food to cook. It was hard to make a decent dinner without the proper foodstuffs."

"I suppose we can thank Rafferty for that too," Norah said in her sinuous voice. "What wonders can we expect next? Oh, yes, something for George. You know, Rafferty, I begin to think you don't like me, what with your marked preference for my little sister."

"Don't be ridiculous, Norah!" her mother said with a gay little laugh. "No one could possibly prefer Georgie to you!"

"I wouldn't have thought so, but there's no accounting for tastes." She was looking at him, a challenge in her vivid eyes, but he kept his expression stoic. "I had a question for you, Rafferty."

This seemed to require a response, and he gave it. "Yes, Miss Manning?"

"What were you doing in my room this afternoon? I didn't send you to fetch anything." Her words were sweetly innocent for a python.

He had two choices—deny it, and brand her a liar, or to come up with some flimsy excuse. He chose the latter. "I was merely inspecting your rooms to make sure the maids had done their work." In truth, he hadn't been up there at all. He'd already searched the bedroom when the family was out and about, and there'd been nothing to find.

"Then perhaps you might explain to me why my diamonds were missing."

He knew exactly what she was talking about—the one necklace that still retained its original stones, albeit in a remarkably ugly setting. He'd often wondered why those hadn't been replaced with paste as well as all her other jewelry.

"What?" Sir Elston thundered.

"Oh, dear," Lady Manning fluttered. "I'm sure Rafferty had nothing to do with it. What about the maids? We have no idea where they came from."

"We have no idea where Rafferty came from," Norah purred. "And besides, the maids had already left by the time I took my jewels out for the evening. It couldn't have been them."

"What are you saying?" Georgie asked in a dangerous voice. "Are you accusing Rafferty of taking your trumpery things?"

Norah smiled like a cat with a pitcher of cream. "Why, not at all. Why should I? After all, he's been in this house for...how long? Five days? But those diamonds are almost priceless. And they're gone."

Nothing was priceless, Rafferty thought, his expression blank. But Miss Norah Manning was willing to pay a high price to rid the house of her nemesis.

"I'm afraid I know nothing about them, Miss Manning," he said smoothly.

"Of course not," Norah said. "But you were in my room."

Sir Elston had thrown his napkin to the table and risen, his round face almost purple with anger. "We'll see about this."

"Oh, dear," Lady Manning fluttered. "A thief in the house? Why, we all might wake up with our throats cut."

"There's no thief in the house!" Georgie cried furiously. "Norah's just trying to get Rafferty into trouble."

"Then it won't do any harm if we search his rooms," Norah said sweetly.

"What if he's already sold them?" Neddy raised his head blearily, more aware of the conversation that Rafferty would have thought.

"He wouldn't have had time," Norah said. "They've only been missing for a few hours. And I suspect I know exactly where my jewels are."

I suspect you do too, Rafferty thought.

By this time everyone at the table had risen, with the exception of Neddy. "Where the bloody hell are your rooms, Rafferty?" Sir Elston said with something short of a bellow.

"Oh, dear, oh dear," Lady Manning fluttered again.

But Rafferty simply bowed. "If you'll follow me, sir."

"You're a beast," Georgie hissed at her sister. "You're just trying to cause trouble for Rafferty!"

"I wouldn't think of it," Norah said innocently. "I just want to know where my jewels are. They're very precious to me."

They were a strange procession past the baize door and down the servants' staircase into the vast kitchen beneath the house. Bertha was sitting at the table, a cup of tea in her hand, and the new scullery maid was scrubbing pots in the huge iron sink. "What's all this, then?" Bertha demanded with the temerity of an old retainer, but no one answered her as they marched down the hallway to the comparatively sumptuous butler's quarters.

There were two rooms—a small sitting room and a smaller bedroom, with his narrow bed neatly made—no sign that anyone had been there since he'd first left that morning.

Sir Elston had gone to the cupboard and begun tossing things about, as Lady Manning kept up a litany of "oh, dears."

"What's this?" he said, emerging, with Rafferty's serviceable pistol in his hand.

"It's a gun," Georgie said unnecessarily. "He has to have something to protect us, doesn't he?"

"Oh, dear, a gun," Lady Manning moaned.

But Sir Elston wasn't interested in firearms, and he tossed it back on the shelf with a singular disregard for the safety of everyone. "I'm not looking for a gun, I'm looking for the Vandevere diamonds. Not *your* diamonds, missy," he informed his smirking daughter. "They're from your mother's family and I have yet to recall they were ever given to you."

That made the beauty pout for a moment, but he knew it wouldn't slow her down for long. As far as he knew, she didn't have the eye to differentiate between paste and real diamonds, but it was unfortunate it wasn't paste that was missing.

"I've heard that criminals hide things under their mattresses," she offered in a silken voice. "Why don't you search there?"

Rafferty leaned back against the wall, perfectly composed. "Would you prefer I do the hunting, sir?" he inquired in his best butler's voice.

"Don't be impudent!" Norah snapped.

"I can look," Georgie offered, starting toward the bed, but her father was ahead of her, and Rafferty breathed a tiny sigh of relief. He truly didn't want to see Georgie diving beneath his covers—he'd never have a peaceful night's sleep again—and he was an idiot to be thinking such things with her irate family surrounding him.

Sir Elston had already thrown back the covers and yanked the horsehair mattress from the wooden frame. There was nothing beneath it.

Norah's smug smile turned blank for a moment, and then she started forward. "It has to be there!" she cried.

"Why?" Georgie demanded, glaring at her sister suspiciously. "Did you put it there?"

Sir Elston was standing straight now, a thunderous expression on his face. "What's going on here? There's something havey-cavey about this entire thing."

"My necklace was stolen!" Norah said stubbornly, the trace of her usual pout back on her face.

"Your mother's necklace!" Sir Elston reminded her in a biting tone.

"Well, if that's all it is, then who cares?" Lady Manning said with a titter of laughter. "It's an ugly old thing—I never wear it."

Her husband rounded on her. "The diamonds just happened to be the most valuable things in this household," he said in a low, dangerous voice. "And if they're lost, then we're lost."

"Don't be absurd, Elston." His wife dismissed his statement with an airy wave of her beringed hand. "We're hardly wanting for the elegancies of life. Now apologize to Rafferty and we'll go back upstairs and finish our dinner. I can't imagine why you insisted on dragging us all away on such a ridiculous pretext. Rafferty has done nothing but take very good care of us—he'd hardly want to steal from us, now would you, Rafferty?"

"No, ma'am," he said politely.

"I'm not apologizing to some damned butler!" Sir Elston grumbled. "Not even Rafferty." He stomped from the room.

"I think you're horrid!" Georgie whispered to her sister.

"You're a stupid baby!" Norah hissed back. And then she met Rafferty's bland eyes, and there was a real threat in their magnificent depths.

He was so tempted to reply with a smug smile, but he wasn't about to give in to temptation. He'd perfected his butler's expression, and he kept it in place as he ushered them out of his wrecked rooms, back to the dinner table. It was going to be a long night.

Chapter Fifteen

RAFFERTY HAD HAD BETTER NIGHTS. The Mannings were cantankerous as they finished their interrupted meal—Georgie kept casting dagger eyes at the beauty, who remained supremely confident despite the look of worry in her fine eyes. Sir Elston grumbled and grouched and made the occasional dark, enigmatic statement, while his wife fluttered and tried to engage everyone in civil conversation. It was an abject failure.

Neddy drank. When it came time for the ladies to depart, his head was down on the table, and Sir Elston faced his family with disgust on his florid face.

"Bring the brandy into my library, Rafferty," he ordered, pushing back from the table. "I've had enough time with this lot."

Georgie's head jerked up, hurt in her eyes, and he wanted to rap Sir Elston over the head. Of all the irksome Mannings, Georgie was an innocent, and she didn't need to be tarred with the same brush as the rest of her family.

"I'm going up to bed!" Norah announced in a strident tone, glaring at Rafferty.

"Good idea," her father said.

"I'm going up too," Georgie announced, but he controlled himself and didn't look her way. It would just lead to trouble.

"Goodness, what's wrong with all of you?" Lady Manning demanded. "Rollo is giving a poetry reading tonight at the Pettigrews—we should all go."

"I've heard your protégé's poetry before," Norah said nastily. "I can happily skip this time."

"And don't bring him back to the house," Manning thundered on the way out the door, "or I'll have Rafferty throw him out."

Lady Manning burst into noisy tears, but her husband had already left, and no one else seemed interested in her plight. Neddy moaned and shifted his head on the snowy white damask, and Rafferty sincerely hoped he wouldn't spew all over it. It was going to be another night of putting him to bed once he got the rest of them sorted out.

But they sorted themselves well enough, the women, including Lady Manning, departing to their various rooms in a huff, while Neddy snored on, oblivious to the family drama.

It was late when he finished in the kitchen. There was no way he was leaving Bertha with such a huge amount to clean up, and the new scullery maid could only do so much. He didn't mind the work—in fact, there was something almost soothing about seeing to the running of this house, carrying the firewood and the hot water and such, but it couldn't go on for long. Stiles's reappearance had changed everything. If he didn't find Belding's cache soon, then Billy was going to take a hand, and God knew what brutality the man was capable of. He'd promised Stiles he'd find it, but it was taking far too long, and Rafferty was beginning to think the money didn't exist. At least, not in this house.

He headed back out to the now-stripped dining room. He'd managed to remove the tablecloth from beneath Neddy's head, all without waking him, and he still lay there, snoring softly, drunk as an owl. To his surprise, Martina was there, leaning over the young man.

"He's a mess," she said, looking up at him.

"Indeed." He sighed. "After I get him in bed, I'm done for the day."

"You're done for the day now," Martina said firmly. "I heard about the raid on your room. You didn't take her bloody diamonds, did you?"

"Do you have to ask?" he said, affronted.

"Well, you are a thief," she said apologetically. "It wouldn't be that unusual."

"I'm trying to save this family, not ruin them further."

"Which reminds me. Why?"

"I feel like it," he said in a dampening tone.

"I know what you feel like, Rafferty. You aren't fooling me," Martina said. "She's too young for you."

"I don't know what you're talking about."

"And too innocent, and well-bred, and sweet, and—"

"I'm not interested. I came here to find Belding's treasure and nothing more. Now I've got Stiles threatening them if I don't move faster, and I've got Georgie mooning after me with puppy dog eyes and..." He stopped talking as frustration overwhelmed him.

"So what are you going to do?"

"Damned if I know," he said wearily.

"Go to bed. I'll take care of Master Neddy," Martina said, flexing her not inconsiderable muscles. The dress had been made especially for her, to take her muscular frame and flat chest into account.

Rafferty hesitated. "He's heavy when he's dead drunk."

"He's just a boy," Martina replied serenely. "He needs someone to look after him." There was a fondness in her voice that was unusual, and he looked at her closely, but the face she turned to him was bland. "Go to bed, Rafferty, and figure a way out of this mess. I won't have you breaking that young woman's heart."

He gave in, leaving her with her task for the night. In truth, he was just tired enough to know he could count on a good night's sleep. Maybe by tomorrow he'd know how to deal with Georgie's inconvenient crush.

He lit the lamp in his sitting room and sank into his chair. He had a copy of Mrs. Beeton's *Book of Household Management* on the table beside him, but he was too tired to open it again. It had proven useful, but right then he had other things to think about, such as what he was going to do with the priceless diamonds that had been hidden under his mattress by that clumsy vixen. She'd assumed he wouldn't notice she'd been sneaking around in the servants' quarters, or that Bertha wouldn't report back to him. It had been simple enough to find where she stashed them, but not time enough to hide them elsewhere. It was a good thing no one had thought to search him.

The meeting with Stiles had been a royal cock-up as well. He didn't need to have Billy peering over his shoulder and threatening Georgie. He should kill him for even looking at her.

But for now, all he wanted was his nice soft bed without the lumpy jewelry beneath it. Kicking off his proper shoes, he stripped off his coat and neckcloth, unbuttoning the buttons that trailed halfway down his shirt. He picked up the lamp and headed into his bedroom and set it down on the dresser before turning to his rumpled bed.

The bed had been remade, though badly, and in the middle lay Georgiana Manning in one of those schoolgirl nightgowns, her hair loose around her sleeping face.

"Shit!" he said, and she opened her eyes, greeting him with a drowsy smile.

"What did you say?" she murmured sleepily.

"Never mind. What the bloody hell are you doing here?"

She sat up, drawing her legs underneath the thin white gown. Too damned thin—why hadn't he seen about getting her proper nightclothes, with layers and layers of cloth to hide her body?

"I came to see you," she said.

"I gather that. Why?"

"Because we're friends. And because they accused you of

stealing Norah's jewels and searched your room, and I wanted to apologize."

"How do you know I didn't steal the necklace?" that was burning a hole in his pocket at that very moment.

"Did you?" she asked. "If you did, it would serve Norah right, but knowing her, she probably lost it and needed someone to blame. Don't you think?"

"Something like that," he agreed. She still hadn't moved from the center of his bed, and he wanted to groan. "You need to go back to your room."

"Why? I suppose you think that because you're a man and I'm a woman that we aren't allowed to talk, but that's ridiculous. You're my protégé—I have to make sure you're all right. Besides, I had a nightmare. About that man with the teeth."

Stiles, he thought. "Martina can sit up with you," he said gruffly. "Are you going to get off my bed?"

"Are you going to make me?" She stretched out her legs, wiggling her toes. "I thought you'd be glad I was here."

"How could you possibly think that?" he said harshly, and a shadow appeared in her laughing eyes.

"We kissed."

"We did not kiss!" His voice rose, and he quickly quieted. "You kissed me."

"It's the same thing. I kiss all my friends."

"Not your male friends. But I forgot, I'm not a man, I'm your butler."

Her disbelieving expression suddenly reminded him that she was older than she looked. "Oh, really?"

He wasn't going to get involved in a discussion of his manhood. "You don't kiss servants," he said sternly.

"But you're not my servant, you're my protégé. And I don't see why I can't sleep in your bed. Norah says that's what real protégées and patrons do."

God help him, was this torture ever to end? "You know why not."

She grimaced, then sighed. "Can't we just cuddle for a little while?"

"No. You're going back to your room and staying there, and you're not coming down here again unless I specifically invite you. This may be your father's house but these are my rooms and I don't want you here."

"But—"

The last bit of his temper shredded. "Georgie, you know perfectly well what men and women do in bed together."

"We don't have to do *that*," she said. "You could just kiss me again...."

"I didn't kiss you in the first place, and it's a lucky thing I didn't. You need to kiss someone of your own class."

"I have. Several times. They weren't as good as you."

For a moment, he was completely silenced. She was innocent, not stupid, but she was being deliberately obtuse. And he was going to kill whoever it was she'd kissed.

"For the last time, I didn't kiss you," he snapped. "Now get off the damned bed and go find your own."

To his surprise and relief, she did, climbing down and landing on the floor, her bare toes just peeping beneath the thin nightdress. "It's too dark," she said.

"I'll light your way." He turned and picked up the lamp, anything rather than look at the enticing shadows beneath the threadbare cloth.

He didn't bother with his coat or shoes—if anyone in the household saw them, he'd be out on his bum before he could utter a word of protest. They were safer going up the servants' stairs, and he led the way, determined not to think about the soft loveliness of her. Damn it.

They saw no one, and he breathed a sigh of relief as he opened her bedroom door and gestured her inside. "Can you light my lamp?" she asked in a chastened voice.

Sighing, he set his own lamp down on the dressing table and

started toward hers, lighting it quickly and efficiently. She was still standing by the door, and he had to be a glutton for punishment, because he said, "Get in bed," when he knew that vision was going to haunt him almost as much as seeing her on his bed would.

"I will," she said. "After you go."

He nodded coldly, heading for the door, but she didn't move out of the way, and he knew he was going to brush by that fiendish nightgown.

"Aren't you going to kiss me goodnight?" she asked as he moved past her.

He froze, looking down at her. She had that mischievous expression on her face again, and he wondered how he could have underestimated her. "You're playing with fire, little girl," he said softly.

"You kissed me once already," she teased him.

Something snapped. "You're about to get burned." And before he could think twice, he put his hands on her arms and dragged her slight body against his damned hard one, setting his mouth against hers.

She was so shocked her mouth was open, and he deepened the kiss, pushing her up against the wall of her bedroom and pressing against her. She made a sound, probably of distress, but he ignored it, using his tongue, kissing her so thoroughly that she felt weak in his arms, and he wanted to lift her up and carry her to the bed, to rip away that flimsy nightgown and place his mouth everywhere, on her breasts, between her legs. He wanted her so badly it weakened him as well, but he just kept kissing her until he had to stop for breath.

He pushed her away from him, and she fell back against the wall, staring up at him with shock and something else which he told himself was horror. He'd done what he set out to do—scared her half to death with her first taste of a real man.

"That's what happens when I kiss you," he growled, furious at himself, at her, at everything. "So keep your distance."

Grabbing the lamp, he closed the door behind him with a decided click, leaving her alone to recover as best she could.

She would hate him now. He'd treated her like a whore—well, no he hadn't, because he didn't kiss whores. But he'd given her a taste of what she should never have to discover. She would marry another man, one who would kiss her gently and worship her, and she would be safe and protected from the harsh realities of life. Maybe his kiss would add to her nightmares—if so, he'd done his job. He'd crushed her, and he'd meant to. It was past time she had a taste of real life.

He gave in to temptation and slammed his bedroom door behind him, then caught a glimpse of his face in the mirror. He looked like a devil, and he felt like one as well. Extinguishing the lamp, he stripped off the rest of his clothes and climbed into bed.

The sheets were soft, rumpled, and they smelled like flowers. They smelled like Georgie, who'd looked so right curled up there. He flung his arms over his eyes, realizing he was out of breath. Realizing his mistake too late.

He may have terrified Georgie, taught her the brutal facts about love and sex among the working classes. But in doing so, he trapped himself, until his very bones ached for her. It was nothing he'd ever felt before, nothing he wanted to feel.

But the deed was done. He needed Georgie like he needed air to breathe. And she would never be his.

HER KNEES WOULDN'T HOLD her up. Georgie sank to the floor, trembling all over, collapsing in a little puddle of her old nightdress. Dazedly she put a hand to her mouth, her lips.

What had he done to her? She knew what happened between men and women—Bertha had explained it to her in frank, sensible terms, and ever since she'd been both horrified and fascinated by the thought.

That was what that kiss was. Not a gentle wooing, a

courtship, a sign of affection. It had been a demand; terrifying, demoralizing.

Electrifying. He wanted her. She no longer had any trace of doubt left, she had felt the desire throughout his body as he'd held her against him, felt the pounding of his heart, the tension in his muscles, the raw hunger in his mouth. He might call her a little girl, but that wasn't what he thought of her.

She rolled onto her back on the thick Persian carpet, stretching. She wanted to cry, she wanted to sing. He wanted her, he wanted her like a man wants a woman. His kiss had left no doubt of that. He wanted to take her to his bed and do things to her.

The kind of things that went on between a husband and a wife. If she had any doubts as to whether he loved her, they were now banished. He loved her and wanted her, and she felt the same way. The answer was simple.

She was going to marry him.

MARTINA STAGGERED a bit under Neddy's weight as she levered him in his doorway and got him as far as his bed. He collapsed onto it, snoring loudly, and she breathed a sigh of relief. She was perfectly willing to clean up after the boy if he spewed, but she could think of things she'd much rather do. He hadn't drunk as much as usual, even though he'd passed out at the dining room table. Martina suspected he'd done so simply to avoid the chaos his family so often indulged in, but for whatever reason, he was merely very drunk, not sick with it.

She stripped him with efficient expertise, then pulled the nightshirt over his head, covering his body. He would be a good-looking man if he lost the puffiness of the alcohol, the weight that circled his midsection. He was still young—in his early twenties, perhaps, but a child in terms of experience. Something had led him to disappear into a bottle and he hadn't emerged, so that his maturity was curiously stunted.

But beneath all that was a sweet young man with some burden too hard to bear. And Martina wondered what she could possibly do to help him.

"Who're you?" His slurred voice startled her as she pulled the snowy white covers around him.

"Your mother's maid," she replied in her deep voice.

"How'd you manage to get me upstairs? Did someone carry me?"

"I helped you. I'm very strong."

He looked at her out of muzzy eyes, then closed them. "Go away," he muttered. "I don't need any help."

"Not anymore," Martina said caustically, but Neddy had already sunk back into a drunken sleep.

She shook her head. "You're a mess, laddie," she whispered. "I just wish I could save you."

Neddy answered with a loud snore. Martina looked down at him, at the elegant lines of his face, softened now with dissipation, and on impulse she leaned over and placed a gentle kiss on his lips.

And then she was gone, before she could see his slack mouth curve in a sleepy smile.

She was a fool, she berated herself as she made her way to the small closet that served as her sleeping quarters, near enough to the women of the house to be on constant call. Pretty young men with broken dreams weren't for the likes of her. There were no happy endings for people like her, no dreamy kisses and sunset rides and all that romantic claptrap, even though deep down she longed for it. Master Edward Manning would either drink himself to death or drag himself out of the morass he'd climbed into. Either way, it would have nothing to do with her.

His lips had been soft and sweet.

But not for the likes of her.

Chapter Sixteen

WHEN GEORGIE WOKE, she stretched out in her bed, feeling gloriously alive. Something in her life had fundamentally changed, and she no longer felt so wretchedly young and useless. Rafferty had kissed her, really kissed her. It had been so different from the timid young men out in the country, snatching a kiss at a cotillion she wasn't even supposed to attend.

The last of her confusion had disappeared. All that mattered was Rafferty, with his strong body and his wicked mouth and his reluctant sweetness.

There'd been nothing sweet about the kiss last night, and she treasured every moment of it. She'd been going about things all wrong, acting like an innocent. Well, technically she was an innocent, and her knowledge was spotty at best, but Rafferty saw her as merely a child.

No, that wasn't true. That was no child's kiss last night. And daunting as it had been, she wanted more. She wanted the rest of it. Mind you, it sounded messy, undignified, and even a bit disgusting. She should view it as her duty, not something to be sought out.

But everything about Rafferty was worth seeking. She'd read

books about soul mates and true love, and he was hers, whether he liked it or not.

He'd tried to scare her away last night—he'd failed. She needed to make sure she didn't scare *him* away. He would know better than she did the kind of trouble a union between the two of them might bring, and he would fight it, and her, tooth and nail.

She sat up in bed, a brilliant smile on her face. He would lose —he was already half gone. And he was hers.

Of course, he was nowhere to be found when she finally descended the servants' stair to the kitchen. Bertha greeted her with her usual disapproval. "That's not the stairs you should be using, young lady."

"Where's Rafferty?"

"Out."

"Out where? He's never here when I ask for him."

"None of your business, Miss Georgie. Leave the poor man alone—he's got enough on his plate with your crazy family. He doesn't need you mooning after him."

"I don't moon after him," Georgie said with great dignity. "I love him."

"Oh, holy Jesus," Bertha moaned.

"Who loves who?" Martina demanded, coming down the stairs with a tray full of dishes.

"Young missy thinks she's in love with Rafferty," Bertha said with a sigh.

"Oh, no," Martina said, and there was real concern in her eyes. "Don't do that, Miss Georgie. He's not the man for you."

"But what if he was?" Georgie said.

"Impossible. For all he's the butler, he's not a very good man. He'll give some poor woman nothing but trouble."

"He's a very good man!" Georgie shot back, offended. "He's done wonderful things for the family, for me..."

"And heaven only knows why," Martina interrupted. "He's a

dangerous man—he belongs with people like Billy Stiles, not a young girl."

"I'm not a young girl, I'm twenty!"

"So very ancient," Martina said gently. "It's only normal to have a crush on the man—he's a great deal more impressive than the usual gentlemen who inhabit your world. But he's not for you." She set the tea tray down. "Speaking of which, your mother says you should prepare to be at home today. Mr. Salton has sent flowers, and he's asked to speak with your father."

Georgie's cheer vanished. Andrew Salton was a lovely man, but the thought of lying in his bed, letting him kiss her, was awful. He was sweet, he was charming, and he didn't love her. "Oh?" she said in a listless voice.

"Now that would be a good match!" Martina warmed to the idea. "He's a gentleman, so he'd treat you like the sweet young thing you are. You could have a very happy life."

But I don't want a very happy life, she wanted to cry. *I want Rafferty.* The illogic wasn't lost on her, and her shoulders drooped.

"Now be sensible, dearie," Bertha said. "As you said, you're twenty now. Time to face reality. You'll marry a good man, a man of substance, have a couple of babies and a peaceful life. It's what every woman dreams of, and it's being handed to you."

"And it's time you were in the drawing room," Martina broke in before Georgie could respond. "Your mother's waiting for you. The first callers have begun to arrive."

She was going to refuse, to head straight back up the forbidden servants' staircase to her room and bar the door, when it suddenly struck her that if visitors had arrived, someone would have to let them in. Without another word, she pushed the green baize door open and headed into the house.

There was no sign of Rafferty when she reached the drawing room, but the Manning women were holding court, and several young gentlemen were leaning on Norah's every word. Only Andrew Salton remained immune to her charm. Suspiciously so.

"Georgie!" her mother called out before she could beat a hasty retreat. "I wondered what had been keeping you. Mr. Salton has come particularly to see you."

Georgie resisted her impulse to bolt and walked into the room, trying not to look too hard at her suitor. She took the only seat left, next to him, just as Rafferty appeared to announce a new caller.

He didn't look at her—of course he didn't. He was the perfect butler, efficient, blank-faced, an automaton. She wanted to kick him. But two could play at that game. She averted her gaze, more out of self-protection than punishment, and laughed inanely at something her companion had said.

Salton looked startled, and she realized he hadn't made a joke, and she immediately sobered. She felt the briefest touch of Rafferty's eyes on her, and she moved closer to Salton, giving him her best dewy-eyed smile.

He wanted to talk to her father. He was going to ask leave to court her, and her father would agree, whether she wanted it or not. Indeed, there was nothing wrong with the match. He was young, handsome, prosperous. Just the kind of husband for a flighty young girl. It didn't matter. If she couldn't have Rafferty then she planned to die an old maid, out in the country, surrounded by cats and books, ignoring the fact that cats made her sneeze and most books were deadly dull. Give her a racy French novel and that made all the difference, but reading racy novels while she lived the life of an elderly nun might prove hazardous to her heart.

By the time she was sixty, she would have forgotten all about him. Maybe. But at least by then, she'd no longer be interested in affairs of the heart, and she could live out her days in peaceful solitude. The very thought made her grumpy.

Rafferty was standing by the door, ready to receive the next callers, and while he was refusing to look at her, there was no way he couldn't hear her. She'd watched Norah at work often enough to understand the art of flirtation, but she'd never put it into action. She did now, laughing inanely at one of Andrew Salton's sallies. Let Rafferty see what it was like if she were to marry someone else. He would scarcely kiss someone like he had last night if he were willing to give her up.

The few peeks she dared take revealed nothing, however, just his perfect posture and his blank face.

She had a lot to accomplish in the fifteen minutes allotted for a polite visit, and she did her best. By the time Salton rose to take his leave, she was feeling almost triumphant, until she remembered he'd asked to speak to her father. He said something to Rafferty, and she wondered how her protégé might respond.

"Sir Elston isn't at home," he intoned in a carrying voice, and Georgie breathed a sigh of relief. She had to get to her father first, to assure him there was no chance that she'd marry a nice man like Andrew Salton. She knew who she was going to marry, and the devil take the hindmost. She wasn't sure how she was going to manage it, but manage it she would—she had no intention of taking no for an answer.

She tried to escape then, but her mother, with a rare show of matronly determination, insisted she sit through all the visits, and it wasn't until the last guest rose that Norah's sweet mask dropped from her face.

"Your new suitor seems quite taken with you," she said with an iron edge to her voice. "I vow, you must be all a-tizzy with the attentions of such a dull young man."

"Don't be unkind," Lady Manning said abstractedly. "He'll be a most pleasant husband for Georgie."

"But I haven't—" Georgie began, but her mother sailed right over her.

"He's got a very Christian reputation. Georgie could count herself blessed that such a proper young man want to court her."

"Very proper," Norah said, her words biting, and Georgie had to wonder what her sister had against Andrew Salton. Maybe it was simply the fact that he didn't fawn over her like every other male on the planet.

Except for Rafferty.

And then her father strode into the salon, looking much put out. "Well?" he demanded with a trace of petulance. "What's happened to Mr. Salton? Has he changed his mind about Georgie? I've been waiting all morning."

"Oh, dear. Rafferty told him you were out, didn't you, Rafferty?" Lady Manning said breathlessly.

Rafferty inclined his head. "I'm afraid I must have been mistaken, sir. I thought you had gone to your club."

"Well, I hadn't," Manning snapped. His shoulders relaxed. "Never mind—if he truly wants her, he'll try again. You're a sly puss, Georgie, beating your sister to the altar."

"She will not!" Norah shot back.

"Then do something about it!" her father said in clipped tones. "Andrew Salton is a more than respectable prospect—he's got money of his own and he is all things desirable in a husband. If you can do better, Norah, then look to it!"

"And you'd let me marry a bore like Andrew Salton?" Norah said cynically. "He's hardly going to repair our fortunes."

"He has enough to make a difference," Sir Elston said. "I made a few inquiries at my club yesterday, and he's quite warm, as they say."

Georgie listened to all this with growing despair. She'd spent her life knowing that Norah would marry well and replenish the always needy family coffers, but she'd never considered that she would meet the same fate.

She was about to announce, quite loudly, that she had no intention of marrying Andrew Salton when something stopped her. Maybe it was Rafferty's determinedly blank face. For some reason he didn't want her to marry Salton. She could work with that.

"I have things to do," Norah announced grandly, sweeping from the room, and her mother followed, leaving Rafferty, Georgie, and her father alone.

"So what do you think, puss?" her father said, his usually

frowning face softening, turning his back on their butler. "Would you consider marrying this man?"

Georgie looked at Rafferty's impassive face, and for a moment her gaze lingered on his mouth. "Yes," she lied, watching him.

Rafferty left the room.

❧

"WHAT'S THAT YOU'VE GOT?" Martina spied Jane moving slowly down the corridor, a heavy-laden tray in her thin arms.

"Coffee for the young master. Not that he'll drink it—he'll probably throw it at my head if he wakes up long enough to notice me."

Martina eyed the tray. "That's not just coffee." A decanter of brandy had pride of place on it, and she sighed. "Give it to me."

"He'll throw it at you."

"No, he won't," Martina said firmly, accepting the tray in one strong arm and taking the brandy off it. "Take this back to the kitchen or wherever you got it, and next time he asks for it, come to me."

Jane shook her head. "You don't know what he's like when he hasn't got his bottle."

"I know perfectly well how men behave when thwarted, and I don't intend to let him get away with it. Go on about your work and I'll deal with him."

"You're a braver soul than I am," Jane muttered gratefully, then scurried down the corridor.

Martina watched her go, then stiffened her shoulders. This was going to be a battle, but one worth fighting. After a light tap, she pushed open Neddy's door.

"Get out, and take your damned coffee with you," came a muffled voice from the darkened bedroom. "Just leave me the bottle."

Ignoring him, she set the tray down and went to the tall windows, throwing back the curtains on the bright fall weather.

There was a shriek of horror from the shrouded bed, and she could hear him diving for the covers she'd tucked around him the night before.

"Close those damned curtains!" he half yelled, half groaned, but she went on to the next window and did the same, before turning to the bed.

He lay there, flat on his back, one arm across his eyes, panting slightly, and she picked up the tray, approaching him. "I've brought you coffee, sir," she said demurely.

Slowly, slowly, he drew back his arm, peering at her. "It's you," he said hoarsely.

"Of course it is," Martina said briskly. "Now sit up and I'll give you your tray."

"Take it away, and yourself with it. Just leave me the bottle."

"There is no bottle, Mr. Edward. You'll have to make do with coffee."

He reached out and tried to dash the tray out of her hands, but she was too quick for him, stepping out of reach. "After you finish your coffee, I'll bring you breakfast—just toast, I think, for today, until your stomach gets used to it."

"Used to what?" he snarled.

"No brandy."

There was dead silence in the bedroom, and she looked at him dispassionately. He was an unprepossessing sight, his eyes bloodshot, the handsome face softened from dissipation, and he was staring back at her with mingled wrath and frustration.

"Listen to me, you..."

"Martina," she supplied calmly.

"You can take the damned coffee and shove it up your..." words failed him, a fact that amused Martina. He flopped back down on the bed. "Bring me a bottle of wine, then," he said grumpily.

"No wine either. Your mother is worried about you."

"My mother doesn't worry about anything but her protégés and her gambling debts."

"And her son. You underestimate a mother's love for her son. But it's more than that. There's a definite shortage of decent men in this world, and I have no intention of letting you ruin yourself any further. You'll have coffee, then toast, then a bath and a shave."

"Who's going to shave me? Our criminal butler?"

"I will."

He looked at her, bleary-eyed, then gathered himself. "I'll have my brandy first."

"Coffee," she said flatly.

"You're a servant!" he snapped, "You do as you're told or you're out on the street!"

"I doubt it. Your sister likes the way I dress her hair. And while you're arguing, the coffee is getting cold. Sit up and I'll bring it to you."

To her surprise, he pushed himself up on the rumpled bed, eyeing her balefully as she approached him. Setting the tray across his lap, she stayed where she was, making no attempt to move out of range.

The first thing he did was pick up the coffeepot, prepared to fling it at her, but she didn't flinch, simply eyed him steadily. After a long, threatening moment, he set it back down. "If I drink the coffee, may I have my brandy?"

She didn't make the mistake of thinking he had given in. Neither had she. "You can have toast. Rafferty can help you with your bath, and then you can join your mother in the yellow salon."

"The moment I'm downstairs, I'll get my own bottle," he snapped.

She nodded. "I can't stop you. You'll have to decide if you really want to keep on like this, useless to everyone, particularly yourself."

"I don't see what business it is of yours," he said sulkily.

"I told you, I don't like waste. I don't like to see handsome young men become an embarrassment to their family and society. You're not too far along the path now that you can't be saved."

"And you have the gall to think you can save me?" he said in biting tones. "Who the hell do you think you are, bloody Joan of Arc?"

"No, sir. I'm the ladies' maid."

He looked at her, stupefied. "And you have the gall to talk to me like this?"

"Yes, sir."

They stared at each other for a long moment, and Martina realized her heart was hammering inside the tight dress. This was far from the first time she'd exerted her will on an upper-class gentleman. Those who came to her previous employer's house were often like little boys, who wanted to be spanked and treated like recalcitrant children. She could simply pretend that Neddy was one of her customers.

No, she didn't want that. She didn't want to think of him as a commercial transaction. He was lost, he was broken, he was beautiful, and she was going to save him. Whether he liked it or not.

And then he poured himself a cup of coffee, the brew still steaming slightly, and he didn't throw it at her, though she knew he wanted to. There was a crafty expression on his face. "Rafferty doesn't need to help me with my bath—you can."

It was meant as an insult, but Neddy didn't know he was dealing with. To her it was a triumph. "Yes, sir," she said, perfectly amiable.

"And shave me,"

She nodded.

"And bring me my bottle when I'm done."

She slowly shook her head. "You'll have to spend the day without it. Unless you don't think you can do it?" He was a gamester, she knew that much about him, and he would be unlikely to resist a bet.

"Of course I can. I just don't want to."

"Really? I don't believe you can. Would you care to place a wager?"

He was growing more alert as he sipped at his coffee. He surveyed her coolly. "And what of yours would I want that I couldn't have already?"

She smiled a dulcet smile. "A gentleman's wager to a lady."

"You're no lady."

"You're no gentleman."

They stared at each other in silence. Finally, he spoke. "One day," he said.

"One day," she agreed.

"And send Rafferty to me."

"He won't bring you a bottle."

"He damned well will, but we have a wager, and I don't like to lose. He can help me bathe."

Martina hid her smile. "Yes, sir," she said with a demure curtsey, and backed out the door.

Chapter Seventeen

RAFFERTY WAS a man who knew his own mind—he'd never been troubled by doubts or second thoughts. He did what he had to do, with no regrets, and that had served him most of his life.

But as he strode down the chilly autumn streets of London, he was infuriatingly aware of a rare case of doubt. One thing was certain—he'd scared Georgie off him last night and her childish crush would be just that, crushed. He wouldn't have to worry about her sneaking into his bedroom or planting kisses on him or watching him out of those soul-searching blue eyes. She was cured.

He wasn't. The very thought of Andrew Salton paying court to her roused an absolute rage in his gut. He'd tossed the man's card and put his floral tribute with Norah's, lost in the mass of bouquets. It was only fitting—the violets he'd chosen were far too delicate for a harum-scarum creature like Georgie, as tone deaf a choice as the sweet pink roses.

He had yet to find a suitable substitute as husband material. Every possibility was either too old or too young, too stupid or too self-consciously clever, too poor or too rich. She needed someone kind and thoughtful, an ordinary man. Just not Andrew Salton. There was something definitely wrong about the man.

There was an absolute parade of eligible young men in the Manning household, all drawn by the Beauty, but they wouldn't do either, though Rafferty couldn't quite pin down why, he only knew that in all of London there was no one worthy of Georgie.

Certainly not a reprobate like him. Not that he was even tempted. That kiss had been instructional, nothing more. It didn't matter that it wreaked havoc with his peace of mind. Peace of mind was overrated.

As if worrying about Georgie wasn't enough, Martina was another problem. She was spending an inordinate amount of time with the young master Neddy, and even if he was newly sober, he was not for the likes of Martina. Rafferty hated to see her heart broken again, as it had been so many times, but his gentle word of warning had garnered him nothing but a laughing and totally false denial. He needed to get out of here, away from Georgie and all the temptation she offered, and he needed to take Martina with him. Not back to that fancified brothel, if he could help it, but somewhere she could bloom.

It was a cool day, without the drizzling rain that had been so omnipresent, and he strode down the street at his usual pace, not the butler's furtive steps, when he realized he wasn't alone. Someone was following him.

He paused, looking in a shop window, searching the reflection for Billy Stiles, but there was no toothy bastard that he could find among the throngs of people moving down the sidewalk. Cursing under his breath, he walked on, ducking down the first alley he came to.

Georgie came into view, and he surveyed her for a moment. She was looking beautiful in one of her new dresses. She was peering through the crowds, looking for him, and he reached out and yanked her into the alley, pushing her, not ungently, up against the brick wall.

"What are you doing?" he demanded, unable to keep the fury from his voice.

She blinked up at him, looking not the slightest bit cowed. "I was following you, of course. Since I knew you wouldn't let me come if I asked."

"Why?"

"I don't know. You just seem to find excuses instead of taking me out," she said, and he cursed inwardly.

"Why are you here?" he clarified, trying to grab a bit of errant patience.

"I wanted to be with you," she said simply.

"Christ," he muttered.

She blinked at his curse. "If you'd let me talk to you, then I wouldn't have to sneak out and follow you."

"I suppose no one knows you're gone?"

A smug smile lit her face. "Of course not. They think I'm lying down with the headache."

"And what if you didn't catch up with me? What if Billy Stiles got to you first?"

Her smile faded somewhat. "I forgot about him. He wouldn't really want to hurt me, would he? I mean, what good am I to him?"

"He'd cut your throat as soon as look at you. The man runs a gang of killers for hire, and he's set his sights on you."

"But why?"

He couldn't answer that. Stiles was a man who could ferret out a man's weakness, and Georgie was just that, whether he like it or not. A weakness, which was why he had to leave her. Billy was never a patient man, and it was taking Rafferty far too long to find the cache. Billy would take his impatience out on someone, someone who mattered to him. She wasn't safe, and she wouldn't be if he was around her. That knowledge had been growing inside him, and he'd kept pushing it away, but the ugly truth was that the longer he was near her, the more dangerous her life would be. He had to find the money.

He managed the best answer he could come up with. "A man like Stiles doesn't need an excuse. For the time being, you should stay put. There's no guarantee that even I could protect you."

"So, I'm to be immured like a nun?" she said.

"Just until I deal with him."

She gazed up at him out of those sweet blue eyes that had a nasty habit of haunting his dreams. "How are you going to deal with him? Are you going to kill him?"

"Yes." He said it without thinking, knowing it was true. He was a threat to Georgie, and for that alone, he deserved to die.

It should have horrified her, made her shrink away, but she simply nodded. "Good. He's a bad man."

Heaven help him! "But right now, you're going back home and staying there."

"But where are you going?" she persisted, and he knew she'd follow him. Would she always follow him, wherever he went? And was that a curse or a blessing?

"I'm taking you back home," he said in his most reproving voice, the one that would make Billy Stiles laugh. "And then I'm going out, alone, to see what can be done."

"About Stiles?"

"About everything." He realized with sudden shock that he was still holding her against the wall, his hands on her shoulders, and he was kneading them slightly, almost caressing them. He practically jumped back, watching as she straightened her dress and looked up at him with that beatific smile that lit her face.

He held out his arm, and she took it happily enough. "That's all right then," she said. "We can talk while you escort me."

"Mmph," he replied as they moved back out among the crowds. He could see Dagger Fanning leaning against a building, a newspaper in his hand. Dagger didn't know how to read, and Rafferty wondered just how many of Stiles's men were out looking for him. Him, or Georgie?

"We could talk about the weather," Georgie said brightly.

"Mmph."

"Or you could tell me why you lied to Andrew Salton and told him my father wasn't at home."

He didn't even blink. "I thought he was gone."

"Then you don't mind if I marry Andrew Salton?"

"Do you want to marry Andrew Salton?" he countered, knowing that was the wrong answer. He should have insisted that it was none of his business.

"You told me I should marry a good man. Everyone says he's a most eligible man!"

"That means nothing. You shouldn't have to marry a man who's clearly wrong for you."

"Mother says he'll settle me down."

"Settle you down? What makes her think that's important?"

"Because of you. She says my feelings for you are most inappropriate, and a good solid husband will rid me of such fantasies."

"What fantasies?" He knew he shouldn't have asked that question the moment the words were out of his mouth, but it was too late.

"That I'm in love with you."

He stumbled for a moment. "Don't be ridiculous," he said gruffly. "I'm the butler."

"So you are. You take excellent care of me," she added, patting his arm.

He looked down into her guileless blue eyes. "Have you forgotten last night? You need a gentleman who'll treat you with respect, not maul you."

"You didn't maul me," she said calmly enough. "You kissed me. I thought that was the way you usually kissed." She smiled up at him. "I liked it."

He stifled his groan. "That's not the way the gentry kiss," he said, knowing it was a lie.

"Well, then, it's a good thing I'm not in love with a member of the gentry."

He wanted to strangle her. He wanted to drag her into the nearest alleyway and give her another lesson in the art of kissing, show her how to kiss him back, show her—

"The right man will come along," he said, unable to keep the frustration out of his voice. "Anyway, it's none of my business.

Whom you marry is your father's decision. I'll be long gone by then." It had to be. There were only a few places left to look—the empty attic with the deserted servants' quarters, the gloomy confines of the coal cellar. Hell, he'd even scour the roof if need be, but he had to hurry things up.

"What?" Her head shot up.

"My time in your household is coming to an end. I appreciate the opportunity you've given me, but I have my own life to get back to. My own problems to deal with."

"You're leaving?" Her voice was so low he had trouble hearing her, but he nodded.

"Once I get Stiles sorted, there won't be any use for me. Then you won't have to deal with my picking and choosing who you should marry. Just not Salton." He wished he could see her expression, but she was staring down at the street, her face hidden by her bonnet. "There'll be other men. It's not like you're in love with him."

"No," she said. "I'm in love with you." Without another word, she started in the direction of Corinth Place, and he had no choice but to follow after her, cursing himself as they went.

They met Martina on the corner of the square, racing in their direction., her shawl blowing in the wind. "Miss Georgie!" she cried out. "Thank God Rafferty found you! Don't you know it's dangerous to go out on your own?"

"I wanted some fresh air, and there was no one around to accompany me," she said, but her voice was curiously listless.

Martina looked at him, a speaking expression in her dark eyes, and he knew they were going to have to have a talk about the situation, something he dreaded. He didn't want to talk to anyone about Georgie, and certainly not to someone who was deluded enough to think he had feelings for her.

"Take her back home," he said. "I'll be back in another hour or so."

He waited for Georgie to protest, but she said nothing, and the anger that was never far away from him nowadays surged back. His lively Georgie...no, not his Georgie...was looking diminished.

He'd made a botch of everything, and it was time to end it. End Stiles, and his bully boys would concentrate on other things —they had no quarrel with him. Find the damned cache, though it seemed as if he'd looked everywhere. He'd done what he could to bring the Mannings back to solvency, but in the end they weren't his responsibility, just an errant whim on his part. They would do fine without him, and if they didn't, so be it. They could sink or swim for all he cared.

"Lock her in her room," he said gruffly, not allowing himself to look at her too closely. "Tie her up if you have to. Just make sure she doesn't leave the house on her own again."

"Yes, master," Martina said in a cheeky voice, threading her arm through Georgie's. "Let's go home, lovey."

And Georgie turned her back on him without another word.

IT WAS a short walk back to the house, but for Georgie it seemed endless as Martina kept up a line of soothing chatter. Georgie only half listened. She felt curiously sluggish, as if she were fighting her way through jellied consommé, and there was nothing she wanted to say or do but throw herself on her bed and weep.

Rafferty was leaving. She knew it wasn't an empty threat— indeed, she'd been afraid this day would come since the moment he first set foot in the house. He wasn't made to be a butler, even though he certainly was a splendid one. No, he was something far grander, like...like a pirate, or a highwayman, or something. And he didn't want her.

Rafferty's kiss...she still wasn't quite sure what she thought of it. She needed him to kiss her again so she could ponder it. Her reaction had been more physical than intellectual. It was the kiss of a man who wanted a woman, she was sure of that much. So why was he leaving?

"We'd best go in through the kitchen," Martina said. "No one else knows you went out."

She roused herself. "How did you?"

"Because Rafferty had ordered me to keep an eye on you while Stiles is still about," she said frankly, heading down the stone steps.

"But why? I don't understand why Mr. Stiles would want to hurt me. He was being pleasant enough at tea." She remembered his unctuous manner and controlled her little shiver of dislike. There'd been something in his flat black eyes, a malice that chilled her to the bone.

"He knows you're Rafferty's weakness."

Georgie lifted her head, a thread of hope spearing the darkness. "I am?"

Martina looked annoyed, though Georgie knew it was with herself. "You are," she said reluctantly.

Georgie scoffed. "He thinks I'm like some overgrown puppy."

Martina's strong mouth curved in a smile. "I don't know as how that's accurate, Miss Georgie."

"What's this?" Bertha demanded when they walked in. "Miss Georgie, have you been out on your own again? How many times must I tell you that—"

Georgie burst into tears. Georgie who never cried, at least not in front of anyone, let out a wail of pure grief. He was going away, and she'd never see him again.

She let them fuss over her. Hug her and soothe her, ply her with hot tea and a cold wet cloth for her eyes, and Martina got her settled back in her bedroom, the curtains drawn, the bed turned down and her pretty dress carefully laid out. The dress she'd foolishly thought would entice Rafferty. By then, her tears had stopped, and she was simply in a state of benumbed misery, and then she thought she might cry again, but sleep overtook her first, and she dreamed of Rafferty.

DAGGER FANNING LAY in a crumpled heap on the ground, unconscious, and Rafferty flexed his bruised and bloody hands. Dagger was a huge man, outweighing him by a good three stone, taller even than his own remarkable height, and he was a bully. Rumor had it he'd killed a woman, one of the whores Belding ran, and when he was sent as a bill collector, bloodshed and death followed. Rafferty had considered killing him—it would be nobody's loss, and it would send an even more effective message than simply beating him to a pulp would. But he'd lost the taste for death, if he'd ever had it. He'd had to kill in his life, more often than he liked, but he saved it for a last resort. He would kill Billy Stiles—there was no help for it. Dagger would serve as a final warning.

He crossed the deserted alleyway and picked up the knife Dagger had pulled on him, the one that gave him his name. It was a nasty piece of business, and he'd managed to slice Rafferty's chest before he'd disarmed him. It was a shallow cut, hidden by the jacket, and he'd sew it up himself if need be, but as far as anyone could tell, Dagger hadn't laid a finger on him.

Word would get to Billy—he probably already knew. It would go one of two ways. Stiles would take the warning and back off. Or things would escalate.

He needed to get the hell away from the Mannings, but for the time being, he didn't dare. He'd put them in danger, and it was up to him to keep them safe. As soon as Billy was in the ground, he'd leave, without warning or a by-your-leave. In a year or two she'd think back on him with acute embarrassment. In a year or two he'd....have forgotten all about her. Of course he would.

Bertha and Martina were looking at him with acute dislike when he came in the kitchen door, and he was tempted to turn around and leave again. Instead, he sighed. "What have I done now?"

"You know perfectly well what you've done," Martina said

sternly. "That poor little girl is in love with you, and you've been treating her like she's getting in your way."

"She is. I can't help that she thinks she's in love with me. What would you have me do, seduce her?"

"Watch your tongue," Bertha snapped. "You won't be talking about Miss Georgie like that!"

He wanted to bang his head against the wall. He had absolutely no idea how things had gotten so bloody complicated. How he was tied to the place, to the girl, in ways that were anathema to him, was something he couldn't fathom—all he knew was he was trapped.

At any other time he would have simply walked away and let things sort themselves out on their own. He didn't want responsibility for a group of helpless aristocrats—he'd walked away from that kind of life years ago and there was no going back. Not for anything less than his grandmother, and in the end, not even for her.

But he couldn't just leave. Whether he cared for Georgie or not, he could scarcely leave her to Stiles's tender mercies. He wouldn't even condemn the Beauty.

"I'll be leaving," he said. "As soon as I judge it safe to do so. Does that please you two biddies?"

Bertha just looked at him. "You'd break her heart like that, would you?"

"As I said before, what would you have me do?"

"Disillusion her," Martina piped up. "That shouldn't be that hard—Lord knows you have practice in it. The women who'd like to cut your throat are legion."

"The problem with Georgie is she'd probably do it."

Martina sighed. "You're right. And every one of those angry women would be back in your bed if you beckoned. You have the devil's own luck."

There was no way he'd consider Georgie's patent adoration to be lucky, not when it was off-limits and too bloody tempting. He stared at Martina. "I'll be done by the end of the week," he said.

'That's five days. You think you can take care of business in that time?" Martina said, her low voice thick with disbelief.

"I can."

"And what business is that, may I ask?" Bertha said, eyeing the two of them suspiciously.

"Keeping the family safe from marauders," Martina said blithely. "Don't you worry, Bertha. This family won't be the worse for having Rafferty as a butler."

"Hmph," said Bertha, her voice derisive. "You just watch out for Miss Georgie. Or I'll have your guts for garters."

Rafferty gave her a wry smile. "Nothing's going to happen to Georgie, I promise," he said, knowing it was the truth. Billy Stiles's rule of the London underworld would come to an end after so short a reign. Someone else would fight and crawl their way upward, but it wouldn't be him. Not anymore.

Chapter Eighteen

IT WAS A SIMPLE ENOUGH MATTER, Georgie thought a few hours later. The faux headache she'd used as an excuse earlier in the day became real, and attending a cotillion was the last thing she wanted to do. She had no idea where Rafferty was, and she didn't care. She was going to stay in her room.

There was no sign of their butler as the family departed, and she watched them go with a deliberately wan expression on her face. If Rafferty reappeared, it would be too damned bad (she savored the word) if he found himself alone in the house with her. But he was nowhere to be seen.

She was practically alone in the house—Bertha would be tucked up in her rooms and Rafferty was off doing whatever it was he did when he was trying to avoid her. And she was hungry. She would go down and raid the larder and if she happened to run into their errant butler, she would be cool and disdainful. She absolutely wouldn't throw herself at him.

She heard the noise from the front hallway, and froze, as remembrance washed over her. Something was in the cellars, making a racket, and this time it couldn't be mice or vermin. Had Billy Stiles invaded the safety of their home, and was now ferreting around in their basement? But why would he? What, in fact, did he want from Rafferty, that he was willing to threaten his employers?

If she had an ounce of sense, she'd run back upstairs and lock herself in her room until Rafferty came home to protect them. But sense had never been her strong point, and besides, she had a strong feeling it was Rafferty himself in the coal cellars.

She didn't bother with her trusty fire poker—she simply headed past the storerooms and the larders to the steep dark stairway and the tiny glow of light emanating forth from it. If it was Rafferty, she was safe—he would never hurt her. If it was that awful man with the teeth, she'd still be safe—Rafferty would make sure no one would harm her. And maybe he'd kiss her again.

"WHAT ARE YOU DOING?" Georgie's soft voice cut across Rafferty's concentration like a saber, and he jumped back from the wall, cursing, to face his nemesis across the darkened coal cellar.

"What in Christ's name are you doing here?" he demanded once he'd caught his breath. "You should be out at the Pettigrews'."

"I had a headache," she said blithely, moving closer. She already had a streak of coal dust across one cheek, and her tawny hair was coming out of its knot at the back of her head. She looked deliciously rumpled, and he knew danger when he saw it.

"You've had too many headaches," he said flatly. "People will stop believing you."

"Oh, I don't think they believed me tonight, but they didn't really want me to accompany them anyway, so it was easy enough. What are you doing?" She came closer, and it took all his determination not to back up. There were three coal cellars in the basement of the house on Corinth Place, and this one hadn't been used in years. What better place to hide a long-lost treasure?

Which he couldn't very well dig with an interested witness. "Why did you follow me down here?" he shot back.

"You answer my question first. Why are you going through the coal cellars? And don't tell me it's to check that we have enough coal—I wouldn't believe you."

"Why else would I be down in the cellars?" he countered reasonably.

"You're looking for something."

He resisted the impulse to curse. "Whatever makes you think that?"

"Because I already caught you in my father's study, and you're always disappearing and showing up in strange places. You're looking for something, and that scary man wants it too."

He hadn't really underestimated her intelligence. He'd just hoped she wouldn't notice. "I'm not looking for a treasure in a heap of coal, if that's what you're thinking," he said, doing exactly that. "This house is my responsibility, and there aren't enough hours in the day to accomplish everything I must accomplish. The good news is there's plenty of coal."

She pushed her hair away from her face, widening the streak of coal dust on her cheekbone. "I don't believe you."

He cursed, silently. "Does Bertha know you're following me around? What about Martina?"

"Bertha's in bed and Martina's gone out. It's just the two of us." She took another step toward him.

He wanted to groan. He'd told Martina to keep an eye on her, distract her from following him around, and so far, she'd failed quite spectacularly.

His own problem was getting worse—the more time he spent with her, the more he wanted her, and he was running out of excuses to disappear. God knew he never should have kissed her.

"Go back to bed, Georgie," he said grimly. A mistake, because she smiled at him.

"I like it when you call me Georgie."

"It's highly improper," he said stiffly.

"I'm highly improper," she said, and he wished it were true. And then she shivered, and he realized how cold and damp the cellars were.

"Back upstairs, Miss Georgiana," he said. "If you go right now, I won't tell Bertha you've been following me."

"You think I'm afraid of her?"

"Anyone with sense would be," he said.

There was a moment of silence as they watched each other across the expanse of the cellar, and he held himself very still, when all he wanted to do was cross the room in two strides and take her into his arms. It was the last thing he was going to do.

"Go to bed, Georgie," he said softly. "Please."

The "please" had done it. She disappeared from the entrance to the room, and he let out his pent-up breath. He should follow her, make certain she made it out of the warren of cellars safely, but he didn't dare. He didn't dare come any closer to her—knowing he'd touch her if he did, knowing he'd be lost if he did. He'd told her he was leaving, he knew he had to, and to hell with Belding's hidden cache. She had much too dangerous an effect on him, and he'd already come perilously close to discovery by the Ormonds. How would they feel to know the heir's cousin was a thief and a criminal, working as a butler in a neighbor's house? They'd probably mind the butler part the most, he thought with a trace of amusement as he heard her footsteps fade away. The Ormonds had been a randy lot going all the way back to the first Duke of Ormond during the time of old Cromwell himself. They were used to black sheep in the family. Just not servants.

By the time he'd cleaned himself up, it was approaching midnight, and all was still and quiet in the house. He had nothing to worry about, and only a few more places to look: the unused servants' quarters on the fourth floor and, as a last resort, the rooftop. The sooner he checked, the sooner he could leave, leave the Mannings to survive as best they could, leave Georgie to marry Andrew Salton.

He barely noticed the pain when he slammed his fist into the wall. How had such a simple job become such a disaster? Just because he disappeared wouldn't mean that Billy Stiles would leave Georgie be. Billy Stiles never gave up on anything, he would assume that if he hurt Georgie, it would lure him back. His assumptions were correct—if Stiles hurt Georgie, he was a dead man.

Maybe he should just kill him and get it over with, but he wasn't a man with a taste for violence, and he preferred a fair fight. But Billy didn't fight fair.

There were still bottles of brandy in the kitchen—for some reason, Neddy hadn't devoured his usual bottle and a half during the day, and he'd looked remarkably sober, if pale and unwell the last time Rafferty had seen him. Doubtless he'd make up for his unaccustomed abstinence that night, and he'd be pouring him into bed once more. In the meantime, Neddy's brandy was his.

Chapter Nineteen

GEORGIE HAD BEEN TEMPTED to go straight from the coal cellar to Rafferty's apartment, Rafferty's bed, but she was uncertain of her welcome. No, that wasn't true—he would yell at her and make her leave, the dratted man. But there was a good chance he'd kiss her again, and even in her innocence she knew that kiss would be even more dangerous than the one the previous night. She made him misbehave, and it was a glorious power to wield. If he hadn't said please, she would have crossed the coal cellar and kissed him, and he would have kissed her back, she was sure of it. And God, she wanted him to kiss her back.

But he'd said please, and she knew that meant not showing up in his bed as well, and besides, she wasn't certain she was ready to strip off her clothes and lie down for him. She knew the details of what that would involve, but a part of her was rightfully wary. Not as strong as the part who wanted to experience it, but her nerve had not quite reached the sticking point.

Her plan was simple. Entice Rafferty to take her to bed and he'd have no choice but to marry her. Her family would be horrified, but she'd never been of much importance in the scheme of things, not like Norah the beauty or Neddy the heir, and they would reconcile themselves soon enough. There should be enough money to buy a small cottage in the country and Rafferty could...what could he do? Without a household to run, he'd have to go back to his old ways, and she'd figured out enough to know those were dangerous indeed. He'd killed men, he'd said. He consorted with people like the criminal Billy Stiles. He'd have to go back to that if he were no longer their butler, and she expected her father would draw the line at that.

There was no sound from the cellars—Rafferty hadn't followed her, and she sighed. She needed a better plan, and there was only one person who could possibly help.

"What are you doing still awake?" Martina had appeared at her bedroom door, looking in to see that her charge was asleep. Tonight, Georgie had tucked herself into bed, piled the pillows behind her and waited. "And what's that on your face?"

Georgie quickly lifted her hand to her cheek and came back with dark powder. "Coal dust," she said.

Martina came into the room and closed the door behind her. "And how did that come about?"

Georgie decided to go straight to the point. "I followed Rafferty into the coal cellars," she said. "He didn't like it."

"I expect not."

"He's searching for something in the house. I'm sure of it."

Martina didn't appear surprised. "Well, if he is, it has nothing to do with you, so leave the poor man alone!"

"Why is he a poor man?" she asked reasonably.

"Because you follow him around like you're a lovesick puppy dog and...oh, no," she finished weakly. "You're not."

Georgie didn't pretend to misunderstand. "I'm in love with him."

"I warned you not to be. He isn't for the likes of you. He isn't for the likes of anyone. Rafferty's a lone wolf, always has been. He hasn't got room in his life for a woman, much less an infatuated little girl."

Fire sparked through her. "I'm not a little girl, and I'm not infatuated. I've considered it quite calmly. I'm in love with him, I'm going to marry him, and you're going to help me."

Martina's sternness vanished, and she sat down on the bed, her full skirts bunched around her. "Georgie, he's not the marrying kind. And even if he were, a young lady does not marry a butler."

"I'm marrying this one," she said determinedly. "I just have to convince him."

Martina laughed, not unkindly. "That's like teaching a dog not to hunt."

"He's in love with me too," Georgie said, sounding more sure than she really felt.

To her amazement, Martina didn't laugh again. "You're deluded, Miss Georgie. Oh, I don't deny that he's got an eye for you. Otherwise, he wouldn't go out of his way to avoid you the way he does. But he's not going to do anything about it. He's not going to ruin you."

"What if I want to be ruined?"

"Bless the girl!" Martina said. "You don't want that. Stay a child until some nice safe gentleman comes along. Rafferty is no good for you, no good for any woman."

"It doesn't matter. I'm in love with him, and I'm going to have him."

"He won't marry you. You'll be a butler's trollop. I can't think of anything much lower than that."

"It sounds lovely to me."

"No!"

"And you'll help me."

"No!"

"Because he loves me too."

"Rafferty doesn't love anyone but himself," Martina said firmly.

Georgie lifted her eyes and looked at her. "Are you so sure of that?"

For a moment, Martina said nothing, as if she were considering an impossibility and finding it possible. "I won't argue with you, Miss Georgie. You must have a plan. What were you thinking? That you might lock him in a room and have your wicked way with him?"

Georgie made a face. "I don't think I could do that. He needs to be the one who locks us in."

Martina sat back. "We'll find you a nice gentleman to marry. Like that Mr. Salton."

"No."

"And you want me to help?"

"Yes, please."

Martina let out a heavy sigh. "Go to sleep, Miss Georgie, and dream safe dreams. That's the closest you'll get to Rafferty, and some day you'll thank God for it. There are separate classes for a reason—the two shouldn't mix."

"You're a snob, Martina."

"Most definitely. Go to sleep now."

"I will if you promise to help me."

"I can't. For your sake and for Rafferty's. It would just lead to disaster."

Georgie's eyes filled with tears. "I want a disaster. I want chaos and madness and passion! Most of all, I want Rafferty! I'll die without him."

"People don't die of love, Miss Georgie. Go to sleep."

"I'll be the first. Help me, Martina."

"I can't," she said. "He's no good for you."

"Then I'll do it myself."

BILLY STILES WAS NOWHERE to be found. Rafferty had headed out into the streets of London, down by the docks where Stiles made his home, but there was no sign of him, when the midnight hours were his usual time to be about. Rafferty could scarcely go to the small fortress where Stiles lived—Dagger

Fanning was out of commission, but there were any number of bully boys out to ensure Billy's safety. He was going to have to get him alone if he was going to kill him, and there was no question about it. Billy Stiles was a threat to Georgie, and as such, couldn't be allowed to live.

It wasn't as if he hadn't killed before. There was the tavern brawl where someone pulled a knife, and it had been him or them. He'd survived that without a trace of guilt, and he'd survive Billy's death as well. His organization would fall apart without him, and he was sure Billy hadn't shared the details of the judge's hidden cache with any of his henchmen. Billy was a man who liked to play things close to the vest, and once he was gone, there'd be no one to threaten the Mannings.

But he'd never killed a man in cold blood before—it had always been in the heat of battle. Billy was too smart to fight with Rafferty—Rafferty was half a head taller and a great deal stronger than Billy. In fact, there was always the strong possibility that Billy had ordered Rafferty's death. Dagger Fanning hadn't been acting on his own.

But the midnight streets of London showed no sign of him, nor of anyone else who might have wished Rafferty harm, and until he finished with that particular threat, he couldn't abandon the feckless Mannings. Couldn't abandon Georgie. No matter how hard staying around her was.

Rafferty moved down the street at an easy pace, acutely aware that he was being followed. It wouldn't be Dagger Fanning—he wouldn't be doing anything for a good long time, and Billy Stiles wouldn't trust him to anyone else. No, it was Billy himself shadowing his footsteps in the middle of the night as he walked toward the docks.

Stiles wouldn't underestimate him—he'd know that Rafferty was well aware of him. Stiles wasn't out to kill him that night—he would have already made his move. No, this would be in the way of a warning, a demand, a threat, but nothing more.

He wished he didn't have so much of the damned gentleman's

code of honor left in him. It would be simple enough to cut back, circle around and finish Stiles quickly and silently. But his august grandmother would be horrified, and he suspected he'd have a hard time living with himself.

He stopped by the bridge and waited, making no effort to disguise his impatience. It didn't take long for Billy to catch up with him.

"Enjoying the night air, Rafferty me boy?" Stiles greeted him, his mouthful of teeth glowing in the moonlight.

"I was," he said evenly. "What do you want?"

"What do you think I want? Belding's ill-gotten gains, that's what. And you're taking a mighty long time to find it. Seems to me I ought to pay a little visit to the house on Corinth Place meself, see what I can find."

"I wouldn't advise it."

"Seems to me that pretty little girl of yours might encourage you to work a little faster. She don't know who you are, does she? None of them do. You'd be out on your arse so fast you wouldn't know what hit you."

"And I wouldn't have access to whatever fucking hiding place Belding decided to use. If I haven't found it yet, what kind of luck do you think you'll have?"

Billy smiled benevolently, his dark black eyes shining murder in the lamplight. "Why, I'd tear the place apart, brick by brick, until I found it. I've got enough men to help me, and there wouldn't be all this shilly-shallying around."

"You don't think the police might notice if you had your men invade the building?"

"The police do what I tell them to," Billy said. "And don't try to tell me the money isn't there. It has to be—there's no place else and everyone knows Belding made frequent visits to the deserted townhouse. I don't think he was looking for companionship from the rats."

"It would have been fitting," Rafferty said. "What do you want from me, Billy?"

"Don't be daft, man. The money, pure and simple. And you're running out of time. Let's say by this time on Monday you'll have the answer, or I'll have to do something about it myself. And I might just take a piece of that little girl as a reward."

"Touch her and I'll cut off your hands."

Billy Stiles sniggered. "Have you fallen in love, old sod? How the mighty have fallen! I never thought to see the time when the cold-blooded Rafferty was brought low by a pretty girl. And I gather she's not even the beauty of the family. Your standards are falling."

"You can have the beauty," he said without a moment's hesitation. "Just keep the fuck away from Georgie."

"Georgie? Now ain't that cute? I'm not staying away from anyone. I want my money."

"Don't you mean your share of the money?" Rafferty countered, knowing full well that any division of the spoils was highly unlikely.

"'Course I do, old sod. 'Course I do." His voice was wheedling. "Monday night. I'll come to collect my share. Or your little Georgie, just to encourage you to work harder. Maybe I shouldn't wait on that."

Rafferty felt no fear, simply a cold, murderous rage that effectively wiped out any stray sense of honor remaining from his privileged upbringing. "Why don't you come closer and say that?" he purred.

"Because you have a knife and you know how to use it. But I'm carrying a pistol meself and I haven't lived to this ripe old age by being stupid," he said smugly.

"Threatening the girl is very stupid," Rafferty said in a low, dangerous voice.

"Threatening me is even worse." He pulled out the pistol, aiming it at Rafferty's mid-section. "Let's just agree to leave each other in one piece, shall we? You agreed to find Belding's cache and split it with me—that's all I'm asking for."

Rafferty controlled his snort of disbelief. "You'll have your money," he said coldly. "As soon as I find it."

"Make it soon, my boy. I never was a patient man." He uncocked the pistol and slid it back in his flashy coat, and Rafferty hesitated. He could kill him where he stood, his knife in Billy's throat, before Stiles could even begin to reach for the gun, and he was sorely tempted. But Stiles was already pulling away, and he knew he'd missed his chance. This time.

Next time, he wouldn't hesitate. Next time, Billy Stiles would be dead before he even opened his mouth, and if that soiled Rafferty's peculiar sense of honor then he'd live with it. Georgie was worth any tarnished standards he still maintained. In fact, he'd give the house one more day. Search the old servants' quarters on the fourth floor again, just to see if he'd missed something, and then take a little trip down to the docks to finish with Billy. He couldn't afford a fair fight—what if, by some fluke, he' lost? Who would protect Georgie? She was hardly Billy's type, but the man had never been accounted stupid. He wanted her because Rafferty wanted her, and nothing would distract him from humbling his ancient enemy.

No, he was about to become a murderer. And he wouldn't feel an ounce of guilt.

GEORGIE LOOKED out over the sleeping city, her brain a torrent of thoughts. Everyone slept, everyone but her, and she yawned, knowing it would do no good. There were nights when she simply couldn't sleep, and she climbed up the servants' stairs and went out through the hinged window to the flat roof, perching up there as the night closed down around her, peace in her solitude. She had no fear of heights—in fact, she liked them. Liked being one with the night, looking down on the world around her.

Rafferty was somewhere down below, not giving one good goddam about her—or maybe he was asleep in that bed, not even dreaming of her. She had to face facts—he didn't really care about her at all, no matter how much she adored him. Oh, she was one of his responsibilities, and as such, he should look after her, but she was nothing beyond that. She might as well be Norah for all he cared.

The dismal truth was, there was no happy ending for Rafferty and her, and the sooner she accepted that fact, the better off she'd be.

Which left her with Andrew Salton. Clearly, he didn't have the money to rescue them from their folly, but he had enough to prove to be a respectable husband. She didn't want him, no matter how charming he was. If she couldn't have Rafferty, she didn't want anyone. Not even to save her family.

She heard the creak on the stairs, and she froze. For a moment, she was tempted to get up and hide behind one of the many chimneys, but she stayed where she was. No one in her family would bother with making their way to the roof, which left only one possibility. Rafferty.

If he was startled to see her sitting there, he didn't show it. He closed the door quietly behind him and stepped out into the moonlight, and she belatedly remembered she was wearing her nightdress. He'd seen her in it often enough, but she pulled her shawl closer around her as she watched him from her perch.

"What are you doing up here?" His voice was low on the night air, and she wanted to shiver. She loved his voice, the deep tones, the warmth.

"I like it up here. I come up when I need to be alone, to think."

"Do you want me to go away?"

"No." She kept her own voice level. "Why are you up here?"

"You left the door to the servants' floor open. It's my duty to see the house is secure."

"Your duty," she scoffed, disappointed. He hadn't come looking for her after all.

"Don't you want me to do my duty? I'm your protégé after all."

"You said you were leaving." She couldn't keep the hurt out of her voice.

"I am," he said reluctantly. "Though I don't know when. Your family is in a mess—I can't abandon you while the wolf is at the door."

"What wolf?" But she knew. It wasn't poverty or starvation, it was Mr. Stiles with all the teeth and that smile that chilled her to the bone. Somehow, they'd gotten his attention, she'd gotten his attention, and they were no longer safe.

"You don't need to worry about it," Rafferty said, moving closer, the moonlight sending a long shadow behind him. "May I sit?"

She ignored the little thrill of pleasure. "If you want to," she said coolly.

"I want to." He dropped down on the flat roof next to her, so close she could put out her hand and touch him. "What are you thinking about? Andrew Salton?" He sounded disgruntled, which pleased her.

"Maybe."

He said nothing and she wanted to kick him. "Are you going to marry him?" The words came out of the blue, and she stared at him, astonished.

"Why do you ask?"

"It would get you out of this house. It would be a safe future for you."

She wanted to cry. "I'm not looking for a safe future," she said stiffly. "And I don't think it's any of your business who I marry. In fact, I'm thinking I might be an old maid, with lots of cats."

His laugh was as soft as the night breeze. "That won't happen. Someone will sweep you off your feet. If it isn't Andrew Salton, then it will be someone else."

"I'm not marrying anyone if I can't—" she stopped herself before the damning words got out.

But she shouldn't have underestimated him. "Georgie," he said gently. "I'm not for the likes of you."

"Who said you were?" she shot back.

"You did."

"Well, I've changed my mind." She could be proud of the firmness in her voice.

"Good to hear," he said softly.

"I'll be a bluestocking, and hold salons, and I'll have no use for men at all."

"It would be a shame if you never were a mother."

She felt the pang, and she flinched. "I intend to be an eccentric intellectual. There's no saying I can't have a baby on my own."

"You need a man for that."

"I suppose they have their uses," she said with a sniff.

He laughed then, and her heart warmed. "If any man tries to take advantage of you, I'll throw him out on his ear."

"You won't be around."

He didn't deny it. He was watching her, and his eyes were warm in the cool night air, and something snapped inside Georgie.

"I'll tell you what," she said briskly. "Since I'm going to want a baby and you aren't going to let any man near me, then you can do the honors."

If she'd managed to startle him, he didn't show it. "I'm not in the habit of leaving my bastards around the place."

"I'll take good care of her."

"What if it's a boy?"

She wondered if he were seriously considering it. She turned to face him, a faint bit of hope filling her heart. "I'll take good care of him, too."

"Now you're talking two children. How am I supposed to manage that?"

"You can be my butler. I'll need help if I'm to have my own

establishment." She'd need money too, but she'd worry about that later.

"I don't think I'm cut out to be a servant for the rest of my life."

"Then you can marry me."

Dead silence. "Georgie," he said softly. "I can't. You can't marry your butler."

"Well, then, we can always live in sin."

She startled a laugh out of him. "There are better men than Andrew Salton," he said, and the faint hope in her heart died.

"Don't you want me?" Her own words were quiet, hopeless.

The moonlight caught his smile. "Who wouldn't want you, dear heart? But it's my duty to keep you safe, not to debauch you."

"Even if I want to be debauched?"

There was an odd look in his blue eyes, and he reached out and cupped her jaw with one strong hand. "No, Georgie." And then, to her amazement, he leaned forward and kissed her gently on the mouth.

It was a far cry from the raw passion of the night before, but it broke her heart, and she rose to meet him, heart and soul, ready to give him everything. His lips were soft, questing, and she wanted more. She needed more.

But then he broke the kiss, pulling back, and she could feel tears fill her eyes. "Then what was that?" she asked in a small voice.

"That was goodbye."

He was gone before she could stop him, getting to his feet with that long, lean grace of his and moving to the heavy door. "Don't stay out too late—it's getting cold," he said, and he left the door open for her.

She sat there, staring after him, and she could feel the wetness of tears on her cheeks. He meant it. He was really going, leaving her, and there was nothing she could do to stop him.

Chapter Twenty

THE CARRIAGE RIDE TO THE CHEVIOTS' that evening could have been worse. For some reason, Rafferty chose to accompany their decrepit coachman, up front, but his manner was as smooth and unremarkable as always.

She didn't make the mistake of thinking his presence meant anything. That kiss on the rooftops had the flavor of goodbye, and she knew deep in her heart that there was nothing she could do to change his mind. She was just a silly girl with an oversized crush, and the sooner she got over it, the better.

She had no real choice, except to marry Andrew Salton. The one saving grace was that it would drive Norah mad, though Georgie had no idea why. Every time the name of Andrew Salton came up, Norah's beautiful eyes would narrow and she'd start pinching. As revenge, it left a lot to be desired, but at least it was something.

Rafferty didn't want her to marry Salton either, though that made absolutely no sense. He kept telling her she needed to find an upstanding young gentleman to wed, and Andrew was the perfect choice. Tonight, she would flirt with all her might, convince him that she was the wife for him. He was a kind, handsome man. She'd be lucky to marry him. Except she couldn't do it.

If he loved her, she'd be a fool to reject him. She'd never been preferred over her stunning sister, and it was a small triumph. If she couldn't have Rafferty, she could have a man who adored her.

The Cheviots' cotillion was an absolute crush, always a sign of a great success, and Norah's coterie of admirers immediately gathered around her, eager for a condescending word from the goddess. Her father decamped to the card room, and her mother, once she'd obtained a partner for her younger daughter, followed suit, leaving Georgie momentarily stranded once the waltz had ended.

But Andrew Salton was there, with his handsome face and brown eyes and charm, swinging her into a waltz before she could decide what to do, and she surveyed him dispassionately as they whirled around the dance floor.

He was more traditionally handsome than Rafferty, broader, with an open, friendly face and a flattering manner that should have made her swoon in delight. The only man who made her swoon was Rafferty.

Not a simple problem to solve, she thought, as Andrew guided her around the dance floor. Fight for the man who'd never love her, or marry the man courting her assiduously. She'd be a fool to turn him down.

She glanced up at him, at his noble profile and the stubborn lock of hair that graced his forehead. He was looking, quite intently, at something at the far side of the ballroom, and Georgie wondered what had caught his attention. There was an expression on his face, one might almost say of yearning, and with the next turn of the dance she followed his gaze.

He was staring at Norah, surrounded by her suitors, with a look of such burning desire that she felt scorched. And Norah was looking back, the same longing on her face.

Georgie froze in the middle of the dance floor, and Andrew stumbled to a stop, his attention finally on her. "Is anything wrong, Miss Georgiana?"

It shouldn't have hurt. She didn't care about Andrew Salton

—the fact that he loved her sister shouldn't mean a thing. Everyone was in love with Norah—after all these years Georgie should be used to it.

But Rafferty knew. Rafferty told her she should marry someone who loved her—he knew that Andrew, like everyone else, preferred Norah.

"I believe my sister has something to say to you," she said, standing perfectly still among the whirling couples.

He looked startled. "I doubt Miss Manning would have anything to impart to me—I barely know her."

"Liar." She used the word pleasantly enough. She pulled away from him and crossed the dance floor, avoiding the swirling couples. It wasn't until she reached the hallway that she began to run.

❧

RAFFERTY WAS PLAYING dice with the other drivers, crouched on the sidewalk when one of the lookers-on said, "Coo, oo's that there?"

He didn't bother to look up. They'd been trying to distract him from his deeply ingrained habit of winning, and he wasn't about to lose focus.

"One of them young ladies just ran out of the building and took off into the night," the man said. "Wonder what she's running from. Not safe out 'ere, if she ain't careful."

Rafferty dropped the dice and rose, ignoring the pile of coin at his feet, and stared around him. "Where?" he demanded. He couldn't be lucky enough that it would be a perfect stranger—he knew it could only be Georgie, running straight into trouble once again.

"She 'eaded that way," the man, nodding toward the east, and Rafferty wanted to groan. Of course she did, headed straight into Stiles's territory without a backward glance.

"I'm out," he said, starting after her.

206

"You'll never catch 'er," the man said. "She was running fast."

Rafferty didn't dignify that with an answer as he took off. He'd been an idiot, letting down his guard. He'd accompanied the carriage for one thing—to keep the Mannings, and Georgie in particular, safe from Billy Stiles and his men, and he'd assumed that as long as she was inside, he wouldn't have to worry. How could he have forgotten how headstrong she was—proper behavior wasn't for the likes for Georgie

There was no sign of her when he turned the corner, and he let out a string of useless curses. Where did she think she was running to, alone in the chill night air? Hadn't he warned her...?

If she thought she was heading home, then she didn't have the sense God gave chickens. But then, Georgie had proved herself to be totally lacking in sense, up to and including her declaration that she was going to marry him. It had almost worked in his favor—if he'd left then, it would have freed him from his unlikely attachment and he could have devoted all his energies to finishing up with Billy Stiles. He assumed he could still keep an eye on her to make certain she was safe until Stiles was done with.

Now she was lost somewhere in the darkness of the city, heading into the worst part of it, all the while he'd stood by and done nothing.

He was a fool, and he had no one to blame but himself. He never should have gotten involved with her in the first place, never agreed to her stupid game, never chosen to be her butler, of all the ridiculous things. It didn't matter that it had given him access to Belding's hiding place—he was beginning to think the legendary cache never existed, and he'd brought Billy's wrath down on Georgie's fair hair for nothing.

What would he do if Stiles caught her? Rafferty refused to think about it—he only knew he would rip Billy's throat out if he put one finger on Georgie's sweet body. Jesus, how did he get himself into such a mess? And where the bloody hell was Georgie?

෩

TEARS WERE BLINDING Georgie as she raced down the empty sidewalks. It was a dark, cold night, with ominous clouds scuttering overhead, but she barely noticed, so intent was she in simply getting away. She'd been such a fool, thinking Andrew Salton was hers to choose or discard at her whim. Chances were that Rafferty was in love with Norah as well—he so clearly disliked her sister that it was probably the reverse side of love. After all, what man was immune to Norah's vaunted beauty?

Her breath was coming in sharp rasps, and she had a stitch in her side, so she began to slow her headlong pace, pressing her hand against her ribs. A light mist had started falling, and she stopped to look around her, into the deep shrouds of darkness. These streets were not well-lit, and they were deserted. She'd thought she was heading toward her home, but nothing looked familiar, everything looked dark and dangerous.

And then she heard the footsteps, slow and steady, behind her, and she turned, certain it was Rafferty come to rescue her from her foolishness once again, only to falter at the sight of the giant who approached her.

He was bigger than Rafferty's impressive height, broader, none of which mattered. What mattered was the huge knife he carried in his hand as he came directly at her.

She turned to run, not daring to waste time in screaming for help, but she was only a few feet away from him, and she felt his hand reach out, the knife slash through her beautiful dress, slowing her. She did scream then, racing down the street with a sudden burst of speed, and for a moment she thought there was a chance she might outrun him. Until a beefy hand came out and caught her arm, yanking her around to drive that vicious knife into her, when suddenly she was free, sprawling on the wet pavement, going down hard.

Two men were locked in a battle—she could see the fierce grimace on the giant who'd followed her, and Rafferty could be no match for him. She wanted to scream again, but she had no intention of distracting him.

"Run!" he panted as he knocked the monster to the ground.

But Georgie wasn't going anywhere. Either Rafferty would win, and protect her, or he would die, and she wouldn't want to live. She could only lie there in the rain and watch them, brutal, savage, horrible, the grunts and the groans shocking in the still night air.

She saw the flash of the knife, carving upward, and she buried her face, unable to watch any longer, sobbing into her hands, when a sudden silence descended. The only sounds were one man's tortured breathing, the noise of a body falling to the pavement, the sigh that could mean nothing less than death.

She braced herself for the hands that caught her arms, letting herself be hauled upright, to face Rafferty's blazing eyes. "I told you to run!" he shouted at her, shaking her, hard.

"I couldn't," she managed to say through chattering teeth. "I couldn't leave you."

At that moment, the sky opened, pouring down on them in sheets of icy rain, and Rafferty swore, something new and peculiar, and scooped her up in his arms. "We have to get out of this," he shouted at her over the noise of the downfall. "And then I'm going to beat you."

She managed a small, weak smile. He did love her. If he didn't, he wouldn't be so angry with her. Burying her face against his chest, she held on, safe for the first time in what seemed like days.

She had no sense of where they were, how long he carried her, and when he suddenly ducked in out of the rain, the surroundings were as dark as the night sky. She felt him lower her to her feet, and she was entirely ready to stand still and be chastised, or even beaten if he really wanted to, but her knees gave way, and she sank to the floor in her ruined gown, feeling the rough wood beneath her.

Rafferty swore, leaving her there, and a moment later, she heard a door slam, and she wondered if he'd abandoned her. It would serve her right, for being such a feckless ninny, but she knew he wouldn't leave her.

She sank down in a little heap, resting her head on her arms, her loose wet hair all about her. Her heart was beating too rapidly, her breath was coming in short, quick bursts as she struggled to catch it, and her limbs felt cold, prickly. She'd seen a man die. She'd almost died herself, and she was in the middle of nowhere with a very angry man. Not that he would hurt her. But she couldn't stop the harsh rasp of her breathing.

And then he was suddenly down beside her, pulling her into his arms, across his lap, cradling her as she gasped for breath and trembled, cold and hot at the same time. "Hush, love," he whispered in her ear, stroking her wet hair away from her face. "Just hush. You're safe now."

But she was frozen, unable to calm, unable to speak, unable to do anything but lie there in his arms and tremble, until he cupped her face in his big, strong hands and kissed her eyelids. "You're safe," he said again, and her breath lurched into a hiccupping sob.

Men hated it when women cried, and yet she couldn't help herself. She let out a wail, and buried her face against his wet shirt, sobbing as he held her, his strong hands stroking her back, calming her as she wept. "He won't hurt you anymore," he murmured against her temple. "He's dead now—he won't hurt anyone."

"I...d...don't want to cry," she stammered. "I don't know why I'm crying so much—I never cry. And I've cried so many times recently, ever since you told me you were leaving."

"I have to leave, Georgie," he said, holding her close. She could feel his heart beating against her face, and she wanted to press closer, to feel him, skin to skin. "You know I can't stay."

"Yes, you can," she wailed. "You can marry me. They won't mind—even Andrew Salton didn't really want me. He's in love with Norah."

"Is that why you ran?"

"It was stupid. I didn't love him. But he lied to me. He

pretended he wanted me, when all the time he just wanted to get close to Norah. Why didn't you tell me?"

"I didn't want to hurt you."

"You couldn't hurt me," she said. "You love me."

"Georgie...!" he began, and there was no missing the weary impatience in his voice.

"You do. You wouldn't have come after me if you didn't. You wouldn't have killed that man!"

"That man deserved killing for a hundred reasons that have nothing to do with you. And, of course I came after you. I'm your servant—it's what I do."

She laughed then, a small, rusty sound. "Does that mean I can tell you what to do?"

He was too smart for her. "No. It means I'll protect you, even with my life. But I'm not in love with you, and you're smart enough to know that. You have a crush on me, because you're a child and I keep getting you out of scrapes. As soon as you find the right man, you'll forget all about me."

"You are the right man."

"Hush," he said again, leaning back against something and carrying her with it. "Just hush. We'll wait till the rain stops and then we'll get you home, and Martina will make a big fuss of you, and by tomorrow you'll be much more sensible."

"Tomorrow I'll still be in love with you."

"I thought I showed you what kind of man I am last night. It was supposed to scare you off."

"You did," she said. "Show me again."

"Christ," he muttered, and she felt his lips against her temple, meant to calm, to soothe. "Christ," he said again, and set his mouth against hers.

It was cold and wet from the rain. It wasn't hard and punishing, like the night before, it was soft, sweet, tasting her, his tongue running along the seam of her lips. His hands came up to her face, and he gently levered her mouth open, to deepen the kiss, and she felt the warmth begin to build inside her. She wanted to kiss him back, but she had no notion how to do it, so she merely let him kiss her, slowly, thoroughly, his heart pounding against hers.

❧

HE SHOULDN'T BE DOING this. The words ran around in his head, while his body paid no attention. He was lost in the touch of her, the taste of her, sweet and untutored and so eager to learn. He wanted to turn her in his arms so that she straddled him, he wanted to reach between her legs and give her a taste of what he could do for her, he wanted to push her down on the filthy floor and fuck her, fuck her till she was out of his brain and his heart and soul.

He pulled back from her, dumping her unceremoniously on the hard floor as he stood and paced several safe feet away from her. He didn't want to look back at her, but he was no coward, and he turned. She had the brightness of tears in her eyes, and he hated himself all the more.

"Why did you stop?" she asked in a small voice. "I didn't want you to stop."

"Another moment and you'd have been flat on your back with your skirts above your waist. I'm not about to take your virginity on a filthy warehouse floor," he said brutally.

"Then where will you take it?" She sounded damnably hopeful.

"I won't. When will you learn that I don't love you, I'm not going to marry you, and I don't even belong working for you? I'll be leaving in a matter of days, and I'm leaving you untouched."

"Too late," she said in that even voice. "You've already touched me."

"It won't happen again."

"Yes, it will."

He wanted to beat his head against a wall, he wanted to roar out his frustration. Instead, he took a deep breath. "You don't want it," he said. "Not really. Not if you knew what you were asking."

"I know perfectly well what I'm asking. I want you."

The words were like a razor blade to his soul, and he could make no response. Instead, he walked to the shuttered door, opening it and staring out into the pouring rain. If it would just stop, he could take her home, put her safely away from him. As long as they were trapped in the darkness, he was more vulnerable than even his worst enemy could wish.

He heard her move behind him, and he closed his eyes in despair. He wasn't a good man, not even remotely. He wasn't a man who ignored pleasure when it was offered to him, he wasn't noble enough to leave her pure and untouched. He'd already touched her, she said. He wanted to touch her everywhere.

He felt her come up behind him, and he opened his eyes, breathing in her scent—flowers and rain and warm skin. He wanted to drink her in.

"Get away from me, Georgie," he warned her in a low voice. "If you know what's good for you, move back."

"You and I have different opinions as to what's good for me," she said, and she didn't sound like the child he kept wanting her to be. She sounded like a woman, a woman he craved with every breath he took, a woman who was warm and yielding.

Frighten her, his brain said. Take her, his body cried out. Pushing her up against the wall, he moved his hands up the bodice of her dress, the whalebone corset like a prison around her ribs, and if he had a knife with him he would have cut it, and the dress, off of her. He covered the swell of her breast his long fingers, and knew it wouldn't be enough. The dress was cut low, and he dipped his hand inside, feeling the warm skin, the pebbling nipple, and he needed to put his mouth on her.

It was a simple enough matter to pull the dress down, exposing her to his hungry eyes, his hungry mouth. She let out a little gasp, but she made no effort to cover herself, she simply stood there, offering herself to him, and he wanted to say no, damned well should say no, but he couldn't. Just a taste, he told himself, and he took her nipple into his mouth, sucking at it.

She let out a cry of surprise, and he would have made himself pull away, but her hands reached up and cradled his head, held her to him, and he sucked harder, using his teeth, and her quiet moan of pleasure went straight to his groin.

He'd never heard her moan before, and it lit a flame that burned brighter still inside him. Common sense and even sanity seemed to have left him, and he ran his tongue over her, drinking her in.

He slid his hands down her body, to her ruined skirts, and began to pull them up, exposing her legs to the cold night air, but she didn't stop him. Why didn't she stop him? He was rapidly getting past the point of no return, and he'd do just what he'd promised he'd never do, and take her virginity on the wet dirty floor of this old warehouse.

With a muttered curse, he tried to pull away, but her fingers tightened on him. "No," she whispered in a rough little voice. "Don't stop."

HER OWN WORDS should have shocked her, but Georgie was past thinking calmly. She only knew she loved the feel of him, of his mouth pulling at her breast. Of his hands as they skimmed up her legs, taking her petticoats with them. She wanted his hands on her bare skin, she wanted to lie naked in his arms, she wanted to do everything she only half understood. When Bertha had explained to her what happened between men and women, she'd been horrified. Now she was melting, wanting everything.

It was cold in the darkness and she was shivering, and she had to hope he wouldn't notice. She couldn't bear it if he stopped what he was doing, if he broke this magic world he'd wrapped her in.

"You're freezing," he said, and he stripped off his proper

butler's coat to wrap it around her. It held his body warmth, it smelled like him, and she breathed it in. He looked very different in his shirt sleeves, wilder, uncivilized, the way she wanted him, but he seemed to have regained some kind of control, for he tugged the front of her dress back up, covering her once more, and took a step away.

"Why did you stop?" she whispered.

"Because...because you're an innocent, and a child, and I don't want you."

"You don't?" she said in a small voice.

"I don't," he said firmly.

There was nothing she could say. The coat still held his body warmth, his scent, and she wanted to bury her face in its folds.

He had his back to her, thank God, so he wouldn't see her weakness, and it was almost pitch-black in the room he'd brought her to. He would never know that he'd just smashed all her hopes and dreams.

To her horror, a tiny sob escaped her, and she clasped her hand over her mouth to try to stop it. She could only see his silhouette in the darkness, but his back stiffened, and he slowly turned back to her.

"Christ almighty," he said, but he didn't sound angry. "Don't cry, Georgie."

"I'm...not," she said, her voice wobbly.

He came back to her then, his arms sliding around her, and she was warmed by the heat of his skin through the thin white shirt.

For a moment, she simply rested against him, content to absorb his heat and strength into her own body. And then shame covered her, and she tried to push him away, but he held her fast.

"Let me be," she cried. "You don't want me, I'm just an annoying little girl—"

"Who says I don't want you?" His voice was low and deliciously dark.

"You did. Just now."

"Well, I lied. I'd have to be a fool not to want you, and I've never been a fool."

"Then take me!" she wailed.

"That's one thing I'm not going to do," he said, tucking her against his chest, the bone and muscle of him.

Closing her eyes, she gave up then, too weary to fight him anymore. He was holding her close, his arms strong and possessive, and she knew this was all she'd ever have of him. It was then that she realized his heart was pounding, as fast as hers, and she took what small comfort she could in that fact.

"I love you," she whispered against his skin.

"No, you don't, lass," he said, his hold on her reassuring as his words speared her heart. "But you'll realize it soon enough."

She wasn't going to argue with him anymore. For the moment, she had him, all around her, and that would have to do.

GETTING BACK into the house on Corinth Street proved surprisingly easy. It was still dark when Rafferty woke her, but the rain had stopped, and the streets were deserted. It was clearly too late for the people who roamed in the night, and too early for the vendors and servants who woke up the great households. She was shocked to see how close they were to Corinth Place, and even Bertha was sound asleep when they crept in. Georgie stood in the kitchen, looking about her with surprise.

"Aren't they worried about me?" she said. "As far as they know, I disappeared into the night and never came home."

"I imagine Martina said something to cover you. She's good at thinking on her feet."

"But how would she know you were with me?"

"She knows I wouldn't let you fall into any danger."

"But..."

"Enough questions. Go on up to bed as quietly as you can and say nothing. I doubt anyone will ask."

It should have been reassuring, if she didn't know that her family simply didn't care, and her shoulders slumped as she turned.

"I should have taken my time with him," he said grimly. "He won't be hurting you again."

She turned to look at him. He was beautiful in the shadowy kitchen, with his blazing eyes and high cheekbones and that glorious mouth that had kissed her. She had never realized a man could be beautiful.

"Did you really kill him?"

He didn't answer her, which was answer enough. "Go up to bed, Georgie, and forget about tonight. Forget everything."

But that was thing she wasn't going to do. His touch on her skin, his mouth on her breast, his strong arms, had started a fire blazing within her, and despite what he said, she was going to cherish the memory.

"Goodnight ...," she said, then paused. "What's your full name?"

"It's Rafferty, Miss Georgie," he said, sounding annoyed.

But she didn't bother arguing with him. She trudged up the servants' staircase, making as little noise as possible, trying to understand her troubled soul. She wanted to cry. She wanted to go back down and throw herself into his arms. She wanted to throw herself on the floor in a temper tantrum like Norah tended to indulge in.

All she could do was climb into bed and wrap her arms around herself, remembering the feel of his arms, his body, his mouth. And she fell into a troubled sleep.

Chapter Twenty-One

RAFFERTY STARTED the day in a foul humor, one he couldn't very well indulge, but he snapped at Jane and growled at Martina. It was the least of his problems. The Manning women were at home to guests, and Georgie had come down late, hollow-eyed and refusing to look at him. Andrew Salton wasn't among the young men who surrounded Norah, which was a blessing. Rafferty was in a thoroughly devilish mood, and Salton had hurt Georgie. He might be tempted to take his revenge.

He headed to the door at the latest summons, opening it to reveal a footman in dark blue livery. Familiar-looking livery. "The Dowager Duchess of Ormond has come to call," he announced in a damnably loud voice, and the buzz of conversation dropped to a whispered hush.

For a brief moment, he considered shutting the door in the footman's face, but he knew he couldn't get away with it. Keeping his expression impassive, he opened the door wider to usher the tiny figure of his grandmother into the house.

She took one long, meditative look at him, wiping out any fond hope that she didn't know he was here, and then nodded. "You clean up well," she said in an icy voice, and swept past him into the salon.

Under any other circumstances, he would have found the Mannings' flustered response to their august guest to be amusing. Liliane Manning had dropped her fan in her hurry to rise and curtsey, and even Norah looked properly cowed. He allowed himself a brief glimpse at Georgie, then wished he hadn't. She was looking at the dowager duchess, the woman with the same vivid blue eyes that were a match to his, and there was an odd expression on her face.

She couldn't have figured it out, he thought. How could a butler be connected to a peer of the realm? If he stood still long enough for Georgie to confront him, he'd simply tell her he was a bastard offspring of the old duke, and she'd have no choice but to believe it. It was far more likely than the truth. And he was a bastard in word and deed when it came to Georgie, even if he was as legitimate as Georgie herself. This would convince her that he truly was out of reach, though in fact he wasn't sure which was lower on the rungs of social acceptability—bastard or butler.

In the ensuing half hour, he might be tempted to think he'd imagined his grandmother's assessing gaze and cryptic words. She had been brought up by high sticklers, and she was social, gracious, and charming, setting the nervous room at ease. Everyone except Georgie, who kept watching the two of them, as if she couldn't believe her eyes. Damn it all!

The dowager duchess rose gracefully when the prescribed time had come to an end, and he wondered if he dared disappear. Her footman had remained in the hallway, standing at attention, his eyes straight ahead, so clearly he had no idea she had come for any other reason than to visit her neighbors. When she rose, Rafferty moved to open the door for her, forestalling the footman, and she paused, looking up at him.

"I have requested the receipt for the wonderful scones Lady Manning is famous for. You will bring it." There was no question of disobedience in her voice, and he nodded, never having seen her famous scones.

"As you wish, Your Grace," he said in a low voice.

"This afternoon." She glanced back into the room, and her eyes lit on Georgie for a moment, before glancing at Norah. "I don't know what game you're playing, but enough is enough."

Fortunately her voice was so low and angry that only he could hear it, though he spared a quick glance into the room to make certain. They were all looking suitably awed by their august visitor. Everyone but Georgie, who was watching the two of them with barely disguised interest.

And then his grandmother was gone, and the room broke into nervous chatter. Rafferty disappeared back into the hallway, out of Georgie's range of vision. She saw more than he would have liked, but he could only play it as it lay.

It wasn't until the last guest left that the dam broke. "Would you believe it?" Liliane said in awe. "The Dowager Duchess of Ormond visiting us! We've come up in the world. I was afraid they disapproved of the heir's attentions to you and sent him away, but it must have been a mere coincidence. Mark my words, she was checking to see if it would be a suitable alliance."

"I'm not going to marry him—he's too much of a boy," Norah said haughtily.

"We'll see. He might not be back from his grand tour in time. Still, it's very encouraging."

"Not interested," Norah said sternly. "Let George have him. He's better than a butler."

"Stop that at once, Norah," her mother decreed. "That's just silliness."

"Talk to George about it and you'll see how serious she is."

Rafferty kept his face impassive when Liliane Manning gave him the receipt for the scones, though he'd had to listen to Bertha's complaints as she laboriously wrote it out, and then he was out in the crisp fall air, heading for Ormond House for only the second time In fifteen years.

He went to the servants' entrance, in the unlikely hope he could simply drop off the paper, but he'd forgotten how gossip spread through a household. The kitchen at the house was positively crammed with servants, from housemaids to footmen to the august butler himself, someone new to Rafferty. He ignored them all, ready to thrust the paper into the cook's meaty hand and beat a retreat, when old Robinson the gardener pushed through the crowd of innocent-looking servants, his old eyes full of tears, and Rafferty felt a pang.

"Master Jamie," he said in a wavery voice. "I thought never to see you again."

He should have looked at him blankly, denied the name, and escaped. But Robinson had put him on his first pony, had taught him how to whittle, had been his companion in mischief. He was an old man now and the other servants were watching them, hanging on their every word.

"Hello, Robinson," he said, and an audible sigh filled the room.

"Her Grace will see you now," the superior-looking butler announced, and Rafferty had no choice. He followed the man from the room, ignoring the excited buzz of conversation when the door closed behind him.

The house had changed little in the ensuing years, but then his grandmother was far from a frivolous creature. She would see no need to change the drapes or the wall coverings if the current were in good shape, and she was sitting in the small yellow parlor she'd always preferred, where he'd endured lectures on his bad behavior and exquisitely formal teas as she tried to drill some manners into a wild boy. When the butler pushed open the door and he saw his grandmother in her familiar chair, it felt as if all the years fell away and he was still an obstreperous child, too wild to accept his role in life.

"Thank you, Adams," her grace said, dismissing the butler. "We'll have tea in a few minutes."

A few minutes? How long was she planning on keeping him here, forcing him through the exquisite ritual once more? At least by now he could carry it off without rattling his cup or spilling his tea.

He heard the door close behind him, and took a step forward. "Grandmother," he greeted her in a low voice.

"You could come and kiss me," she said with some asperity, and he did so, his lips brushing her papery-thin cheek. His grandmother blinked, as if she had something in her eye, but showed no other reaction.

"Sit down, Jamie," she said. "You hurt my neck looking up at you. When in the world did you grow so tall? It doesn't run in our family. Your cousin is not that much taller than your father was."

He said nothing as he sat gingerly on one of her spindly chairs, having no answer. "Did you tell him?"

"He just left for his grand tour. I'll tell him when he returns."

"There's no need. I don't intend to make any claim on the family."

"And what if the family wants to make a claim on you?" she countered.

"It would be foolish. I'm the child of your youngest son, with two uncles and five cousins between me and the title. You don't need another heir."

"What if I want one?"

"I don't belong in this life anymore. It's been too many years."

"Are you going to try to convince me you belong as a butler?" she scoffed.

"I've done a good job."

"You've been there a week at most. Hardly a proper amount of time to shine in your new profession. What did you do before you fell in with the dreadful Mannings?"

"They're not dreadful," he protested instantly. "They're just foolish."

"As I said. The mother is an idiot, the older girl, while a great beauty, looks to be a harridan, and I've heard stories of the brother's drunkenness. Only the younger girl seems halfway presentable."

He resisted the impulse to protest. Neddy was a drunkard, Norah was indeed a harridan, and their mother foolish in the extreme. Trust his grandmother to know quality when she saw it, in Georgie's presence.

"They're my responsibility," he said in a reproving voice.

"They're beneath you."

His laugh was sharp and cynical. "I don't think so."

"What have you been doing these last fifteen years?" she demanded, changing tack. "Why didn't you come to see me?"

He ignored the faintly plaintive note in her voice. "I've been a sailor, a horse trainer, a highwayman, and a thief," he said defiantly. "This is the first honest job I've held in years."

She took it all in with no visible response. "How very adventurous of you," she said. "And did you enjoy it?"

"Yes."

"Then what made you seek honest work? Or do I already know the answer to that impertinent question?"

"What do you mean?"

"That girl is in love with you."

He wanted to snarl, but one didn't snarl at one's grandmother, particularly one as impressive as the Dowager Duchess of Ormond. "I don't know what you're talking about."

"She couldn't keep her eyes off you this morning. And you couldn't keep your eyes off her. I can hardly approve, but at least she seems to be better quality than the rest of her family."

"You're a snob."

"Of course I am. Would you expect anything less? So, when are you going to cease this ridiculous masquerade and come home? You may marry the girl if that's what you really wish—I'll talk to your uncle about it. Since he's the current duke, he'll have something to say about it, but I can handle him."

"Grandmama..." he said, then stopped. He hadn't used that word in over fifteen years, and he wasn't going to start now. "Your Grace, I have no interest in marrying."

"I like 'grandmama' better. Are you planning on breaking that girl's heart? She's clearly set on you, and while you can do better, you could also do a lot worse. There's something pleasing about the girl, and I'm certain the rest of our family will welcome her with open arms. As they'll welcome your return."

"I'm not returning." His words were short, clipped.

"Don't be ridiculous. Sooner or later, someone is going to recognize you, and the scandal would be appalling."

"You've never been worried about scandal in your life. You simply rise above it. And I expect my disappearance at age sixteen caused enough of a scandal already."

"And just why did you leave?" she demanded. "You left no note, you were just gone."

"I didn't want to join the church or the army, and my uncle was determined to whip me into shape. Besides, no one needed me around—I was just one of too many cousins."

She pressed her thin lips together in rampant disapproval, eyeing him, and then her mouth softened. "I want you back, Jamie," she said in gentle voice. "I don't think I could bear it if you were to disappear again."

"I won't." He'd made his decision, and abandoning his grand-mother wasn't in the cards. "I'm not going to rejoin the family, but I'll keep in touch, visit."

"From the Mannings' house?"

"No. I'm leaving that job. I've been there too long."

"You've fallen in love."

"No!" The denial was forceful, too forceful. "I have a job to do in that household, something that had nothing to do with being a butler. It's almost finished, and the sooner I'm away from Georgie, the sooner she'll be over her little crush."

"Georgie? What an extraordinary name. Still, she has a certain charm about her. And you've decided to break her heart."

"Her heart is none of my concern," he said sharply.

His grandmother said nothing for a moment, but her disap-proval was rampant. "You were always a kind boy, even if you were wild. I'm sorry to see you've lost that quality."

He had no intention of feeling guilty. The women in his life tended to come and go—there was no room for a wife. It would be easy enough to steer Georgie's affections in another direction. As soon as he found someone worthy of her.

"You don't know her—I do. She'll get over it quite quickly."

His grandmother's bright blue eyes, so like his own, were dark with disappointment, but she accepted her defeat gracefully. "You'll quit this absurd job?"

"Soon."

"But you refuse to come home. Where will you go?"

"I'll be fine."

"Where will you go?" she persisted in a flinty voice.

"I'll let you know."

"You'll disappear for fifteen years again. I hate to tell you, my boy, but I don't necessarily have another fifteen years to wait for you."

He said nothing for a long moment. "You're a worthy adversary, Your Grace."

"Grandmama," she corrected.

"I promise I'll tell you where I'm going. In truth, I have an old farm in Hampshire where I usually hole up. I imagine I'll be going there."

His grandmother said nothing for a long moment. "And I can't dissuade you otherwise?"

"No."

She sighed. "You always were a stubborn boy. The tea should be here by now—I don't know what's keeping them." She looked around her.

"They're probably listening at the door."

The speed with which the door opened attested to the accuracy of his supposition, and his grandmother gave the butler a ferocious frown. "It took you long enough," she said flatly. Rafferty surveyed him with professional interest. He was a much better butler than Rafferty was—adept at handling his grandmother and serving tea. Rafferty always managed to slop the tea slightly.

"I beg your pardon, Your Grace. There's a young lady wishing to see you."

"A young lady? How extraordinary! Did she come alone?"

Rafferty closed his eyes in frustration. There was only one possibility.

"Yes, Your Grace. She's insisting—"

The door pushed open behind him and Georgie rushed into the room, her hair coming down from its simple arrangement, her cloak barely clinging to her. "I beg your pardon, Your Grace," she said, hurriedly curtseying, "but we need Rafferty back home. Immediately!"

Georgie was no match for his grandmother. "Do you indeed, child? I collect you're the youngest Manning child. What urgent need do you have for your butler?"

Georgie blinked. "My mother requested him," she said after a moment's hesitation. "He's needed."

"So you said and your mother sent you out to procure him. How very strange. Sit down, child."

"I can't."

"Sit down." His grandmother didn't raise her voice, but Georgie immediately sat, cowed, and it took a lot to cow Georgie. "Never mind the tea, Adams," she instructed the butler. "It appears that Mr. Rafferty is needed at home for some desperate assignment, and he and Miss Manning won't be staying. You may go."

"But Your Grace..." Adams was horrified at this breach of good behavior.

"That is all." The door closed behind the man with a little more noise than expected, as the butler evinced displeasure at his summary dismissal.

"And now you," his grandmother said, turning to look at Georgie. "Do you always barge into things like a harum-scarum young lady? It won't do at all, I'm afraid. You'd best learn to behave as soon as possible, and I doubt your mother could put any sense into you."

"Why must I learn to behave?" Georgie asked, completely without guile. "I don't matter."

The Duchess sniffed. "I'll have to leave it up to you, Rafferty, to calm her wild Indian ways."

"I've tried," he said wryly.

"Try harder. Otherwise even I can't persuade the Duke."

In another minute, she'd claim him as her grandchild, and he couldn't afford to let that happen. Not if he were going to escape the trap he'd set for himself by coming here.

"I should take Miss Georgiana home," he said, rising. "It's growing late..."

"Very well. But bring her back to me when she's civilized. I was always a harum-scarum child myself."

Belatedly, Georgie rose, managing a clumsy curtsey, and he was about to take her arm and escort her out of the room when the Duchess spoke again. "Come here, child."

Georgie cast a questioning glance at Rafferty, and he nodded. She approached the Duchess carefully, as if she were a basket of snakes.

"Closer!" the woman demanded. "My eyes are still strong but I want a good look at you. You have a stubborn chin."

"Yes," said Georgie meekly.

"But you're pretty enough, though no great beauty like your sister."

Georgie swallowed. "Yes, Your Grace."

"But I think you'll do," she pronounced finally. "Though it won't be easy for you."

"What won't?" she asked, but Her Grace had had enough.

"Take her away, Rafferty. It's time for my nap." And he ushered her from the room.

There was no question whether they should leave by the main entrance, and he didn't say a word to her until they were well on their way. He looked down at her, glowering.

"Have you run mad? What in the world made you come after

me, and without Martina to keep you company. My...the old lady must have thought you were a perfect hoyden."

"Not perfect," she said with a trace of her old impudence. "But I couldn't leave you there. I know what she wanted."

"You do?"

"She wants to hire you as her butler!" Georgie said. "And I know why!"

"Why? My charm of manner? My stalwart frame?"

"Your eyes. You both have the same eyes," she said.

He didn't show his reaction. "And why should that matter?"

"Because you're clearly related to her. You must be some bastard offspring of her family, and she wants you there because—"

"If I were an Ormond bastard, they'd want me a thousand miles away," he said. "Not living cheek by jowl. You're wrong, Georgie. You've let your imagination run away with you again."

"Then why did she specifically say you were to bring her Bertha's receipt? Why were you sitting in her presence?"

"She's democratic in her principles."

Georgie's scoffing laugh was answer enough.

"Let me assure you that she has no interest in me becoming her butler, or any other kind of servant. She's merely an eccentric old lady who wanted to find out more about the Mannings. The heir Is smitten with your sister, you know."

"Everyone is," she said glumly.

"They've sent him off on his grand tour to get him away from temptation, but just in case that doesn't work, they wanted to know more about your family."

"And you told them? Of course you did—how could one say no to such a formidable woman? That's what she must have meant when she said I would 'do.' That I'd be the proper sister-in-law for a duke."

"I don't think that's going to happen."

"Good," Georgie said. "Because Norah doesn't deserve everything she wants."

"And she wants to be a duchess?"

"Doesn't everyone?"

"Do you?"

"No. I want to marry a butler."

He froze, halting their forward stride. "Stop that," he said testily.

"You know it's true."

"I know you're a silly little girl. We're almost back at Corinth Place, and I want you to behave yourself."

"Like we did last night?"

"Forget last night. God knows I have."

Her face whitened, as if from a blow, and the familiar guilt assailed him. He wanted to take her in his arms and tell her he hadn't forgotten, that it had just flamed his hunger into something ravenous, but he kept silent. She was a child, he told himself. She needed to face the ugly truth.

But by that time they'd reached Corinth Place, and there was nothing more to be said. She started up the broad marble stairs, now devoid of dirt and lichen, and turned to look back at him, as if expecting him to join her.

It was the last thing he was going to do. "Go on, Miss Georgiana," he said formally. "That's your door, and this is mine." Without another word, he turned and took the side path down to the basement.

The kitchen was thankfully deserted when he let himself in, and he breathed a sigh of relief. He had a lot to think about. One thing was certain—whether he liked it or not, he'd regained his acquaintance with his aging grandmother. She was right—he couldn't simply disappear for another fifteen years. She would now have to be part of the few people he trusted, the only member of his makeshift family who was actually related to him. He wondered how she'd react to the truth about Martin.

And that left the problem of Georgie and her inconvenient crush. The crush he'd taken advantage of, time and time again. One of these days he was going to give in entirely, and he'd hate himself afterward. She was someone he wanted to protect, not ruin. But she was so damned tempting.

He heard the crash all the way down in the kitchen, and his first thought was Neddy hitting the bottle again. He'd been surprisingly sober the last few days, but those things seldom lasted. But then he heard the beauty, screeching in full voice. There was no sound from Georgie, but she was most likely the object of Norah's wrath, and he took the servants' stairs two at a time till he reached the second floor.

"We have no money for your little megrims. I can't imagine you asking Father for a cottage in the country. Apart from how shocking it would be, we're destitute."

"Then stop demanding new clothes all the time!" Georgie shot back.

"You're the one who got new gowns, not me," Norah hissed. "And I wonder what you had to do to get them."

"You're a witch. It's no wonder no one wants to marry you!"

"I've got a great many more suitors than you have. Even Andrew Salton would rather have me—you're just a fallback."

"I hate you!"

Norah reached out slapped her sister hard across the face, and Rafferty had had enough. He'd been listening to the sisters quarrel with a mixture of annoyance and amusement, but Norah had gone too far. She raised her hand to slap George again but Rafferty moved swiftly enough to catch it, yanking her away from Georgie. Norah responded by slapping him, and he was so sorely tempted to belt her back that he clenched his fist. He didn't hit women, even those begging for it.

"You'll not hit your sister," he said in a low, menacing voice.

She looked like she wanted to slap him again, but something in his eyes stopped her. "Such a knight errant," she mocked. "You two deserve each other. I've had enough of both of you." Yanking her hand free, she stomped away from them with a fraction of her usual well-contained grace.

"I hate her," Georgie said with a sniffle. "She was lying in wait for me when I came upstairs, ready to attack. At least I'm not sitting around waiting for the axe to fall. I've come up with a plan, and everyone would be a great deal happier if I were out of the picture."

"Don't let her bother you, Miss Georgie," he said in his best, avuncular voice. "She's just jealous."

Georgie gave a watery laugh. "The beauty of the season is jealous of her awkward younger sister? I don't think so."

He wanted to tell her she was beautiful, but he didn't dare. Society would always flock to the striking Norah, whereas he was inexorably drawn to Georgie, with her wide eyes, her sweet mouth, her softly rounded body. All of which were off-limits to him, he reminded himself.

"What's all this about a cottage in the country?" he said, not bothering to his the disapproval in his voice.

"Nobody wants me here. You think I'm a tedious child, and I'm not, but you won't believe me!" They were standing too close, and he could smell the faint scent of lavender that always accompanied her. He took a quick step back, away from her.

"You'll marry a nice young man," he said gently, hating those words. But anything was better than immuring herself in the country, away from her family. "And you'll be very happy."

"I don't want to marry anyone except you. I love you."

He had to stop her, anyway he could. "Don't be a child," he said, knowing the words were cutting. 'You're too young to know what love is."

"I am not! I love you and if I can't marry you, I won't marry anyone!" she shot back, and the tears in her blue eyes almost unmanned him.

"Then maybe the cottage in the country is a good idea after all," he said, his tone sharp, and he half expected her to wince with the cruelty of the blow. He had no intention of letting her throw her life away, even if her father could be persuaded, but he wasn't about to tell her that. She needed to give up her romantic illusions —he was a bad man, not love's young dream.

But she pulled herself together with dignity, her eyes still bright with unshed tears. "I'm so glad you approve," she said in an icy voice, and she turned and walked into her room, slamming the door behind her.

He wasn't alone in the hallway, and he turned to see Martina looking at him with a reproving expression in her dark eyes. "You cocked that one up for sure," she said. "Doesn't the girl have enough trouble with that bitch of a sister?"

"She doesn't need me making things worse," he said bitterly. "The sooner I'm out of here, the sooner she'll get over it."

"Will she? I think you underestimate a woman's heart."

"She's not a woman, she's a girl!" he protested.

'Where do you think women come from?" Martina asked archly. "You need to make up your mind."

"I already have!" he snapped. "I need to get away from this madhouse and its inhabitants."

Martina said nothing, but her expression was answer enough.

Chapter Twenty-Two

THE NEXT DAY, Martina rushed into the darkened bedroom with a flurry of skirts. "What's wrong with you, Miss Georgie? We're leaving in half an hour and I haven't had time to pack for you."

"I'm not going," Georgie croaked in a hoarse voice. "I'm sick."

"Oh, no!" Martina began to draw the curtains, letting light into the room, and Georgie moaned loudly, turning her face into the pillow. "What's wrong?"

"I have a putrid sore throat," came the weak reply. "I can barely swallow, my head aches, and I feel feverish."

"But we're all leaving for the Hendersons' country estate! You can't stay behind!"

"I can't go," she said with a trace of firmness. "I'm too sick. We can't afford to have Norah catch it."

"It's simple enough, then," Martina said, drawing the curtains back again, plunging the room into darkness. "I'll simply stay behind."

"You don't have to," Georgie said pitifully. "I'm certain a few days in bed and I'll feel right as rain."

"Don't be silly, of course I'll stay behind," Martina's voice was firm.

"What's Georgie doing?" Norah appeared in the doorway. "We'll be late. Get out of bed!"

"Miss Georgie's sick, Miss Norah," Martina said calmly. "I'll be needing to stay behind and look after her."

"Noooo!" Norah shrieked. "I need you with me. No one else can do my hair half as well."

"But Miss Georgie is—"

"I don't care what she is. She'll be fine. Bertha can look after her."

"Bertha can look after whom?" Liliane appeared in the doorway, and Georgie emitted a heartfelt moan of misery. "She's gone off to visit her sister—I told her to since we weren't going to be at home."

"Well, then, those two slatternly girls can look after Georgie!" Norah snapped. "I'm not doing without my maid because Georgie's been selfish enough to catch an ague."

"Do without your maid? Don't be absurd, of course Martina's coming with us. You don't need her here, do you, Georgie?" Her mother stayed in the doorway, loath to come any closer to the patient.

"No," Georgie whispered. "I'll be fine."

"You can't leave her here with just Rafferty," Martina said, and Liliane looked troubled for a brief moment, then brightened.

"He's already gone off as well. After all, the man deserves some time off considering that he's not being paid. The two housemaids will look after her—after all, she won't want to eat anything and it wouldn't involve much more than bringing her an occasional cup of tea."

"What if she gets worse?" Martina demanded, just the tiniest note of asperity in her rich voice.

"Oh, she won't," Liliane said carelessly. "Georgie's strong as an ox. In fact, I expect she'll be fine by this afternoon. She should come with us—"

"No!" Norah shrieked again, and Georgie slunk down deeper into the bed. "I'm not letting her make me sick too—I have too much to do. She can stay behind—she wouldn't want to make anyone else sick."

"But what if she gets worse?" Martina persisted.

"Then one of the maids can go for the doctor," Liliane said. "Not that we have the money to spare, so it would be far better if we dispensed with him. A nice long nap and a cup of gruel will do wonders, I expect."

"Who's making the gruel?" Martina said.

"I'm sure one of those girls can manage. I'll have my husband leave a note for Rafferty—he's gone out someplace. We'll only be gone three days—everything will be fine. Georgie doesn't want us to change our plans for her, do you, Georgie?"

"No, Mama," she croaked.

Martina stood there, not moving for a long moment. "You mean we're going to simply take off and leave Miss Georgie behind?"

Liliane eyed her with hauteur. "That's exactly what we're going to do. This party is too important—the Viscount Canfield will be there and he's been most particular in his attentions. Georgie wouldn't want to interfere, now would you, Georgie?"

"No, Mama," she said again.

"Then come along, and let the poor girl get some rest. Don't worry—she'll be fine. Georgie is as strong as an ox."

Georgie let out a faint whimper of agreement, and Liliane gave her a brilliant smile.

She waited for the door to close behind her vociferous family, and then managed a creditable coughing fit. Not enough to alarm them, though the thought of her family being worried about her was remote indeed. And then she snuggled down in the bed, hugging herself happily. She was going to have Rafferty all to herself. There was no limit to what she might accomplish.

§&.

THE AUTUMN NIGHT had a decided chill—winter was coming, and Rafferty huddled in his coat as he strode down the street back to the house on Corinth Place. The moon shone brightly overhead, but there was no one about—Corinth Place was down on its luck and there were no glittering parties to fill the streets with carriages and party-goers. The Manning house was typical of the rest of the buildings on the square—like a grande dame gone to seed. No one would make the mistake that there was anything worth stealing from its fallen grandeur.

He ducked down the back steps to the kitchen, letting himself in and shutting the door behind him. The house was cold—the other servants were gone, the family off to some house party in the countryside, and he breathed a sigh of relief. No Georgie to pop up and distract him, and she was so very distracting. With luck, she'd find the perfectly sweet young man to adore her and treat her with the exquisite care she deserved. He couldn't imagine such a man, but one had to exist.

Except a sweet young man would be bowled over by her. She needed someone a little older, old enough to get her out of the scrapes she was always falling into, old enough not to get carried away by her flights of fancy. She needed someone to love her, completely, but someone who wouldn't get cozened by her wild imagination.

He knew what she needed, and she wasn't getting him. He'd told her straight out, he wasn't the marrying kind. It would be one thing if he didn't have his history behind him...no, none of that mattered. She wasn't for him, no matter how damned tempting she was, and days without her would soon set his wavering mind to rights.

The kitchen was icy—no great fire in the stove, no lights to brighten the darkness. Not that he needed them—he'd grown used to navigating in the dark, and he moved through the deserted house on silent, sure feet.

He hadn't meant to come back that night—his plans were simple. Do one last sweep of every nook and cranny, and if

Beldon's cache was there, he'd find it. He'd told Billy Stiles as much—this was the last chance, and if it wasn't there, he was giving up. Billy hadn't looked pleased.

"If you can't find it, maybe me and my men can," Stiles had said, his flat black eyes drilling into him.

"You're not to touch the place. The family is under my protection," he said, controlling his rage with an effort.

"That doesn't say much. Who've you got to stand by you—a catamite and a cook? I'm tired of waiting."

"I've got three days. If it's there, I'll find it."

Stiles had made a harrumphing noise before flashing his teeth at Rafferty. "I'll give you that," he said. "And not an hour more."

He wished he could believe him, but Billy wasn't the kind of man who sat around and waited. Rafferty had put him off long enough, and by the time the Mannings returned, they were going to be in very grave danger. There'd been a family slaughtered in Mayfair last year, killed in the midst of a robbery, and if the police suspected it was Stiles and his men, they weren't doing anything about it. Stiles wouldn't hesitate hurting Georgie if he thought it would get him what he wanted. Hell, he didn't even need that incentive. Billy liked to hurt women.

Knowing that, Rafferty couldn't just go off and get a well-deserved rest. He needed to use every spare minute he had looking for the damn money.

He moved through the darkness on silent feet, heading toward the top floor and the servants' rooms. Only Martina slept up there, and she'd gone through everything with a fine-toothed comb, but another set of eyes might pick up on something new. He moved past the closed bedroom doors, heading for the back stairs, when he heard a sound.

It was just a small scuffle, probably nothing more than an errant mouse. But it had come from Georgie's room, and there was no way he was simply going to walk on by.

He pushed the well-oiled door open silently, peering into the stygian darkness, and saw nothing. He was about to close it again, when he heard the scuffle, and something moved by the fireplace.

He always carried his knife, even when dressed in full butler's regalia, and he slid it out, prepared for anything, when a dark figure rose from the floor, and he half expected a ghostly moan. He was about to fling the knife when the creature spoke, stopping him cold.

"Rafferty?" came Georgie's strained voice in the darkness, and he dropped the knife, shaken.

"What the hell are you doing here?" he demanded, moving into the bedroom in a blur of speed, catching hold of the dark figure. It was Georgie, all right, wrapped in a dark blanket, and he wanted to shake her. "Why didn't you say something sooner—I could have killed you!"

"I didn't know it was you," she said, her attempt at sounding practical belied by the tremor in her voice. "I thought you might be the man with the teeth."

"This house is supposed to be empty. Why aren't you with your family in Kent?"

"I was sick," she said in a stronger voice.

"You don't sound sick."

"I'm better now."

Damn the girl. "And they just left you behind?"

"They thought Jane and Betsey would look after me, but they never showed up."

"I told them they could take the next few days off." He clutched the heavy blanket wrapped around her shoulders. "Why are you wearing this?"

"I was cold, and I couldn't get a fire started, and there were no candles...."

He released her, striding to the window and pushing open the curtains. The bright moonlight flooded the room, and he could see the frost on the edge of the glass. He turned back to her. "It's a wonder you don't catch pneumonia in this freezing house. What in the world were your parents thinking? That I'd take care of you? Where's Martina?"

"Martina went with them—Norah insisted. I told you, they thought Betsy and Janie would look after me, but I never saw them, and they probably didn't even know I was here." Her teeth weren't chattering, but he could tell it was taking her a great effort to keep up the pretense of warmth. "Can you start a fire?"

He looked down at her, not bothering to hide his frustration. Were her parents complete idiots, to leave her in the dubious care of a man? But then, to them he wasn't a man, he was only a servant, and therefore no threat to their younger daughter.

They had no idea. "We're getting out of here," he said abruptly.

She blinked. "Why?"

"Because it's not safe. Anyone can see the house is empty, and it's ripe for thieves and burglars." *And Billy Stiles*, he added silently.

"Don't you want to stop them?" she asked.

"I would if you weren't here. It's too dangerous to wait around here hoping no one comes to investigate. Where's your heavy cloak? It's cold outside."

"Er...I don't really have one," she confessed. "Won't this blanket do?"

He growled, low in his throat, and stripped off his heavy winter cloak, pulling it around her unresisting body. "That'll do until we get where we're going," he said grimly, ignoring the chill that ran over him. She must have been freezing, huddled up in that blanket.

"Where is that?"

He didn't bother to enlighten her. This night was turning into a disaster, and all it would take would be for Billy Stiles to show up with half a dozen of his men. Which he'd swore he wouldn't do, which meant he'd be there any time now. If Georgie had been where she belonged, he could have stayed there and made sure Billy and his mates didn't do too much damage. As it was, the best he could do was get Georgie the hell away from there and hope for the best.

"Come along," he said. "We can't afford to waste time." He took her arm, thanking God it was encased in his heavy wool coat, and steered her from the room.

§

THE COAT WAS warm with his body heat, and it smelled like him, masculine and delicious, and she had to behave herself and not snuggle down in it the way she wanted to. He was angry—well, she'd expected no less. He'd been doing his best to avoid her, and now he was stuck with her. She knew she ought to feel guilty about it, and a small part of her did. But most of her was simply reveling in the warmth of his coat around her and the strength of his arm as he led her through the inky blackness of her deserted home.

He seemed to have cat's eyes, seeing in the dark with no trouble where she would have stumbled and fallen. To her surprise, he didn't take her to the front door, but instead headed toward the side door and the tangled garden, guiding her through it with barely disguised impatience.

And then they were out in the chilly night air. A wind had blown up, tossing her loose hair about her, and the bright moonlight had disappeared behind a bank of clouds, plunging the street into darkness. Still, he led her on, sure-footed and silent, and she could feel the disapproval coming off him in waves.

Guilt assailed her. "I'm sorry," she offered in a small voice, but he said nothing, moving determinedly forward.

"Do you really think the man with the teeth will come to our house?" she tried again.

"His name is Stiles, and yes, I think so. You're just damned lucky I decided to check the house before I went home."

"Home? What do you mean? Isn't Corinth Place your home?"

"Not by a mile. Now keep your head down and keep quiet. We don't want to draw any unwanted attention."

"You're mad at me," she said, ignoring his warning.

He stopped, so quickly she barreled into him, but he caught her before she could fall against his big, warm, safe body. "If you were anyone else, I would have left you in the deserted house. Now stop talking and keep up."

She stopped talking.

They were in a better part of town. The street was well-lit, the buildings looked more prosperous, and there were carriages and well-dressed couples all around. He paid no attention to any of it, and she could do nothing more than try to keep up with him, his hand strong on her arm. She barely had time to observe the building they stopped at—it was tall, white granite, and fairly new if she had to guess. He dragged her to the front door, pulled it open, and ushered her inside.

They were greeted by a long, sweeping staircase and several closed doors, and he went to the first one, using another key, and opened it onto darked rooms. Yanking her inside, he closed the door behind them, locking it, sealing them in.

"Where are we?" she whispered as he moved her into through the foyer.

"What does it look like? Rooms for let." A light flared, and he lit a candle, one small argument against the darkness.

She looked around her. It was in better shape than the house on Corinth Place, with good furniture, paintings, and expensive curtains that blotted out the moonlight. "Whose rooms are they?"

"None of your business." He moved through the room, lighting candles. There was a fire banked in the hearth, and the room was pleasantly warm.

"Won't we get caught being here?" she persisted.

"No." He reached behind her and pulled his heavy coat off her shoulders, then stared at the woolen dress she was wearing.

"Why are you wearing that rag—I thought I burned all your old dresses?"

"This was the warmest I had. I couldn't start the fire and I was freezing." She was suddenly aware that her hair was loose down her back, and she put a quick hand to it.

"Listen to me very carefully. I have to go out. You're to stay here and go to bed."

"No!" she protested, suddenly panicked. "I don't want to be here all alone; what if the owner comes back?"

"He won't. There's a bedroom beyond the dining room—go there and get some sleep. I'll be back by morning." His voice was implacable.

"But..."

"No arguments. I'm angry enough to beat you right now, and it won't take much more to put me over the edge."

She was silenced only for a moment. "You wouldn't hurt me," she said confidently.

"Just don't push me. If you aren't here when I get back..."

"I will be," she said. "I promise." The very thought of going out alone into the night air was terrifying. She hesitated. She wasn't used to him being angry with her. "Do you have to go out?"

"If you don't want your house destroyed, I do," he snapped. "Why in the world didn't they take you with them?"

"I told them I was sick," she confessed.

"For God's sake, why?"

"Because I wanted to be with you."

There was no missing the frustration in his eyes. "Well, you bollixed things completely. Get in bed and stay there! I'll deal with you when I get back."

He locked the door when he left, effectively locking her in, and she stuck out her tongue at his receding back. She was tired, she was hungry, and she was guilty, and she wanted Rafferty to take care of her, not to yell at her. She picked up a candle and wandered through the rooms.

They weren't sumptuous by any means, but there was a casual elegance about them that reminded her of something, and she explored the dining room, library, and small salon before she finally found the bedroom. She stopped in the doorway.

The bed was large, welcoming, and she breathed a sigh of relief. Curling up beneath those heavy covers seemed an absolutely delightful thing to do, and she walked over to it, sitting down and bouncing slightly. It was going to be very comfortable. Leaning down, she removed her beautiful walking shoes, then stood, reaching behind her to loosen her skirt. She could dress and undress herself—she'd learned to when they'd lost their lady's maid, and it took only mild contortion to strip down to her chemise, then she folded her dress and petticoats in a neat pile. The dress was ugly, but it was warm, and there was a slight chill in the bedroom, although it had a similarly banked fire. Without hesitation, she pulled down the covers and climbed into the bed, snuggling in. If the owner came back, he'd be very surprised to have a stranger in his bed.

But she knew the owner wouldn't be back till morning. Somehow, some way, this place belonged to Rafferty. She could smell him in the sheets, warm skin and masculinity. She could sense him in the air. She had no idea how he managed to acquire such a place, but she didn't doubt her guess was right. The only man who was going to find her in his bed was Rafferty.

Chapter Twenty-Three

"WHERE'S YOUR LITTLE GIRL, RAFFERTY?" Billy Stiles greeted him from behind Sir Elston's desk. He was drinking the man's expensive brandy, the one indulgence the baronet had left, and his feet were on the top of the desk.

"She's in Kent with her family, of course," he said, moving into the room warily. He didn't trust Stiles further than he could throw him, and he could see the anger and frustration in his flat black eyes. "You know where they've gone—that's why you decided to ignore my warnings and have your men search this place themselves."

"And doing a fine job, aren't they?" he said with specious joviality. "I haven't heard any crashing or breaking. No one will be able to tell we've been here."

"I can."

"Well, that's just too bad, ain't it? It's your fault you haven't found anything. Been too busy sniffing around that girl's ankles. That's one thing I don't understand, old son. Why go after the young one when the other's such a beauty? You've always had an eye for the best, and that girl of yours is nothing special."

Rafferty looked at him calmly, resisting the strong temptation to tell him to keep his mouth shut when it came to Georgie. He already knew she was his weakness, and he couldn't afford to be weak. Not with an enemy like Billy Stiles. "You've got it all wrong, Billy. I'm not interested in either of them, but I've got a role to play if I'm going to find our money."

"Unless my men find it tonight."

There was a resounding crash from the kitchen and Rafferty hid his wince. Bertha would have his guts for garters if she came back to a disaster.

"Oh, dear," Stiles said. "They might be getting a bit impatient."

"Then you can imagine how I feel. Searching the place day after day, coming up with nothing. Except this." He pulled Norah's ugly diamond necklace from his pocket and dangled it in front of Stiles.

The man snatched it, peering at it closely. "This ain't paste?" he said suspiciously.

"No, the real thing. Found it in the attics."

"Pretty piece," said Stiles, taking it. "But where's the rest?"

"I told you I've searched everywhere. It's not here."

"You'd like me to believe that, wouldn't you? You'd go your own way and then come back to claim it when you think I'm not looking. The money's here, and it's mine."

"Ours," he corrected softly.

Stiles gave him a sour look. "Ours," he agreed reluctantly. "But I'm thinking it shouldn't be fifty-fifty since it's taking you so damned long to find it and you won't let me tear this place apart like it needs to be."

"That would be stupid. Someone would tell Bow Street and you'd be shit out of luck if you weren't well ahead of them. And even tearing this place apart is no guarantee that the money will show up."

Stiles gave him a sour look but didn't reply. "Are you going to help my men?" he demanded. "They're getting more and more riled up."

"I'll be cleaning up your mess—I'll be able to see if they've overlooked anything. Are you almost done?"

"Why in such a hurry, old sod? The night is young."

Another crash sounded from the kitchen, and Rafferty wondered what would happen if they actually found Belding's treasure. He could only hope so—it would leave him free to disappear without worrying what would happen to Georgie. Once he left, she'd stop thinking about him, and she'd find someone kind and honest to marry. Someone the opposite of him.

"I've got things to do," he said roughly. "Make sure your men put everything back when they finish." That wasn't going to happen, and he was going to spend the next two days tidying up the mess they made. Though he had no idea what the hell he was going to do with Georgie. She'd probably offer to help!

Stiles grinned at him, his teeth shining in the lamplight. "Of course they will. Trust me."

That was the very last thing Rafferty was going to do.

AFTER TWO SLEEPLESS HOURS, Georgie came to a very simple conclusion. She was going to have to seduce James Rafferty.

Not that she knew much, if anything, about seduction. Her only acquaintance was in the pages of racy French novels, and it was always the man who did the seducing. Unfortunately, it was clear she couldn't count on Rafferty to do his part. He was determined to protect her, and she was going to have to find some way to overcome his scruples. She was here in his bed, all wrapped up and cozy, and she was tired of waiting.

She had a perfectly natural hesitation about the act, of course. The way Bertha had described it sounded messy and embarrassing, but Bertha had assured her that men were crazy for it, and after a while, women even liked it too. She had her doubts, but she suspected what women really liked was the cuddling afterward, not the actual deed itself. And she'd go through all manner of distasteful things to feel herself wrapped in Rafferty's arms, have him kiss her again, gently. She wanted him to kiss her roughly even more—there had been something irresistible about the way he'd pushed her up against the door and claimed her mouth. Maybe those kinds of kisses were the reason women agreed to the whole mess—she knew she would.

But she had to make him want to kiss her. Want to lay her down on the bed and do the things Bertha had described in a matter of fact voice. She was a grown-up woman now—she could survive the act of copulation as so many others did. And it would be Rafferty touching her, Rafferty lying on top of her, Rafferty...

She'd found a basin of water and managed a makeshift bath, and then she looked at her reflection in the mirror. She looked ghostly pale in her plain white chemise, devoid of any of the laces or embroidery that decorated Norah's underclothing. It wasn't fair—she was going to go to bed with someone before her beauteous older sister did. She was the one who needed bridal underwear.

Her plan was simple. If Rafferty could be persuaded to debauch her, then he'd simply have to marry her. She'd be ruined for anyone else, thankfully so, and Rafferty would have no choice. It didn't matter that he said he didn't care for her—that was clearly a lie. He wouldn't kiss her, he wouldn't be providing her with pretty things, he wouldn't fight so hard to keep away from her if she didn't matter.

She was young but not that naïve—most butlers would take what was offered quite happily. Rafferty's diffidence only meant that he cared about her.

She turned from the mirror, a disconsolate frown on her face. It was inescapable—she was no great beauty like her sister, but for some reason Rafferty seemed to prefer her, when all her life she'd been simply the younger sister, easy to forget. Even Andrew Salton had been lying to her.

But when Rafferty looked at her, he saw her, really saw her. And she'd go through anything to keep it that way.

She was starving—stuck up in her room, she hadn't eaten anything but the stale toast from her untouched breakfast. If she was going to seduce Rafferty, she needed some sustenance; it wasn't going to be easy. Grabbing her candle, she made her way through the rooms until she found the small kitchen in the back. Did Rafferty cook for himself? She had made some progress with Bertha's tutelage, but she was going to have to learn more if she was going to take proper care of him.

She was good at toast, and there was half a loaf of bread in the scullery, but the big stove was banked down, making it a more dangerous task than usual. She burnt her hand, but success was finally hers, though making a pot of tea proved beyond her capabilities. She took her jam-smeared toast back into the salon, curling up on the window seat near the banked fireplace. The place was getting colder, and she shivered slightly as she tucked into the bread. And then she saw the brandy bottle.

If she were about to go through an ordeal, a little brandy might be just the thing to lessen her fears. She wasn't really frightened—Rafferty would take care of her. But Dutch courage was never a bad idea.

Except when she had three glasses. By that time she was deliciously warm, having stirred the coals with a fire poker that reminded her of the night she'd found him in her father's office, looking for the mysterious treasure he talked about, one that probably didn't exist. She had just started singing to herself when she heard the key in the lock, and she knew her time had come.

He looked tired, and bad-tempered. "I told you to go to bed," he said abruptly, locking the door and divesting himself of his warm coat.

"I was waiting for you."

His reaction wasn't promising. "I'm here now. Go back to bed."

"Where were you?"

"None of your damned business."

This was looking more difficult, and she wanted to snap back at him, but she controlled her irritation. "Was anyone at the house?"

"Your old friend Stiles was. It's a bloody good thing he didn't find you there—he's not known for his gentlemanly behavior."

"You're not doing too good a job yourself at the moment," she said sulkily. "He's your fault, not mine."

"True enough. He'll be gone by morning and I'll take you back."

"I want to stay here. This place belongs to you, doesn't it?"

He didn't look surprised. "It does."

"How does a beggar afford rooms in this part of town?" she demanded.

"I told you, I'm a liar and a thief. Everything I've told you has been a lie."

"You keep telling me you don't care about me," she pointed out. "Is that a lie?"

"Go to bed, Georgie."

She couldn't help but warm to the sound of her name in his deep voice. "Not without you."

Silence filled the room, the only sound the muted crackling of the fire. He stared at her, and she couldn't read his expression, but it definitely wasn't promising. "You're a child," he said after a moment.

"I'm twenty years old. Most women are married by my age. I want you to take me to bed."

"You want me to ruin you," he said, and there was no missing the exasperation in his voice. "That's the last thing I'd do."

This wasn't going well. "Why?"

"I've been trying to look after you, not destroy you...."

"Why?"

"My life is complicated enough without an overgrown girl in love with me," he snapped.

"Well, at least you admit that I love you."

"It's a crush, nothing more. If you were just out in society, you'd find someone more suitable and—"

"I found someone more suitable. Andrew Salton. And he was in love with my sister. In fact, you're the only man who's ever preferred me. I'll have to make do with you." She'd hoped to coax a smile from him, but he was deadly serious.

He was also beautiful, with those mesmerizing blue eyes, haunted now. "There will be plenty of men who prefer you to her. You haven't given it a chance."

"I don't want to...."

"I'm not arguing with you, Georgie. You've thrown my life into disarray and I need to get it back. As soon as Stiles finishes with the house, I'm taking you back there, and you'll help me clean up the mess he made."

"Of course," she said sweetly. "If you tell me what he's looking for. What you've been looking for—don't pretend you haven't. You were searching down in the coal cellar, you were looking through my father's office. What is it you're looking for?"

He looked at her in frustration. "It's none of your business."

"It's my house. Of course it is."

"If I tell you, will you go to bed?"

"Of course," she said promptly.

He sighed, leaning against the door. "I used to work for a man who had a great deal of money. Ill-gotten money, and he hid it before he died."

"And you think he hid it in our house? Why?"

"It was his house before he...was killed. He often stashed things there, and we've searched everywhere else. It's somewhere at Corinth Place, and Billy Stiles is determined to find it."

"And you?"

"I'm determined to find it too, just to get Billy off my back."

A cold certainty settled down around her. "So that's why you agreed to become our butler? Because you needed to search the house?"

"You gave me the perfect opportunity. With any luck, I should have been able to find it in a day or two. But as far as I can tell, it's nowhere."

"But why did you take such good care of us if you were only there to find some stolen treasure?" she said, fighting the disappointment that filled her.

"Temporary insanity," he said irritably. "If I'd known you were going to read all sorts of foolish things into my efforts, I never would have done so."

"So you're supposed to share this so-called treasure with Mr. Stiles?"

"I don't think sharing's in the picture. He'll take it all, and I'll let him. I don't need the damned money."

So much for being a beggar. She glanced around the room slowly, her brandy-infused glow fading in the wee hours of the morning. "Do you live here alone?" she asked abruptly. What if he had a wife, or a mistress? What if she was making an absolute fool of herself...?

"No," he said, and her heart sank. "I have someone who looks after me. A valet cum butler."

She couldn't help it, she laughed. "The butler has a butler? No wonder you were so good at your job."

He said nothing, and in the distant night air they could hear the bells of the new clock tower. It was four in the morning, and suddenly Georgie was very cold and tired. "I want to go home," she said.

"Stiles isn't finished. I'll take you back in the morning. Go back to bed and get some sleep."

She looked at him, at his haunted face and high cheekbones, at his unsmiling mouth and shadowed eyes. That's what she ought to do—leave him alone and go to bed, forget her dreams.

She climbed off the window seat, and her diaphanous gown floated around her. "I don't want to sleep," she said, and before she could think better of it, she crossed the room and reached up to him, sliding her arms around his neck. He didn't move, simply looked at her.

"What are you doing?" he said in a rough voice.

"Seducing you." Reaching up, she pressed her mouth against his.

He didn't move, didn't react, simply stood there as she kissed him, his mouth cold and unmoving. She pulled away. "I'm not doing a very good job at this," she said. "I really don't know what I'm doing."

"Go to bed, Georgie," he said in a low, gravelly voice.

She looked up at him, and knew she'd lost somewhere along the way. He really didn't want her—it had all been a part of his lies.

She knew her eyes filled with tears but she blinked them back, starting to pull away. "I'm sorry," she said in a small voice. "My mistake."

"No," he said with a growl. "Mine." He slid his arms around her waist and brought her up tight against him, and his mouth sank down on hers.

SHE WAS A FAR from a tiny woman, but she felt small and delicate in his arms, and she sank against him like she was coming home. The damned shift was practically transparent, and he could feel her breasts, her hips, against his body, and he knew he was surrendering. Surrendering to the aching need that had haunted him for the last five days, that stole his sleep and his common sense, and left him helpless to resist her when he knew he must. She was just a determined girl with an ill-advised crush, and he was going to take her to bed and do everything he dreamed about to her.

And then he was going to leave her.

He caught her face in his hands, holding her there, as he kissed the smooth planes of her cheeks, her forehead, her eyelids, wet with tears. She was crying, and he knew he ought to stop, but it was too late. They were salty tears on her lips, and he licked them off. And then he scooped her up in his arms and started toward the bedroom.

He didn't have to do this, he told himself. He could set her down on the bed, tuck her in, and leave. She wouldn't come after him. She'd used up her courage for the night, and she'd let him go.

Go where? He was going nowhere but to bed with Georgie, mistake though it was. He wasn't a man built for abstinence, for noble self-denial. He wanted this woman more than he could remember wanting any woman in his life, and he was going to take her.

Kicking the bedroom door shut behind him, he set her down on the bed. One low candle was burning, and it would gutter out soon, and he wanted to light a dozen more, so he could see her. But he didn't want to let go of her long enough to find the candles—she felt too good in his arms, smelled too sweet, and he laid her down in the middle of his big bed, following her down.

He wanted to take her then, to rip off her chemise, shove open his pants and plunge inside her. He needed surcease so badly, but he couldn't do that to her. She was a virgin, and he'd never taken one to bed before. He needed to woo her, arouse her, tease her. He had to make her his in every way possible before he got what he needed so badly, and the first step was getting rid of the blasted chemise that was getting in his way. It was flimsy, old, like most of the clothes she'd worn before he replaced them, and he wanted to rip it from her body. He didn't. The shift had a drawstring neckline, and he loosened it, his fingers deft and gentle, and slowly drew it down, exposing her full, perfect breasts to the moonlit room.

She gasped nervously, but didn't try to cover herself, and for a moment, he simply looked at her, drinking her in.

"Change your mind," he said, in a gruff voice. "Tell me no."

He could see her eyes glittering in the darkness. "Yes," she said. "I love you."

If he had any sense, he wouldn't let her say it, but some small part of him wanted to hear it. Women had often told him that they loved him, particularly in bed, but this was different. This was the first time he believed it.

He covered one breast with his hand, and the nipple was tight and beaded against his palm. He knew he should get her used to his touch first, but temptation was too strong, and he put his mouth on her as she let out a little squeak of surprise. He sucked at it her, using his teeth, using his tongue as his fingers toyed with her other breast, and he could feel the response surging through her.

"Oh, my," she whispered in a choked voice, and he smiled against her breast.

He was drawing the chemise down her body, and she made no attempt to stop him. Moving his mouth to her other breast, he pulled the garment off her hips, and she lifted them up so he could pull it away. And then his little chatterbox started to talk.

"I know what you're going to do," she said breathlessly.

"You do?"

"Bertha explained it to me years ago. And I really don't mind."

He slid his hand across her waist, down over her softly rounded belly. "You don't?"

She was biting her lips. "It's going to hurt."

"Yes. The first time."

"The first time?" she echoed. "You mean we'll do it more than once?"

"Usually," he said, as his long fingers slid into the tangle of curls at her apex and she jerked, then forced herself to lie still.

"But it doesn't hurt that much?"

"I don't believe so. But I've never been a with a virgin before."

"You haven't?" She sounded pleased but then gasped as his hands slid further between her legs. His touch was sure and practiced and slowly she began to relax, some of the tightness in her body loosening.

He moved up again, so that he could kiss her, distract her, as he began to coax some dampness from her. She continued to chatter.

"Most women find this perfectly acceptable," she said, in a tight voice as his fingers delved deeper. "I've heard some even grow to like it."

He hid a smile from her. "Occasionally."

"Do women tend to like it when you do it?"

He kissed her forehead, nuzzling her lazily. "Mmh-hmm," he murmured in agreement.

"Do you think I'll like it?" She was sounding nervous, the perfect time for him to pull away, leave her, which he would do, if he weren't such a very bad man.

"Maybe." It was a taunt, one he shouldn't give in to. No woman has ever left his bed unsatisfied. Georgie was more important than all the faceless other women, and he intended to leave her screaming his name before the night was through.

He wanted to taste her badly, but he wondered if she'd be too shocked. Bertha probably hadn't explained that, but he found he couldn't resist temptation.

"Just lie there," he said, in a gravelly voice, moving down her body. Her legs were tight together, and he laughed. "It doesn't work that way."

She relaxed her legs a fraction. "Are you going to do it now?"

"Do it?" he echoed, amused.

"What Bertha told me."

"Let's leave Bertha out of this. No, I'm going to get you ready."

"How?"

He started to move her legs apart, but she resisted. He kissed her then, full and hard and deep, holding nothing back, and she rose to meet him, her legs falling open.

He caressed her, with his hands, his mouth, working his way down her body until he reached her mound. "Don't be too shocked," he said, his voice light with amusement.

"Why would I... Oh, my God!" He had put his mouth

between her legs, and she jerked, trying to close herself off from him.

But he was prepared, holding her legs apart as he went down on her. She was sweet, delicious, and he'd forgotten how much he loved it. Loved this with her and her squeaky protests. She was shoving at his shoulders, trying to dislodge him, but he found her sweet spot and sucked, and she let out a loud, frightened moan.

He continued, using his lips, his tongue and his teeth, and at some point, she stopped fighting him. Threaded her fingers through his long hair and held him against her. It was easy to tell when she was near her peak, her breathing was short, her hips were moving, restlessly, and she stopped talking in full sentences, coming out with choked phrases like "oh my God" and "don't" and "more."

The "more" was permission enough. He brought her to the edge, holding her there, until she broke, letting out a satisfying scream. He moved then, wiping his mouth on the bedclothes as he surged over her. He was still dressed, and he tore away at his clothes, kicking out of them while she lay there and trembled in continuing reaction.

He couldn't wait any longer, and he started to move over her, when she reached out, stopping him, and he wanted to howl in frustration.

"Shouldn't I...do something?" she whispered in a strained voice. "Or do I just lie here and let you do it?"

He took her small hand in his, and he put it on his cock. She tried to shrink back but he held her there. Getting her used to the feel of him, the heat and hardness that needed her so desperately.

"This will never work," she whispered.

"Trust me," he said, when he knew that was the last thing she should do. He was about to ruin her, and he damned well couldn't stop himself, particularly when her fingers wrapped around him and explored him until he was ready to explode.

And then he was over her, between her legs, heavy and hard and desperate.

Her tear-drenched eyes flew open. "I don't..." She gasped. "I'm not ready... I'm afraid."

He started to pull back, knowing he should, but she put her arms around him, pulling him close. "Don't leave me."

He wanted to growl his frustration. She was killing him, but he held still, so close to heaven and yet so far. She looked at him, and there was no hiding the fear in her eyes, and he began to pull away.

"I want you," she said in a raw whisper, clinging to him, and his last qualm left him.

"Hush," he said, and he pushed into her.

Her cry was short and sharp as he broke the barrier, and he held still for a moment to get her used to the feel of him. She was panting slightly, and he kissed her softly and sweetly, and she let out her breath, accepting his invasion, accepting him.

He could've finished then and there, but he was greedy. He wanted to make her climax again with him inside her, wanted everything from her, and he began to move.

He started to pull out, but she clutched at him. "Don't... stop," she gasped, and it took all his battered self-control, not to see slam inside her.

But he moved slowly, rocking her back and forth, drawing a nascent response from her. She felt so good beneath him, and he wanted more. He wanted her to love him, and she swore she did.

It changed faster than he could have imagined, the slow rocking turning into something fiercer. She was arching up to meet him, their bodies sweat-slick in the early morning air as he thrust into her, harder, deeper, needing her and everything she was, loving her.

Her cry signaled her release, and she tightened around him, pulling his own response from him. He pulled out, though it killed him to do so, and spilled on the warmth of her skin, holding her as she shuddered against him.

He didn't give a damn about the mess; he pulled her against him, into his arms, listening to her racing heart, her rapid breathing, as he held her. For a moment, she was stiff in his arms, and then she sank against him, clinging to him.

"Did you survive?" he whispered when he found he could talk.

"I'm not sure," she whispered back.

"Do you want to do it again?"

"Again?" she sounded horrified. And then she gave a rusty little laugh. "Yes, please." And they did.

Chapter Twenty-Four

SHE WAS ALONE in the bed. Georgie opened her eyes, staring around the shadowy room. Daylight was filtering through the curtains, and she could hear the sounds of the city outside the window. She pushed herself up slowly.

She was achy, sticky, tired, and strangely close to tears. Where was Rafferty? No, she shouldn't call him that—that was his butler's name. He wasn't her butler, he was her lover, and all sorts of conflicting thoughts assailed her. Where was he?

There was a knock on the door, and she quickly dove beneath the covers again, unaccountably shy of this man who'd done so much to her body. But to her shock it wasn't Rafferty peering in the open door.

"You awake, miss?" the man said. "I've got a bath ready for you if you'd like, and Rafferty brought some clothes back from your house Then I'll make you a nice hot breakfast and we'll get you on your way."

She stared at him, nonplussed. "Who are you?"

"I'm Rafferty's man, Jenkins," he said easily. "He told me to take care of you while he looked after business. I've got tea and toast first to give you a little sustenance. You must be tired." There was no salacious meaning beneath the words, but Georgie could feel her face flush.

"Tea would be very nice," she said in a choked voice.

He came in the room, carrying a small tray. He didn't look like a servant, but then Rafferty didn't look like a butler. "Rafferty'll be back for you in an hour, so you can take your time, miss. Just don't let the bath get cold."

"I won't." She took a bracing sip of tea, and felt a little bit of her lost strength pour through her. She wondered how she was going to get from the bed to the bathtub—there was no sign of her discarded gown or her chemise, and she knew she had no choice but to wrap herself in a sheet like some ancient Roman goddess. She needed Rafferty. She needed him to smile down at her, she needed his arms around her. Instead, she felt like an interloper, a stranger in a strange place.

The bath was heavenly, so warm that she wanted to cry. Tears felt very close, and she wondered why. She'd made her choice last night, she'd managed to seduce him after all, and she didn't regret it. She just wanted him back, to tell her everything was all right, to tell her he loved her.

But there was no sign of him.

By the time she got back to the bedroom, wrapped once again in an abandoned sheet, the room had been changed, the bed made, the curtains open to the bright autumn day, the fire crackling in the fireplace. Her clothes lay neatly folded on the bed, including one of her new dresses.

She bit her lip. It was too bright a color for her mood—she'd prefer the old dark one to hide away in, but it had disappeared along with her old chemise. She looked and saw that a new one had been provided, clearly stolen from Norah's clothes press. It was made of whisper-fine batiste with tiny blue bells embroidered at the neckline and hem, a far cry from her own utilitarian undergarment, and she bit her lip as she surveyed it. Once more, Rafferty was taking care of her.

She dressed quickly, barely struggling with the fastenings, and surveyed herself in the mirror. Her hair was a mare's nest, tangled down her back, and she looked around until she saw silver-backed brushes on the washstand. Doing what she could with her hair, she braided it down her back, and then, straightening her spine, she stepped out into the main room.

She'd expected to see Jenkins. Instead, she stopped short as she saw Rafferty sitting in one of the chairs, drinking coffee.

He rose, and she didn't want him to. She had to fight the urge to turn and run back into the bedroom, but some latent bravery returned, enough to allow her to scoot across the room and drop down into the chair opposite him. This was not going to be pleasant, she knew it. There was no expression on his face—she might as well be a stranger, and she wanted to cry.

"I take it Jenkins looked after you?" he said in a neutral voice, settling back in his own chair.

"Very well. Thank you for bringing my clothes."

He merely nodded. "We'll go back to the house as soon as you're ready. It's a mess, but the girls are already working on it, and it should be habitable by tonight."

"Did they...did they find the money?" she ventured.

"No."

Silence fell. She needed him to smile at her, to tell her he loved her, to say something that would make this awkward interview better, but he said nothing. When she last saw him, they had been naked in each others' arms, and she'd been so happy.

But now he looked at her, and his extraordinary eyes were cool and emotionless. "You needn't worry about last night," he said, and she felt fresh color flood her face. "There won't be consequences. Martina will look after you."

"Wh...what do you mean?" She really didn't want to be talking about it in such a clinical manner, but he was giving her no choice.

"It's easy enough to fake virginity for your husband. No one need ever know you had a slight slip from grace."

The words were like a dagger in her heart, and grief shut down around her. He didn't care. Last night hadn't mattered to him, it was just another household problem to be solved. "What if I'm pregnant?" she said defiantly.

"You won't be. I pulled out. If there's any chance it didn't work, then Martina can see to that also."

She just stared at him in shock as he rose, draining his coffee and setting it down on the table. "Are you ready?"

She wanted to scream at him, throw something at him, hit him. But he simply stood there, seemingly barely aware of her, and she rose as well, a little unsteady, and moved past him to the door, saying not one word.

There was a hackney waiting for them, and he helped her in, then followed her inside, sitting far too close in the confined quarters. They travelled back to Corinth Place in an uneasily silence, and when he helped her out, he said one thing that was her death knell.

"I warned you, Miss Georgiana," he said in a low voice. "I'm a thief and a liar and a very bad man. You should never have come near me."

And there was nothing she could say.

HE HATED HIMSELF. Despised himself for giving in to temptation, not once but twice, for taking her and her innocence and reveling in the triumph. He'd wanted her so long, refusing to admit it, but once he did, he'd been almost insatiable. It was only the knowledge that she must be sore that kept him from going for a third and even a fourth time. She'd been so lithe and luscious in his arms, so sweetly curious and gloriously responsive, and he knew that despite his worst misgivings, she had to love him, at least a little bit.

And instead of comforting her the next day he'd been cold and dismissive, trying to push her away from him. It was that, or she'd be on the table with her skirts up to her ears, and he couldn't afford to give in again. The harm was done, but he had to do what he could to remedy things.

At least Martina would be there to see to things, to look after her and make certain she was all right. It had killed him, but he hadn't spilled inside her body, which would help avert pregnancy. If by any chance it hadn't worked, he'd do what he had to do, and ruin her life. But that was unlikely.

In fact, he'd found that if he bedded women and then didn't return for more, they grew particularly irate. All he had to do was keep his hands off Georgie and she'd despise him soon enough. Which would be a relief, wouldn't it?

By the time they reached the house on Corinth Place, his worst fears had been realized. The house had been ransacked, and Rafferty went from room to room in a mood so far beyond sour that he could only wish that Billy Stiles would show up. He was in a mood for violence, and there was no one he could take it out on. He'd already destroyed Georgie's sweet smile—the expression on her face was nothing short of heartbreak.

But her heart wasn't truly broken. She'd had a tumble with a servant, nothing more, and there would be no repercussions. She might think she was in love, but he knew better. It was simply childish infatuation, nothing more.

Except he was finding it harder and harder to think of her as a child after last night. She'd laid in his arms, warm and pliant, she'd welcomed him into her body, she'd held him as he found his release. She'd been shyly adventurous, doing what he'd told her, and she'd looked him with such adoration that it made him want to hit somebody. Where the hell was Billy Stiles when he needed him?

She'd gone straight to her room, and he hadn't seen any sign of her all day. It was no surprise—he'd been too busy driving Jane and Betsey to attack the appalling mess Stiles's henchmen had left behind to even think of her more than once or twice. A minute. The less he saw of her the better—he was having trouble keeping his distance, and he took out his own self-loathing on the girls, who accepted it naturally enough.

He did loathe himself. He should never have touched her, never have given in to overwhelming temptation. But her mouth had been so sweet against his, her eyes so full of longing, and for some unknown reason he'd wanted her too badly to stop himself. If he'd even stopped at the first time...

Even that hadn't been enough. He still wanted her, if he were honest. And she'd never let him touch her again—he'd seen to that quite effectively. She hated him, as he deserved to be hated, and that knowledge should have satisfied him.

Christ, he needed to get away from her. He hadn't seen Billy since early this morning, when they'd finished with the house. Maybe he was ready to give up his quest, and Georgie would be safe enough to leave behind.

And she could marry some young whelp who didn't appreciate her and have babies and be happy and he wouldn't ever have to think about her again.

He slammed his fist against the walnut paneling and then swore.

"You all right, Rafferty?" Jane asked.

"Fine," he barked back. "Can either of you cook?"

"'Course we can. Eggs and toast and the like."

"Then one of you make dinner for Miss Georgiana. See if she needs anything."

"Don't you usually look after her?" Janie asked.

"I'm too busy," he snapped. He'd broken the skin on his hand—he was going to have to bandage it. At least he hadn't broken any bones against the iron-hard wood.

But half an hour later, Jane informed him that Miss Georgiana didn't want any food, and she was, in fact, just sitting in a chair in her bedroom, staring at the fire, and he swore.

"Go home," he told the two girls. "We can finish this up tomorrow."

Neither one was about to put up any objection, and by nine

o'clock, the house was deserted. He went to the kitchen, sliced fresh bread and covered it with jam, made a pot of tea, and headed up to Georgie's bedroom. If she was sulking, so much the better —he just needed to make sure she had enough to eat and that she truly hated him, and his work for the day would be done.

He didn't bother knocking at her door, simply pushed it open and strode in carrying the tray. Jane was right—Georgie was sitting in a chair staring into the fire, no expression on her face.

"If you've finished sulking, it's time to eat something," he said, not the most promising beginning of a conversation.

She turned her head to look at him with awful majesty. "Go away."

"I'm the butler. It's my job to look after you," he said stubbornly.

"You did that last night," she said bitterly.

That stopped him for a brief moment. And his own uncertain temper rose. "I did what you asked me to do."

Her face was stony. "Always the perfect butler. Go away, then."

"Not until you eat something." He brought the tray over to her and before he realized what she'd intended she flipped it out of his hands, the tea pot flying.

"You're behaving like a child," he said.

"You always tell me I'm a child," she snapped. Damn, she was furious! Hell hath no fury like a woman scorned. "I'll behave like one if I feel like it."

He decided to try a different tactic. "Listen to me, Georgie. I'm sorry about last night—I should never have touched you...."

"Don't you dare apologize!" She sprang up from her chair and he took a hasty step back. "I...I..." And then to his horror, she burst into tears, sinking back into the chair again, and all his cool determination vanished.

"Georgie," he said, and like an absolute fool, he pulled her up and into his arms, wrapping himself around her.

He could feel her momentary struggle, and then she sank

against him, crying like some heartbroken child, and he wanted to beat whomever had made her so unhappy. But that was himself.

"You need to forget last night," he said in a low, soothing voice. "It was a terrible mistake—forget it ever happened. I was a bastard to touch you, and I'll regret it for the rest of my life, but it's over. It'll never happen again, and you can go on to a happy life with some nice young man who'll adore you as you deserve to be adored."

He felt her stiffen in his arms for a moment, and then relax as she pulled free of his embrace. He didn't want to let her go, but he knew it was the best thing. Tears were streaked down her pale cheeks, but she raised her head and smiled a bright, false smile. "I've already forgotten," she said, moving to the chair and sinking back down again, seemingly in control of herself once more. "I'm sorry I tossed the tray. I would have liked tea and toast."

He couldn't believe her. She was entirely calm, in control, smiling at him with her usual smile—no, it wasn't her usual smile. That was loving, besotted, adoring. This smile was merely polite.

But he believed her. "Then we won't speak of this again?" he said tentatively.

"There's no need to. Good night, Rafferty."

It was a goddamned dismissal, worthy of his grandmother the dowager duchess, and some unruly part of him rebelled at her perfect manners. He didn't want her calm and in control. He wanted...he wanted...

He had no choice. Channeling his grandmother's august sangfroid, he backed from the room without another word.

SHE WATCHED HIM GO, waiting for those wrenching tears to return, but something had dried them. A terrible mistake. He never should have touched her. He would regret it for the rest of his life.

She must have been truly awful in bed. There was a knack to

it, she'd figured that much, but she'd known and done nothing but lie there. No wonder he was disgusted with her.

He'd made her feel such things, such glorious, terrifying things, and he must have hated it. Hated her. Because otherwise he would have taken her back to bed tonight, and let her feel all those wild and petrifying emotions again. She'd sat in her chair waiting for him to come to her, and instead, he'd been full of excuses and self-recrimination. He was lost to her, she knew it when he'd held her in his arms like she was a broken doll, and he wasn't coming back.

She could survive. What choice did she have? He was going to leave—she knew now that he'd entered their household only to find some hidden cache of money. It had nothing to do with her. It had nothing to do with the clothes and the shoes he'd found for her, nothing to do with her feckless family. He'd been using them all, and now he was done.

He might even be gone the next morning when she woke up. She wouldn't be surprised if she was alone in the house, waiting for her family's return. Even Martina would disappear somewhere, and they'd be back where they were. And it was all because she'd made such a botch of things.

The French novels were woefully short on detail when it came to the mechanics of making love, but she knew that men didn't pay women to just lie there. There had to be more to it, but the very thought made her tremble in anticipation. If doing nothing had led to such a cataclysmic reaction, then what would happen if she...if she did what he did? Touched him, kissed him, licked him. Put her mouth on him?

She could go to bed and weep. She could bewail her mistakes and accept her fate—married to a man she didn't love who couldn't begin to make her feel the things Rafferty did.

Or she could find out more. She wasn't a coward, and she wasn't one to accept defeat so easily. So she'd lost the battle. There was still a war to be won, and she intended to do it. She suspected she couldn't ask Bertha for details, but Martina had been uncommonly frank. Surely she would tell her what she needed to know?

She would have to bide her time, and hope and pray that Rafferty stayed where he was. That horrid man Styles didn't strike her as the kind of man who gave up easily. Rafferty wouldn't leave them, leave her, if there was still danger. For now, all she could do was sleep. And plan.

IF HE PUNCHED another wall he would break his fist, Rafferty thought as he stared at the wood paneling that covered the dining room. He was sorely tempted anyway. Upstairs lay a girl...no, a woman...that he wanted so much he ached with it, a woman he absolutely must not touch again. He'd been a bastard and a half for touching her the first time, and he wasn't about to do it again. She wasn't for the likes of him, and he wasn't the kind of man who had room for a woman in his life. He'd always comforted himself with the thought that she'd forget all about him once she was married, but a woman never forgot her first lover. And he wondered how he could fight Billy Stiles with a broken hand.

Catholic priests had the right of it—didn't they whip themselves as an act of contrition? He needed someone to take a horsewhip to him. At least that would get her off his mind.

She looked so small and sad up there in the room, staring at the fire, and he couldn't tell whether she was still horrified by the things he'd done to her or wanting more. He'd bet on horrified. She'd been a total innocent, and he'd given in to impossible temptation. And he was still tempted.

Beyond tempted. The house was empty. She was upstairs, alone. She thought she loved him. If he were totally without conscience, he'd be up there right now, taking her to bed.

But he wouldn't. He...cared about her. The only thing he could do for her now was leave her strictly alone.

He punched the wall.

Chapter Twenty-Five

IF HER PARENTS thought there'd been anything irregular about leaving Georgie home alone to Rafferty's tender ministrations, they didn't show it. By the time they returned, the maids were in residence, Bertha had returned, and Georgie had risen from her specious sickbed, bright and cheerful enough to convince anyone of an uneventful sojourn.

She would have congratulated herself on her impeccable play-acting, but Rafferty seemed to be oblivious to her gallant efforts. He moved through the house smoothly, treating her with polite deference when she'd asked about his bandaged hand, and made no mention of leaving. She'd had to make do with that.

She wasn't able to do anything with Rafferty—she was now firmly Miss Georgiana to him—and even though she longed to throw herself into his arms she behaved with perfect propriety. So he wanted to pretend the night hadn't happened? She wished him luck—she had no intention of letting it go. She wanted more. His touch was oddly insistent—if she closed her eyes, she could feel him, his hand on her breasts, his mouth on hers, his body pressing hers down into the mattress. She could feel him inside her. He'd been hers, and then gone, and she wanted more.

Martina came bustling into her room, a morning tray in her

capable hands. "How are you feeling this morning, Miss Georgiana? We missed you in Kent."

Georgie tried to look bright-eyed and cheerful. "I'm feeling fine. It was just a temporary indisposition."

Martina set the tray down and pulled the curtains, letting in the gloomy autumn light. "I can just imagine..." she was saying as she turned, and then the words dried up for a moment, as she stared at her. Then she seemed to pull herself together. "I can just imagine you had a nice time without your family breathing down your neck," she said in a studiedly casual voice. "Did Rafferty look after you?"

"Oh, he wasn't here much. Jane and Betsey took care of me, not that I needed taking care of. I really can manage on my own."

"Of course, you can, Miss Georgiana. You're looking a bit pale still. A walk would do you some good, get you fresh air. Shall I ask Rafferty to escort you?"

"No...er, no, I don't think so," she stammered. Rafferty didn't seem to want to have anything to do with her and she wasn't about to force herself on him. Not until she decided exactly what she was going to do.

"I'm going to kill him," Martina said with deceptive calm.

"Martina..." Georgie began, but Martina had raced from the room like a cyclone, leaving her alone, and she slid out of bed and poured herself a cup of tea, her toes freezing in the early morning air. How had Martina known? Was there some scarlet sign about her that announced to the world she had lost her innocence? Where in the world had she gone?

"You rat bastard!" Martina found Rafferty on the fourth floor, among the deserted servants' bedrooms.

He didn't bother denying it. "Don't you think I know it?" he replied. "I never should have touched her."

"Then why did you? Did she throw herself at you?"

He wasn't about to tell her the truth. "She was too tempting."

"You're a man who can resist all sorts of temptation. I thought you were looking after the girl, when all this time you were just trying to get beneath her skirts! Shame on you, Rafferty. She's just a child."

"She's not a child," he snapped. "Apart from that, you're right."

"So you spent the last two days rolling in bed with her."

"It was just once. One night," he amended truthfully. "I told her it would never happen again."

"And she believed you? You need to leave here, Rafferty, before you do any more damage. She thinks she's in love with you!"

"Don't you think I know that?"

"Then why did you seduce her?"

He started to deny it, then shut his mouth. It didn't matter that she'd thrown herself in his arms—he was man enough to resist even the strongest temptation. And that's what she had been—more temptation than he'd known what to do with, and he'd given in like a fool. "I'm never touching her again."

"You think that excuses you? What if she's pregnant? Did you pull out?"

"Of course I did," he said irritably. He didn't want to be making excuses to Martina, he didn't want to be thinking about Georgie all the time. She haunted him, his dreams, his waking hours, and Martina was right, he should get the hell away from her. But he couldn't, as long as Stiles posed a threat.

"You need to tell her what to do when she gets married," he said.

"I don't think we need to worry about that—she's nowhere near ready to look at anyone else but her beloved Rafferty. Damn you!"

"I've tried to talk her out of it," he snapped.

"Try harder! What if she's pregnant?"

"She won't be!"

"Withdrawal is never a sure thing. Will you marry her if she is?"

"I'd ruin her life."

"You already have!" Martina slammed the door behind her as she stomped off to rejoin her young mistress.

§

SHE SHUT the door carefully behind her. She'd regained her calm, and she smoothed her dark chignon and brushed her skirts as she approached the bed, as if girding herself for war.

"First of all," she said in voice far removed from her subservient maid's voice, "Did he hurt you?"

Georgie didn't attempt to dissemble. "Of course not!"

"Don't lie to me, Miss Georgiana! Whose idea was this?"

"Mine, of course. If it had been up to him, he wouldn't have touched me," she said earnestly.

"Ha!" Martina scoffed. "That's not what he said. And he knew what he was doing—he never should have come near you!"

"I don't want to talk about it."

"Well, you have to. You need to know what to do when you go to your marriage bed, we need to plan what to do if the stupid man didn't take careful enough precautions, we need to…oh, God, don't cry."

"I'm not," Georgie said, blinking back tears. "It wasn't his fault, it was mine. And I'm never getting married so it shouldn't matter…."

"You should get married right away, in case there are any unexpected consequences. What about Mr. Salton?"

"He's in love with Norah."

"Fool," said Martina loyally. "Is there anyone else who might do?"

Georgie shook her head. "I'm never getting married," she said again.

"You are if you're pregnant," Martina said firmly.

"Then I'll marry Rafferty."

"He's not the marrying kind. Don't worry—he'll find someone for you," she said.

"I don't want anyone but Rafferty."

"Child," Martina said in a kind voice, "he doesn't want you."

&

"CHILD, HE DOESN'T WANT YOU." The words ran round and round in Georgie's brain. It was a death knell to her hopes and dreams, and she felt crushed, shattered, wounded to the heart. She needed time to think, time to come to terms with Martina's brutal words. They were kindly meant—a necessary warning, and they had the unmistakable ring of truth. He didn't want her, and the sooner she accepted that dreadful truth and how to leave him alone, the better.

What was wrong with her? This was no surprise—Rafferty had done nothing but try to avoid her since he entered the household, denying her adolescent passion and treating her like a younger sister. Or mostly—that had been no brotherly night in his bed. But if he didn't want her, why had he touched her, taken her? Was she just so desperate that he'd taken pity on her and deflowered her as an act of charity? She could feel the warmth stain her cheeks as she considered it, and she threw herself down on her bed, burying her face in the pillows.

She didn't cry. It was past the time for tears. The situation was disastrous, and she couldn't bear to think about him and his certain reluctance to touch her. Maybe men simply couldn't resist a female in deshabille, one who was throwing herself at his feet. Maybe she disgusted him, and that's why he threatened to leave. Maybe he'd never wanted her at all.

She rolled over on her back, flinging her arms outward. She couldn't bear it, if it were true. She could simply hide from him, let him leave without ever seeing him again. Part of her wanted to —her shame was absolute. But she wasn't someone who hid from disaster. If she didn't find out the truth she would...she would...

She climbed off the bed, landing on the floor in her beautiful shoes. Why had he given her the shoes? The dresses? Norah would tell her that he pitied her, and it seemed the dismal truth. She took off the shoes and left them neatly by the bed. If she was going to have this out with him, then she didn't want to feel beholden to him from her head to her toes.

It was late morning, and her mother and Norah had left for their morning visits. She was allowed to stay home, being not quite out, and it was one other injustice. Some nights she was to stay at behind and be demure, at others she could go out and even dance. Dance with Andrew Salton, the devious bastard. No, he wasn't that, he was simply in love with the wrong person, as she was. Though from the look on Norah's face, this particular passion was requited.

She moved silently down the stairs. How she would get Rafferty alone long enough to ask him the all-important question was a conundrum, but she would manage it somehow, if she had to ask him in front of Bertha, who would likely kill him.

Of course, there was no sign of him, and Bertha was in the midst of baking bread with no time for her foolish questions. Georgie moved through the rooms—her father's abandoned study where she'd found him at midnight that first night, through the salons and the dining room where he would stand stiff as a poker while her family discussed him. He probably hated her for causing him so much trouble.

She heard the clink of glassware, and the sound of someone moving behind the dining room wall, and she walked into the hallway on silent feet. Rafferty was in the butler's pantry, a narrow closet with cupboards on three sides and sideboards to rest the food. He was standing in the back of the long room, polishing their wineglasses, but he looked up when she filled the doorway.

He had no way of escaping, or he probably would have run her over in an effort to get away from her, she thought miserably.

His face was grave, impassive as he looked at her, and he set the glass down, tossing the rag beside it.

"Did you want me for something, Miss Georgiana?"

"Do you?"

He momentarily looked confused, and she heard a sound overhead, her brother and Martina in a laughing conversation in the upstairs hallway. She stepped into the room and closed the door behind her.

"I'm working," he said reprovingly, and she knew the truth, but she had to ask him anyway.

"You don't care a fig for me, do you?"

He didn't blink. "You're my mistress and my patron. I'm very grateful for the chance you gave me."

"But that's all," she persisted, dreading his answer.

"What do you want me to say?"

That you love me! That you can't live without me. But she said nothing.

He sighed and leaned back against the counter at the end of the small room. "Georgie," he began, and she wanted to cry. "I'm leaving tomorrow."

"It's my fault," she said. "I forced myself on you when you didn't want anything to do with me. I was childish and stupid and you're desperate to get away from me...."

"I'm not desperate to get away from you. And you're not childish and stupid, you simply have a crush on me. It will vanish the moment I'm gone," he said gently.

"Did you ever want me?" she asked, her voice tight with strain and unshed tears. "Or did I force you. Dear God, did I r...r...rape you?"

He laughed then. "Dear girl, I want you as much as a man can want a woman. But I'm no good for you, and you'll realize that in time."

The tears were inching down her cheeks now. "You're really going?"

"I have to."

"And I'll never see you again? You'll never touch me again?"

A dark, unreadable expression crossed his face. "Georgie," he said, and his own voice was hoarse. "Leave while you still can."

"Or what?" she said through her tears, defiant in her misery.

"Or lock the door."

The pantry was wide enough for two people, but he brushed against her as he moved past, and she watched in silence as he turned the key in the lock. His eyes met hers, and she could see the heat in them, as he came back to her, sliding his arms around her and lifting her in the air as he kissed her.

If he wanted her he'd be hard, and she reached down to touch him, braver than she thought she could be. The feel of him was overwhelming, and she let out a little sob of relief as his hands moved up her legs, pulling her voluminous skirts out of the way as he lifted them.

"This changes nothing," he said in a gritty voice. "I'm leaving tomorrow. Are you sure you want this?"

"I want everything you'll give me," she said in a choked voice, and his mouth came down on hers once more.

He set her on the counter, pushing her skirts out of the way, his hands deft and merciless as they touched her, aroused her, readied her, and before she knew it he was pushing inside her, fast, hard and deep. Her arms were around his neck, and she buried her face against his shoulder, holding on as he held her there, balanced against the cupboard, surging into her. She was crying, knowing this was the last time, but heat was building inside her, strong and sure, and her fingers dug into his arms, clutching tightly, refusing to let him go.

He pulled her away from the counter, holding her up as he slammed into her, and this was darker, faster than before, a conflagration of desire that even he could no longer deny. He thrust into her, holding still as he filled her, groaning, and she shattered at the feel of him inside her, the feel of his seed inside her.

He shuddered against her, and she held him tight, fighting

back her tears. She was shaken, weak, but he pulled out of her, setting her down on the floor, and her legs could barely hold her.

"Oh, God," he said bitterly. "I'm an idiot. Why did I do that?"

It felt like a slap across the face. She pulled back, staring up at him in hurt and disbelief. "Because you love me?" she said.

"I don't love you! How many times must I tell you that? I want you—who wouldn't? But it doesn't change a thing. I'm leaving tomorrow, and nothing is going to change that. Not even this."

"This" was said in a tone of disgust, and it was the last straw. The warm glow that had filled her body had now vanished, and she felt small and wretched. Turning her back on him, she went toward the door and turned the key, hearing the lock click open.

"Georgie..." he said, and there was regret in his voice. But she had had enough of his regret, and she ran out into the hallway, heading for the safety of her bedroom.

Chapter Twenty-Six

GEORGIE DRESSED in her old gray dress, warm against the brisk fall weather. If she'd had a choice, she wouldn't have worn the shoes he gave her, but the old ones were long gone and she had no choice. She waited down in the kitchen until Bertha had disappeared into the larder, and she slipped out into the city streets, her bonnet pulled low over her face.

She felt...gutted. She no longer had any doubt that he wanted her—that time in the butler's pantry had banished all the doubts. But he was still leaving her. He would never touch her again, and by tomorrow he would be gone. And all she could do was walk blindly through the streets of London, awash in misery.

She walked, it seemed like miles, all the way to Green Park, her jacket pulled tightly around her. It was too early in the season for the weather to be so cold, but it matched her bleak outlook. It wasn't until the rain began to spit from the sky that she turned back, keeping her head down as she made her way back to Corinth Place.

Unfortunately, keeping her head down wasn't the best way to find the right direction, and when she should have turned onto Corinth Place she instead found herself down by docks. Gone were the stylish couples strolling arm in arm, gone were the gentlemen with their carriages. She was in a rougher area of town and this time there was no Rafferty to rescue her. It served her right.

"Well, well, what have we here?" came a familiar voice, and Georgie felt a sinking feeling in the pit of her stomach. Looking up, she came face to face with Billy Stiles's enormous teeth, and she stopped, momentarily panicked.

There was nothing to be frightened of, she reminded herself. This man wouldn't hurt her—Rafferty had warned him away, and only a fool would go against a man like their makeshift butler.

"Good afternoon, Mr. Stiles," she said politely. "I was just on my way home."

"You were headed in the wrong direction, Miss Georgiana," he said with a certain pleased malice. "Allow me to accompany you the rest of the way." He took her arm in one meaty hand, and she tried to pull away, to no avail. "Does Rafferty know you're out wandering?" he said in a jovial voice. "I wouldn't think he'd want you down in my territory, all on your own. Unless you were looking for me?"

"I...I got turned around," she stammered, tugging at her arm. "Rafferty was with me, we must have gotten separated...."

"Rafferty's at the Duchess of Ormond's house. Perhaps you could tell me why?"

"I have no idea. And now I really must go home...."

"Not yet, Miss Georgiana." His voice was implacable. "We'll go for a nice cup of tea and you'll tell me what our mutual friend has been doing. You see, he's looking for something for me, and I worry he's not being diligent enough in his task.

"He has no idea where the money is!" she said hotly.

"Oh, he told you about that, did he? He's been a talkative fellow, now ain't he? What else did he tell you?"

How could teeth seem malevolent, Georgie thought absently. He wasn't about to bite her. "He just said he was looking for it, that's all. I don't know anything else."

"I'm not sure I believe you, Miss Georgiana. I think our friend cares a little too much for you, enough to make him indiscreet."

"Your friend doesn't care about me at all," she said bitterly.

"Oh, have we had a lover's quarrel? Never you mind, he'll come racing after you the moment he finds out I have you, and maybe I'll finally get some satisfaction."

"He can't find the money if it's not there."

"Well, that will be too bad for you, now won't it? I'm a patient man, but my patience has run out."

"You looked yourself and couldn't find it!" she said desperately. "How do you expect Rafferty to perform miracles? If it's not there, it's not there."

"Oh, it's there all right. All I have to do is give the man enough incentive and I expect to have it in hand by the end of the day. You'd best hope so, Miss Georgiana. Because you're not going home until I have it, and if it takes too long, I might be tempted to see what Rafferty finds so appealing about you."

"Rafferty doesn't care about me, I told you." Couldn't he hear the ring of truth in her voice?

"We'll see how long it takes him to come after you. Then we'll decide. If I were you, I'd hope I was wrong. If you're of no value to me, then I'd have to get rid of you."

"You could let me go home," she said in a small voice.

"Can't do that. You'd tell the police and I'm already paying enough to keep them off my back."

"What are you going to do with me?" she asked.

His toothy grin merely widened.

THE NIGHT WAS CLOSING EARLY around the house in Corinth Place when Rafferty returned from his grandmother's house, and thankfully there was no sign of Georgie. Bertha was in her element, ordering her two assistants in the kitchen, and he didn't make the mistake of asking her where Georgie was. The less he saw of her the better—even the trace of her scent in the air sent the blood pounding in his veins, and he suspected Martina knew it. He knew what was wrong with him—he was infatuated, and right at the time that he'd finally managed to drive her away. He needed to get away from her—that would erase her from his mind and soul quite effectively. But until then, he was growing more and more obsessed, avoiding her with ferocious dedication. He had to leave, he told her he was leaving, but he wasn't quite sure he could.

He was an idiot, and he knew it, but he was well and truly trapped. He couldn't leave this place without satisfying Billy Stiles —it was too dangerous to the family, and to Georgie in particular. He'd been fool enough to betray himself to Stiles, and he knew that Georgie mattered to him. Stiles wouldn't dare touch her, but that would only last so long. Sooner or later, he was going to break the leash on his partially civilized behavior and then God knew what would happen. Billy Stiles had cut more throats than most of his men could even count, and he wouldn't hesitate...

"Where is everyone?" he demanded of Bertha, who fixed him with a stern eye.

"Miss Norah and Lady Manning are still out visiting or whatever they call it," she said irritably.

"And Georgie?"

"Miss Georgiana," she corrected. "Never you mind where she is. It's a good thing she's not hanging around after you—maybe she's finally over you. You leave her alone."

He knew what was wrong with Georgie. He'd botched it when he took her to bed, and the time in the butler's pantry had sealed it. She was a gently bred girl, she was probably horrified by the whole experience and she couldn't face him.

He had butler duties to perform, and he headed for the still-room, but something stopped him. He wasn't going to be able to move ahead until he was sure she was safe.

He moved silently up the backstairs, heading toward the bedrooms. The doors were closed, keeping the heat inside, and when he reached Georgie's, he hesitated. He told her he wouldn't see her again. Wouldn't touch her again. Could he keep that promise? He knocked on the door.

There was no answer, and he knocked a little more loudly. Finally he pushed the door open to find the room deserted, and a feeling of foreboding came over him. She was probably in the library, reading one of her French novels, but there was no sign of her. Anywhere.

Finally, he knocked on Neddy's door, pushing it open to see Neddy and Martina curled up on a sofa, a pack of cards between them. "Have you see Miss Georgiana?"

Neddy looked up, a lot more sharp-eyed than he'd first been. In fact, he hadn't passed out at the table or been carried to bed in days—Martina must have worked her magic. "Where's Georgie?"

"I don't know. I can't find any sign of her in the house."

Martina had jumped up, smoothing her skirts. "Do you suppose she's gone out? She would have asked one of us to accompany her."

"That's the last thing she's going to ask me," he said bitterly.

"Why shouldn't she?" Neddy asked, his new sobriety inconvenient.

"You know she has a crush on Rafferty," Martina said patiently. "I told her it was a waste of time."

"What did you say?" Rafferty demanded.

"My sister's in love with the butler?" Neddy demanded, sharp-eyed.

"It's infatuation, nothing more. I told her he didn't care about her and she finally believed me," Martina said.

"And now we can't find her," Rafferty said bitterly.

"You don't suppose she's gone out on her own?" she asked.

"That's exactly what she's done," Rafferty said. "I'm going to beat her."

"I beg your pardon!" Neddy said frostily.

"I'll explain it to you later," Martina told him. "In the meantime, we need to find her before Stiles does."

"Who the hell is Stiles?" Neddy said.

"Later," Martina said. "We need to go."

Neddy rose. "I'm going too. She's my sister, after all."

Martina merely nodded, and Rafferty observed the two of them with no particular surprise and no room for worry. Georgie was missing, and that was enough fear to keep him going until he found the wretched brat. Whether he was going to spank her or kiss her was the question, so maybe it was a good idea that her brother was searching too.

Night had already fallen, the streetlamps sending a fitful light to guide him. Neddy and Martina had headed toward the parks, though the thought of Georgie alone in a park after dark terrified him. She was so bloody fearless, and too innocent to realize her danger. Her being anywhere after dark, alone, without him to protect her, was enough to send cold shivers through him, and he moved faster. He had people he could ask, down by the docks, and he pushed through the thinning crowds, heading toward the slums, when a carriage pulled up beside him.

"Rafferty, me boy," came Billy Stiles's jovial voice. "Out on the town, I see, when you ought to be home searching for my money."

Rafferty stopped in his tracks. "What do you want, Billy?" He didn't make the mistake of thinking this was a coincidence.

"The question, my boy, is what do you want? I have a young lady here who is most anxious to return home."

Ice formed in his veins. "Let her go, Billy."

"Oh, I think not. I'm tired of waiting—I told you that. It's time for you to bring me my money."

"I haven't got your money. I've got money of my own, I can give you that..."

"Don't be ridiculous! Belding had a fortune tucked away in that house—your paltry money couldn't touch it. I want the money that's owed me. If you don't want your throat cut in an alleyway, you'll get it for me."

"First give me Miss Manning."

"She's fine where she is, ain't you, darling?"

He could see her then in the dark confines of the coach, and if she'd looked terrified he would have lost his mind. Instead, her eyes met his, and there was no missing the anger in them. For Stiles, or for him? For both of them, he suspected. It would be no more than he deserved.

"I'd like to go home," she said politely enough.

"And so you shall, me darling, if your lover would just take care of business."

"He's not my lover," she said in an icy voice.

"I'll bring you the money tonight," Rafferty said rashly. "Where do you want me to come? Your house?"

"Oh, I don't think so. Too many people about—if my men knew I'd found Belding's pot, they'd want a piece of it."

"I thought you were planning on sharing it," Rafferty shot back.

"Now why would I do that? Meet me by Landon Bridge and I'll bring you the girl. But no tricks. I can slice her throat faster than you can stop me." He leaned over and caught Georgie's chin in his hand. "Though I'd like to have a taste of her before I do it. See what you find so exciting about the other half."

"Get your hands off her."

Stiles released her with a little laugh. "Shall we say midnight, then? Why not be melodramatic with our little play?"

Rafferty wracked his brain. It would take time to get the money together, and too much of it was in land, but no one knew for sure how big Belding's cache was, and in the darkness he could fool Stiles long enough to kill him. "Ten o'clock," he said recklessly. He didn't want Georgie in his hands for a minute longer than necessary.

"Too many witnesses. Midnight, at Landon Bridge. And I don't need to warn you to come alone."

"I'll bring Martin."

Stiles snorted. "Fat lot of good he'd do. Certainly, bring your catamite. But since you two are so close, I wonder you'd want to bother with this young lady."

"Touch her again and I'll cut off your hands."

Stiles merely laughed, and his teeth shone in the gaslight. "Midnight."

❧

SHE WAS GOING TO DIE, Georgie thought. She was sitting in a room full of noisy men and women, and no one was paying any attention to her, thank God, but the ropes around her wrists and ankles were too tight, and the strip of cloth wrapped around her face was cutting into her mouth. All she could use was her eyes, and she didn't want to be seeing half of what she was seeing. Where was Rafferty? She had no idea of the time, but he would be there, she knew he would. By Landon Bridge, wherever that was, carrying a fortune's ransom.

Billy Stiles wasn't going to let them go. Why should he, and risk retribution? Her ears were working too, for all that everyone seemed to have forgotten about her, and she heard Billy quite clearly. "You stay in the shadows, and when I give the signal you shoot him. I'll cut the girl's throat and we'll be gone before you can say Bob's your uncle."

"Why don't I shoot her too?" the man had demanded.

"Because you won't have time to reload," Stiles said patiently.

"I could bring two guns."

"Because I want to see if the upper classes bleed blue."

"Do they?" the first man said in wonder.

"No, you fool. Because two guns would make you clumsy, and I don't want any mistakes. I want this over and done with."

"But what if he really can't find the money? Won't killing him mean he'll never find it?"

"Jonesy, when I want to explain my thinking to you, I'll let you know," Stiles said. "Go and bother someone else—I've got some drinking to do."

She watched as the heavyset man walked away. Of course Stiles had set a trap—she should have expected it. And Rafferty would expect it as well—he knew Stiles of old. He wouldn't just walk into the night to be shot. Maybe he wouldn't come at all, leaving her to her fate.

It would simplify his life, after all. She was just a tedious responsibility, one he was tired of. He was sick of her following him around and looking at him with calf's eyes. Martina had had it right—"he doesn't want you," she'd said, and those words had been a death knell in her heart. Maybe she didn't care if Stiles cut her throat after all.

Yes, she did. Because Martina was wrong. When it came right down to it, and she was staring death in the face, she couldn't believe that he didn't want her. Oh, he might not love her—she was inconvenient, silly, smitten. But as for not wanting her, that was blatantly untrue. He wouldn't have kissed her. He wouldn't have... She blushed at the memory, feeling it warm her cramped body.

His hands on her—she could still feel them. The feel of him inside her, his mouth on hers, the wall of the pantry against her back. He would rescue her, and he would fall in love with her. She would make it happen. At least if she was going to her death, she was going to believe that with all her heart.

The hours passed in a blur of pain and misery, but she didn't cry, tempted though she was. Now was not the time for despair. She had to keep her wits about her if she was going to survive the night and not get in Rafferty's way. When they finally cut the ropes that were binding her ankles and pulled her to her feet, she fell, collapsing to the floor to the great merriment of those around. Stiles hauled her up again.

"Time to go, missy. Your lover awaits."

Her feet felt numb, her ankles screamed with pain, but she had no choice. With her hands still bound in front of her, she stumbled after him, his hand heavy on her arm, out into the midnight air, the hulking man beside him.

It was a good thing he was too greedy to share the money—the two of them would make better odds for Rafferty. Unless the man did as Stiles told him and shot from the shadows. She still had the gag around her mouth, but she suspected she could scream anyway, make some kind of warning noise. The smartest thing she could probably do was trip and go flat on the filthy street. Unless she was going to be a true heroine and leap in front of the gun, exchanging her life for Rafferty's.

It was a lovely thought for a brief moment. He would weep over her body, in despair that he hadn't realized how much he loved her and now she had died for him, but she dismissed the idea. Touching though it was, she wouldn't be around to enjoy his remorse, and she staggered after Stiles in the cold night air, trying to think of some other way to warn him. The night was still and quiet, and they passed few people as they made their way through the filthy neighborhoods. That, or everyone gave them a wide berth. She had no idea which was Landon Bridge, but it turned out to be a small bridge crossing an offshoot of the Thames, and he placed her in the shadows.

"You'll be a good girl, now, won't you?" he said cheerfully, a light in his eyes. "I'm looking forward to this. Oh, not the money, though I've waited long enough for that. No, Rafferty's been an itch on my arse for too long now, and I'm finally getting rid of him. As for you, I'll give you your choice. You can join my girls, or I can cut your throat. I'll make it fast if I can—no one ever said Billy Stiles wasn't a thoughtful bloke."

There was no way she could answer him. She really didn't want to bleed to death on a filthy London street, but at the moment she was more worried about Rafferty.

She didn't see him, but Stiles knew when he was there. "That you, Rafferty, my boy?" he called into the darkness. "Aren't you going to show yourself?"

"And give you a perfect target? What kind of fool do you think I am?" came his disembodied voice.

It happened so fast she didn't have time to fight. Billy grabbed her and pulled her against his stocky body, and she felt the sting of the knife against her throat. "I can finish her in a trice, Rafferty, if you don't show that pretty face of yours. And you'd best have my money."

"I've got it," came a familiar voice, but the young man who stepped into the small pool of light was a stranger. He was carrying a heavy box and he set it down on the ground where he stood.

"It's my old friend Martin," Billy cooed. "Should have known he'd bring you into it. Bring the box over here, there's a good lad."

"Let her go, Billy," came Rafferty's voice from the darkness.

"Not a chance. You'd shoot me as soon as look at me. Don't you trust me, Rafferty, my boy? After all we've been together?"

"Let her go," he said again, his voice like steel.

"I don't think—" An explosion rent the night air, and fire spat out from beneath the bridge as Billy's accomplice shot into the dark. She tried to pull away, but Stiles held her tight.

"That Jonesy?" Rafferty's voice came floating back. "He never could hit the broadside of a barn. See to him, Martin."

The young man headed for the bridge, a small gun in his hand, and in the still night air, Georgie could hear footsteps as Jonesy ran away.

"That just leaves you and me, Billy," Rafferty said in an amiable voice. "Why don't we end this now?"

"You're forgetting I have the lady."

"I'm not forgetting. Let her go and you can have the money."

"But we both know that's not Belding's cache. He would have at least twice as much money tucked away there, which you should have been able to find."

"It's not there," Rafferty said flatly.

"Then whose money is this?"

"Mine."

"Not enough."

"It'll have to do."

Stiles suddenly ripped off the enveloping gag, freeing

Georgie's voice. "Want to tell him goodbye?" The knife pressed against her throat.

She was going to die. It didn't seem real, but it was happening, and she could think of only one thing to say. "I love you, Jamie," she said in a choked voice, and closed her eyes.

The explosion was deafening, the fire burned her, and she fell to her knees, then her stomach in the filthy street as she was flattened beneath Billy Stiles's body. He didn't move.

She couldn't hear a thing, she couldn't breathe, and she closed her eyes, struggling uselessly against the heavy weight. A moment later, she was free, and Rafferty was there, pulling her into his arms, holding her so tightly she would have protested if she hadn't liked it so much. He was talking to her, but she couldn't hear a word, she just put her arms around him and clung tight, safe and loved, if for only that moment.

He reached down and cradled her face, and there was blood on his fingertips as he brushed her skin, and some of his words began to penetrate the blank fog. "You're...bleeding," he said, pushing her loose hair away from her face. "I was afraid...hurt you...love..."

He said "love" but she couldn't hear the rest of his muffled words. She put up her hand to her face and it came away smoky and bloody. A moment later, he'd scooped her up in his arms, holding her tightly.

"Is...hurt?" came the truncated words of the young man, and Georgie turned her face to look into Martina's dark brown eyes. She stared in wonder, and the young man smiled wryly. "You'll...be...fine," he said. "Just let...Rafferty...care of you."

It was too much. She closed her eyes and fainted.

Chapter Twenty-Seven

"YOU'RE AWAKE, THEN, MISS GEORGIE," came Martina's low voice, and Georgie opened her eyes blearily, then wider. The young man by her bedside was fluffing the covers, plumping her pillows, fussing over her with the care that Martina had showed, all as if this was perfectly normal. "We were that worried about you—you never struck me as the kind of girl who'd faint dead away, but this time you had reason to. You've been asleep for so long we started to think the worst."

Georgie picked up on the key word. "We?"

"Of course, miss. We were afraid Stiles had...well, he'd threatened, and Rafferty was half mad with worry when you disappeared. What in heaven's name made you go out all alone, without Rafferty or me?"

"Who are you?" she demanded groggily, but she knew full well.

"I'm Martin." He hesitated. "Martina's twin brother, if that makes you feel any better."

"No, you're not," she said, all of Billy Stiles's odd comments finally making sense.

"No, I'm not," he agreed. "And I'd better go change before Bertha finds out and raises a fuss. Though I expect she knows."

"Bertha knows everything," Georgie said gloomily. "She won't be shocked."

"Are you? Shocked, that is?"

Georgie considered it. "No," she said finally. "You helped saved my life last night."

"Rafferty saved you. I was just a distraction. You stay where you are, and I'll see about a bath for you. The girls will bring up the water."

It answered the question she was too afraid to ask. Where was Rafferty? Didn't he care that she was finally awake? She lay back among the pillows. "Where is he?" she said finally.

"He left a while ago. He had some things to see to, he said." Martin started for the door, striding like a young man, and she blinked.

"Is he coming back?"

There was kindness in Martin's eyes. "I don't know, Miss Georgie."

She would have thought the bath would make her feel more human, but despite the delicious soak in the tub, her stomach was still churning. Where was Rafferty? Now that Stiles was dead, he had no reason to stay in Corinth Place, unless he wanted the money himself. But he already had money—he'd been ready to trade his own for her safety. Surely that meant something.

It meant he was responsible for her, and nothing else. She dressed in one of her new dresses, too weary to protest, and slipped on her beautiful leather shoes. Her reflection gave her no solace—she looked exhausted and almost tearful, and she quickly stiffened her back. If Rafferty was leaving, she would give him no reason to repine. It must be true, he really didn't love her. She'd mistaken his sense of responsibility for more tender feelings. She'd thrown herself at him, time and again, and he'd resisted as much as any man could.

And she wasn't going to sit around waiting for him. Grabbing her shawl, she made her way up to the fourth floor and the window to the roof, climbing out gingerly to look down over the windswept city. It was warmer than it had been, and down below, people were going about their business without the faintest notion that they were being watched. She searched, but there was no sign of Rafferty on the busy streets below. Maybe never again.

She leaned back against the chimney, closing her eyes. She missed the countryside, the fresh air and the sunshine. The sun must shine as often in the city as it did in the country, but it didn't seem like it. All of London seemed mired in a gloomy miasma, and the smoke pouring out of the chimney pots only made it worse. At least this one chimney wasn't belching soot like all the others—it was quiet and unused, newer than the other chimney pots with no smoke stains or heat or...

She turned around, staring up at the chimney, then glanced out at the skies around her. Each chimney, on every house, was pouring out thick, black coal smoke. Every single chimney but the one she rested against, the one that stood on the edge of the roof, above no fireplace or hearth.

Rising, she examined it more closely. It was no wonder there was no smoke—the chimney pot was sealed tight. She knocked her fist against it, but the satisfying thud told her it was far from hollow, and she knew without question, she'd found the missing money.

The last thing she wanted was for someone else to find it. Wrapping her shawl around her, she climbed back through the window and pulled it tight behind her. As long as Rafferty didn't know where the money was, there was a chance he would stay and search for it. Once he found it, he would be gone, if he hadn't gone already.

She went back to her room, closing the door behind her. She had to think, undisturbed. He'd searched for days, he'd even been out on the roof with her and hadn't noticed the defunct chimney. There was no reason she should tell him—she could just pretend she'd never made that astonishing discovery, and maybe he would stay. Maybe he would learn to love her.

But that was a child's reckoning and she was no longer a child. Sooner or later she would have to let him go.

§

IT WAS close to midnight when Rafferty returned to the house on Corinth Place. He'd had a busy day seeing to the aftermath of Stiles's death. All he needed was his men coming after him, intent on retribution, but it turned out Stiles's hold on Belding's old gang had been peripheral at best. Especially once they learned he hadn't planned on sharing his windfall. He had to reject their very flattering offer to join them, all without offending, and it had required several hours of careful negotiations.

And then there was his grandmother to deal with. She was a stubborn old woman, determined to have him rejoin the family, but he wasn't joining anything. He was leaving London and all the responsibilities behind, going back to his sprawling farmhouse in Hampshire where he only had to worry about the livestock. He was leaving Georgie to find a husband and have a real life.

He didn't want to think about Georgie. He hadn't seen her since he'd carried her home after she'd fainted, and he knew he'd see horror in her eyes when he did. She'd seen him kill a man in cold blood, a man who was threatening to cut her throat. It had been a close thing, but he was an excellent shot, and he'd never had any doubt he could make it. She might not have faith that she'd been in no danger from his gun.

He'd given up on finding Belding's long-lost money. He didn't need it, and Stiles's men accepted the fact that it was gone —there'd be no trouble from that direction. There was nothing holding him back from leaving.

Except for Georgie. He was a fool about her, he knew that. In the end, he'd become as besotted as she was, and the sooner he left, the safer he'd be. Every time he touched her he got in deeper, and he might start thinking foolish things if he didn't escape. He had complete faith that she could have a happy life with some kind young man. She wasn't for the likes of him.

The kitchen was dark and deserted as he made his way to his rooms. He didn't have much to pack—he'd leave his butler's uniform behind—and he'd leave it up to Martina to say his good-byes. He couldn't stand to see the look in Georgie's eyes when he left her.

He knew the moment he entered his room that she was there, and he walked through to his bedroom to find her perched on his bed. She was fully dressed, and he knew a moment of regret.

"What are you doing here?" he demanded roughly.

She didn't appear discomfited by his greeting. She swung around and put her feet on the floor. Stockinged feet, and he remembered the feel of them in his hands, so delicate, so strong.

"I've come to give you what you want," she said with a misplaced dignity.

"I don't want you," he lied, gritting his teeth.

She flushed. "Not that," she said. "I've found the money."

He just stared at her for a long moment. "No, you haven't," he said in flat disbelief.

"It's on the roof. You never thought to check up there, and I found it. At least I think I did," she added in an unemotional voice. "One of the chimneys doesn't lead to any fireplace, and the chimney pot is new and sealed. I can't imagine anything else that would be hidden up there."

He stared at her in disbelief. "When did you figure this out?"

"This morning. You've been gone all day so I couldn't tell you, but I thought you'd want to know. Now you can have it all for yourself and not have to share with Stiles."

He said nothing, watching her. "Why are you telling me this?" he finally asked her. "Looking for the money is the only thing keeping me here."

She held very still, as if she were about to make a great leap. "Because I love you. And love means wanting the best for some-one, and letting them go when they want to leave."

"Georgie, you don't love me," he said wearily.

She rose from the narrow bed and came toward him, and he knew if he put his hands on her he wouldn't let her go. She came up to him, standing on her toes to place a soft kiss on his unresponsive mouth. "Goodbye, Rafferty."

And she was gone.

He knew what he was going to do—there was never any question in his mind. He'd already stripped off his coat, and he didn't bother putting it on again as he bounded up the stairs two at a time, pushing through the baize door to the bedrooms. He moved past Georgie's room with only a moment's regret and then headed for Neddy's. He knocked softly on the door, then pushed the door open and stopped.

Neddy was lying in bed with Martina, both of them fully clothed, both of them sound asleep. Rafferty only hesitated a minute. "Wake up," he said with a fair amount of force.

Neddy sat up in bed, blinking in the dim light. "What the hell do you want?" he demanded. Martina sat up beside him and then swiftly climbed off the bed.

"I must have fallen asleep," she said with a fair attempt at innocence. "I'm so sorry. Did you want something, Rafferty?"

She was going to get her heart broken, and he resisted the temptation to lecture her. She knew what she was doing, she knew the dangers, and there was nothing he could do to help her now. "I've got something for Neddy," he said, eschewing the proper "Master Edward" that he usually used. "Come with me."

If Neddy was discomfited by the form of address he didn't show it. Climbing out of bed, he slipped on his shoes and started toward the door. "Bring your coat," Rafferty said. "It's cold out there."

"Where are we going?"

"Up on the roof. Your sister has made a discovery."

"Where is she?" Neddy demanded, suddenly suspicious. "If you've done anything to harm her..."

He'd already done a great deal to harm her, but he wasn't about to tell him. "She's gone to bed. The rest is up to you."

"What's that you've got in your hand?"

"A fire poker. You'll see why."

Without another protest, Neddy followed him from the room, Martina taking up the rear. Neither of them balked at climbing out on the roof, and Rafferty found the chimney almost immediately. "Here," he said to Neddy, handing him the fire poker.

"I'm not about to destroy the chimney..." Neddy protested.

"It's a false chimney. Just break the chimney pot."

It wasn't the smartest thing to do, in the end. Coins and jewelry scattered on the rooftop, and Rafferty watched as a ruby necklace skittered over the side of the roof and down four stories to the grounds below.

"What the hell is this?" Neddy exclaimed.

"Part of the household. I believe you were told that everything in the house went with the sale. Therefore, this is, I believe, your family's."

"There's a bloody fortune here. How will I explain how we got it?"

"No need to explain. No one's going to question you too closely. It should be enough to get your family out of the River Tick."

Neddy sat back on his knees, staring at the pile of gold in wonder. "I should say so. Martina, look!"

But Martina was looking at Rafferty with wonder in her fine brown eyes. "You sure you know what you're doing, Rafferty?" she asked.

He moved out of Neddy's hearing. "I don't need it," he said. "And this will ensure that Georgie will be all right. She can wait and marry someone she loves."

"You're a thief—you always need money."

He shook his head. "This means I can leave with a clear conscience."

Martina shook her head. "I don't know that your conscience is that clear when it comes to Georgie."

"She'll get over me, the moment I'm gone. You can make sure she does."

"I don't know where I'll be," she said slowly.

"Does he know?"

She shook her head. "Don't look at me like that—I'll tell him. But that will be the end of it and I'm not quite ready for that. We're a fine pair, aren't we, mooning over the two of them?"

"I'm not mooning over anyone," he said stiffly. "And she's already well on her way to getting over me. I just don't want her marrying the wrong man."

"I think that's a given," Martina said. "But I'll do what I can."

"That's all I ask."

"Martina, come and look at this," Neddy called over, and Martina moved back to the chimney, leaving Rafferty to watch. It would be well, he thought. Not that there was a future for Neddy and Martina, but Georgie would be free to find the perfect young man to adore her and give her babies. And he'd be free. It was everything he wanted, wasn't it? Of course it was.

The next morning, Rafferty was gone.

Chapter Twenty-Eight

MARTINA CLIMBED THE STAIRS, balancing the breakfast tray carefully as she went. It was a dark, stormy day, perfectly matching her mood. She should be delighted—the impoverished Mannings were no longer impoverished, Billy Stiles was dead, and Neddy cared about her.

But Neddy didn't know who she was, and it was past time to tell him. Rafferty had disappeared, leaving nothing but his butler's uniform behind. And she was going to have to tell Georgie he was gone.

At least there was one happy ending in the Manning family, for Norah, the one who least deserved it. She would marry Andrew Salton now that a marriage settlement was no longer necessary to ensure the Mannings' future. There was nothing for Georgie. Rafferty was a fool and a half—the girl wasn't going to fall in love with a proper young man. She was going to love Rafferty till the day she died, Martina was sure of it. And that left two miserable human beings among the people she loved.

And she was doomed to join them. At least she had a real reason for heartbreak, not a bunch of foolish notions about society and what it demanded. Georgie didn't care one bit about society, and yet she was being sacrificed on its altar. And Rafferty refused to understand.

Georgie's door was shut against the morning chill, and Martina knocked softly. There was no answer, but she pushed open the door, moving into the shadowy room. "Good morning, Miss Georgie," she said softly, setting down the tray and moving to the curtains, pulling them back to reveal the gloomy day. "You've slept for hours past your usual time, so I thought I'd go ahead and bring your breakfast tray. Bertha said I was to tell you to get up and not be such a slugabed, and I—"

Georgie hadn't moved, or responded, and Martina's words petered out as she approached the bed. Georgie lay there, pale with fever-flushed cheeks, and Martina put a quick hand to her forehead. The girl was burning up with fever.

"Georgie!" she cried, and Georgie opened her eyes for a moment, then closed them again.

"I think I'm sick," she said in a soft, raspy voice.

"I'd say you are. I'll send for the doctor. Don't you worry, you'll be right as rain in a couple of days. You just lay still until the doctor gets here."

Georgie tried to sit up and failed, slipping down in the bed, and then she started coughing, great hacking sounds that broke Martina's heart. "You can send Rafferty for the doctor," she managed to wheeze, and Martina would have given anything to be able to lie.

"Rafferty's gone, miss," she said.

Georgie's eyes opened fully, staring at her, and then closed again. And those was the last words she spoke for two weeks.

IT WAS A STRANGE, nightmare time, Georgie thought later. She would go through stages where she was shivering with cold, followed by unbearable heat, and her coughing was so bad it felt like she was ripping her throat out. People came and went, but she was only vaguely aware of them as she travelled down the path of her sickness. She only knew that Rafferty wasn't there.

But slowly, slowly, she began to emerge from the cocoon of illness, and when the doctor declared her well enough to allow visitors, she finally sat up in bed and faced the shambles of her life. Rafferty was gone, disappeared as if he'd never been there, and all she had to show for it were a few pretty dresses and a wonderful pair of shoes.

"You're finally better," her mother announced as she breezed into the room, an extravagant new dress flowing around her. "I declare I was so worried about you I could barely eat. I would have come to see you, but you know I'm sadly sensitive to suffering, and it wasn't the thing. But now that you're well, you can get up and celebrate with us." Her mother stayed by the door, in case Georgie's illness was catching.

"Celebrate?" she echoed in a raspy voice. "You mean my recovery?"

"Oh, that too, of course!" her mother said hastily. "I declare, we've been so worried about you we haven't had a chance to celebrate our good fortune. And you must not have realized it, but Rafferty has left us. Such a handsome man," she said with a soulful sigh. "But we have a delightful new butler. Not as good-looking as Rafferty was, but full of such dignity that even I feel awed. You shan't have him for a project, but it's time we focused on getting you married as well."

"I'm never getting married," she said in her raspy throat. "I'm going to live in the country with cats and books and be very happy."

"Oh, not that again. You'll change your mind soon enough once you meet the right man."

She had met the right man, and he was gone. She watched her mother go in a sail of silk and closed her eyes. Two more weeks in bed seemed like a fine idea, but Martina knocked at her door an hour later, a worried expression on her face.

"Are you feeling up to getting dressed, Miss Georgie?" she

asked. "The family is celebrating in the drawing room and they want you to join them."

What were they celebrating? She didn't really care. "I'd rather stay in bed," she said listlessly.

"The doctor said you were well enough to come downstairs," she persisted, flinging open the curtains to let in the fitful autumn sunlight.

"The doctor was wrong. I'll come down tomorrow."

There was a wealth of sympathy in Martina's dark eyes, and, for a brief moment Georgie thought back to the young man who'd saved her life. Had she dreamed that?

But in truth, she didn't care. She lay back and closed her eyes, shutting out the daylight. Rafferty was gone, and nothing else mattered. Martina tried a few more times, but Georgie simply closed her eyes, shutting out everything.

It continued this way for several days. Much to Georgie's dismay, her body grew stronger and lying in bed was growing tedious, but she was loath to leave the sanctuary of it. She didn't want to join in her family's celebration, which seemed to infuse the entire household with revolting good cheer. She just wanted to hide away.

It was the morning of the fifth day when she heard the footsteps approach her bedroom door, firm, determined footsteps, and her door was flung open, revealing a stern Bertha.

"It's time you got up, Miss Georgie!" she announced, brushing flour off her apron. "It's time for you to face the day and get on with it, and no more nonsense."

Georgie had sat up in bed, and she looked at her as tears started in her eyes. "Oh, Bertha!" she said brokenly, and she began to cry in earnest. "He's gone, Bertha!" she wept. "I'll never see him again!"

Bertha held her as she cried, patting her shoulder and murmuring comforting things. "There, there, Miss Georgie. It's not the end of the world. You knew he was never going to stay for long."

"But I love him!" she cried.

"Of course you do, " Bertha said. "Anyone could see that. But no butler is going to marry the young lady of the house."

"He's not just a butler."

"No, we could all see that. But he's gone, and he's not coming back."

That bleak truth should have sent her off in waves of fresh tears, but for some reason, it dried them. She'd mourned long enough. Now it was time to do something.

She pushed her tangled hair away from her face. "I'll come down," she said wearily. "What are we celebrating? I hope it's Norah's upcoming marriage to Andrew Salton."

"That's not what they're celebrating, you silly goose," Bertha said fondly. "They're celebrating the money."

"What money?" Georgie echoed.

"Goodness me, you mean to tell me you don't know?"

"Know what?"

"Your family's come into a fortune," Bertha said. "Your mother's spent the last two weeks shopping and it hasn't put a dent in it."

"Came into a fortune? How?" She sat up straight in the rumpled bed.

"It was up on the roof, of all places! Master Neddy found it. He figures it must belong to the old judge who once owned this place, but since he was a criminal and died without heirs, he said he's keeping it."

"He can't!" Georgie protested. "That was Rafferty's money."

'I don't think so, Miss Georgie. He left after Master Neddy found it and he made no mention of taking any. He was just anxious to be gone. But see, you do have something to celebrate. There was a fortune hidden in that chimney pot—who would have ever thought such a thing?"

"Who would?" Georgie echoed. She pushed the covers off her legs and swung them around. "I'm getting up."

'Thank the Lord,' Bertha said.

"Don't thank him just yet. I'm going after Rafferty."

For a moment, Bertha said nothing. And then she grinned. "You find him, lass, and teach the man a lesson or two."

"Don't worry," she said grimly. "I will."

❧

Two days later

"Do you suppose she'll convince him?" Neddy said, as he watched the elegant carriage disappear into the London traffic.

"I gave them clear instructions to the house in Hampshire," Martina replied. "If anyone can change Rafferty's mind, it's Georgie. He's in love with her and he just won't admit it, and Georgie's not going to settle for anything less. I'm surprised you don't mind."

"His connections have a lot to recommend him," Neddy drawled. "And I've broadened my opinion on suitable alliances. Which brings me round to a question."

Martina's stomach tightened in a knot. She'd known this was coming—they were growing closer and closer, and the truth couldn't be put off for much longer. He'd be horrified, disgusted, and her heart would be broken. Rafferty had warned her, but she'd fallen in love with the drunken little boy anyway. Not so drunken—he hadn't touched the bottle in weeks, and seemed to have no interest in it. Weeks of talking, and playing cards, and flirting, and kissing. Weeks of her lies.

"Oh, don't ask me questions," she said brightly, trying to avoid the inevitable. "We've just got George safely off to claim her true love—I don't want to worry about anything else."

"Nothing to worry about, my dear," Neddy said. "It's easy enough. You know I've bought a house on Clarges Street. I want you to come along with me and be its mistress."

Martina kept the distressed expression from her face. "You mean be your housekeeper?"

"No," he said gently. "Become its mistress, and mine."

She could hide the truth no longer. She could simply disappear, never tell him, but that wouldn't be fair to either of them. "I don't think that would be a good idea," she said carefully. "I haven't had a blameless life."

"Who has? Give me one reason why you don't want to live me."

"It wouldn't be good for you."

"Now you're acting like Rafferty, and we just sent Georgie off to make him see reason. Allow me to be the judge of what's good for me."

"I lived in a brothel!" she said abruptly.

He simply nodded. "I know you've had a hard life. All the more reason to make it easy. Come with me."

"I can't!" she said, tears filling her eyes. They were in the middle of London, outside of the house on Corinth Place, and she was going to have to tell him. And what would he do? At best, he'd simply walk away from her in disgust. At worst...

He caught her, his hands on her upper arms, holding her gently. "Tell me why, my dear. I thought we understood each other tolerably well—what's troubling you?"

"I'm not what you think I am," she said brokenly, afraid to look into his dear, kind face.

"Then tell me. What's this deep dark secret?"

She pulled free and turned her back on him, taking a deep breath. "I'm not really a woman," she said. "I'm a man."

She heard him make a strange noise, and she wondered if he was going to be ill in horror at the thought. "I'm so sorry I didn't tell you," she said, starting to turn. "I understand if you're disgusted, if you hate me, if you...are you laughing?"

He wiped his streaming eyes. "My dear, what kind of idiot do you think I am? I've known since the day I stopped drinking. Now will you stop this shilly-shallying and kiss me?"

"In public? For all to see?" she demanded, shocked.

"In public. For all to see," he echoed, and pulled her into his arms.

Chapter Twenty-Nine

RAFFERTY WAS SPRAWLED in a chair by the fire in the great kitchen, a glass of brandy in his hand. He'd been drinking too much for the last few weeks, and it was not improving his dark mood. He should be a happy man—all his troubles were over. Billy Stiles was dead and his men weren't interested in revenge. He'd walked away from his temporary madness of working as a butler, and he'd left Georgie behind to fall in love with someone suitable. He'd even been insane enough to give up Belding's cache to the impoverished Mannings. Not that he'd needed it, but could one ever be too rich?

He was back at the sprawling farm that had been his home away from London for the last five years, the place of peace and tranquility. He'd had enough of London to last a lifetime, and it would take a great deal to lure him back there.

Maybe he'd go back when Georgie got married, just to see that she looked happy and in love. Enough to close that chapter in his life.

Because he still wanted her. He'd been so sure that once he'd gotten away from her, he'd forget all about her, but she lingered in his dreams, in his waking moments, when he least expected her she came and whispered in his ear, and only the brandy would silence her. And the brandy didn't help his none-too-charming temper.

The door opened and Jenkins came in, carrying an armful of firewood. "You'll be needing to get a boy for this kind of work," he intoned. "It's beneath my dignity as your valet."

"I thought you were my butler," Rafferty drawled.

"Not much call for a butler in a farmhouse."

'Not much call for a valet for a farmer."

"Are you dismissing me, Rafferty?" Jenkins demanded haughtily.

"Not if you bring in more wood. It's going to be a cold night."

Jenkins sighed, dumping the wood by the fireplace. "You've been in a right foul mood since you got here," he pointed out. "Don't you think you ought to do something about it?"

"About what?"

"About the lady. You've been like a moonling, wandering around the place like a bear with a sore paw. Why don't you go back for her?"

"You said it yourself, she's a lady," Rafferty growled.

"She doesn't care."

"She would, sooner or later."

Jenkins made a disgusted noise and went back out the kitchen door, slamming it behind him, and Rafferty cursed. Everyone was disgusted with him, almost as much as he was himself. He had to get over the deadly case of the doldrums before all the people who worked for him quit.

He reached for his glass of brandy, then shoved it away. His temper was none too sweet already, and the brandy only made it worse. He was happy, dammit. Everything had gone his way, and he was finally free to continue his peaceful country life.

Maybe he needed a woman, but he couldn't think of any that appealed to him apart from a certain long-legged, golden-haired, child-woman that he couldn't stop thinking about. Maybe he'd become a goddamn monk. He heard the sound of the carriage through the thick stone walls of the farmhouse, but he didn't stir from his place. Jenkins would get rid of whoever it was, leaving him in peace.

He closed his eyes and then opened them again as the heavy door was thrust open, and the woman he loved, his earthly nemesis, burst into the room.

"Rafferty!" she cried. "I thought we'd never find you. Martina isn't the best person at giving directions, and then your grandmother grew peckish, and we're here much later than we thought we would be."

She set the large basket she was carrying down on the table and began to unpack it. "I wasn't sure what food you might have, but I brought eggs and Bertha made you a loaf of bread, but I saw you have chickens and I'm so glad! I adore chickens. The coachman is bringing in the rest of the supplies and—"

"Did you say my grandmother?" He broke through her spate of words. She was nervous—she always talked too much when she was nervous.

"Mr. Jenkins is bringing her in. She is very cross with you for just taking off, and why didn't you tell me you were the grandson of a duke? Doesn't that make you an honorable or something?"

"Honorable is the last word to reply to me," he said, dourly, rising from his seat, just as his grandmother's tiny figure appeared, accompanied by Jenkins, two footmen bearing firewood and baskets, presumably of food, and a tall, thin stranger took up the tail of the procession.

"There you are, Jamie," the dowager duchess greeted her errant grandson "You've been remarkably hard to find."

Georgie was busy unpacking the baskets and boxes until the table was laden with food. "Do you have a cook?" she asked brightly. "Bertha has been teaching me, but I still have a lot to learn, though I expect I can manage something for dinner."

Rafferty ignored her, focusing on the stranger. "And who the hell are you?" he demanded.

The man look like he'd been bitten by a snake. "I am the

Reverend Oswald Pettiforce and I would remind you to watch your language. There are ladies present."

"Oh, we're used to it," Georgie said cheerfully.

"What are you doing here?" Rafferty demanded.

"He's here to marry us, of course," Georgie said.

If he didn't know her so well, he wouldn't have seen the traces of anxiety in her beautiful blue eyes, and part of him melted at the sight. He steeled himself. "No," he said flatly.

"We've got a special license," she said.

"I don't care."

She looked as if she'd been slapped in the face, and she set down the ham she'd been holding. "All right," she said, and she walked out the door into the cold night air.

"You idiot," his grandmother said, as the heavy door closed behind Georgie. "That girl is worth ten of you."

"I know it. That's why I'm not going to marry her."

"So now you're noble and self-sacrificing. She doesn't want a good man, an honorable man. She wants you."

Picking up his glass of brandy, he flung it against the fireplace. The dowager duchess didn't even blink.

"Don't you understand," he said, in a tight, angry voice. "I'd destroy her. She'll be trapped out in the country, shunned by the ton and possibly her entire family. I can't ask her to do that. Better to break her heart now and get it over with."

"And what about you? I know you're in love with the girl—it's as plain as the nose on your face."

"I'll survive," he said grimly. "The best thing I could do for her is to let her go, no matter what I might feel."

"Idiot," his grandmother said again.

"If I love her, and I'm not admitting it, then I wouldn't want to bring her down to my level."

"If you love her, you'll go after her and never let her go."

He stood there, staring at her, his breath coming unevenly.

"Excuse me, but is there going to be a wedding?" The

Reverend Pettiforce demanded in a fretful voice. "If not, I'd like to return to my home."

The dowager duchess turned to look at her grandson. "Well, Jamie? Are you going down in history as the first saintly Ormond? Or are you going to take what you want?

❦

SHE TRIED EVERYTHING, Georgie thought. Thrown herself at his feet, even brought his grandmother along with her for extra ammunition, though, since the carriage belonged to the duchess, it was more accurate to say she'd been brought along.

All for nothing. She'd been wrong all this time, he didn't love her....

The door to the carriage was yanked open, and Rafferty stood there, a thunderous expression on his face.

"What are you doing in here?" he demanded.

"You... You said you didn't want me."

"I said I wasn't going to marry you," he corrected.

A sudden light filled her eyes. "You mean I can be your mistress? Oh, that would be perfectly fine. I'd enjoy being a fallen woman."

"You're not going to be my mistress," he said, his voice grumpy. "I've changed my mind. Assuming I even have a mind left after dealing with a hoyden like you."

She eyed him warily. "Changed your mind about what?"

He looked absolutely furious, never a good sign, but hope was stirring within her. "Remember when you told me that true love meant letting someone go?" he said.

"Yes," she said uncertainly.

"Then I guess I don't love you enough, because there is no way in hell I'm letting you get away from me ever again. That unpleasant man will marry us with my grandmother and Jenkins as witnesses, and you'll have to live with the consequences. I need you, Georgie. I can't let you go."

Her smile was dazzling enough to light the universe. "Really? Truly?"

"I'm in love with you, Georgie. And I'm tired of being noble."

"I would think so. You're a bad man, or so you told me. Do the bad thing and marry me." And she jumped from the high carriage into his arms.

He caught her, holding her tight. "No one will accept it if you marry your butler," he warned her. "We'll be outcasts."

"I know," she said cheerfully.

"I'll ruin you."

"Yes, please," she said, and she kissed him.

About the Author

Anne Stuart has been writing since the Dawn of Time. She's been published by every major publisher, and made the *NYT, USA Today,* and *Publisher's Weekly* Bestseller lists. She's won numerous awards, including four RITAs, as well as RWA's Lifetime Achievement Award, and she's known for her dark heroes, black humor and hot sex.

Follow her on her website at Anne-Stuart.com social media at:

 facebook.com/author.annestuart

 x.com/TheAnneStuart

 instagram.com/Annestuartwriter

Also by Anne Stuart

THE FIRE SERIES
Consumed by Fire
Driven by Fire
Wildfire

THE ICE SERIES
Black Ice
Cold as Ice
Ice Blue
Ice Storm
Fire and Ice
On Thin Ice

THE HOUSE OF ROHAN
The Wicked House of Rohan
Ruthless
Reckless
Breathless
Shameless
Heartless
A Rohan Family Christmas

TROUBLE AT THE HOUSE OF RUSSELL
Never Kiss a Rake
Never Trust a Pirate
Never Marry a Viscount

DON'T LOOK BACK—THE MAGGIE BENNETT BOOKS

Escape Out of Darkness

Darkness before Dawn

At the Edge of the Sun

HISTORICAL ROMANCES

The Devil's Waltz

Hidden Honor

Lady Fortune

Prince of Magic

Lord of Danger

Prince of Swords

To Love a Dark Lord

Shadow Dance

A Rose at Midnight

The Houseparty

The Demon Count Novels

The Spinster and the Rake

Lord Satan's Bride

Angels Wings

Demonwood

Cameron's Landing

Barrett's Hill

To Catch a Thief

WOMEN'S FICTION

When the Stars Fall Down

ROMANTIC SUSPENSE

Into the Fire

The Widow

Silver Falls

Still Lake

Shadows at Sunset

Shadow Lover

Ritual Sins

Moonrise

Nightfall

Now You See Him

Special Gifts

Break the Night

The Fall of Maggie Brown

Winter's Edge

Hand in Glove

Tangled Lies

The Catspaw Collection

Against the Wind

Return to Mariposa

SUSPENSE

Seen and Not Heard

ANNE STUART'S GREATEST HITS

Cinderman

The Soldier, the Nun and the Baby

One More Valentine

Blue Sage

Night of the Phantom

Falling Angel

CONTEMPORARY ROMANCE

The Right Man

A Dark and Stormy Night

Wild Thing

Rafe's Revenge

Heat Lightning

Asking for Trouble (formerly *Chasing Trouble*)

Lazarus Rising

Rancho Diablo

Crazy Like a Fox

Glass Houses

Cry for the Moon

Partners in Crime

Bewitching Hour

Rocky Road

Museum Piece

Heart's Ease

Chain of Love

Against the Wind

Return to Christmas

COLLABORATIONS

Dogs & Goddesses – with Jennifer Crusie and Lani Diane Rich

The Unfortunate Miss Fortunes with Jennifer Crusie and Lani Diane Rich

SHORT READS

Night and Day

Burning Bright

Dark Journey

Date with the Devil

The Monster in the Closet

The High Sheriff of Huntingdon

Risk the Night

Under an Enchantment

The Gunslinger and the Lady (formerly *Dangerous Touch*)

Kissing Frosty

Sultry

Saints Alive

Goddess in Waiting

Blind Date from Hell

A Midnight Clear

Blackheart's Long Night

Claus and Effect

The Road to Hidden Harbor

MANGA

A Dark and Stormy Night

Night

www.ingramcontent.com/pod-product-compliance
Lightning Source LLC
Chambersburg PA
CBHW021351260626
47153CB00024B/406